ISBN-13: 9798848870176
ISBN-10: 1477123456

Cover design by: Art Painter
Library of Congress Control Number: 2018675309
Printed in the United States of America

REDEEMING LOVE

By

Darla Kinion

CHAPTER 1

This is not happening! There is no way possible the person that is staring back at me in this mirror is getting married in just a few short hours!

Honestly, I will have black and blue marks all up and down my arms if I don't stop pinching myself.

I had been practicing writing how my name would look on paper. Something so funny when I think about it. I mean, really, that is something schoolgirls do. Not grown women. Not that I would *think* they would anyways.

"Mrs. Robert Davis"

"Mrs. Holly Davis"

"Mr. and Mrs. Davis"

Mr. and Mrs. Davis always seemed to be something older people would be called, like his parents. But in a few short hours that is who we would be, Mr. and Mrs. Davis!

Husband and wife.

My ears longed to hear Toby pronounce us to the church.

"Ladies and gentlemen, I now present to you for the first time, husband and wife, Mr. and Mrs. Davis!"

My hands were shaking so much. I was barely able to put my make-up on.

Mother had been in my room several times this

morning making sure we weren't forgetting anything. I think she was as excited as me.

We had an appointment at the salon to get our hair done. Memaw, Patty and Mrs. Davis were going to be there as well.

My dress was already at the church as well as my shoes. Nails were done yesterday.

The caterers had called. Everything was going to go off like a breeze!

Every girl dreams of a wedding day. Not me! I definitely had not!

Nope, I never expected that I would get married.

I had only ever loved one boy in my life. I never would have thought that he even noticed me. Even if we did live next door to each other.

I was sure I was not the marrying kind.

Not the kind that a nice boy like Robert Davis would want to marry anyways.

He was BMOC and could have had any girl in high school.

He dated a few of them. Then he left them all, me included, to join the Army.

I'm sure most of those girls cried their eyes out when he left without making one of them his wife.

Boy, am I glad he didn't!

I had home privilege, sort of.

Not that it did me any good. He never even looked in my direction. But I sure looked in his. Any time and every time I got the chance.

He was so good looking!

I mean, red hair.

Broad shoulders.

Played football.

To me he was just gorgeous.

And lucky me, I had a front row seat.

We had been neighbors ever since I was about four and he was about six.

Sometimes he would say hi to me, but I was too bashful to answer.

Sometimes I would half-wave back if I didn't think Father was looking.

Mostly I just looked at him through my window and dreamed of a handsome red-headed boy knocking on my door and taking me out on a date in his blue and white car.

But he never did.

Not one single date with him in that stinking car!

Not one!

But I did get the next best thing. I got to own the car, for a while anyways.

What a goofy kid I was. I blushed even thinking about it.

His mother must have thought I was a nutcase.

She probably laughed her head off at me that day I bought the car from her.

I mean, "I would like to buy Roberts car. Here's the money."

"Ok. I'll get the keys."

"I can't drive."

"Oh okay, you are some kind of weirdo, please go home little girl."

No, she didn't say that. She was too graceful. But I am sure she probably thought it.

What kind of weirdo buys a car they can't even drive?

Me!

I guess I am a kind of weirdo after all.

And in a few short hours I will be Robert Davis's one and only weirdo.

CHAPTER 2

My hair had always had a slight curl to it. Nothing to make it look good or anything but too curly to straighten all the time.

I usually wore it pulled back in a ponytail but had decided to try curling it for the wedding.

Patty had curled her hair for her wedding just a couple of weeks earlier. She looked gorgeous! She always did.

She had such grace and style about her.

She knew what clothes went together with which shoes and what hairstyles were in.

Me on the other hand, I had never really given it much thought.

She was truly the closest thing I had to a sister, so it was always a treat when she and I could shop together.

It was nice shopping with Mother too, but it was just more of a sister thing with Patty.

Her dress had been so lovely.

She and her mother had spent hours getting just the right dress.

Oh, how beautiful she looked. It had a long train and was long and flowy. The capped lace sleeves that came up and covered the bodice, it was so dainty. She looked so regal.

She had curled her beautiful blond hair and had it

all pinned up with ringlets flowing under the veil.

Her colors were lilac and yellow.

All the men had yellow cummerbunds and Toby had a lilac one. Patty's cousin and I both wore flowing yellow dresses with purple lilacs on them.

Her bouquet was made up of yellow roses and baby's breath. She'd had two purple roses in there as well. She stopped and gave one to her mother and one to Aunt Jessie when she got to the front row where they were sitting. They both cried when she handed them to them. It was so sweet.

Toby looked as if he was about to bust out of his tuxedo. He was bursting with pride. He looked at Patty as she walked down the aisle and beamed. He looked like he might faint when Pastor Taylor asked, "Who gives this woman to be joined with this man?"

I really didn't know why he was so nervous. Patty's parents adored him! And why wouldn't they?

He had graduated from college just two years ago and now he was a very much sought-after evangelist. He and Patty were going to be going all over preaching and singing in churches everywhere. He truly was a dynamic preacher and singer. He had already been going out on his own while Patty finished her schooling. She and I had graduated a year ago in May, and now they were having their June wedding.

June 21st, 1974.

They were going to be going to honeymoon in a cottage by the lake. A family friend had offered to let them use it as their wedding present to them.

They were going to be staying a week. It was up in the mountains and a little secluded.

Just what a newly married couple would need to

get to know each other. It was going to be a lovely time for both of them.

One of Patty's friends sang a love song and then they spoke their vows.

Josh looked like he was going to pop a button while he stood there.

And then Pastor Taylor asked them to kneel to pray for them. When they did, all was revealed.

Josh tried his best to not look guilty, but he didn't do a very good job of it. Uncle Joey shot him a look and Josh would not look back. He had a smile on his face like the cat that ate the canary.

Several people started snickering as they realized what was written on the bottom of Toby's shoes.

One shoe said "HELP" and the other shoe said "ME".

What was supposed to be a solemn moment was not quite so solemn after all.

Pastor Taylor and the rest of us were oblivious to what was going on until the reception.

By then no one cared anymore. Not even Uncle Joey.

The barn had been set up with all kinds of tables and chairs. The decorations were lovely.

It was a coming home of sorts.

Patty and Toby were the best-looking bride and groom that I had ever seen. They were meant to be. Everyone knew it. You would have to be practically blind not to see how much in love they were.

Food!

So much food!

This was not a catered affair.

No! Every neighbor, friend, acquaintance that they both knew, showed up with food.

The truly only remarkably fancy item there, was the cake.

It was a four-tiered chocolate cake that would feed an army.

It was decorated with royal white icing with yellow roses and little purple lilacs.

It was so scrumptiously decorated. So beautiful. Almost too pretty to cut.

Aunt Jessie had planned on making it, but they insisted that she let someone else do it. They wanted her to be part of the wedding, not the one that had to run around and make sure everything was being taken care of.

There was only one person that she would allow to help, and at her insistence, that was my future mother-in-law.

She and Aunt Jessie knew each other from the Tuesday morning Bible Study. They had known each other for years and had exchanged recipes and cooking tips for as long as they could remember.

Sara had insisted on making the cake for the wedding. And of course, she used Aunt Jessie's recipe. After all, it was Toby's favorite, chocolate!

Everything went off without a hitch. Well, one hitch. They were finally married.

CHAPTER 3

A week in the mountains for a honeymoon sounded delightful.

Robert and I would not be going to the mountains for our honeymoon.

We were going to drive to the ocean and stay in a hotel and on the beach. We both loved the water and had found a little hotel right on the beach, more of a resort or spa.

Grandmother and Grandfather Abernathy had insisted on paying for it as a wedding gift. We told them it was too much, but they insisted.

I was so anticipating seeing Patty and Toby when they got home.

We all were.

They were due to come home on Saturday. They wanted to start preparing for a few services they were going to be holding, after mine and Robert's wedding.

It did not go as planned!

The honeymoon had not been as glorious and joyous as it had seemed it should.

The first three days were lovely. Then Patty got a miserable sunburn on the fourth day. Then Toby had brushed up against some poison ivy while they were on a hike. They had been miserable for the last couple of days and decided to come home early so Toby could go see a doctor.

I felt so bad for them. We all did.

Toby had been staying at home while he was preaching.

With Patty still in college there was no use in the added expense of an apartment. They decided they would stay with Patty's family after they got back.

They weren't sure if they should find an apartment or what they were going to do yet.

As evangelists, a lot of their time would be traveling from one place to the next. They weren't sure what their finances would be since they were going to be taking love offerings as their pay.

That might not be a lot since they were just starting out.

They would still have to pay for gas in the car and keep it repaired. It was getting older.

Toby had put a few miles on it in the last year while he traveled. Luckily for him, he knew a good mechanic, Robert. Well, and Lance, Roberts brother. They knew that car very well!

Patty was glad they were home. She could hardly move. She was so badly sunburned. She needed help.

But Toby was so sick and hurting from his poison ivy that he didn't have the strength or will to move his things over.

He dropped her off at her mothers and he went to his.

After a few days of some TLC from their mothers, and a cream from the doctor, they were feeling much better.

On Monday Toby was feeling well enough to load up the Fairlane and move in with his new wife and in-laws.

Our wedding was on Thursday and I was so glad that Patty's sunburn had subsided. I couldn't wait to see her in the maid of honor, well, matron of honors dress.

It was a red chiffon dress with a strappy bow-tie sleeve. I was worried it would rub her shoulders, but they healed up nicely before the wedding.

I wanted to get married on a day that held a lot of significance for me.

Robert and I talked it over and he said that a Fourth of July wedding with all the fireworks would be the best wedding ever.

Aunt Jessie and Uncle Joey were more than happy to let us use the barn for the reception.

"We just had one reception there, why not another one. We were going to have a party there anyways. Let's make it count," Uncle Joey had said.

I was really surprised that I wanted to have the wedding on the 4th.

It just seemed like the thing to do.

So, I did.

There had been a lot of healing since that first 4th of July just six years earlier.

But that was a lifetime and a different person ago.

I knew that I would be able to get over the trauma of 4th of July's because of what happened a few years ago.

That is when my life really took on meaning.

That is when the healing began.

That is when I met the two most important people to ever make a change in my life.

I had met the Lord Jesus Christ and had asked Him to be my Savior and I had finally met Robert Davis.

My life would never be the same.

Not that it would ever be completely easy or without pain, but it was never going to be the same as it had been.

And as much as I loved Robert Davis and was ready to spend the rest of my life with him, I knew that I could make it without him as long as I held on to Jesus.

CHAPTER 4

Mother called for me to come downstairs so we could get to the salon.

Mrs. Davis was going to ride over with us.

Patty, Memaw and Aunt Jessie were going to meet us there.

Usually the salon would be closed today, just like every other business, but they made an exception for us.

After all, it was the 4th of July. Everybody had that day off.

We had 9 o'clock appointments. They had scheduled us for 2 hours. Mamie had been doing Mother's hair for a long time. She asked her girls if they wanted to help. Luckily for us, they did.

Patty, Memaw and Aunt Jessie had shown up right before we arrived and were getting their hair washed. By the time we were all done we looked like six of the most beautifully coiffed women walking around in our everyday clothes. If anyone had seen us, they would have thought we were putting on airs.

By this time, we were starving. The bagel and coffee Mother and I had eaten was finally wearing off.

We decided a burger was in order. The wedding was in five hours and it would even be a little later before we would eat and have divine lemon chiffon cake.

We would have to be at the church by four to get dressed.

The wedding was at five, and if everything went as planned, we would be eating by seven and fireworks by nine.

We hurried to the Burger Joint and ordered food, to go!

Sara said she would need to bring food home to the guys. If we ordered it to go then we could all eat when we got home.

Memaw thought to go was a good idea. They could eat while they drove back home.

The guys had been left in charge of setting up tables and getting anything the caterers were going to need when they got there.

Aunt Jessie had made sandwiches for them before she left so they wouldn't starve. Doing it like this would give them time to get home, check on everything, make sure all the sweets were ready and have the cake ready to assemble.

Aunt Jessie had told Sara, "If you are going to decorate my son's wedding cake, then I am doing the same for you."

They had struck up a deal!

I carried our food in while Mrs. Davis and Mother carried her food home.

I had everything ready to eat when she got back.

After a quick prayer, we ate the most glorious cheeseburgers ever. They were the exact same burgers we got every time we were there, but they always seemed to taste so much better when we were hungry.

And we were.

I joked that I had better not eat the whole thing or my wedding dress might not zip up.

"At least the veil will still fit," Mother laughed.

We both ate every bite.

I'd made sure Mrs. Davis didn't buy any burgers with onions.

Not on my wedding day!

She laughed and said she would not do that to me! She said she would let Robert know that he could eat onions tomorrow.

I told her no! "You tell him he can eat onions when we get back from our honeymoon.

She laughed and promised she would tell him just that.

I could not believe I was marrying someone who liked to eat onions.

But then again, it was Robert Davis! He could eat onions or anything he wanted as long as he always loved me as much as I loved him.

CHAPTER 5

Mother and I both wanted to take a bath and rest a bit before we went to the church.

Memaw, Pappy, Uncle Joey, Aunt Jessie, and Josh would have to come back for the wedding.

Memaw and Pappy had gone over the night before to help make sure that everything was taken care of. Between them, Uncle Joey and Aunt Jessie, I knew everything was in good hands.

They beat us to the church by only a few minutes.

Toby and Patty were already there. She was a vision of loveliness. With her hair pulled up and curled like it was. In her red dress and navy pumps, she looked just gorgeous.

Mother thought it was hilarious that I would have a red, white, and blue wedding.

I explained that we were getting married on the 4th of July, what better colors to get married in. She tried to let me know that just because it was the 4th, we didn't have to use those colors; we could use any colors we chose.

I chose red, white, and blue!

Mother and Patty helped me into my dress.

I guess I was more of a girl than I thought I was.

I didn't want a heavy dress because it was the

middle of summer. I didn't want to be so hot, but I still wanted to have that Cinderella wedding dress.

Mother and I had shopped at three different places then we finally ended up back at the first place and bought the first dress I had tried on.

It was flowy and twirly and felt oh so light. It didn't quite go to the floor more of a midi style. Which was fine by me because then I could see the red wedge heels that I was wearing.

Grandmother Abernathy stopped in and gave me a string of beautiful pearls that had belonged to her mother for the something old.

Mother had bought me combs with rhinestones and babies' breath on them to wear in my hair for the something new.

I knew just the thing I needed for the something borrowed, something blue!

Pappy had it.

He always had it.

I was sure if I asked, he would not mind.

Memaw went and got him for me.

"What do you need sweet baby girl?"

"Well, Pappy, I need something only you can give me. I need something borrowed and something blue. Do you think you would be willing to part with it for just a little while?"

A big grin spread across his face. "For you, anything."

He reached into the back pocket of his tuxedo and pulled out his navy-blue bandana that he always had with him and handed it to me.

"Is this what you needed?"

"Yes," I squealed with delight.

I hugged him and he hugged me right back.

I took the bandana and rolled it out and tied it around my bouquet.

It looked lovely mingled with the white ribbons.

We were all just about ready when I heard her.

Lisa was bringing her down the hall.

Hannah would soon be bursting into my room. A fireball of energy.

I couldn't wait to see how sweet she looked, all dressed up for the wedding.

I had asked Memaw and Mother before I said anything to Lisa. I had wanted to make sure it wouldn't be awkward if I asked her to let Hannah be my flower girl.

They said they didn't think that it would be a problem.

I asked and Lisa agreed.

I couldn't take my eyes off of her. She was the cutest little thing. Lisa had curled her hair and had put red white and blue ribbons all up in it to hold it in place.

"Well look at you," I declared. "You are a vision to behold."

"I know," she giggled. "I am a vision and mommy said I had better behave myself or I would be in big trouble. I am going to behave myself. Did you know it's my birthday today? I am six years old today."

"I know. That is fantastic."

"I know. I had birthday cake and ice-cream. And I am going to have a party tonight to have my birthday."

"No, Hannah," Lisa said, "I told you, we are going to a party after the wedding. We are having a birthday party for you on Saturday."

"I get two parties?"

"I, uh, no. Just the one. But we are going to a party tonight. Remember for Miss Holly and Mr. Robert?"

"Is it their birthday too?"

"No. I, uhm, I tell you what, I will explain it later. How's that?"

"Ok. Holly, I mean Miss Holly, I like your dress."

"Well thank you. I really like yours too. Does yours twirl a lot like mine?"

With that we both swished our dresses around.

"Yep," she giggled. "I have my basket and flowers. I will be careful and behave myself when I throw them down."

"Well, good for you."

"Yep, I practiced at home. I threw them in the air and mommy said that is not how it is done. She showed me. But I think my brother ate one of the flowers."

"He what," Lisa exclaimed? "When did he do that?"

"When I throwed them in the air and he catched one and I think he ate it 'cause I couldn't find it. I think it was blue or red, it could have been white. But he will be okay mommy.'

'I am sure he will." She sounded exasperated.

Before long everyone was ready for the wedding to start.

No one knew what was to be expected.

Well, except Patty and myself, and we had not told a living soul.

It is good to have a sister.

CHAPTER 6

Pappy took my arm as the organist began the song I had been longing to hear forever!

"Here comes the Bride"

That was me!

I know I was beaming but I couldn't help myself.

The whole congregation rose to their feet as Pappy and I began the walk down the aisle.

The red, white, and blue flower petals were strewn everywhere. I could see little Hannah in her twirly little blue dress. That, along with her little white socks and red shiny shoes made here look like the little firecracker that she was.

Patty looked beautiful. What more could I say? Her golden hair with that red dress and her navy shoes made this a real 4th of July wedding.

Toby was standing there waiting for me to get to my groom.

Then there was Wheels. Well, Lance. He was getting used to being called "Wheels" though.

He was Robert's best man.

Robert had said that Lance was the best man that he could possibly have stand up with him on our wedding day. He was a true hero in Roberts eyes. Not just his, but everyone else's as well.

Vietnam had taken his leg, but he didn't seem to let

that stop him or even slow him down, much.

He wasn't always in the wheelchair. Only when his good leg was giving him a lot of grief from where the shrapnel had taken a good bit out of it.

Today was a good day, so far. He was standing behind Robert and was smiling, waiting. Right there to be the best man to his big brother.

Then I caught his eye. He was looking straight at me. I couldn't take my eyes off of him. I wanted to run down the aisle to him. To have him take my hand and never let go.

I wanted him to look at me the way he was looking at me this very moment for the rest of my life. My heart doubled in size and I am sure it showed on my face.

Pappy leaned in, "Holly, you look so happy. You are in love with this young man and it shows. From where I'm standing, he's just as much in love with you it looks like," he whispered.

"Do you really think so," I asked, not breaking my gaze?

"He is looking at you the same way I still look at your Memaw. Yes, I really think so."

I believe I smiled even bigger.

The music stopped as we got to the front pews where our mothers were seated.

I had loved watching Patty give her mother and future mother-in-law a rose. I asked her if she would mind if I did the same? She didn't mind it at all.

I had Pappy stop so I could give a rose to each of these two beautiful women. I had a white rose for each of them.

Then Pappy took one more step with me holding

on to his arm.

Toby stepped forward.

"Who gives this woman to be married to this man?"

He was so serious.

I listened to him ask the question and my mind began to race.

I didn't feel like a woman. I felt like a little girl playing dress up and that it was all a dream. A dream I didn't want to wake up from. But it wasn't a dream. I was brought back to reality when I heard Pappy start to speak.

"Her mother and all the rest of her family give her to be married to this fine young man. He had better take good care of her too. There are a lot of us!"

He winked at Robert as Robert stepped to take my arm and walk me to the altar.

"I will sir," he said to Pappy, "you can count on it."

Toby started speaking and I was half listening. I could hardly take my eyes off of this handsome man that I would soon be calling husband.

After a few minutes Toby announced that there would be a special song.

He nodded to Patty, presuming that she was the one that was going to be singing a wedding song.

She had told him that when he got to a certain point that there was going to be a song. What she didn't tell him was who was going to be singing it.

Patty left her place and went and got a microphone and brought it to me then she went to the piano.

You could have heard a pin drop. They were all surprised. Not as much as I was though!

I had let Patty talk me into singing to my future

husband at my own wedding.

I was a puddle of Jello!

I had never sung in public before. I had never sung anywhere out loud, in front of anyone before. Except for Patty that is.

The only place I had ever let one note come out of my mouth was in the shower where no one was supposed to be listening.

But someone was.

Patty!

She heard me singing in the shower one day when I thought I was alone in the dorms and had taken a coveted shower.

I thought she was still at work. She had stood outside the bathroom that day wanting to know who was singing. Imagine both our surprise when I walked out! She realized it was me and I realized she had heard me. There we both were!

She wanted to know why I never sang with them.

I explained to her because I can't sing.

She explained to me that I was so wrong. I could sing and I was pretty good at it. I would not believe her.

That is not anything I had ever been told and I was too scared and embarrassed to believe that it could be true.

She kept on so much about it that I started to want to believe her.

She bought a tape recorder and made me sing the song I had sung in the shower into it.

She played it back and I didn't recognize the voice that came out.

It wasn't half bad.

After a little, no, a lot, of coaxing, she convinced me that it would be a special treat if I was to sing to Robert.

She had the perfect love song.

We practiced for the rest of the school year. Neither of us told a living soul.

So as much as everyone else was surprised, they weren't nearly as surprised as I was.

In a million years I would never have expected myself to be standing in front of people, singing a love song to my soon to be husband. But then again, I had never expected to have a soon to be husband.

I turned to him and sang the beautiful love song that Patty and I had practiced for months.

"Whither thou goest I will go,
Wherever thou lodgest I will lodge,
Thy people shall be my people my love,
Whither thou goest I will go.
As in the story long ago
The same sweet love story now is so,
Thy people shall be my people my love
Whither thou goest I will go!"

Patty came back and took the bouquet from my hand.

Toby spoke a few more moments, then he had us kneel to pray.

Robert had thought it was funny that Josh had written on Toby's shoes.

So much so that he had done the same to his own shoes.

"She's" "Mine"

Twitters started in the auditorium. Even Robert was giggling.

After the prayer was said we were ready to exchange vows and rings.

Uncle Jerry's youngest son, who was six, had been given the job as ring bearer. He had been standing there so quietly and respectfully the whole time. He went to hand the pillow to Lance so he could untie the ribbons and hand the rings to Robert, or that is what he was supposed to do, but no, suddenly he started to growl.

Lance looked at Robert with a "I don't know what to do in this situation" kind of look.

Robert turned to the little boy and knelt down in front of him while he still growled and would not let go of the pillow.

"What's going on buddy," he asked him?

He stopped growling long enough to explain.

"I am the ring bear. I have to growl because that is what bears do. Grrr."

"Well, you are doing an excellent job as the ring bear. That is some good growling too, but could you please hand the pillow to Lance so he can get the rings off of it?"

"Sure, but I already took them off," he told him.

"You did? Uh, where are they?"

"In my pocket."

"In your pocket huh? Can you get them for me?"

"Sure."

He started reaching into all of his pockets.

By this time the whole congregation is snickering as they watched what could have been a disaster.

"Here they are!"

He pulled them out with such a proud ta-da moment.

"Thanks bud. Now if you could go stand by Lance for just a few more minutes, we are all going to go get some cake."

"Sure."

He moved next to Lance who was shaking with laughter, as so were many of the people that had come to watch.

"We're gonna have cake," he said as he looked up at Lance.

Everybody lost it.

We were all giggling by now.

It didn't take long though before everything settled down.

After all the I dos were said, Robert and I exchanged rings.

Toby pronounced us "Man and Wife" and with the biggest grin he told Robert, "You may kiss your bride."

And he did.

My heart melted into his at the very moment and I knew we had become one.

CHAPTER 7

The reception in the barn was what to be expected. Even more so!

There was so much food and deserts.

So many people.

Aunt Jessie joked that she would never ever have thought of having a 4th of July party catered. But, seeing how much easier it was than having to do so much cooking she might consider it next year.

We all knew that was never going to happen.

As good as the food was, and it was, it still couldn't match barbecued burgers and hot dogs to celebrate the 4th of July.

I really didn't want to leave Robert's side or even let him out of my sight for one second, but I had a birthday present to deliver.

I had heard it through the grapevine that Miss Hannah wanted a piano for her birthday, and she was not going to be getting one.

I had not wanted to overstep my boundaries. I might have given birth to her, but she really was Lisa and Tony Henderson's daughter. They were truly her parents. And they loved her and were doing an awesome job of raising her and her little brother. So, before I got her anything, I made sure to clear it with them.

They both gave their blessings.

Lisa had explained that they weren't getting her the piano because they had already purchased her presents and this one was a surprise that she had added on last minute.

I made sure to get her the biggest and best piano that we could find. We made it extra special and had her name put on the bench. We also gave our little ring "bear" a big wheel.

They were both in hog heaven!

So many presents and cards and excitement.

Josh and some of his friends had set up the fireworks out in the open field as always.

Promptly at 9 we all went out to watch the glorious display. It felt like home.

Everyone was there.

Everyone that we loved.

With the exception of Sam.

He would always be missed. But truthfully, he was there. In every smile, in every laugh, in every hug and in every thought. And this celebration. The celebration of freedom and love of country was clearly meant for men like him and Lance and Robert, and every man or woman that had sacrificed so that we could celebrate as we were.

It felt like life would never be better than this moment as I stood there watching explosion after explosion and holding Robert's hand as he held mine.

After the fireworks were done, there was still cake to be had and so many presents to open.

The cake was so divine. Lemon chiffon cake with white icing and red roses and blue trim.

Robert had surprised me. He said he didn't care what kind of cake we had as long as it wasn't coconut. Lemon was his favorite but if I wanted chocolate that would be fine too. Just not coconut.

I was more than happy. Lemon was my favorite and I hated coconut as well.

His mother shared her recipe with Aunt Jessie, and she made this wonderful luscious cake for us.

I was in cake heaven right along with my new husband.

Mother and Aunt Jessie said not to worry about opening all the presents tonight. We could open them when we got back from our honeymoon.

Our honeymoon! What a divine word.

We were going to be driving to the coast and staying for 7 glorious days.

Grandmother and Grandfather Abernathy had been so generous by taking care of the cost for us, but we were more than surprised when Grandfather handed Robert an envelope.

He told Robert to make sure we had a good time.

He hugged him and told him to please always take care of me and to love me.

Robert assured him that he would do just that.

They left not too long after that.

We got ready to leave ourselves.

We had quite a drive and we still had to stop by our houses to pick up our luggage and change clothes.

We went to leave and found the car highly decorated.

Cans of all kinds and a few shoes were tied to the back and "Just Married" had been written in shoe polish on the back window.

Josh denied everything but it was hard to believe him with the shoe polish streak on his pants.

Lisa and Tony were loading two tired kids into the car to leave when they motioned for us to come to the car.

Lisa hugged me and Robert and Tony shook our hands.

They congratulated us on our wedding and wished us many blessings.

Lisa looked at Tony and he handed me a card. Lisa explained it was a wedding gift but to please not open it until we got back from our honeymoon.

I promised her I wouldn't.

They left and we went to say our goodbyes before we headed out to start our new adventure.

We headed to our homes while we held hands and shared looks while we listened to cans hitting the road behind us and smiled at the road before us.

Mr. and Mrs. Robert Davis.

Life was definitely good.

CHAPTER 8

Robert dropped me off in front of my house before going next door. We were going to change our clothes before heading out. It had been a long day, but we thought for sure we could stay awake for a couple of hours to get to our destination.

Serenity Bay Resort and Spa! It was a highly recommended resort.

It sounded lovely!

I hurried in and changed my clothes and freshened up while Robert did the same.

I had just finished touching up my make-up and shaking the pins out of my hair letting the curls fall where they may when Robert knocked on the front door.

I took one last look and hurried down to let my new husband in to gather his new bride and her belongings.

I opened the door and there he stood.

Just like I had dreamed for so many years.

Robert Davis.

I flew into his arms and he kissed me once more.

After we loaded my bags in the car, he showed me that my Grandfather had handed him an envelope full of cash.

$500.00!

"What are we going to do with that?"

Robert shook his head, "I don't know. We don't really need it do we?"

"No. That was so generous of them. They have already paid for the Resort. I think we can manage the rest. Let's think about it. Maybe invest it or something. We don't have to decide that tonight, do we?"

"No, not tonight. We will figure it out. We have more important things to think about tonight."

He winked at me.

I blushed.

As he drove, I let my thoughts wander.

I remembered the day he finally asked me on a date.

It was two days after Easter just a little over three years ago.

I remembered that Easter night. It was when I realized that I had a need for a Savior because of his testimony.

I had been running from and blaming God for the sins my father had perpetrated on me for so long, that I had failed to realize that I was as much in need of a Savior as he had been.

That night, when Robert showed up at the church and told how God had delivered him and had set him free, I knew that I wanted that. I had wanted that freedom from the chains that were binding me.

I wanted the same peace and joy that exuded from those around me.

How I had gone so far in my life around people that knew the answer, but I just couldn't accept it.

So many of them had told me.

Tried to persuade me to surrender my heart to Jesus.

To make him Lord of my life.

I felt like Agrippa with Paul, so many times, almost they could persuade me, but yet I still could not let go of the hurt and pain.

That is until I realized what Robert had gone through and what he had been delivered from, then, then, I was persuaded.

I knew I had been set free that night. If I could have floated, I would have.

So many people that loved me and surrounded me that night were as happy about my decision as I was.

Their prayers had been answered. I had come to know the Lord at the foot of the cross as I knelt at an altar and gave it all to Him.

The cross that I had loathed for so many years had now become a beacon of home. A place of refuge.

I remember that day, two days later, while I was sitting in the window seat, just contemplating life, and the decision I had made, when I saw him coming across the lawn.

Was I dreaming?

Was this for real?

Was Robert Davis coming to my front door?

I heard the doorbell and then the knock.

I hurried to answer the door and promptly fell out of the window seat.

Mother had beaten me to the door. As she welcomed him in, there I was trying to pull myself up off the floor.

She was leaving to go to her Bible study, so she told him to come on in, not realizing that I was in such an embarrassing position.

My foot had fallen asleep and I had not realized it.

He hurried over to help me up.

I realized at that moment he was even more handsome and muscular than I had ever remembered.

We sat back on the window seat together.

It was rather awkward!

We neither one knew where to start the conversation.

Finally, "So what brings you over," I asked.

"Well, you do."

"Me?"

"Yeah you! My mom told me you would be home for another week. That you, Pastor Toby and Patty would be going back to college next Monday."

"Yeah, that's right. Toby is preaching at the church one more Sunday and then we are going back to school."

"Well, then, I figured I had better not let one more day go by without coming to see you. My time is going to be limited and I am tired of letting life happen to me."

"Okay. So how can I help you with that?

"Well, for starters, would you like to go on a date with me?"

"A date?"

"Uh, yeah, a date. We could go have lunch today if you would like. I would really like to get to know you. I mean, I know you, but I would like to get to know you better. Would you like to have lunch with me today?"

"Today?"

"Too soon?"

"No. Not too soon. I mean, today would be fine.

Where would you like to go?"

"I will leave that up to you. We can get a burger or go just anywhere you like. How about I be here by 11:30 and you let me know where you would like to go. Oh yeah, would you mind driving. I am no longer a car owner. Some girl bought my car."

He winked at me when he said that.

I blushed.

"Sure, I'll drive."

My heart was doing cartwheels inside my head.

I had a date with Robert Davis.

What was I going to wear?

What was I going to say?

What was I going to do?

He saw himself out while I just sat there.

I was so glad that he didn't see me fall again when I stood up and tripped over my own two feet.

I would have died on the spot!

CHAPTER 9

I immediately called Patty.

I was so excited I didn't know how to get the words out.

"Slow down girl. Now start over. Slower, so I can understand you."

I took a deep breath. "Patty, he asked me out on a date. Well, a lunch date."

"Who?"

"Bobby, I mean Robert. You know, the man that spoke on Sunday night. Robert Davis. He just walked right over to my house and asked me out on a lunch date. Can you believe it? I can't believe it! He asked me out on a date. I don't know what to do."

"Did you tell him you would go?"

"Yeah, I said I would go. I'm gonna go. I mean, I mean, well, you know what I mean. I don't know what to wear or anything."

"Where is he taking you?"

"Well, it's more like I am taking him. He asked if I'd drive since he doesn't have a car right now. And as for where, he is leaving that up to me. Where should we go?

"Where do you want to go?"

"I don't know. I mean, we could go get a burger, but it is always loud at the Burger Joint. Not personal at all. It would feel like we would be talking over each other. I know a little place that I have been a few times that has really good food and it is a lot quieter. Paulie's Bistro. It is really a quaint little place. I just don't know if he likes quiche and such."

"Did he say you could pick the place?"

"Yes,"

"Well then, problem solved! If he is letting you choose then Paulie's it is. Next time he can choose."

"Do you really think there will be a next time? I mean, what if he goes with me today and realizes that I am a real goon?"

"I tell you what, go on the first date and see how that one goes. You might think he is a real goon and not want to go out with him again."

"Yeah, I don't think that will ever happen."

I thought to myself, "If he were to ask me to marry him at lunch today, I would most likely scream yes!!!!"

After a bit more conversation with her we decided that one of the midi dresses that I had would suffice or even a pair of bell bottoms. I chose the dress. It made me feel like a girl and I wanted to look and feel my best for my first date with Robert,

I couldn't help but sing and hum while I got ready. "I wanna be Bobby's girl. I wanna be Bobby's girl"

I had practically two hours before he would be back over, and I took advantage of every minute.

Hair fixed. Check

Nails painted. Check

Bath. Check

Brush my teeth. Check

Deodorant. Check

Make-up. Check

Pretty dress. Check

Perfume. Check

I was ready with five minutes to spare.

I remember thinking that if I sat in the window seat, I would see him when he walked over.

And I did.

I was getting out of the seat to answer the door and my shoe got tangled in the hem of my dress which caused me to fall flat on the ground one more time.

This first date was not getting off to a great start.

And now the butterflies were doing flip flops in my stomach and I felt like throwing up.

I answered the door instead.

CHAPTER 10

"You clean up nicely," Robert said when I finally answered the door.

"Thank you."

I could barely whisper. I am sure my face had turned ten shades of red at the compliment.

My heart was pumping blood through my heart so fast that I was sure he could hear it pounding.

"So, did you decide where you would like to eat?"

"Have you ever heard of Paulie's Bistro? They serve a good variety of food. Would you like that? If you don't, we could go anywhere else. We don't have to go there. But it is good food and a very nice place."

My mouth wouldn't stop.

Robert grinned, "Paulie's sounds great. I am sure they have something there that I can eat."

"Here, you drive." I handed him the keys to my car.

"Are you sure?"

"Why not? You didn't forget how to drive did you?"

Why was I being so snarky?

Robert grinned at me again, "No. I didn't forget."

He took the keys and opened my door for me.

It took him a minute to figure out where everything was on the car.

Before long we had pulled out of the driveway and were headed to Paulie's for our date.

I was sitting right next to the door.

What was I so afraid of?

It was Bobby, I mean Robert for goodness sake.

Yes, it was Bobby for goodness sake!

"Do you want to listen to some music?"

"Sure, I told him."

He turned on the radio. It was set to cassette. Just as it came on, I died a thousand deaths.

"I wanna be Bobby's girl. I wanna be Bobby's girl" blasted through the speakers. Loudly.

I could not get it turned down fast enough.

"You must really like that song," Robert smiled.

"A little," I cringed, hoping he wouldn't notice that my face was redder than ever.

"I like it too," he said, "turn it back up."

So, I did.

After telling him where Paulie's was it didn't take us long to get there.

Paulie recognized me right away.

"Hi Miss Holly," he said as he side-kissed me. "Who is the gentleman you are with today?"

"This is Robert Davis. He is my neighbor. I mean my date. I mean, he is my neighbor, but today he is my date as well."

"Nice to meet you neighbor Robert Davis."

They shook hands.

"I believe your grandparents are finishing up. Would you like to sit in their area?"

"Sure. Why not?"

I could not think of a reason that would suffice in saying, "No. I don't want anyone to know that I am on a date with Robert right now. I want it to be personal and private and just ours for the first time to be together ever."

But "Sure. Why not," is what came out.

Thankfully he did not seat us right next to them and luckily, they were finishing up just like Paulie had said.

I excused myself and went to say hello.

They were as happy to see me as much as I was happy to see them.

I had to explain that I could not join them because I was on a date.

They looked over in Robert's direction and he nodded and smiled and gave a little wave.

They seemed to understand and did not even come over and introduce themselves.

They left and I went back and sat with my date. Robert Davis.

The menu was the same as it had always been.

Robert asked what I suggested. I never really thought about it, what was good and what might not be good. I am sure it was all good, but I giggled a little and told him I had a confession to make.

"I have only eaten here a few times. And every time I get the same thing. The spinach quiche and salad. My Grandmother does the same. I look at the menu repeatedly. It all sounds good but that is what I always get. My grandparents were creatures of habit. Grandmother always got the spinach quiche just like me and my grandfather always gets the French dip sandwich and salad. So really, those are the only two things that I know."

"I know I've looked at the menu several times and it all sounds good. But that French dip sandwich sounds good. I think I will try that."

We ordered and waited and waited, neither one of us saying a word.

They could not bring the food out fast enough.

"Oh, this is really good," he said after the first bite. "You want to try a bite? That way next time we come here you might want to try something different instead of the quiche."

"Did you say next time we come here?"

"Yep."

"So, you want to have a next time with me?"

"Yep."

"Really?"

"Yep."

I didn't know what to think or say.

"So, you think this date is going well?"

"Nope."

"Then why do you want to have a next time with me?"

Robert put down his sandwich and looked straight at me.

"Holly, I am going to tell you something. It is a bit embarrassing for me, but here goes. When you and your family moved in next door, you were just a little girl, three or four, I think. I had just started 1st grade. Lance was still at home. I came home from school and Lance told me all about the new family that had just moved in.

He told me all about you.

He thought you were cute.

I had to see for myself, so I came over to your house and just walked right in. There you were sitting on the end of the stairs playing with your dolls while the moving men moved furniture everywhere.

You were cute, just like Lance had said.

I don't even know if you noticed me or not that day.

I turned around and went straight home.

I found Lance and told him I had seen you. I told him what I had done. I then told him you were my new girlfriend. To which he promptly socked me in the nose and proclaimed you for himself.

I didn't get mad. I just sat him down and put my arm around his shoulder and explained to him that you couldn't be his girlfriend because I had already been to your house and now you were my girlfriend.

And besides, I told him, he wasn't your type. I was your type because you liked older men. And I was an older man, so you liked me and that is how it was going to be.

I let him cry it out that day. And after that, you were my girl."

I chuckled at this story.

"Well, Holly, as time went by, I never did have the guts or the opportunity to ask you for a date. And since you have been my girlfriend for such a long time, I think we should have a few more dates to make sure that I had as good of taste as I thought I did. Don't you agree?"

"Well, Robert, having not known all this time that we were such an item, I guess it would be the right thing to have a few dates. I am not going to be the one that messes up such a long-standing relationship like we've had over one lousy date."

"So, you think this is a lousy date."

"Yep."

We both laughed.

After the ice was broken, we talked a good long

while.

Mostly about our mothers becoming such good friends.

I told him how glad I was to have him back home safe but probably not near as much as his mom and dad.

We talked about everything banal while we finished our food.

But then it came time for dessert.

That is when I knew that we were meant to be for ever and ever.

"So, what is good for dessert here?"

"Well my grandfather always gets the chocolate mousse. But my grandmother and I always get the lemon tart. Again, they have many things but these two are the only ones that I know about."

"Well, I think I know which one I'll be having."

"The Chocolate Mousse?"

"No. I love lemon desserts. They are my favorite. I am going to have the lemon tart. And a cup of coffee."

"Same here!"

It was a lovely first date after all!

We had lunch the next day and the day after that. We were going to go to the movies on Friday night, but we ended up getting a burger and soda and taking it to the park and eating there.

We ate and walked around the park until it started getting dark.

He held my hand and we talked. I remember that a breeze blew past me and I shivered a bit. He pulled me closer and put his arm around my shoulder and rubbed my arm.

"Your arm is cold. I didn't realize how chilly the

evening had gotten."

"I have a sweater in the car."

We walked to the car and he opened the door and got my sweater for me. I started to take it from him but he held it so I could put my arms in it. I turned away and slipped one arm in and then I remember he helped me guide my other arm in. As he finished helping me. He gently spun me around to face him and pulled me close to himself.

Oh, he smelled so good.

He wrapped his arms around me and held me tightly to his chest.

My head rested on his heart and my arms went around him.

I remember him reaching down and tilting my head back as he leaned in to kiss me.

My heart was beating out of my chest. I had waited so long for this.

He leaned in and kissed me. He kissed me like I had been wanting him to do all my life.

I didn't want this night to ever end.

We walked and talked, and he held me close to his side and every little bit he would kiss me.

After a while he said he needed to take me home.

I wanted to protest but he was adamant that we go.

I thought maybe I had done something wrong. He barely spoke to me all the way home.

I remember thinking, "What have I done?"

He didn't get out of the car right away. After a couple of minutes, he finally spoke.

He wouldn't look at me at first.

"Holly, I know you probably think I am a jerk right now for bringing you home like this. Would you let me explain why?"

"Okay," I said as I looked at my hands in my lap.

He reached over and took my hand in his, "Look at me," he said. "I brought you home because I really, really like you. Your kissing me and me kissing you like we did was stirring up feelings in me that were not very respectful of you. The old Robert would have probably taken advantage of those emotions and to hell with everything.

But I am not that person anymore.

I really am trying to be a Godly man. A man worthy of you.

I want to honor you in every way.

I couldn't spend any more time alone with you tonight. It would not have been the right thing to do.

Holly, I really want to get to know you.

The real you.

I want to know who you are.

I want to know who you want to be when you grow up.

I want you to know me like that too.

So, we are going to have to have a few more dates.

I know you are going to be going back to school on Monday. I am staying here and will be getting a job.

I want to start college next year myself. I have been talking to Toby and he thinks between our Pastor and Pastor Taylor endorsing me that I could possibly get into the same school you are going to next year. That is if you wouldn't mind dating a freshman?"

My hands and my heart were trembling. Much like I had been trembling every time he had kissed me.

"I would like that. Robert, can I make a confession to you as well?"

"Holly, you can tell me anything."

"Promise not to laugh?"

"Is it going to be embarrassing?"

"Yes."

"Then I can't promise that. But I promise to try and not to laugh. Will that be okay?'

"I guess. Okay. Well, you told me of how when you were a little boy that you told Lance I was your girlfriend?"

"Yeah."

"Well, when I was a younger girl, I always wanted to be your girlfriend. I never thought you even knew my name. So, you said, you wanted to know what I wanted to be when I grow up. Let me show you."

I leaned over and turned on the car and turned on the tape player and rewound it to the very first song and hit play.

"This is what I have wanted to be my whole life when I grow up."

He didn't laugh.

He looked at me and said, "I know we have only been dating a very short time. A very short time, but I need to go get something from my house.

Will you wait here? It might be a couple of minutes."

"I'll wait."

He sprinted across the yard and into his house. I waited patiently. After about 15 minutes he came back carrying some rolled up papers in his hands.

"Now it's your turn to promise not to laugh."

"I won't." I crossed my heart.

Robert turned on the lights and slowly unfolded paper after paper. Each one had pictures or notes on them.

It was pictures drawn by a little red headed boy in love with a little strawberry blond girl.

Some said Holly is my girlfriend written in crayon.

One or two declared an undying love.

One or two announced that he was going to marry this girl Holly when he got bigger.

Then the teenage years where the writing turned to pen. A young man wishing that the girl he could see sitting in her window seat would give him the time of day. She probably doesn't even know I am alive.

Some even declared how he was going to ask certain girls to go on dates with him so that I would find out and get jealous.

But then as he matured a little, he realized that I still sat in the same spot every day and would always wave back at him if he waved at me.

One of them said he could never understand why I never looked happy. He vowed to change that.

Someday I will marry her if she'll have me. I will be the best thing that ever happened to her.

My heart melted as I read them.

Tears rolled silently down my face.

I wiped them away.

"Holly, I know that we have only been on a few dates. And normally, if there is such a thing, it would be way too early to tell anyone this, but Holly, I am in love with you. I think I always have been."

I looked up and looked so deep into his blue eyes.

I knew that I could trust him with my heart.

I knew that I had to tell him.

If he could still love me after that, then maybe, just

maybe, I could tell him how much I loved him as well.

CHAPTER 11

I remember asking him if he was sure he really wanted to know everything about me. He assured me that he did.

I told him to please turn off the lights in the car. We rolled down the windows a bit and listened to the silence for a moment. The smell of jasmine and roses were in the air.

Spring, the smell of newness.

I told Robert something that night that very few people knew.

Truthfully only a handful of people knew the whole truth and nothing but the truth.

I started at the beginning, leaving out nothing. He reached over and took my hand as the story unfolded.

I told how I had blamed myself for so long for what happened. But that I had come to realize that it was not my fault.

He interjected that it was not my fault. None of it was.

I continued on to the part where I found out I was pregnant after Father had died. How I had gone to live with my Aunt and Uncle until I had the baby.

How she had been born and when.

I told of being able to hold her and kiss her and cuddle her, even if but for a brief moment.

I told him how my arms have never felt full since that day.

I told how I had given her up for adoption and that I had also found out who adopted her. I didn't tell him who she was or who her parents were.

I didn't feel that it was right to do so at that moment.

I told how I had never felt clean or worthy for anyone to love me.

Then I looked at him and said, "That is until you poured out your heart on Sunday night. When you spoke about all you had gone through and what God had done for you, that is when I knew, all the things that people have been telling me about how much God loves me started to make sense. I am still struggling with forgiving him. I know that I am supposed to, and I am truly trying, but it is very hard.

I wanted you to know all this about me because I really am not the girl that you should want to be with.

I am used property.

I know you just said that you love me.

But after hearing all this if you want to change your mind I would understand."

"Holly, no, no, I would not change my mind. You are so much the girl I want to be with. I have loved you for so long. I can't imagine not loving you.

I dream about you every night.

Your beautiful face.

Your smile.

Your laugh.

Holly, I love you more now than I ever thought possible.

I can only speak for myself.

I love you and I always will.

What I don't know, is if you even feel a little of what I feel. Do you have any feelings for me at all?"

"Robert, I can't remember not loving you either. I love you so much that my heart doesn't seem large enough to contain it. Please kiss me one more time?"

This time he leaned in and tenderly kissed me until I melted.

I knew that he loved me.

I could feel it when I laid my head on his shoulder and we just sat there and held hands.

I knew it when we woke up the next morning in the same position.

My head on his shoulder, holding his hand.

We would have probably slept like that all morning if mother had not woken us up by knocking on the window.

"Oh my. I am so sorry Holly. I didn't mean for us to fall asleep out here like this. I am so sorry."

"We didn't do anything wrong," I laughed. "Come on inside and I'll make us a cup of coffee. How do you take it?'

"A little cream."

We were going to get along just fine!

CHAPTER 12

"Hey, sleepyhead, you have been awfully quiet. What have you been thinking about?"

"About us."

"Was it good?"

"So far. I was just remembering that first day when you asked me out. I was so nervous. I had been waiting for you to ask me forever and when you actually did, I was so nervous that I almost threw up."

"Well now, that is what a guy likes to hear. "Remember when you asked me out on a date? It made me want to throw up.""

"No, not because of you silly, because of me."

"I'm just kidding you."

"I had never been on a date with anyone. Ever. Not only was it because you asked me, I wasn't sure what to do on a date."

"Like how you introduced me to Paulie that first time. "He's my neighbor." I couldn't tell you were nervous at all. No, not at all."

"Now you are teasing me. Now I know who I really married."

"Hey, I was just as nervous as you. I had wanted to ask you out for a long time. I'd had four cups of coffee that morning while I built up the courage to ask you. I knew your mother would be leaving soon to go the Bible study with my mom. My mom told me to tell your mom that she was ready to go when I got there. But your mom must have known it because she was about to walk out the door when I rang the bell. She told me you were by the den, to come on in. I was pretty surprised when I came in and you were sprawled out on the floor."

"My foot had fallen asleep. When I was getting up to answer the door it betrayed me, and I fell. I was so embarrassed. Luckily you didn't see me fall two more times before you came back over."

"Pretty clumsy huh? I'll have to remember that. Just kidding. But really, I was probably as nervous as you that morning. Just because I had been on a date before, I had never been on one with you. And when I saw you lying there, I knew that I had to be with you, forever. Somebody had to take care of you!"

"Forever it shall be then. How much longer until we get there do you think?"

"It is just up the road. Shouldn't be long."

"Good. It has been a long day. If it was going to be much longer, I was going to suggest that we pull over and take a nap at a rest stop. Wouldn't be the first time we slept in this car. Remember that?"

"Oh, I remember. I was so embarrassed. Here we were, two grown people, that had just poured their hearts out to each other. Big talk about respecting each other and then promptly sleep together!"

"We didn't sleep together! Well, I guess we did huh?"

"What did your mother ever say to you after I went home?"

"Not a single thing. I am sure she knew that it

was as innocent as it looked. I mean, we had papers all over us and we were fully clothed. She never even mentioned it. Did your mother ever say anything?"

"Why would my mother say anything?"

"They are best friends remember. Just because she didn't say anything to me doesn't mean she didn't say anything to your mother."

"I see. Well, if she did, she didn't say anything to me about it. I think we are here."

"Oh, this is nice. It is little bungalows lined up right along the ocean. Can't wait to see what it looks like inside."

"Me too! We are going to have to do something extra special for your Grandparents! This is really nice."

We had no idea how nice it was.

It was the honeymoon suite.

So very secluded and right on the ocean.

We followed the bell hop in the car to the end of the row of bungalows.

Bungalow #21.

He unlocked the door for us and carried in our bags and put them in the bedroom. He made sure to point out where everything was. It had a fully stocked kitchenette and a little dining table. It also had a little sitting area with a television. Then he opened the back door off the dining area to reveal another world. Another sitting area and a secluded beach for a back yard with an ocean view.

Robert tipped him and he left. I had stayed outside to enjoy the wondrous vision that was laid out before me.

The moon was shimmering off the ocean and the

stars were sprinkled everywhere. It was a full sky. It matched my full heart.

The sounds of the waves as they beat on the shore kept perfect rhythm. It was made perfectly complete when Robert came back out and came up to me and wrapped me in his arms.

We stood there for what seemed to be forever just taking it all in.

Then he turned me around and tilted my head just like the first time he had kissed me, and we kissed and we kissed and we kissed, and I melted into him.

CHAPTER 13

I was so nervous. More than I thought I would be. A lot more!

We went inside and Robert asked if I wanted to get ready for bed first or should he.

I told him he could.

We began to put our clothes away. It didn't take him very long. When he was done, he went in to get himself ready.

I finished putting my things away while he was in there. I carefully laid the beautiful negligee out that I had brought with me for this very special night. As I looked at it, my stomach started doing flip flops.

Robert came out looking so handsome. It had been a long time since I had seen a man in pajamas. And I don't think Uncles and cousins should count. He was just so gorgeous.

"It's all yours."

I walked past him carrying my things and he stopped me and kissed me one more time.

I smiled and hurried into the bathroom to get ready hoping he wouldn't see how scared I truly was.

He put the suitcases away while I was in there.

It took me forever it seemed like. My ears were on fire as I worried about what was going to happen after I came out. I wiped tears away and almost decided that maybe I should just stay in there until he fell asleep.

Tomorrow night would be as good of a time as any to do what I knew he wanted to do.

It wasn't like I didn't want to, but I was so scared. I was so unsure of myself. It wasn't like I didn't know what was going to happen. I had experience of sorts. But this time it would be something freely given, not taken.

Robert knocked on the door.

"Everything ok?"

"I'll be right out."

I guess he wasn't going to fall asleep.

Slowly I unlocked the door and stepped out. He was there waiting for me.

"Are you ok?"

"No. I'm not ok. I don't think I can do this."

"It's ok. I understand."

He took my hand and we walked into the sitting area. He sat on the loveseat and guided me down beside him.

"Let's just sit here for a while. We have the rest of our lives to do this."

I scooted in as close to him as I could. He wrapped his arms around me and held me. I was shaking like a leaf.

"It's going to be okay."

He kissed me so tenderly and then held me some more.

At some point I must have quit shaking and settled into his arms. I don't remember falling asleep, but I did.

I woke up the next morning lying next to my husband in our bed. Still fully clothed.

He was laying there looking at me.

"Good morning sleepy head! It is after nine. I thought you were going to sleep all day!" He smiled at me and kissed my forehead.

"How, I mean, when, I mean, how did we get in here?"

"After you fell asleep, I picked you up and carried you in here. I figured you would probably sleep better in a bed than in a chair. Looks like I was right."

"Did we?"

"Holly, no, we didn't. I would never take advantage of you like that. I love you with all my heart. When you are ready you will let me know and then it will happen. But, no, sweetheart, we didn't. How about some coffee?"

"Oh yes. Coffee sounds divine. Do you think they have some here so we can make a nice big pot of it?"

"Let's go look!"

Then he kissed me once more and we made a pot of coffee. We went outside and watched the world unfold before us as we started our new life as husband and wife. With the ocean and coffee and God what could go wrong.

Life was good!

CHAPTER 14

Both Robert and I were early risers. So, getting up at 9 a.m. seemed as if we had slept half of the day away. Which wasn't entirely true. We hadn't really fallen asleep until probably four or four-thirty. But nonetheless, we were awake and starving.

We dressed and went to find a restaurant that was still serving breakfast. We stopped in at the lobby to see what they recommended and was told that the resort had a great restaurant and it was still serving breakfast or even lunch if we liked.

We liked.

It was a sweet little place and we were seated right away.

We looked over the menu and after a few minutes we decided on breakfast.

"And what will you have ma'am?"

"I will take a toasted bagel with cream cheese and more coffee please."

"Really? Really? That is all you are going to have. I thought you said you were starving. I'm starving."

"And what will the gentleman be having?"

"I will have the number four breakfast."

"And how would you like your eggs?"

"Over easy."

"And your steak?"

"Medium rare."

"And did you want hash-browns or home fries?"

"Fries."

"Do you prefer maple syrup or a flavored syrup for your pancakes?"

"Maple."

"White or wheat toast?"

"Make it white. No, can you make it a bagel?"

"Yes sir, we can."

"Then make it a bagel. And more coffee. Oh yeah, and a tall glass of milk."

"Ok. We'll have that right out to you."

"Really? Really? You were that hungry?"

"I'm starving. Like a bear. Like a ring bear."

We both giggled as we remembered my little cousin growling.

"I love to hear you laugh and see you smile. That is what I am going to live for. For the rest of my life it is going to be my goal to make you smile and laugh."

We clinked our glasses of water together and toasted each other.

"To joy."

"To laughter."

"To love."

Clink!

I really had no idea that he could eat that much.

I made sure to point out that the only thing that was left on his plate was the bagel.

"I am saving it for later."

"Later?"

"Yeah, for an afternoon snack."

"Oh, dear Lord. You think you are going to need an afternoon snack! Dear Lord help us."

"Yep! What are we going to do when we leave here?"

"I don't really know. To be honest I don't know what is around here. One thing I think we should do is find a car wash."

"Oh yeah! We need to get that shoe polish off the car and those cans. I am not sure if there were that many left hanging on there, but we need to get that cleaned up. What are we going to do after that?"

"How about let's come back and swim in the ocean. I have never been swimming in the ocean before. It should be gloriously hot this afternoon and that should cool us off. How does that sound? You can even eat your bagel then too!"

"Well that sounds like a plan to me! I was wondering when I was going to make time to eat this bagel."

"Well, now you know."

CHAPTER 15

The girl at the lobby desk told us where we could take the car to get it washed. She also gave us some brochures for things we could do in the area.

Robert had been right. There was one lonely can left hanging off the car and two shoes that had seen way better days.

We cut all of that off before we went to the car wash.

It wasn't too far. We opted to go through the car wash instead of hand washing it. It cleaned it really well.

The attendant congratulated us as we paid for the extra heavy-duty stuff to make sure we got all the polish off. He assured us it would all come off. And it did!

We drove back to the spa and went inside.

"I've been thinking. Let's call the restaurant and check on room service."

"You're hungry again?"

"No. And besides, I still have my bagel, remember?"

"Oh, I remember."

"What I was trying to say is, let's see if we can order dinner and have them bring it to us. How does that sound?'

"Ooh, that sounds nice. I know there is a menu in

there. If they have a menu then I am sure they will do room service. Let's look and see what they have."

"I bet they have bagels," he teased.

"Don't worry. If I get hungry for a bagel again today, I will just have a bite of yours."

"You think I will share my bagel with you? You already had a bagel today."

"And you had everything else. And yes. I think you will share your bagel with me."

"Why do you think that?"

"Because you love me!"

"Yes, yes I do. I would give you the whole thing if you wanted it. That is how much I love you."

"I would never want you to do that. I wouldn't take the whole thing because I love you too."

He kissed me.

I love this man so much!

After looking over the menu, we decided that a lobster dinner for two would be delicious!

Robert called and asked if we could have it delivered and set up by six that evening.

"No problem sir."

Then we were ready for the ocean.

Robert said he would go to the lobby and get us some sodas to drink while we were on the beach.

I told him I would try and be ready when he returned.

And I was.

I had hoped he would like the bikini that I had picked out.

It was a little skimpy, but it wasn't meant to be seen by anyone else but him anyways. And after all, he was my husband.

I had a cover up over myself when he returned.

I told him I would get us some glasses and ice down the sodas while he got ready.

I had just taken them outside and sat them on the table when he came out with some towels.

I could not take my eyes off him.

He looked gorgeous.

He had on a muscle shirt and a pair of swim trunks. Every muscle he had was showing.

Now I knew why I always felt so secure in his arms.

My heart started to thump in my chest.

"Come on. Let's go set the towels on the beach and try out that water."

He carried the towels and I carried the sodas.

Before long we had everything set up the way we wanted it.

He took off his shirt and I realized that I still had my cover up on.

I slowly let it drop onto the towels.

Now it was his turn to look.

I hoped he liked what he saw.

"Oh, my Holly. You are beautiful. So beautiful."

"Do you like it?"

"I love it. But more so, I love the person wearing it."

He reached out and took my hand and we walked into the ocean.

He held me close and kissed me as we just stood there.

His kisses were tender and loving and wonderful.

I knew that he wanted me. I wanted him too. I was trembling so bad. I was so scared.

"Holly, I want you so bad," he whispered.

"I know. I'm so scared though. I don't know why. I

am feeling things inside my body that I have never felt before and it is scaring me."

"We won't do anything you don't want to do. But let's go back to the room and just kiss and see if you want to go any further."

I agreed.

We walked back to the room, stopping to get our things along the way.

He dried me off before we went inside and then we closed the door behind us.

I knew that I was going to give myself to this man.

I was scared and I was trembling. But Robert was a man of his word.

He was kind.

He was gentle.

He took his time as we made love for the first time.

We fell asleep in each other's arms, only to be woken up by the knocking on the front door as our dinner was delivered.

CHAPTER 16

Saturday morning, we awoke with the sunrise.

We had spent the rest of the night getting to know each other after we devoured our delicious dinner.

Once I knew that I could fully trust Robert then I knew that I could fully give myself to him.

We went for an early morning swim and came back inside to warm up with a nice hot cup of coffee.

After a good breakfast we spent the day just walking around the town looking in the shops and seeing the sites.

We ate lunch at a little shack on the wharf. It was the most divine fish and chips.

This quaint little town was full of characters and the ocean. Well the ocean was what poetry was made of. The way the sunlight hit the waves and the crescendo that echoed as they hit the jutting rocks.

It was like a symphony.

After we had went out to do a little sightseeing, we realized we had seen a lot of churches in the little town. We knew we would be going to one of them, so we stopped in at the lobby when we got back to the spa that afternoon to find out what the local churches were.

The girl at the front desk told us of several in the area. But she told us that her church was having a guest speaker on Sunday and they would be glad to have us.

We told her we would be delighted to go to her church since she had invited us.

She told us where it was and what time the services were. She told us that she was sure we would enjoy the speaker. She had heard him preach before and thought that he was a dynamic preacher. He would be preaching in the morning and evening service.

We were looking forward to going now.

Robert had one more year before he was to graduate.

He and I had many discussions over the past three years as to what he was going to do when he graduated.

We had prayed and we'd had Toby and Patty pray with us looking for guidance.

It was easy for Toby and Patty and even Robert at some point to say they were waiting on the Lord to reveal what it was He wanted us to do.

Many times, Robert would tell me, "I am doing everything in my power to be still and listen, to try and hear what the Lord is telling me. I want to be that man, that righteous man, the one that knows where his foot is supposed to go."

We would read the Word together. He would read and re-read a passage. He would discuss it with me.

All four of us had spent so much time learning the Word of God together. It was starting to make sense. I was starting to want to read it more and more, but I could not keep up with them. Sometimes I felt like it was over my head.

Robert felt as if he had a calling on his life. That he

was supposed to either be a preacher or an evangelist like Toby.

I was just happy to be Roberts fiancé, well wife, now. So, whatever he felt he should do, I was willing to do with him.

They seemed to have a relationship with the Lord that was so much deeper than mine.

Not that I didn't want it, I just wasn't sure how to get it.

I knew that I had a long road ahead of me before I was to get to where they were.

Fully trusting in God.

I did trust Him. I did love Him. But it felt like I was holding something back.

Even after three years I still felt like I was taking baby steps.

Just what was missing I didn't know.

Sometimes I thought that maybe it was because I still didn't feel like I was worthy of His love. Even though I accepted that He loved me, I couldn't help but feel that I didn't deserve it.

I would pray at night and feel all was well but when I would lay down the thoughts would run around in my mind reminding me of what I had done.

I would sometimes cry myself to sleep over it. I would try to tell myself that the Bible said that since I had confessed my sins He was just and would forgive my sins.

What more could I ask for? Maybe I was not going to be the one that had that kind of relationship with Him.

But I truly wanted it.

All I could tell myself was one day, maybe this God

that Toby, Patty and Robert could hear talking to them would talk to me and I will hear His voice and will know it.

I wasn't going to give up.

I was going to keep on praying and believing and hoping that He loved me as much as He loved them and that I would be able to be the preacher's wife or evangelist's wife that He wanted me to be.

CHAPTER 17

Waking up as Mrs. Robert Davis was getting to be more lovely by the moment.

I so loved this man.

How could I not?

Who couldn't fall in love over and over again each morning to a man after your own heart? Whose first thoughts each morning was first of you and then coffee?

Sunday morning Robert and I both were excited to get up early.

We put a pot of coffee on after we took our time getting out of bed. Then we took a dip in that cool wonderful ocean. Then coffee to warm us up.

Our thoughts turned to church. We opted to go to Sunday School. Afterall, if they were not teaching the Word in Sunday School then we might not want to stay for the morning service, no matter who the special speaker was.

I knew Robert was excited to hear someone preach as an evangelist. The more he talked about what he felt God was calling him to do, the more I felt like he thought it was to be an evangelist, like Toby and Patty.

I wasn't sure what I felt about it. I just knew that I would follow Robert and go wherever life took him.

After a quick bite to eat in the restaurant we

headed to church. It wasn't too far of a drive, about 10 minutes. As we drove, we thought we saw someone walking up ahead that looked familiar. We slowed down and sure enough it was the girl from the spa that had invited us to church. Robert pulled up alongside her and asked if we could give her a lift. She hesitated for a moment but decided to take a chance on us.

"Thank you," she said a little timidly.

"You are so welcome," I told her. "I am so sorry. I forget your name?"

"Oh, it's Amy. Amy Pinkerton."

I turned to shake her hand.

"Well, nice to actually meet you Amy Pinkerton. My name is Holly, and this is my husband, Robert. You should have told us you needed a ride to church this morning. We would have been more than happy to pick you up."

"Oh, it's no problem. I walk pretty much everywhere I go. Luckily for me the places I go are not too far from where I live. The only time it's a bother is when the weather turns bad. Then I just stay home pretty much. Well, except for church. If the weather is bad, someone usually comes and gets me."

"Do you guys get a lot of bad weather here?"

"Not often. Sometimes. But not often."

"How long have you been going to this church? Did you grow up here?"

"Yeah, I grew up in this little town. I have been going to church here a little over three years now. Ever since I moved back here. There, there's the church."

We pulled in and we all got out.

Amy told us Sunday School was going to be

starting in a few minutes.

She took us inside this quaint little church.

It was like going home.

It felt like church as soon as we walked in.

"Amy, good morning! So glad to see you this morning. Who is this you've brought with you?"

Amy introduced us, pretty much to everyone as it seemed everyone knew her.

She was beaming as she spoke to them. She seemed to stand much taller and prouder as she maneuvered her way around.

Three little girls came running to her.

"Miss Amy! Are you ready for Sunday School?"

"Yes I am. How about you? Did you study your lesson? Who knows their memory verse?"

All three hands shot up.

"Let's go then. Will you both be ok? I have a class to teach."

"We'll be fine. We'll find our class."

Just as we were about to ask what class we should go to, the special speaker showed up.

"What are you two doing here?"

"I could ask you two the same thing. What are you two doing here?"

I didn't care why they were there. I was just happy to see Toby and Patty walk in the doors.

Hugs and handshakes all around.

Then the Pastor of the church walked up.

After Toby introduced us to him and his wife, we all went to Sunday School together.

We knew that we would be staying for the service.

Any church that would have Toby as their special speaker truly taught the Word of God.

CHAPTER 18

There wasn't much time to talk to each other between Sunday School and church service. We all found a place up front to sit together.

Amy noticed us and came to join us with a couple of other young ladies.

The pastor introduced them to Toby and Patty and us.

We told him that we knew who Amy was. She was the reason we were there today.

"Well now, that sounds about right. Our little church has grown a lot because of this young lady. She invites everyone to come to church."

They sat by us as the service began.

After the song service and a few preliminaries, the pastor introduced Toby and Patty.

Amy leaned into me, "Have you ever heard them before? They sing so good together and his preaching is like nothing else."

"I have heard him before. He is my cousin."

"Your what?"

"Yes, he is my cousin. His wife Patty is my best friend."

"Did you know they were going to be here this morning?"

"No. It was a great surprise that they were

the guest speakers that you told us about yesterday. Thank you so much for inviting us."

She beamed, "Thank you so much for actually coming. I ask a lot of people. They don't always come."

"Their loss!"

We settled back to hear Patty and Toby sing a new song.

And Amy was right. They did sing beautifully together. Patty came back and joined us as Toby began to preach.

"Good morning," he began. "This morning I received a happy surprise. I always expect to get something from a church service whenever I walk through the doors. I was pleasantly surprised this morning when I walked in and there was a couple of visitors to your beautiful church that I had not expected to see here.

Just a few short days ago I had the privilege of marrying two of my favorite people to each other. Would you two stand up?" He pointed to Robert and me.

We stood up.

"Ladies and gentlemen let me introduce to you my cousin Holly and her new husband, Robert. Mr. and Mrs. Robert Davis."

The church applauded.

We sat down and Toby continued.

"Would you all please stand for the reading of the Word?"

The congregation stood.

"Open your Bibles to John 8 starting with verse 1."

"1. Jesus went unto the Mount of Olives. 2. And early

in the morning He came again into the temple, and all the people came unto Him; and he sat down and taught them. 3. And the scribes and Pharisees brought unto Him a woman taken in adultery; and when they had sat her in the midst, 4. They say unto Him, Master, this woman was taken in adultery, in the very act, 5. Now Moses in the law commanded us, that such should be stoned: but sayest thou? 6. This they said, tempting Him, that they might have to accuse Him. But Jesus stooped down, and with His finger wrote on the ground, as though He heard them not. 7. So when they continued asking Him, He lifted up Himself, and said unto them, He that is without sin among you, let him first cast a stone at her. 8. And again he stooped down and wrote on the ground. 9. And they which heard it, being convicted by their own conscience, went out one by one, beginning at the eldest, even unto the last: and Jesus was left alone, and the woman standing in the midst. 10. When Jesus had lifted Himself up, and saw none but the woman, he said unto her, Woman, where are those thine accusers? Hath no man condemned thee? 11. She said, No man, Lord. And Jesus said unto her, neither do I condemn thee: go, and sin no more."

Then Toby prayed and we were all seated.

"This morning's service is kind of a heavy subject.

A lot of people get their feathers ruffled when you talk about this woman.

They think the subject is taboo.

We shouldn't bring it up.

I want to tell you something about this passage. It has nothing to do with the kind of sin that had been committed. This passage is not about the sin as much as it is about the sinners.

Now we have a group of characters in this story.

Let's start with the main character.

That would be Jesus.

Let's assume that in every Bible story that Jesus should be the main character.

But in this story, He is especially crucial.

Here he was, in the temple, preaching and teaching. He had a good audience. Now I am going to let you in on a little secret, as a minister, I would be lost without an audience. I need one or I wouldn't have a job. Your pastor can attest to this.

Well, Jesus had an audience.

He actually was preaching to a group of church people.

The people that he was addressing that morning were Godly men, they just didn't recognize God when He was in their midst.

As a matter of fact, they considered this man Jesus, a fake man of God.

A blasphemer.

They hated Him and were always looking for a way to entangle Him. Hoping that at some point they would be able to destroy Him.

Take Him down.

Get rid of Him.

But today was not going to be that day.

Now, for some reason, this group of men, these Scribes and Pharisees, knew of a certain woman that was a common woman.

Now, the Bible doesn't say *how* they knew of her, it just says they did.

They knew exactly where to find her and what she would be doing and when. They knew what she was doing was a sin.

It was a sin yesterday when she was doing it.

It was a sin a week ago when she was doing it.

And it would still be a sin tomorrow.

It had not seemed to be an issue up until this moment in time.

Now, in this particular sin, it takes two.

I have often wondered why they only brought her.

Makes you think doesn't it?

Why not bring the man?

Clearly, he was as much at fault as she was.

But I am going to tell you, that in this story, the sin did not matter.

The story could have easily read, this woman was caught in the middle of lying. She is a known liar. She lies all the time.

Or, this woman was caught in the middle of robbing someone, she is a thief. She steals from people all the time.

The sin is not the main crux of the story.

It is the sinner.

Now let's talk about the next character or group of characters, the Scribes and Pharisees.

These men, these holy men.

Men that knew the Word, well the old testament anyways.

Men that taught the Word.

They were men with a bunch of head knowledge, but not a lot of heart knowledge.

They truly had the author of the book right in their midst and didn't recognize Him.

They were so blinded by their hatred. Blinded by their desire to destroy this man, Jesus.

He spoke the words they knew, and it pierced their souls. It convicted them and they didn't like it. So, they plotted and schemed every chance they got to try and convict Him with His own words and actions.

"What better way than to have Him do or say something contrary to the Law. Moses law!

The laws that God Himself had given to Moses."

But wait, He was God.

He knew the law.

He was the law.

And finally, the woman.

Now this woman had a title.

As much as these men, these Scribes and Pharisees were known by their title and by their actions, and as much as Jesus was known, so was this woman known.

Everyone in town probably knew her business.

I am sure she was shunned by the women in this town and by anyone who would not want to be associated with her.

Much like the woman at the well. A woman. Despised and rejected.

But then Jesus.

Much like Nicodemus, the tax collector, despised by men.

But then Jesus.

Aren't we all so glad that there has been a "But then Jesus" point in our lives?

I know I am.

So now, they have taken this woman, caught in the act of sin, and brought her to the feet of Jesus.

They want Him to condemn her, to justify their actions.

But then Jesus.

He didn't react to their presentation of sin at His feet.

Instead, He stooped down, and started writing on the ground with His finger, acting like He hadn't even heard them.

Now, I have read this passage over and over again. Nowhere in here does it tell what He wrote.

He could have been writing the law of Moses, you know, the very thing they were trying to ensnare Him with, those pesky 10 commandments, He starts writing.

1. *You shall have no other Gods before me.*

2. *You shall not have any graven image.*

3. *You shall not take the name of the Lord your God in vain.*

4. *You shall remember the Sabbath and keep it holy.*

5. *You shall honor your father and mother.*

6. *You shall not kill.*

7. *You shall not commit adultery.*

8. *You shall not steal.*

9. *You shall not bear false witness.*

10. *You shall not covet.*

Most of them probably thought, "I have held every one of these commandments!"

Then maybe Jesus added a Proverb.

"As a man thinketh, so is he!"

So, they stand there watching Him write.

Possibly realizing that maybe they had not committed sin so that man could see it, but in their hearts, in their minds.

Remember, Jesus may have written the word, but these men had memorized it. That is how they knew to twist it.

To justify themselves.

Maybe while they were standing there, the Holy Spirit pricked their minds and reminded them that these people that were standing around them, looking at them, maybe they didn't know the sin or sins that they had committed, but they remembered the verse when the Lord said to Samuel when he was showing him who would be king.

"Man looks on the outside, but God looks on the heart."

Maybe the Holy Spirit reminded them of the 139th Psalm that told them the truth. That there was nowhere they could hide, no place that they could go that God could not see their very thoughts, their very hearts.

Then it says, He lifted Himself up and spoke to them.

He addressed their sin.

The very thing they are condemning this woman of, not the adultery, but the sin.

Now, I want to interject something here. If you think I am wrong, so be it, but I do not believe there are degrees of sin. I have not read anywhere in this book that one sin is more heinous than another.

Sin is sin.

Sin is what separates us from God.

I also do not believe that if you only sin a little or you didn't commit a big sin, thinking, well, I only told a little lie, I didn't kill someone, so even if I don't make it to heaven, my section of hell won't be as bad as someone that has killed someone.

Nope, that's not in there either.

Sin is sin!

But these righteous men, these holy men, seemed to know better.

That is, until Jesus called them out on it.

They were condemning her of doing something that they had probably been guilty of. And if not of this sin at least one of them.

But then Jesus, lifting Himself up, addressed their sins. He knew their hearts. He knew what they are thinking.

"He who is without sin, go ahead, cast the first stone."

Then He knelt back down and began to write again.

Maybe this time He started naming names.

Maybe this time He let them know what was in their own hearts.

As their consciences were pierced, as they were convicted, one by one. they let the stones drop out of their hands and they left, until after a while, it was just Jesus and this woman.

Do you really think when He stood back up and looked around that He was surprised that they had all left?

Do you think His first thought was, "Wow, that really worked!"

Do you think that it was for anyone else's benefit at that very moment when He looked at the woman and asked her, "Where are your accusers?"

Do you think He didn't already know?

He knew.

When she answered Him, "there are none," He already knew that as well.

"Neither do I condemn thee, go and sin no more."

I would love to think that as He lifted her up off the ground that all her shame, her guilt, her sin, fell at His feet.

That when she came up, after being so completely guilty, so beat down, that every chain, every shackle, every condemnation that had been thrust upon her, was now laying at the feet of the Master, the Redeemer.

She was no longer a woman with the title “Adulteress”.

She had a new name, it was Redeemed.

It was new creation.

It was child of God.

Let’s see what that next verse tells us, verse 12.

“Then spake Jesus again unto them, saying, I am the light of the world: he that followeth Me shall not walk in darkness, but shall have the light of life.”

Oh man, what a promise of God.

If we are followers of Christ, then we no longer live in darkness but have the light of life living inside of us.

You know, I am sure there are many here today who feel that condemnation in your heart.

Just like the Scribes and the Pharisees that day felt it.

Just like the woman felt it.

Just like the woman at the well felt it.

Just like Nicodemus felt it.

Just like I have felt it.

We are sinners.

God’s word tells us that “All” have sinned, and we “All” have come short of the Glory of God.

All, not some. All!

You can leave here today like the Scribes and Pharisees did, taking all your guilt and condemnation with you. They didn’t have to, but they did.

Or you can come to this altar and lay that sin, that guilt, at the feet of Jesus.

You can leave it there.

Don't pick it back up, leave it there.

Jesus knows your very heart.

He knows that we may not have Scribes and Pharisees around anymore to condemn us.

To taunt us.

To tell us that we are not worthy of Jesus love.

That we can't be forgiven of our sins because they are too heinous.

Maybe you have given your heart to Christ, but you are still living under condemnation.

Maybe you are being tormented.

Satan is just standing there waiting to throw stones at you.

Still condemning you.

Still lying to you.

Still deceiving you.

He wants to see you still bound in the chains of your condemnation!

Don't believe him!

Don't let the lies of the devil keep you from living a delivered life.

A redeemed life.

A life full of the light of life.

Jesus said, you do not have to live in darkness any longer. He told us, *"Come unto Me, all ye that labor and are heavy laden, and I will give you rest. Take my yoke upon you and learn of me; for I am meek and lowly in heart: and ye shall find rest unto your souls. For My yoke is easy, and my burden is light."*

We can drop those chains that bind us, that keep us

thinking that we are not deserving.

That we really have not been set free.

But we have!

I have been!

You have been!

We all can be set free!

We can all find that freedom here at the foot of the cross.

Just as "All" have sinned, "All" can be set free!

We can leave these things, sin and grief, there at Jesus' feet!

And as we follow Him, we can be filled with His light, the light of life.

I am going to open the altars this morning for anyone that would like to come and give your heart to God.

To anyone that is feeling the condemnation of the deceiver, the one that would steal, kill, and destroy.

I want you to quit listening to him and come and be set free.

He whom the Lord sets free is free indeed!

Come to the altars this morning and be set free indeed!"

Many came to the altar that morning.

I, myself included.

I was so tired of being deceived.

I did not want to live under the condemnation any longer.

I was tired of not walking full of His light.

I knew that I was saved.

I knew that I had been forgiven.

I knew that I was a Child of God.

I *was* one of the redeemed and I was going to take

ownership of that.

The chains came off that morning and I was filled with the Holy Spirit and a newness in my heart. I would not be walking in the dark ever again.

I was going to start living for the Lord.

Not just doing lip service but I was going to give Him Lordship in my life.

I was redeemed!

CHAPTER 19

We had invited Amy to join us for Sunday dinner, but she had plans with her two friends. So, Patty, Toby, Robert, and I joined the Pastor and his wife at a little café not too far from the church.

By the time everyone had gone from the church it was much later than usual, so we had missed a big church crowd. But it was still bustling.

We only had to wait a few minutes to be seated.

The pastor's children had been invited to spend the afternoon with a couple of their friends, so it was more of a couple's luncheon.

Pastor Marks and his wife Terri had been the pastors of the little church going on five years they told us as the conversation started. As it turned, out they knew Pastor Taylor and his family.

That is how Toby and Patty had gotten the invitation to come and preach.

We were laughing about which one of us had been more surprised at seeing the other one this morning.

"Amy, the girl who invited us, told us that her church was having a special speaker this morning and asked if we would like to come and hear him. We had no idea that it was you two. She didn't say and we didn't ask. How crazy is that?"

"I know. We walked in and I thought my eyes were

playing tricks on me. I didn't realize this was the town you were honeymooning at."

"You are on your honeymoon," Terri asked?

"Oh, yes. We just got married on the 4th. With all the excitement I guess we didn't think to ask where they were going to be preaching this weekend."

"You never told me what town you were going to, just that it was a Spa Resort. With both of us getting married so close together I don't think our heads were on straight for the last few weeks. I am so happy you were here today. It made it so much nicer."

"I am too."

"Now, how do you know each other again?"

"Well, my husband and Holly are cousins. That is how I met her, was through him. Then she and I were roommates in college. And then Robert, her husband, and her, were neighbors and then they really met a little over three years ago at church. They fell in love and got married about two weeks after we did. We were married on the 21st of June and they were married, like they said, on the 4th. That's about it in a nutshell."

"What she said."

We all laughed.

The food was delicious, or we were just starving. But the time spent together was even better.

After a while the conversation turned to what all of us were going to be doing as a ministry.

"Patty and I are going into full time ministry as evangelists. I have felt like that is the call that God has placed on my life. Patty and I both feel like that is where He is leading us. I know it isn't going to be easy.

But I feel God has been speaking to me, well to both of us really, for a long time.

Holly, do you remember when you were staying with us and, I think it was a New Year's Eve service, Sam and I both felt God was speaking to us.

My brother Sam really felt like God had called him to the mission field. Turned out that his mission field was Vietnam."

"Oh yes. Vietnam was his mission field. If it wasn't for him, I don't know that I would be here," Robert said. "He is the one that pointed me to the Savior. He led many young men to Christ before he lost his life. So many men owe their walk with God to Sam. I know that if he hadn't lived it out in front of me, then I wouldn't have wanted anything to do with it. But because he really practiced what he preached, it stirred something up inside me and I had to have it."

I let them talk.

I knew that something had changed in me during the prayer service that morning. Something that I could not explain. I wanted to talk it over more in private with Patty and Toby and of course Robert before I talked to anyone else.

After a few more minutes Robert was telling of the night that he had given his testimony in church that Easter night. It seemed like a lifetime ago, but it also seemed so new.

Maybe because it was.

My walk with the Lord, my personal walk with the Lord, was only three and half years old. I may have been raised in church, but that didn't mean I knew what it meant to be saved. I mean, really saved.

But that night I did.

That night something changed in me.

And as great as that was, knowing that my sins had been forgiven, and that I was clean, it felt even more complete since I prayed this morning.

I don't know what came over me. What was different?

When I started speaking in a different language and I didn't care who saw or heard, it was as if chains were falling off of me. I did not want to have that bondage ever again.

I wanted that joy, that peace, oh my, that is what it was, it was peace that passed all understanding.

Now I knew what that verse meant.

Oh, I loved that, peace.

A stillness in my soul and yet I felt more alive, like electricity was bursting through me.

I was never going to be able to express this.

If I couldn't understand it myself, how was I ever going to be able to express it to anyone else.

Pastor Marks said to Robert and Toby, "That must have been when Amy heard you. She is the one who told us about you. She moved back here, when was that Terri, sometime in May wasn't it. About three years back. We didn't know her when she lived here before." He looked at his wife, "Do you think she would mind us telling a little of her story? She has shared a lot of it with the church a few times. Do you think she would mind?"

"No, I think she would be okay with it."

CHAPTER 20

"Amy moved back here like I said a little over three years ago. She had run away from her foster home when she was around 16 years old.

She had been severely abused by her mother and stepfather.

He used to beat her and do terrible things to her and her little brother.

No one that knew anything about it ever seemed to intervene on their behalf.

One day, her stepfather had been drinking, a lot.

After he had beaten Amy he went after her little brother. I think Amy said she was almost 15 when this happened. Her little brother was only 10.

Her stepfather was the boy's real dad. I guess it didn't matter to the dad.

He had beaten him with a belt buckle and had swung it so hard that the prong on it struck him in the temple and stuck in his head.

Amy had been trying to stop him from hitting him, but she was no match for him. After her brother fell to the ground, with the belt still stuck in his head, he pushed her off of himself and had his way with her.

He told her that it was all her fault that her brother had died. That if she had not pulled on his arm like she did it would not have struck him where it had.

All the while that he is telling her this, he is holding her against her will and hurting her. All she could do was lay there and try and fight him off while she watched the life flow out of her brother.

Her mother came home and found him passed out drunk with her only son dead and her daughter destroyed.

Amy said that the county put her in a foster home. She didn't even get to go to her brother's funeral.

At the trial, her mother tried approaching her and begged her to tell them that she had caused it.

To please not testify against her stepfather.

When she refused to do as her mother asked, her mother spat at her and told her that she got what she deserved.

He was found guilty and is spending a life sentence in prison.

Amy's mother was so angry at her that she never even tried to get her back.

The foster home was no picnic either. The family had a teenage son and daughter. They were just a little older than Amy.

They tortured her and said horrible things to her.

If Amy said anything to the foster parents, the kids always denied it and she was called a liar.

She figured that being out on her own would have to be better than living like this. She packed up her meager belongings in a bag and left. She had no intentions of ever coming back to this place.

She survived on the streets somehow. I don't know what all she did, but she survived."

"Thank God she did," Terri interjected. "That girl is the most on fire for Christ person that I have ever met."

"Yes, she is. That is how she came to us. I remember her coming to church that first Sunday.

She was not dressed like any regular person that had visited our church. Her clothes were worn and tattered, but they were clean.

She was clean, well, as clean as she could be.

It was close to the end of May, or somewhere in there.

She sat in the back and you wouldn't have really known she was there except for the fact that she just cried all during the service.

There was a dear old lady in the church that noticed her. Jane Lindstrom. Sister Jane. She was a widower and all her children had moved away. She really spent her time just loving on people, and Amy was a people if there ever was one.

She had gone back and sat by her about mid-way through the service. She just sat by her and put her arm around her and loved on her.

When the invitation was given, Jane asked her if she wanted to go to the altar and pray?

Amy couldn't get there fast enough. I don't even remember what I preached about that day.

But I don't think it mattered.

After the service, Jane sat with her and they talked for a while. Jane took her home that day and fed her and clothed her. She had clothes from her daughter, they were a little dated, but they were clean, and they were in a lot better shape than what she was wearing.

They were both back at church that night and we found out that Jane had insisted that she stay with her if just for a little while.

She has been in every church service since then barring some problem. Most Sundays she even walks.

She wasn't raised in church. She knew very little about God or His saving grace until right before she came back.

Seems she had been in some town where you were preaching Toby.

It was Easter service. You were filling in for the pastor there."

"That would be our pastor. Pastor James. Toby was filling in for him for three weekends. Easter evening service was when Robert came back to church. Well, he had actually been there that morning as well, but hardly anyone knew it."

"You must be the man that brought the Bible back home?

She said that she had been in the morning service. She told us that she had been so tired. She was just trying to find a place where she could rest.

She didn't even realize that it was Easter Sunday until she walked in.

There were so many people there.

That is usually the case. Christmas and Easter services are usually full.

She said that she found a place to sit on the back pew.

The people were friendly enough. She thought she would be able to get some rest and some sleep, maybe ask for a few bucks from some of the people when they left so she could get some food."

"Hey, I do remember her. Robert, remember when we met at the Burger Joint and that girl was just standing around outside. She looked like she wanted to talk to us, but she wouldn't. I remember asking her if she was hungry and she asked me how I knew that?"

"Oh yeah. Man, she looked a mess. I knew I did, but she looked even worse off than me. I guess that is what living on the streets does to you. I am sure I looked that bad just a few months earlier. What did you tell her, something like, nobody told you, but she looked like she might be hungry, that is why you asked, or something to that affect? I think she finally agreed to let you buy her some food."

"Yep. She ate every bite."

"She sure did."

"She was gone by the time we left to go to the church. I looked around and didn't see her so I figured she must have gone on her way. I remember praying for her."

"That pretty much lines up with what she told us. She said after you preached that morning you asked for anyone that wanted to come to the altar and pray. She told us she had wanted to go so bad but that she just felt like she wasn't worthy. She said she looked at all the dressed-up people in the church and a lot of them went and prayed but she just couldn't do it.

She said she left and walked around town trying to find a place to rest. It was late in the afternoon when she said she ended up by a burger place and of all the people in the world, the person who had been preaching showed up with some soldier guy.

She was totally taken by surprise when the man that she'd heard preach that morning approached her and asked her if she was hungry.

She told us she was starving but didn't realize that her hunger for a Savior was what was driving her that day.

You fed her and she said it was one of the best burgers she had ever had."

"Burger Joint," we all said in unison and in agreement.

"Well, she said after she ate, she headed straight back to that church to see if it was going to be different that night than it was that morning.

She told us it was both the same and different at the same time.

She didn't know what a church service was supposed to be like.

That morning was the first time she had ever been inside a church in her whole life. She really didn't know what to expect.

She said she sat in the back again, hoping no one would notice her. There weren't as many people there that night, but she said she was amazed that there were so many young people sitting at the front. She didn't know that teenagers even went to church, much less sat at the front like they would want to be there.

You must have a had a testimony service.

She said that one by one people all over the church stood up and told about this God that had done so much for them.

How he had changed their lives.

Then she talked about some guy with a cross came in and a couple of the teenagers came back to help him carry it forward.

She described it as an old rugged thing.

You had them put it up front.

Then you asked the guy that you had been eating

with to come and talk.

Robert, I think she must have been talking about you from what I'm hearing."

"Yep. That was me. I was the soldier. Well, ex-soldier."

"She said you looked like you'd seen better days. But when you started talking about all the things you had been through, and how this God had helped you, how you felt like a new person, all because of the cross, that rugged looking thing, how that man Jesus, that Toby had spoken of that morning, had given up His life so that she could be saved. How He'd paid the price by dying in the cross, but even more that He was no longer dead, that was someone that she wanted to get to know personally.

When you asked people to come down and pray that night, she almost didn't go but she said she couldn't stay sitting there. She wanted to know that love and peace and forgiveness that you had been talking about. She said she wanted to feel clean.

She hadn't felt that way in so long.

She said so many people came and prayed with her. Most of them young people, teenagers.

They prayed with her until she finally felt like every burden, every sin, had been lifted from her.

She told us that even though she knew that maybe her clothes weren't that clean and that she probably needed a bath, she never felt cleaner in her life than she did at that very moment."

"I feel horrible. I didn't even notice her that evening. There were so many people down there that night praying at the altars. I prayed with as many as I could get too. Oh, man, I wish I had seen her.

I remember that night because of the young people in the church. So many of them were down there praying for others. Knowing that these kids played an instrumental part in her salvation means a lot to me."

"Well, after that night, she still didn't have a place to stay and the only food that she'd had in a few days was the burger you had bought her.

But there was something that compelled her to make it home somehow.

Something Robert said made her feel as if she needed to go home.

She wasn't sure why.

She told us she really didn't want to, but that it was in her heart, her thoughts.

She couldn't get away from it.

But she didn't have a way of doing it.

She said she stayed by the burger place and somebody else bought her a meal the next day. It was some lady that invited her to come to some Bible study that she taught on Tuesday mornings at the very same church."

"Oh, my word, how bizarre is that? I am sure that had to be my mother, or possibly yours Robert. They are the ones that teach the Bible study on Tuesdays."

"Knowing them both it could have been either one of them."

"Whoever. it was had a friend with her that had a tin full of cookies and she gave them to her."

We knew who it was. It *was* our mothers.

"She decided to go. She told us that they had accepted her that day as if she should have been there all along. They were the kindest ladies that she had ever met. There was an older lady that asked her to come home with her and she would make sure she had a home cooked meal before she headed out.

She insisted on letting her take a bath and she washed her clothes for her.

She said she had never been fed such glorious food in all her life.

By the way, do you people have a cookie problem in your city?

Amy said that this woman insisted that she fill up her tin with more cookies and they were just as good as the ones she had left.

Amy told us that she couldn't figure out why these women were so nice to her. She didn't deserve to be treated so kindly.

She couldn't figure out why she was even letting them. She waited for the other shoe to drop.

She figured when this woman's husband came home from work that she would need to leave, but they had both insisted that she spend a couple of nights and get some rest before she left.

It had been so long since she had slept in a bed, and never one as great as this one.

The temptation was too great. Her fears that something terrible might happen were overcome by the promise of a bed with clean sheets and a hot meal.

She stayed the night and the next and the next.

The man owned some kind of fixture shop, like sinks and toilets and such. He asked her if she would like to earn some money for her trip?

He had her come down and clean the place, you know, sweep and mop and clean in general. He paid her $150.00.

She told him that it was too much.

He insisted that she take it. He said he hadn't had such sparkling toilets in a long time. She had earned every penny.

She had stayed with them until after Sunday morning service.

The older couple took her to the bus stop after they fed her a nice Sunday dinner.

The lady had made sure she had clean clothes, a little bag with soap, some deodorant, a toothbrush and toothpaste, you know, the things we take for granted, in it.

When they got to the bus station, they did even one better. The couple went to the counter with her and paid for her ticket. She tried to protest but they just smiled at her and insisted that she let them bless her.

They told her it brought them nothing but joy to be able to do this for her.

They had also presented her with a Bible.

They gave instruction to read it and study it and that it would change her life.

She had told them what her life had been like. She says she didn't tell them everything though.

She said she asked them why she felt so compelled to go home and they couldn't answer her.

All they would tell her was that if she felt like that is where God was taking her then that is where she needed to be.

They did tell her that if she ever felt like she wanted to come back their way, to please come by. There would always be a place for her.

They just loved on her and treated her so kindly.

She has said on more than one occasion that these people are who she pictures God to be like. Love.

Then she got on the bus and came home.

She didn't start coming to church here right away.

She said that when she got off the bus, everything in her wanted to get back on it and go back to where she came from.

She knew she was home, but it didn't feel much like home.

She was going to need a job, so she started walking the streets looking to see if anyone had a sign that they were hiring.

After about two weeks of sleeping wherever she could find she finally heard that the Spa was hiring for night shift to run the front desk.

The man that owns it goes to our church. He is a very good Christian man. He loves God and for some reason, even though she had no experience, he offered her the job.

He even let her stay in one of the rooms until she could get a place of her own.

Like I said. He felt like that is what God was telling him to do.

Turned out that God was right.

She turned out to be one of his best workers after just a few weeks.

She was reading her Bible like this couple had told her to.

They had told her to start in Ephesians. And since they had been so nice to her, she decided to do like they had suggested.

The owner happened to come by and saw her reading the Bible.

She thought he was going to fire her for reading on the job.

He didn't of course. Instead they started talking and he found out that she had just gotten saved and had not been to church since she had returned.

He invited her to come to his church sometime.

She wasn't sure that she wanted to do that. She still didn't have decent clothing. If it wasn't for the uniform they gave her she would only have rags to wear.

He told her that the people in his church would not care what she wore or what she looked like. They would just love on her.

And that is what he did.

He changed her shift so that she worked days and gave her Sundays and Mondays off.

She still didn't know why she had felt like she was supposed to be there.

Why she was compelled in her heart to come home.

That is until one Monday, on her day off, she had walked to town and was looking in the shops when she saw a familiar face.

She wanted to run and hide.

She said fear was making her shake to the bone.

There was no place to hide.

She decided that it was now or never.

She wasn't going to talk to her, but she wasn't going to let that fear overtake her either.

As she passed by her, her mother reached out and grabbed her by the arm.

"So, you thought you would just be able to sneak back in town unnoticed huh?"

"No. I have been here for a while. And I didn't sneak back."

"Oh yeah, for a while now huh? Where have you been hiding? I haven't seen you."

"I haven't been hiding anywhere. I have been working."

"Who in their right mind would give you a job? You are nothing but a liar and a piece of white trash."

Amy said everything in her wanted to lash out. To tell her mother exactly what she thought.

But she didn't.

She said a peace came over her.

She said the fear, the panic, the worry, the anger, all of it just seemed to melt right out of her.

All of a sudden, the words from the Bible that she had been reading every chance she got, began to fill her heart and her mind and she said that she felt nothing towards this woman, her mother, other than pity.

She said that, over and over in her head, it was like a still small voice was speaking to her.

She knew the verse and she has come to know that voice.

Ephesians 4:32, Be ye kind one to another, forgiving one another, even as God for Christ's sake hath forgiven you.

It was like a broken record.

Be ye kind.

Be ye kind.

Suddenly, she said she felt compelled to hug her mother and tell her that she loved her and forgave her.

Her mother pulled away and told her that she didn't love her and that she never had. She told her that she wished it had been her that died instead of her brother.

The words struck her like a knife.

But that still small voice kept speaking to her.

Be ye kind.

Be ye kind.

She turned to walk away and as she did, she told her mother one last time that she loved her and that she forgave her.

She didn't see her again until the following Saturday.

After she had gotten off work, she decided to take a walk into town again.

And there was her mother again.

When she saw Amy, she stood up and called her by name.

Amy turned to see who was calling her. When she realized it was her mother, she thought maybe her mother wanted to talk things over. That maybe this encounter would be different.

It wasn't.

She hadn't quite made it to her when her mother yelled out, "So you love me do you? Well I still don't love you!" She started running towards her with a knife.

Luckily someone saw what was happening and pulled Amy to safety just as she lunged at her.

She was drunk, extremely drunk.

When Amy was pulled to safety, her mother had tripped and fell on the knife.

Amy hurried to her.

The person that had pulled her to safety helped her turn her mother over.

She was still alive.

She looked at Amy and with as much hatred as you

could imagine, she asked her again. "So, do you still love me?"

Amy began to weep over her mother and took her hand and told her yes, she still loved her.

Her mother died right there on the street before the ambulance got there.

The police came and questioned her, and the witness told everything that had happened.

They took her back to the spa and called Curly, he was the owner, and told him what had happened.

He and his wife came and stayed with her for a while until she fell asleep.

The next morning, she showed up at our church.

Jane didn't live that far away from the Spa. So, after they got to know each other, Jane insisted Amy come and stay with her.

She was lonely and her kids wouldn't mind.

Amy talked to Curly about it.

He gave her the best advice that he could.

Do it!

He knew Jane and knew that she was a good Christian woman and he also knew that she would love on Amy.

So, Amy did. She moved in with her.

And true to what Curly knew, Jane poured more love onto that girl.

She showed her how to study the Word of God.

Amy loved her so.

Jane passed away about six weeks ago and Amy had to move out and find an apartment.

Curly offered to let her stay at the Spa again but Amy wouldn't hear of it.

She was now a manager at the Spa. Curly has

taught her a lot about running the business and he pays her a good salary."

"Just curious then, if she has a good salary, why doesn't she get a car and drive herself to church and places?"

"She has a car. Jane gave Amy her car a long time ago. Put it in her name and everything."

"Then why doesn't she use it."

"She doesn't know how to drive. I think Jane was teaching her, but she died before she could finish, I guess. It's also an older car. Probably needs a lot of work."

"Well, that makes sense."

"Yep. Anyways, about a little over a year ago, Jane talked us into letting her teach a Sunday School class. We were needing teachers and she said that she thought Amy would be good at it. We had no reason to doubt her and we offered Amy the class if she wanted it. We knew she was the one we wanted in there when she responded, "Can I pray about it first?"

Those girls love her.

She holds them to the fire.

Makes them learn their lessons and their memory verses. She wants them to be able to teach the class someday she said."

"We are so glad that God sent her our way. Our daughter loves her."

CHAPTER 21

We finished our lunch and Patty and Toby followed Pastor Marks and his wife home so they could get refreshed for the evening service.

Robert and I went back to our little honeymoon cottage.

"That was quite a story huh," Robert asked?

"Yes, yes it was. It really makes you think. I mean, I would never had known that she had lived through so much horror. Who does that to a child?"

"Holly, you went through horrible things yourself. Nobody knows why people do the things they do. Well, we do. They are void of God. They have no reason to not do what they do since they are not accountable to anyone but man."

"Yes, but even then, they have to take responsibility for their own actions."

"Only if they get caught. Your father didn't get caught for a long time and when he did, it was almost instant judgement for him. Just like Amy's mother. Neither one of them had an opportunity at the last minute to repent and turn their hearts over to God.

Your father knew of God. He knew the consequences of his sin. Eternal separation from God.

Eternity in hell.

But what about Amy's mother? Amy had never

been in church before they said. What if the same was true for her mother?

It's kind of like what Toby was talking about this morning. All have sinned and all can be saved.

But all haven't heard."

"That's true. You know, I know that the Bible tells us that we have to forgive to be forgiven. I still struggle with that.

I don't want to hate him, but there are times when those emotions just overwhelm me. I don't know how to get over it. There are times when I think I'm doing okay and then there are times when I think I'm drowning.

It is like little flashes of memory that will all of a sudden pop up in my head. Something I thought I had pretty much hidden so long ago, then suddenly, there it is. Those are the times I feel so alone. Like my salvation isn't real. I don't know why I can't "just get over it".

It seems as if Amy did and she had a lot worse done to her."

We pulled into our little driveway and decided to take a quick dip in the ocean before we had to get ready for church.

It was only four in the afternoon and church didn't start until seven. We might even have time for a nap.

The water was glorious. The waves washed over us as we played and swam in that wonderful water!

Robert took a shower and then took a nap afterwards.

I took a shower after him, but instead of relaxing me, it seemed to revive me.

I went back outside in the sunshine to let my hair

dry.

While I sat there, I decided to read my Bible.

I really hadn't taken the time to do that since our wedding.

Where was it that Memaw told Amy to read?

Oh yes, Ephesians!

Why not start there?

I mean, I had read the Bible, bits and pieces of it.

Robert was always reading his. Just like Toby and Patty. But I had never studied it like they did.

I opened it up and began to read.

Ephesians chapter 1!

I read the whole thing through!

What had Pastor Marks said?

When Amy had seen her mother that day, it was like she could hear the verse being spoken inside her head?

This was it!

That verse was right there.

If she had never been to church before and that was the only book in the Bible she had been reading, then what a wonder that the verse right there in chapter four was brought to her memory.

Wow!

What if she hadn't read that particular book?

What if she hadn't read it at all?

What if she had ignored that voice?

Wow!

I have got to show Robert this!

"Robert," I said as I hurried into the room, "did you know that Amy was remembering a verse she had read when her mother stopped her on the street that day?"

"What," Robert mumbled into his pillow. "What?"

"You know, Pastor Marks told us at lunch that when Amy's mother stopped her on the street that day, how Amy said she wanted to run, but she didn't, and then she heard like a voice in her head telling her to be kind? Remember that?"

"Yeah," he said as he tried to clear the cobwebs from his nap.

"Okay then. Did you know that is a verse in Ephesians? You know the only book in the Bible that she had been reading? Did you know that?"

"Yeah. It's Ephesians 4:32, I think, anyways. I would have to check my Bible."

"No, no you won't. See, I have it right here. How did you know that?"

"Well, it's in the Bible, and I read my Bible. I study it. I want to be able to preach it. I can't preach or even teach something that I don't know myself, right? So, I study and study some more. So, I guess that is how I knew it was in there."

"Oh, well, okay then. Then, okay, tell me something? How did she remember that particular verse at that particular moment, you know, right when she needed it? She could have ignored it right? She could have not been nice to her mother, right? I mean, people would understand. After all her mother and stepfather had done, people would have understood, right? God would have understood, right?"

"Holly, slow down. Let me wake up a bit. That is a lot of questions to wake somebody up with. Why are you asking me this anyways?"

"I couldn't sleep. So, I went outside to dry my hair

and decided to read Ephesians. I figured that if my Memaw thought it was such a good passage to tell Amy to start reading the Bible at, then why not? So, I did!

Then as I was reading, it has a lot of good stuff in there, I came across that part, and it hit me, that is the verse that Amy had in her head that day. Why that verse?

Why did she even remember it?"

"Well, that is how God talks to people sometimes. He speaks to us through His Word. The Bible.

At that very moment it seems like Amy needed to hear that. The Holy Spirit spoke it into her. He reminded her of the verse that she had read.

Just like if at that very moment, she was angry at her mother and wanted to lash out at her, she didn't. In that same chapter, I think it says to be angry and sin not."

"It did say that. I read it. It's in there."

"Okay, so if she had needed to be reminded of that part of the chapter, the Holy Spirit would have reminded her of that."

"Okay, then why didn't He tell her about something else in another book? Why that one?"

"Did you ever have a test in school?"

"Yes."

"Were you ever given a test on something you hadn't studied or learned?"

"Not that I can remember, no."

"That is because you don't get tested on what you don't know. Only on what you studied.

That is how life is. We as Christians are going to have tests. Not just Christians. Everyone. We are going to have life. Mostly everyday life. On occasion severe life. Like you with your father, like Amy with her parents and the death of her brother. Like me and Lance in Vietnam. We are going to have life. And it is how we answer those questions that come up in life that determines our walk.

If we study the book, then we'll know the answers. People who don't study it won't.

We are to study the Word so that when the fiery darts that the Devil throws at us come our way, we can stand on the Word of God, the promises, the directions, and we can make it.

Amy was being tested that day and the answer to the test was "be kind. She had the answer to the test that day because she had been studying the book.

Did that answer any of your questions?"

"Mostly."

"Only mostly?"

"Yep. You know what?

"What's that?"

"You are not only handsome you are pretty smart too."

"Well thank you. And you, you are a little sunburned. How long were you out there?

"About an hour."

"Well, you might want to put something on it so we can start getting ready for church."

"Oh yeah. Let's get ready. Get up and help me put some of my cream on the back of my shoulders."

"My pleasure."

CHAPTER 22

The little church was full for a Sunday night service. Possibly because there was a guest speaker. And possibly because the people there loved to go to church.

Robert and Patty sang a couple of songs and Patty did something I don't think I had ever seen Patty do.

She addressed the congregation.

Toby stepped away after introducing his new bride and let her talk for a little bit.

As she spoke you could see her come alive as she told of how she and Toby were just newly married but that they were so glad that God was calling them to be evangelists.

She laughed as she said she wasn't sure she was going to be very good at being a vagabond, a gypsy so to speak. But what better way to see this great country of ours than to be led by the Master into places unknown to them.

She told the people that night, that she might not be looking forward to the traveling, but she was sure looking forward to what God was going to be doing.

She spoke to the youth that night and encouraged them to dig into the Word of God. To get a righteous hunger down in their souls to want to devour the Word of God. To make it their goal to live for God, to live holy lives, lives worth living, so that when they faced the fiery darts of the devil that they would be able to stand.

I nudged Robert when she said that part.

He nudged me back.

After a while Toby spoke and his sermon was just as dynamic as the morning service had been.

Amy and one of the girls that she had been with that morning were back that night and they sat with us again.

I think she was surprised to see us back that evening.

She smiled when she sat down.

"You came back!"

"Yes, we did! We had to hear more of Toby's preaching. Thank you so much for inviting us."

"Well, I am just glad you came. Like I said this morning, I invite a lot of people but not everybody comes."

"Well, you keep on inviting them. You plant the seed and God will bring the increase," Robert told her.

"Exactly! Not everybody hears when the Holy Spirit speaks to them. They ignore the wooing, or they just flat out say no! But nonetheless, God still speaks to them. All I can do is be His voice sometimes. I can't make them hear."

"Ain't that the truth," Robert agreed!

"That is what I try to emphasize to my little Sunday School Class. That they need to learn how to hear God when He speaks to them. To be like Samuel. To learn to be a willing vessel when He calls them. I have been teaching them that God knows them. Not only collectively but especially individually. He is not going to speak to the crowd what He has just for them to hear, to learn to become. He loves us all, but He loves us one by one."

"That preaches," Robert told her.

Then the service started.

After the service was over Amy's friend had to leave which meant Amy was going to walk home by herself.

Robert stopped her from leaving.

"We'll take you home."

"You don't have to do that. I walk home by myself all the time. Don't worry."

"It isn't a worry. It would be our privilege."

We had been discussing getting a burger at the local burger place.

Pastor Marks said he and his wife were going to take the kids home. They had been swimming all afternoon and they were exhausted. Terri gave Toby a house key and told them to just let themselves in and they would see them in the morning.

Amy rode with us and Toby and Patty followed us.

It wasn't too crowded, but it was one of the only places open this late and we were all starving.

Burgers, fries, and drinks all around.

We sat and visited a while.

Toby told Amy that he was so glad that she had told Pastor Marks about them.

"He didn't have you come right away. I told him a while back."

"We know. He told us. But being the pastor, he had to do his due diligence and find out more about us. He called my pastor and asked him if he knew us since it was in the area that you told him. Worked out pretty good though. My pastor and your pastor are friends. As a matter of fact, they graduated from the same college that we graduated from. Well, except Robert. He has another year still to go. Pastor Taylor vouched for us. The only problem was I was still in College. I had pretty much booked up my time until now, waiting for Patty to graduate. Then we had a wedding to plan. He had contacted me about a year ago, but this is as soon as I could get here."

"That is pretty cool that you came the same weekend that your cousins were going to be here."

"It's even funnier. Neither one of us knew the other was going to be here in this particular town this weekend."

"Yeah, Toby and I just got married in June and they just got married last Thursday. We all had been so busy planning weddings and such that we hadn't touched base.

I mean, we knew they were coming to a Spa Resort. We just didn't know it was here."

"And Robert and I knew that they were going to be preaching somewhere this weekend. We just didn't know it was here."

"Wow. Now I really am glad I asked you. I mean, you asked me actually. I guess it was a divine appointment as such."

"I guess so."

Toby and Patty said they would come by in the morning to see us when we parted ways.

It was getting late and they didn't want to make a disturbance by coming home so late.

We took Amy home, even though she insisted that it wasn't that far. As a matter of fact, it wasn't too far.

It was right on our way to the resort.

It was a cute little duplex about two blocks from the Spa.

We pulled up in front of her little home and was pleasantly surprised.

"Amy, is that your car?"

"Uh, yes."

"Then why don't you drive it instead of walking everywhere?"

"It is too long of a story. Short story is it doesn't run right now. I don't have the money to repair it and I don't quite have my license anyways. So, I walk."

"Oh, okay. We'll see you tomorrow."

"Oh no. I'm sorry. Tomorrow is my day off. Larry Cowen is on tomorrow. He is a very nice guy. He will take good care of you."

"Oh, I'm sure he will. You enjoy your day off."

"Oh, I will. That is if you think laundry is fun," she laughed. "Laundry is my least favorite chore. I would rather scrub my floors and wash dishes than do laundry. It's a dirty job, but somebody has to do it."

We all laughed in agreement.

We waited for her to get inside then we went home.

Both of us were silent for the rest of the drive.

CHAPTER 23

"Hey sleepyhead! Good morning!"

Ugh. Robert was too cheerful this morning.

You cannot be that cheerful without first having coffee.

I needed coffee.

Well, after morning kisses, then I needed coffee, with a little cream.

Perfection!

We had stayed up late after we came home from dropping Amy off.

A midnight swim and some alone time with each other was a perfect ending to a perfect day.

As we laid together, we talked about all that had happened that day.

Everything!

But in the end the talk had turned to Amy.

"So, what do you think about Amy?"

"I don't really know. She is one of the sweetest, grounded young ladies that I have ever met. For someone who has gone through as much as she has, you wouldn't know it. There is something about her that makes you just want to be around her."

"Yeah, I think she is pretty grounded myself. Holly, I know we haven't really talked about it, but I would like to do something to help her."

"Help her? What do you mean? Help her how?"

"Did you notice her car?"

"Really? How could I not notice that car? What do you think the odds are that she has the exact Fairlane that we gave to Toby and Patty?"

"That was pretty cool. The same colors too. It was probably the same year. It looked it."

"I wonder what is wrong with it?"

"It could be anything. I sure would like to get my hands on it and find out."

"I'm no mechanic, but even I could see it needed new tires."

"Yeah, some tires. Probably a new battery. Could just be a few miner things."

"Or it could be some major things."

"Yep. We won't know until we look at it huh?"

"Yeah. Until we look at it," I yawned. "Wait, what? Until we look at it?"

"Yeah, in the morning. Don't you think we should at least look at it and see what the problem is?

"I really hadn't thought about it. Clearly you have."

"Do you think Toby would stay and help me?"

"Work on a car? I think you would have a problem if you tried to stop him.

What are you going to do if it needs a lot of work? Pastor Marks said she couldn't afford to fix it."

"I know. But we can."

"We can? How is that?"

"Uh, remember that money that your Grandparents gave us?"

I had totally forgotten all about that.

"Oh Robert," I rolled over to face him, "yes. Let's do it. That is exactly what we should do with that money."

I could see the moon shining on his face and I couldn't resist.

So, we were up a little later.

And now, this morning, I was still sleepy.

But we had company coming and a lot of work to do.

So, kisses, coffee, and car!

And breakfast!

CHAPTER 24

We were just finished getting ready for the day when Toby and Patty got there.

We showed them around the little cottage.

"Nice. Ooh, that's nice."

Patty loved it.

But when we went outside and showed them our private little ocean then she was really impressed.

They both were!

By this time, we were all starving!

Breakfast it was!

It was going to be a feast! Both Toby and Robert were champion breakfast eaters!

And they were starving.

Patty and I were hungry, but Toby and Robert had it down to a perfection.

While we ate, we asked if they had to get back home today.

They said they had nothing pressing.

Robert ran our plan by them.

"You're kidding? She has the exact same car? What are the odds of that?"

"I know huh? Would you feel up to helping me with it?"

Toby looked at Patty, "Would that be okay?"

"I don't care. I think it is a fantastic idea! Do you

think she will let you do that?"

"I don't know. The only way we will know for certain is to go and find out."

So, it was settled.

We took both cars. They followed us in the Fairlane and pulled up behind us.

I am sure Amy didn't know what to think when she answered the door and we were all standing there.

"Good morning!"

"Oh my! What are you all doing here?"

"Well," Robert began, "we were wondering if you would let us do something for you?"

"For me? You want to do something for me?"

"Yeah." He pointed over his shoulder at the Fairlane.

"Oh, my word! Whose car is that?"

"Well, it used to be Roberts, then when he went to Vietnam, Holly bought it. Then she got a newer car and they decided that we needed to have it. They gave it to Patty and me."

"Now that is quite a story."

"And that is the short version!"

We all laughed.

"Okay, then, what kind of favor do you want?"

"No, not what we want. It is what we want to do for you. You see, Robert and I were talking it over last night and we wondered if you would let them look at your car to see what all is wrong with it. I mean we can see it needs tires. Do you know what is wrong with it?"

"Uh, no. I know nothing about cars. It has been sitting here for a few weeks. It had been running right up until a couple of weeks before Mama Jane died.

She is the one who gave me the car. I had to have it towed here. She is the one that drove it. I don't have my license yet."

"Have you driven at all?"

"Oh yes. I have a permit. Mama Jane was teaching me. But the car quit working on us, and she passed away before we could get it repaired. I figured there was no point in pursuing it now. What would be the use in having a license and no car?"

I think Patty and I both had the same idea at the same time.

"Ok, how about this. You let the guys work on the car and we will let you drive around in our Fairlane to refresh your memory and then we will go get your license."

"Oh, I couldn't let you do that?"

"Why not?"

"Yeah, why not." Patty chimed in.

She couldn't think of a reason why not.

After she found the key and Robert and Toby took over the car repair, Patty, Amy, and I had driving lessons.

She didn't do too bad. Mama Jane had been a good teacher!

"Mama Jane was a pretty good teacher. She was a stickler when it came to studying. I was surprised that she gave me the car. She said her kids didn't want it. She was one of the kindest women that I ever knew. She took me in for a while you know?"

"She sounds like a very nice woman."

"She was. She truly was. She knew the Word of God like nobody I knew. She showed me how to study the Bible. We would talk for hours on what it meant to apply the Word of God to our lives. How important it was to study it so that we would have it when we needed it. She said it was the right thing to do. The Bible tells us to write it on our hearts. That is what I am trying to do. I can't get enough of it. I want to be able to live it out in front of everyone that I meet. I want my life to be an example that God would be proud of."

"You are humbling us right now. I feel ashamed that I probably don't read and share it near as much as you do."

"I am sure you and Pastor Toby know the Word way more than I do. But I will tell you, I just can't get enough of it. It is like a hunger down in my soul. When I was seeking to be filled with the Holy Spirit, I locked myself up in my room as soon as I got home every day. I fasted and prayed for a week. Once I was filled with the Holy Spirit, it was like the scriptures opened up and seemed to jump off the pages."

"Like electricity!"

"Yes, just like electricity. I couldn't get enough of it."

We had driven around for a while and decided to stop and get some fish and chips to take back to Amy's.

We told her that after we ate, we were going to go get that license.

"I don't think I can afford it really."

"Don't you worry about that. It can't cost that much, and we will make sure you are taken care of.

When we got back with the food, we found the boys elbow deep in grease.

"What is the prognosis." Amy asked. "What is it going to take to fix it?"

"Tires."

"Tires? You mean it wouldn't run because it needed tires?"

Robert looked at me and shook his head and smiled.

Truthfully, Patty and Amy were thinking the same thing, but I said it first.

That didn't make sense. Surely it needed something besides tires to make the car run again?

"Well, tires and gas."

"You mean it had just run out of gas? That is why it wouldn't run," Amy asked?

"Well, no. Now all it needs is tires and gas. It needed a new battery and a tune-up. It needed coolant in the radiator and a couple of hoses. It needed power steering fluid and brake fluid and a few other miner things. But now, it only needs tires and gas," Toby said.

"You got all that done in three hours?"

"Well, it's not like we didn't know what could be wrong. We have both worked on that Fairlane out there. Let's eat. I'm starving!"

We ate!

Afterward they towed the car to Sears and got new tires on it and bought a gas can to fill up to keep in the trunk and filled the car up while we took Miss Amy to get a long overdue right-of-passage.

A driver's license.

She started to protest that it was too much and that she could never repay us.

We told her that at some point there might be someone that needed something that she would be able do for them.

So that was it.
Amy Pinkerton was now a driver!

CHAPTER 25

Patty and Toby decided to stay with us that night. After all, the couch in the living room was able to be made into a bed.

We ordered lobster dinners for room service for all of us.

"How were you able to pay for all those repairs for Amy's car if you don't mind me asking? I'm not trying to be nosy, but I know you are going back to college in a couple of months and you are going to have to have an apartment while you are there. Did you find a wad of cash somewhere?'

"Well, sort of." Robert chuckled. "Holly's grandparents gave us some money for our honeymoon, and we didn't need it for the honeymoon. We weren't sure what we were going to do with it. Probably invest it. We had prayed about it when they gave it to us. So last night we were talking and we both felt like that is what God would have us do with it. We even ended up with $50.00 left over."

"Yes, and Robert and I were talking. We know that you both are now going into full time ministry as evangelists. That car loves gas."

"Yes, we know," Patty nudged Toby.

"So, he and I talked about it on the way home. We want to give it to you for your ministry. A love offering if you will. It isn't much but we feel like it is an investment. Not like the stock market or such but in the kingdom of God. Will you take it?"

"Are you sure? I mean, you could put it up and save it for when you get back to college."

"No, we are sure. This is what we are supposed to do with it."

Toby took it and put it in his wallet.

The food was delicious!

Toby and Patty had never had Lobster before, so we got to show off our skills from our one time eating it.

Luckily, we had extra swimsuits and we all took an evening swim and sat around a campfire that we built on the beach. It was a lovely ending to a perfectly lovely day.

Toby and Patty left to go home after a hearty breakfast.

Amy was beaming when she saw us come in.

"The car is a dream! I cannot thank you enough for what you did for me!"

Patty and Toby hugged her and then they were on their way.

Amy asked if we were going to be doing any site seeing?

She told us of a few quirky little places. Not such touristy places that she thought we might enjoy.

She said that there was a little place pretty much about two miles from the church that served tacos for a really good price. Taco Tuesdays were the best.

"Why not? Who doesn't like a good taco? And especially if they were on sale."

We were just heading out when the owner, Curly came in.

"Amy, who's car is that? Do we have a special guest that I don't know about?"

We left as she was telling him all about what had happened and showed him her new license."

He was just as happy for her as she was.

You could tell he thought the world of her.

He made her call and get insurance on it.

He even paid for the first six months.

He told her, "We can't let total strangers come in and take care of you when we can help."

Amy was not able to stop crying pretty much all day.

The tacos were delicious, just like she said. We brought her some back for her dinner.

She was overwhelmed.

"God is so good to me!"

"God is good to all of us. We just fail to notice sometimes and give Him the thanks that He deserves.

The rest of our little honeymoon was glorious.

Saying goodbye to Amy was the hardest.

We got to spend more time with her in the evenings. She even drove us to church on Wednesday night.

Everyone oohed and awed at her new wheels. Well, her new old wheels.

She really was a treasure.

We told her that if she was ever in our neck of the woods to please come and see us. Maybe even stay with us.

She told us she already had a standing invitation to stay with some friends she'd stayed with when she first heard Toby.

"They go to your church. Brother and sister Lewis.

They are an elderly couple, they made me promise, that if I ever come back to town, I was to stay with them. Do you know them?"

"You might say that. I believe you are talking about mine and Toby's Grandparents. He owns a porcelain store."

"Yes, that's them."

"Sister Lewis writes me letters all the time. I just love them. They are two of the first people to really show me what God is supposed to be like. They even gave me my Bible. My very first Bible."

We hoped we would see her again.

She truly was one of God's treasures here on earth.

We were definitely going to miss her.

CHAPTER 26

Yes, we hated to see it end but we had to get back.

Robert and I had to be back at work on Monday to finish saving money for his schooling.

Well, not really for schooling. That was covered by his GI Bill. But we hadn't heard if we were going to be accepted into family housing or not. We figured we had better save every penny when we got back just in case.

I would be working full time when we got back to college while Robert went to school and worked in the evenings.

I didn't have a job lined up yet, but I figured I should be able to get one.

We would figure it out no matter what.

God would provide. We were sure of that.

Pastor James as well as Pastor Taylor had been talking to some of the churches again trying to persuade them to let Robert come and preach on Sunday evenings, just like Toby had done.

We were hoping that they would be open to that.

Robert had preached at our home church a couple of Sunday evenings. He was as dynamic a preacher as Toby was.

Only problem was, who was going to sing?

While we were driving home that very issue came

up.

"You know, I haven't told you something that I meant to tell you. That I should have told you a lot sooner."

"Oh yeah. What's that?"

"You have a beautiful voice."

I know I turned ten shades of red.

"Thank you. That was the very first time I ever sang in public. Showers don't count."

"They do for me. You do know I can hear you when you sing while you take a shower right?"

Uh, no. I had not thought about that.

"I am so sorry. I will try to be quieter."

"Why would you try and be quieter. You sing really good!"

"No, I don't."

"Yes, you do. Why do you think you don't sing good?"

"I would really rather not say. Let's just leave it that somebody from my past a long time ago told me I couldn't. So, I didn't."

"Holly, you know that was a lie from Satan. He was trying to stop what God placed in you. To think he almost succeeded! Would you be willing to practice some songs with me so we can sing in churches as we minister?"

"You really want to sing with me?"

"Yes Holly. If you would sing with me."

"Well, I guess we could give it a go. But I have to confess. I do not play an instrument. Nothing. So, what are we going to do about that? I mean I guess we could sing without music if we had too."

"Why would we have to do that?"

"Like I said, I don't play an instrument."

"Well, are you going to be in for real surprise. I do!"

"You play an instrument? Really?"

"Why do you sound so surprised? Did you think I was just another handsome face?"

We both laughed.

"What instrument do you play?"

"Instruments! I play the piano and the guitar. My mother made me and Lance take lessons. I might need to practice a little, but it can't be that hard. I mean I won't be near as good at it as Toby and Patty, but I think we can do it. Are you game?"

"I guess. Why not?"

And it was only why not because I couldn't think of a better reason than "why not."

We pulled into the driveway and were surprised that no one was home.

Mother had gone out for a while and we had the house to ourselves for a while.

Robert and I were going to be staying here until we left to go back to college.

We unloaded the car and were in the process of doing some laundry when we heard the doorbell.

Robert answered the door while I finished loading the machine.

"Robert!"

I could hear my new Mother-in-law as she greeted her baby.

"Where is my new daughter?'

"What, I don't even get a hug?"

"Oh, sorry baby." She hugged him.

"Now where is my daughter?"

"Holly," Robert yelled, "your new mommy wants

you."

"Oh, stop with that."

I came from the laundry room. She covered us with hugs and kisses.

"I am so glad you are home. So, tell me everything."

"No," Mr. Davis said, "they can tell us all when we have dinner tonight. We are having BBQ at the house tonight."

He looked at me and winked then he gave me a hug.

"Nice to have you both home, daughter. That has a nice ring to it. Daughter. By the way, that is where your mom is. She went to get some things to make salad with for tonight."

He led his wife to the door. As they walked out, he hollered over his shoulder, "See you guys in a while"

"Do you think we will have time for a nap?"

"Or something." He winked at me.

We ran upstairs.

CHAPTER 27

Overwhelmed is what we were.

Everybody showed up at Roberts house for the barbecue. Well, his parent's house.

I was going to have to get used to saying that.

My house, or my mother's house, anyways, was now Roberts house.

At least for a few more weeks, then we would be on our own. Mr. and Mrs. Davis.

For right now we would be just fine.

Uncle Joey and Aunt Jessie were there. They had even brought Josh and his girlfriend, Janey. Hmm. I wonder what happened to Sabrina, I think that was her name? Oh well, I am sure I would get the scoop later.

He really was growing up.

He was going to be seventeen here soon. He was looking more and more like his big brothers when they were his age.

I am sure the girls are all over him. Just like Sam, but I think, the way he is looking at Janey right now, that he may be a one-man girl, just like Toby.

Memaw and Pappy were there. Even Grandmother and Grandfather Abernathy were there.

I couldn't wait to tell them what we did with the money. I hope they would be pleased that we used it to help someone rather than on ourselves. I am sure they would be.

It had been such a pleasure these last couple of years getting to really know them.

Every chance Robert and I had we would have lunch with them at Paulie's.

Grandfather had even got Robert to go to the dark side, not all the time, but sometimes. They would both enjoy a chocolate mousse instead of his lemon tart. But then we would always have to get a lemon tart to go.

They had even come to church a few times when Robert was preaching. They seemed to really enjoy it too. He was a good preacher.

Just like Toby, when he preached it seemed as if the young people couldn't get enough of the messages he brought.

I loved watching the young people get excited as they listened and would come and pray at the altars. Not just for each other, but for anyone that would come down for prayer.

Just like they had done for Amy. Not even knowing the impact they had on her life. But because they were willing to pray for anyone and everyone.

So many new relatives were there as well.

Aunts and Uncles and cousins galore!

One of my favorite new relatives was Lance.

It was so good to have him home.

What, it's been about a year now that he came back. But he was in and out of rehab to learn how to walk on crutches and a couple of surgeries as well to try and get the other leg stronger.

He sometimes seemed to be somewhere else, like

his mind was a thousand miles away. Any loud noises seemed to make him jump a little.

He hadn't even stayed outside on our wedding night to watch the fireworks. He disappeared somewhere.

I guess we could all understand.

It had been hard on him losing his leg like he had.

But it was even harder losing his friends.

They were out on patrol when they were ambushed.

He told Robert, pretty much like what happened to him, the only difference was they couldn't get out.

He said he was talking to one of his buddies, telling him to get lower when a sniper got him.

"I tried to pull him a little more to safety not realizing he was already gone when my buddy on the other side of got hit as well.

I was trying to get them both to safety, when I heard one of the newbies screaming. He was on fire. Something had exploded and he had caught on fire.

I knew my buddies were gone so I left them to go help the kid.

The kid had started to run so I tackled him down and put out the flames. He was in agony, still screaming. I put my hand on his mouth to quiet him down. He finally settled down. I thought he was going to be okay, but he was just really in shock.

I heard them calling on the radio that they were sending in reinforcements, but they were going to be about thirty minutes out. We had to hunker down until they got there.

"I pulled the kid to where my buddies were and laid him beside them. He looked a mess. But at least he'd quit screaming.

We started taking fire again before the reinforcements got there.

I saw a couple of guys afar off and got them both. Then Daryn, he got a couple more of 'em from where he was at.

We thought we were going to be okay because the firing had pretty much stopped.

Then, just as the reinforcements got there, it started back up.

We had only had a fifteen-minute breather. Long enough for me to hold the hand of the kid while he kept telling me he was going to be alright.

I knew he wasn't, but I just kept agreeing with him, right up until the last.

Daryn came to join me and he brought a couple of more guys with him. From where we were, we had a good view.

We fought them off for a good 4 hours or more until we got them all or they were on the run.

We were carrying the dead and wounded to an open area to get them to the choppers.

I was on my way back to help get more of them when I heard the explosion go off.

The two guys that Daryn had brought over were laying out on the ground. Both of them were screaming. I ran to them. They were in bad shape.

I helped get them to the chopper and loaded, then I went back for more.

I'd made it to the chopper with the help of Daryn who had been helping too. We were going back one last time when another explosion hit.

This time we weren't so lucky.

Daryn was gone. He had taken the brunt of the explosion. My left leg was just dangling there. My right leg was burning, full of shrapnel. I fell to the ground. I knew we had to get back to the chopper.

I couldn't leave Daryn there. I pulled him to the choppers and a couple of medics ran to us and put me on the chopper with all the rest of them, but they left Daryn.

They were only taking the wounded this time around they said. I was the last one on there.

The rest, as they say, is history."

What he forgot to tell Robert, or his parents was that he had helped to get fifteen men to the choppers and transported out. If he had not done that, they would probably not be alive today. He really was a real-life hero.

It was hard to watch him not be himself. But after what he had been through it was going to take some time.

All we could do was pray for him.

The one thing about him, he was still one of the best mechanics around.

He did seem to get excited when Robert started telling him about Amy's car and what all they had done to it.

Grandfather and Grandmother Abernathy were equally pleased that we had put the money to such good use.

"You are good people," Grandfather said.

"We are so glad that you are not angry that we used the money for someone else."

"Angry? Why would I be angry? Didn't I tell you to use it to make your honeymoon fun? Did you have fun helping this girl?"

"Oh, yes! Because you blessed us, we were able to bless someone else. Thank you again so much for all you did for us. The Spa was great!"

"Did you meet Curly Hartwell. He is the owner. He and I go way back. We went to college together. He was a minister as well, but his first wife got very sick and he had to quit to take care of her. They had grown up in that little town, so they went back there. Her parents helped them open the Spa Resort. It was right on the ocean and it helped her for a while.

She died, what, I think about fifteen years ago. He was a widower for a while. I think he just got remarried maybe seven years ago.

Very Godly man. He really knows his Bible. He walks the property every day, he and his bride, and prays for each of the visitors in his cottages."

"Oh, yes, we met him. He is the reason we were able to meet Amy, the girl we were able to help. He had hired her to run the front desk. He is a pretty awesome man, him and his wife both."

"We are going to have to get back down there and see them. It's been a while. I wonder if they will keep our suite for us?"

"Which one is your suite?"

"Number 21 of course. It has the best view of the ocean and the most privacy.

He calls it the honeymoon suite, but truthfully, they are all the same on the inside. The only thing that sets this one apart is the seclusion. Which suite did they put you in?"

"Why, the honeymoon suite, of course!"

"For the seclusion," Robert chimed in.

The food was delicious just like we knew it would be.

It was getting late when everyone headed home.

We made sure everything was cleaned up and put away before we went home.

I hadn't had a chance to get alone with Josh and talk to him.

Mostly because his little friend stuck to him like glue. I couldn't get the scoop if she was standing there.

Also, because there were so many people to get to know.

The only two that were missing from the homecoming were Toby and Patty. They were off holding a revival somewhere and they had left to get there that morning.

They were going to be gone all week is what Uncle Joey said.

Aunt Jessie hoped they would be able to come home before their next weekend service. But she was pretty sure it would be over a week before they saw them. They were supposed to be preaching the following weekend at another church and be home on Monday, but only for a few days.

I was going to miss them.

We weren't going to be seeing much of them before we had to leave but at least they were doing what they felt God had called them to do.

All we could do was pray that God would keep them safe.

CHAPTER 28

That night for the first time in over a week I pulled the picture album out from under my pillow.

My routine had been messed up for over a week.

I hadn't taken it with me on my honeymoon. It didn't seem like the thing to do.

It was the first time I had gone to bed at night before looking at her beautiful little face.

"Whatcha' got there." Robert asked.

I hadn't really told him about the album. I hadn't brought it up because, well, I didn't really know why.

He knew I had a daughter and he knew that I knew who it was. I, for some reason, just had never told him who she was or showed him the album.

I guess now was going to be that time.

"Remember so long ago when I told you that I knew who my daughter is?

"Yeah, I remember."

"Well, this album is photos of her."

"Photos? How did you get those?"

"It is a long story. Do you want to hear it?"

"I want to hear anything that has to do with you. I want to get to know everything there is to know about you. If this is something you want me to know, then yes, I want to know it."

I started at the beginning. Well, sort of, I had

already told him about giving birth to her and how I had seen her and got to hold her. What I hadn't told him was how Memaw and Pappy had been her guardian angels for all these years and that they were the ones, especially Memaw, that were keeping me informed about her for so long."

"So, your grandparents know who she is?"

"You do too."

"I do? How do I know her?"

I opened the album and began to show him her pictures.

"Hey, that is Lisa and Tony's little girl. She was our flower girl."

"Yes, she was."

"And they are okay with you being around her and all?"

"They don't know that I know. They don't know that Memaw and Pappy know. We haven't told them."

"Don't you think you should?"

"No. Why?"

"Well, I don't know. I just think it would be the right thing to do."

"Why. I have no intentions of ever trying to take her from them. They love her. They have loved her ever since they met her. I think they loved her before she was even theirs."

"What do you mean by that? "

"Well, I loved her as she was growing in me and knew I couldn't keep her. They were waiting for her for almost as long as I was and eagerly took her in and loved her."

I told him the first time that I saw them with her. How I had wanted to take her from them and run out of the store. She was mine. I knew it. Memaw and Pappy knew it. Lisa and Tony did not.

As I looked at them, I knew in that moment they were the right people to raise my daughter.

I could see the love all over their faces. They were meant to be her parents. They were meant to be the ones who raised Hannah.

I came to terms with it, really, long before I laid eyes on her after that.

Memaw and Pappy would love on her and they loved on Tony and Lisa.

"Really Robert, you've met them, they love on everybody."

"Yeah, they do tend to do that. They are pretty special."

"That they are! I don't think they were trying to be deceitful, just trying to put my mind at ease. So that I would know she was being taken good care of. I needed to know it, to see it. The pictures gave me hope. Not so much for me, but for her.

Robert, I am going to tell you something about myself."

"Something else? Besides this?"

"Well, including this."

"Okay, then spill the beans my sweet wife. I am all ears."

"Well, after I had Hannah, well, before I had her really, because of what was being done to me and now having had a baby, I just couldn't imagine anyone ever loving me or even wanting to be with me. I didn't hold out hope."

"Oh babe, come here."

He pulled me close to him.

"I am not looking for pity. I just want you to know that I had figured that is what my life was going to be like. I never in my life dreamed that you would fall in love with me and ask me to marry you. I had been in love with you for so long. You were who I dreamed of. Then Hannah came along, and I could see her pictures, and so then my dreams were complete.

Now it is like I have the best of both worlds. You, to love me and let me love you, and to be able to see little Hannah."

"Okay, I won't pressure you into doing something that you don't feel right about. Just pray about it and we'll do what you feel the Lord is telling you."

"Robert, I am afraid."

"Afraid of what?"

"God doesn't really talk to me."

"He talks to you all the time."

"No, He doesn't."

"Yes, He does. Remember at the Spa when you started reading Ephesians and the words seemed to jump off the pages?"

"Yeah, that was so amazing to me. It was like they just came alive that day."

"Well, that is the Holy Spirit, God, talking to you. Like when we all knew that we were supposed to help Amy, remember? We all knew it. It was like the Holy Spirit, God, was speaking to each of us."

"Yeah, I just knew that I knew that it was what we were supposed to do. Somehow, we were supposed to find a way and help her. To bless her. And we did."

"Yes, we did. That is God talking to you. When we pray, when we earnestly seek after God, when we make our petitions known to Him. He answers us.

Somehow, He answers us.

If it is when we are reading the Word of God and the words just seem to jump off the page or if we are asleep and we dream dreams that we thought would never come true. He is speaking to us.

There is a peace in knowing, even in the midst of the storm. He is speaking to us.

We just have to learn how to listen. We need to learn his voice."

"You are so smart Robert."

"No, I am just a sheep."

"A what?"

"A sheep."

"How is that? How are you a sheep?"

"Well, the Word of God tells us, *"My sheep know my voice, and hears it!"*, I was smart enough to listen to His voice when He told me I was supposed to marry you. I am a good sheep."

"Then I guess I am too. Because I knew down deep in my knower, that I was supposed to say yes. So, I did."

"Robert."

"Yes?"

"Kiss me!"

"Yes!!"

CHAPTER 29

Surprisingly we all made it to church on time. Even Sunday School.

Pastor James was happy to see us back.

He told Robert that a lot of times newlyweds miss church for the first few Sundays after they get married.

Robert smiled, "Well, that would probably not bode well with God considering I am trying to get a job working for Him."

They both laughed in agreement.

"Well, when you graduate, you'll know where He is leading you. Hopefully back here, maybe not forever, but for a while.

We are starting to really grow and will be looking for an associate Pastor in the next year or two. I think you'd be a good fit. You and Holly pray about it. When the time comes, you will know where He is leading you."

"I appreciate that. We are praying. God will lead us and show us where we are supposed to be. Wherever it is. I want to be in the center of it."

"Good man!" Good man!"

We went inside and found our class.

We were now in the "young marrieds" class.

It felt strange going into a class that we had never

been in before.

Thank God for familiar faces.

Lisa and Tony were there.

"I am so glad you guys are here. We were kind of feeling out of sorts in here."

They seemed happy to see us too.

"Who is the teacher in this class," Robert asked.

"Well, funny you should ask. That would be us," Tony smiled.

He reached over and shook Roberts hand.

"So happy to have you here today. Newlyweds are you, now, huh."

He winked to let Robert know he was joking.

Then he started the class in prayer and introduced us.

It wasn't like we didn't know them. Robert had grown up in this church and knew practically all of them.

We just didn't know them as married couples.

We had been single a lot longer than most of the people in this class. A couple of them looked like they had barely just got out of Highschool.

We were the newbies.

After class we went to find a place to sit in church.

We had been sitting with Memaw and Pappy for so long, that seemed to be the appropriate place to sit.

We were there before many of the others had gotten out of class.

I could hear her as she came running down the aisle.

"Hannah, no running in church."

"But I want to see Miss Holly and Mr. Robert."

"I know. But still, no running in church."

She beat her mother there by a mile.

The sweet little face that I loved to see was right there.

"Hi Miss Holly. Hi Mr. Robert. See my dress. It is my red wedding dress. It still fits me and everything and I didn't get it all messed up and Mommy said I could wear it today. Look, it still is twirly. See!" She twirled so we could see it all swishy.

"Do you still have your twirly dress Miss Holly? I liked your dress, but it wasn't red like mine. Do you still have it?"

"Oh yes, I still have it."

"How come you didn't wear it? See, I wore mine."

Before I could even really answer her, new subject.

"Where's Pappy?"

"You know, I don't know where he is. He should be here in a minute I'm sure."

"Yeah, I'm sure too. Hey, my brother didn't eat the flower."

"What flower? Oh, yeah, from the petals that you were throwing. He didn't eat it?

How do you know?"

"Because I found it. He bited it, but then he didn't eat it. I found it in his toy truck."

"Well, then, good for you. And good for him for not eating it."

"Yeah, it was a red one."

"Pappy," she squealed as she ran to him.

"Hannah, quit running in church!"

"Pappy, look, I am wearing my red twirly wedding dress. I wore it to my wedding. You remember that?"

Pappy laughed, "Yeah, I remember. Who did you marry?"

"His name is Ring Bear. He had to go home to his house. I don't know where that is though."

"Hannah, I've told you before that you did not get married. That Miss Holly and Mr. Robert got married. You were only in their wedding. You weren't the bride. You were the flower girl and the little boy was the ring bearer. Remember that I explained that to you."

"Bor-ing,' she said in a little sing-song voice.

We were all trying not to laugh. Lisa looked frustrated.

"Come on Little Miss Twirly red dress. It is time for you two to go to Children's Church. You and MJ give Pappy and Memaw one more hug and then off we go."

"I will see you both after Children's Church. And if you are both really good then I have Lifesavers for both of you."

"I want red," Hannah yelled as she led them away.

"Me too," yelled MJ, "I want green."

"Green is not red," Hannah explained to him, "green is just green and red is the best kind."

"I just want green."

CHAPTER 30

Mother had put a roast on in the slow cooker that morning before we left for church. So, dinner was going to be ready when we got home.

It was delicious too.

Robert and I cleaned the kitchen so she could go to the office like she was prone to do.

For the longest time I knew she would go in there after she got home from church on Sundays, if not right after church then sometime after lunch. I didn't know why until one day we were talking, and she said she liked to go in and study what she had learned in church that day.

She said it had started when she first got saved and she wasn't sure of all the things she was learning so she wanted to study it out.

Write out questions that she might have and see where she could find the answers in the Bible.

It had become such a habit that she just kept it up.

It helped her a lot when she would teach the Women's Bible Study.

We told her we were going to go get the car cleaned after we finished cleaning the kitchen.

When all was said and done, that is exactly what we did.

It wasn't like it was terribly dirty, but we wanted to

make sure to wash it to get all the sea salt off of it.

We were cleaning out the inside, throwing things away when Robert came across the card that Lisa and Tony had given us.

"Hey, we forgot about this."

"That reminds me, we have all those presents that we need to open and letters to write to thank everyone. What is in it? They asked us not to open it until after the honeymoon remember? Open it."

"Let's wait until we get home so we don't leave it in the car again."

We finished cleaning it, inside and out.

It really didn't take long so we were home in less than an hour.

"That didn't take long," Mother said when we walked into the house.

"Yeah, just a quick clean up from the trip. Nothing big."

"Did you guys take all the gifts from Uncle Joey's?"

"Oh, yeah. They are in the den. Do you guys want to open them now?"

"No, not today. We just weren't sure if we were going to have to go out there and get them or if someone had brought them here."

"There here. Ready whenever you are. I am going to go next door and see your mom. I'll be back in a while. We need to talk about what we want to start teaching in the new session of the Bible Study."

"Hey, do you remember a about three years back a young girl coming to the Bible study? She said there were these two ladies that had fed her, I'm sure it would have been at the Burger Joint one day and invited her to your Bible Study. One of them gave her a tin of cookies. Does that ring a bell? She would have been a homeless girl around 19 or so."

"I do remember her. Mom took her home with her and let her stay with her for a few days. When she brought her to church on Sunday there had been a complete change in her. Now what was her name? Jamie or..."

"It was Amy."

"Yeah, Amy. That's it. Wait how did you know her name was Amy?"

"You are not going to believe this."

Robert and I told her the whole story.

"You're kidding me? Sara is going to be so happy to hear that. Do you mind if I tell her?"

"No, go ahead. Mom, we told her if she ever came back this way to please come and stay with us. That's okay right?"

"Oh, Holly, that is more than okay. See you guys in a bit."

After the door closed behind her Robert looked at me and then he looked upstairs. He grinned a little crooked grin and nodded.

"Race ya," I said.

CHAPTER 31

True to her word she didn't come back for a while and Robert got to enjoy each other's company for a while.

Then we took a nap.

It was about five o'clock when we heard mother come back home.

Robert nudged me.

"We better get up and start getting ready for church here in a bit. Do you think it would be okay if I took a shower?"

"Well, it's okay with me. Why are you asking?"

"I don't know. I mean, it's not like it's my house."

"Well, it is your house. And my house. And my mother's house. We'll figure it out. But if you want to take a shower, take a shower."

He kissed me and went to take a shower.

I remembered the card in my purse, so I went and got it and brought it back upstairs.

Mother called out from the kitchen, "Do you guys want to eat a roast beef sandwich before church or after church?"

"I don't know mom. Robert is in the shower right now. I will let you know when he gets out."

"Okay baby."

I went inside my, well our, room and got the card

out of my purse. It was heavy.

What had they put in there, cash?

Then I wondered if I should open it or wait until Robert got out of the shower.

I decided to wait.

He came into the room in a towel.

"Hey Mr. Naked."

"Hey beautiful wifey! Whatcha got there?"

"I remembered the card that Lisa and Tony gave us so I went and got it. I wonder what is in it?"

"You know how to find out?"

"How's that?"

"Open it!"

"Oh yeah, I know that. By the way, my mom wants to know if we want to eat roast beef sandwiches before or after church?"

"Uh, hmm, can it be both. I mean, I could eat."

I laughed.

I called down to her, "Robert said he would like a sandwich before and after if that would be possible."

She laughed and called back up, "I think that is doable. How about you?"

"I think I will wait until after."

"Okay, I will make him one now and bring it to him when I come up to get freshened up for church."

"Thanks mom. I will let him know."

"You better get some clothes on or my mother is going to see you naked when she brings you a sandwich."

He threw his towel at me.

He was completely dressed, well except socks and shoes before she got upstairs.

Robert thanked her profusely for staving off

starvation for him. She laughed and said she would be ready in about 30 minutes. If we wanted to, we could ride together.

That was okay by us.

She went to get ready.

By now I knew that I had to get ready for church.

The card was going to have to wait.

That sandwich looked awfully good.

"Hey, can I have a bite of that?"

"My sandwich?"

"Yeah, your sandwich."

"The sandwich your mother lovingly made for me?"

"Yes, that would be the one."

"I mean, I know we are married and such and we are supposed to share, you know, what's yours is mine and what's mine is yours, but this sandwich is sure good. I don't know."

"Give me a bite of that sandwich! Please! Pretty please with a cherry on top!"

"How can I resist that. You can have the rest of it."

"Awe babe, I don't want the rest of it. Just a bite."

"Okay, just a bite!"

"Oh, that is good."

I went and got ready for church.

Robert joined me in the bathroom to brush his teeth before we left.

"Gotta get rid of this roast beef breath."

We both laughed as we brushed our teeth.

CHAPTER 32

Church had been awesome. So many young people were coming to the church. It truly was growing.

It was exciting to see so many young people praying at the altars. There were always new faces with them.

They were hungry and they were coming to be fed.

They were coming to the right place.

Pastor James asked if Robert would want to preach next Sunday night and he readily accepted.

It was all he could talk about on the ride home. It was all he could talk about while we ate another roast beef sandwich.

Robert and I cleaned up before heading to bed.

We got ready for bed and we noticed the card sitting there.

"Should we open it now? It is getting kind of late."

"Sure. Let's see what they have to tell us. Maybe it is good marriage advice. Did you know they were the young married couple's teachers? I didn't"

I opened the card.

It was a beautiful card.

When we opened it up to read the inside that is when a folded letter fell out.

We finished reading the card. It had such a lovely sentiment.

I set it aside to see what the letter said.

"This is probably all the marriage advice."

But it wasn't.

Dear Holly and Robert,

First off, congratulations on your new marriage.

We are so happy for you both.

We have been watching you for a while and it seems as if God really has His hand on you, both of you.

We are praying that you would be yielded vessels in His service.

I am sure you are wondering why this letter is so long.

We have a lot that we would like to say to you, but we aren't sure how to start.

I hope you are not reading this on your honeymoon!

We don't want to be intrusive on your honeymoon! So, if you started reading while you are on your honeymoon, please put this down and read it when you get home.

Please!

This letter is a hard letter to write.

We honestly don't know where to start.

We don't want to intrude on your privacy and if you don't ever want to bring up what we need to talk to you about, please feel free to just put this letter away and it can be out of sight out of mind.

Okay, since there is no better way to put this, here goes.

Holly, please don't think that we are speaking out of turn.

I am sure you have told your husband all about yourself as much as he has told you all about himself.

If there is ever a first rule in marriage, that should be one of them.

Do not keep secrets from your spouse!

So, Holly, here is hoping that you have told Robert

about your past.

We want you to know that we know you are Hannah's mother."

What?

Holly looked at Robert.

Keep reading," he told her.

"We weren't sure at first, but we had our suspicions.

Well, we didn't until you started coming to church with your mother and grandparents.

Speaking of them, they are some of the most down to earth, Godliest people we have ever met in our life.

You are truly blessed to have them in your life.

Both sets of our grandparents are passed away. So, it is pretty awesome that yours took such an interest in our Hannah. We had met them at the hospital the day after she was born, but of course you know that.

We could not hold our excitement back that we were there to get our new baby.

They were so happy for us. We are not sure if they truly knew at that moment that it was your baby that we were going to be picking up, but they knew the minute they saw her in church.

How could they not recognize her? That little birthmark on her neck was a telltale sign.

After that they were in love with her as much as we were.

But honestly Holly, we all know that even if it had not been your baby, they would have reacted or acted the same. That is just who they are.

But when you showed up that Sunday morning and Hannah came running up there looking for her Pappy, and you went white as a ghost, we knew something was up.

You reacted that way a lot, at first.

Then you seemed to get used to her coming up there.

We have to admit, we were a bit jealous. She loved her Miss Holly and we could tell you had a connection with her.

Then about six months or so ago, you turned your head just right and we saw it.

You looked just like Hannah, or should we say, she looked just like you.

We went home that day and talked about it.

We wondered what the odds were that you were not her mother.

That possibly someone else might be.

That Tuesday morning after Bible study, we asked if your Memaw, our Memaw, the one and only Memaw would have lunch with us. Her and the one and only Pappy.

They did us one better, they invited us over for dinner that night.

We got a sitter and went.

They were a little disappointed that we had not brought the kids with us, but we needed to ask them a few questions of course and didn't feel it would be appropriate to ask in front of them.

We really didn't know what we were going to ask and what their answers were going to be.

It was around Christmas. Their house smelled of cookies. I have come to find out, their house always smells of cookies.

After we had a lovely dinner, we knew we needed to just ask.

We weren't angry about it. We weren't even upset. We just wanted to know.

Tony was the much braver one.

I remember that he told them that we had some questions and if they could, would they answer them?

We told them, no pressure. If they didn't feel free to say, then we would just let it be.

So over coffee and some of the best cookies ever, we asked.

Your grandmother, bless her heart, was at a loss for words. And as we all know, that is a hard thing to do, put Memaw at a loss for words.

After a minute or so, they got their composure.

They countered with a question.

We told them every question we had and why we had it.

Pappy reached across and took your Memaws hand and said, "We need to tell them."

And they did.

They told us that it was your baby and that you had given it up for adoption and that they realized it was your baby for the same reason we suspected, the birthmark. Well, that, and they say she looks just like you did when you were a baby.

You must have been a beautiful baby, Hannah sure is.

And we know she will grow up into a beautiful young woman because you are.

Robert, you are a very blessed man.

We don't really know if it is the right thing to tell you that we know or if we should have just let it go, but we prayed about it, a lot, and felt that we should let you know that we know.

Please don't be angry at your grandparents for telling us.

They would only tell us that you loved Hannah and

that you were glad the we were raising her.

Oh, and one more thing. She did tell us about the dolls.

She loves every one of them.

She has every one of them that you have given her.

She names them all baby at first until she can come up with a good name. The last one's name is Abigail.

We wondered if we should be worried that the dad might show up some time to try and take the baby, but they assured us that would never be a problem.

Anyways, we guess we just wanted to let you know that we know, and we hope that is not weird for you, for either of you.

We only have one request, please don't tell her.

She knows she is adopted.

We have told her that much.

We have tried to explain it to her in a way that she could comprehend, the same with MJ.

That God and their Love Mommies gave them to us.

Thank you for the gift of Hannah!

We pray that God blesses you over and abundantly with another Hannah because of your gift to us.

We pray God blesses you both over and abundantly!

Love,

Lisa and Tony Henderson

Holly wiped the tears that were flowing down her face.

She just sat there holding the letter.

Finally, Robert took the letter and folded it and put it back inside the card.

"Where do you want to put it?"

"The same place I put all the important letters I get."

I took it from him and pulled the album from

under my pillow and put it to the back where the other letters that I held so dear to my heart were kept.

I looked at her pictures as Robert sat beside me, holding me.

"Isn't she the prettiest little thing."

"Yes, just like her mother."

We sat and looked at her pictures for a little bit and finally it was time to go to sleep.

Tomorrow was a workday and we were about to embark on life, or was it about to embark on us. Too early to tell.

He held me as we fell asleep in each other's arms while the moon streamed in on us through the window.

CHAPTER 33

As lovely as the moon had been the sunlight was blinding.

Neither one of us wanted to get out of bed, but we didn't have a choice.

Mother had already gotten up to make breakfast and coffee.

Honestly, I could care less about the breakfast, but coffee was what we needed.

She had made us both sandwiches to take to work and we were out the door.

He dropped me off at Pappy's and took the car on down the street. I guess he could have ridden to work with Lance, but he was already gone when we left.

With both of them working there it was pretty convenient if they could ride together.

Robert said he would make a point to talk to Lance about it.

Cooper's Auto Shop.

They were the two-best mechanics in the place.

The owner, Cooper Owen, was getting up there in age and was trying to sell the place but he wasn't sure if he was ready to retire just yet.

He would talk about it then change his mind.

Then something would happen, and he was ready again.

One of these days he would pull the trigger and sell the place. Then what were they going to do?

If he sold it, who knows, the new owner might not like to have a vet working for him.

These days, a lot of people still held a lot of hatred toward the military and especially Vietnam Vets.

But, today, they both had jobs.

Pappy was happy to see me that morning.

"We missed you last week. I sure am glad to have you home."

He hugged me.

I was quiet.

I wasn't sure yet how to put into order the letter we had read last night.

Should I be mad at them for telling them or should I be glad that it was finally out in the open?

I decided to talk to him about it.

"Can you make time to have a conversation with me today?"

"Sure, baby girl. How about I take you to lunch? We can grab a burger."

I thought of the wonderful sandwich I had in my bag and thought to myself, "The sandwich can wait until tomorrow.

"You're on."

It was a hectic morning.

Jedediah, Pappy's new guy, had called in late and so he was busy on the floor and I was busy getting the books in order.

By lunchtime we were both starving.

We left for lunch after everyone else had eaten because we weren't sure how long we would be.

Pappy drove.

It was just down the street, so we weren't going to die of starvation.

Seems like they had a new kid in here every few months. I guess that is what made it what it was, simply a Burger Joint where you could get a good burger, fries, and a soda.

Pappy ordered the double-double cheeseburger, loaded, a large-fries and a large soda.

I ordered a single cheeseburger with no onions, medium fries, and a large soda.

We took our seat and Pappy jumped right on in.

"So, what do you need to talk to me about baby girl?"

"Well, I'm not really sure how to start."

"Start anywhere. You can talk to me about anything. You've only been married a little over a week. I can't imagine it being marriage problems already. So, it must be something else. What is it?"

I was just about to say when they brought us our food.

Pappy unwrapped his burger. It was huge. I was about to take a bite of mine when a couple of onions fell out.

"Stop Pappy. Check your burger. I think I have your onions."

Sure enough, I did.

I scraped them off, all of them, and gave them to him.

He took a great big bite.

"Go ahead and talk. I can eat and listen. Don't want to be rude, but I am hungry."

I laughed as I took a bite of my now onion-less burger.

It was so good. I didn't realize how hungry I had

been until that first bite hit my mouth.

"We'll wait. I am just as hungry as you are, and I want to eat it while it is hot."

We ate in peace.

They were so good.

It was the kind of burger that just dripped grease down your arm if you didn't hold it just right when you ate it.

So good!

We finished our burgers. I don't know how he managed it, but Pappy even beat me eating that monstrous burger against my little one, and not a bit of grease on him.

He waited for me to finish before he asked me again to tell him what I was needing.

A full stomach and just sitting there with him made it almost impossible to broach the subject, but I knew it was now or never.

"Well, I wanted to talk to you about a letter that I got, well that Robert and I got."

"Okay, what was the letter? Did you not get student housing? Your Memaw..."

"No, not that kind of letter. Let me explain."

I told him everything the letter had said.

This time he didn't interrupt. He just let me keep talking.

Finally, when I was done, he looked at me and said, "Okay, so what do you want to know baby girl?"

"I want to know why you told them?"

"Well, because they asked."

"I don't understand. Is that really a reason? I don't understand?"

"Well, would you have us lie?"

"No, but I don't really know how to feel about the fact that they know. Do they hate me? Do they think I was a horrible person? Did they think that I was someone that got that way because I had a lot of boyfriend and such? I mean, what did they think before you told them?"

"Told them what Holly?"

I lowered my voice, "How I had gotten that way."

He lowered his voice, "They didn't ask."

"You didn't tell them?"

"That is not something for us to tell. If you want them to know you will have to tell them that for yourself. They just wanted to know if the baby was yours and we confirmed what they thought.

Did they say something in the letter to make you think they thought less of you because of it? They don't strike me as that kind of people."

"No. As a matter of fact, they were glad that I had given them the baby."

"Yes, they are grateful for that. They only asked one thing of us and that was to please not tell her that we were her great-grandparents. We promised them that we would not ever tell her. Her and that little brother of hers are the cutest little things. MJ, has a new slingshot you know. I gave it to him."

He looked so proud of that fact.

"Yeah, they asked me not to tell her that I was her mother. I won't ever do that. She is too cute. Did you tell them that I was the one giving her the dolls or did they figure that out on their own too."

"They asked and we confirmed."

"Well, I guess that answers a lot of questions. Are you sure they don't think I am a horrible person?"

"I am sure Holly girl. Now let's get back to the store. Your husband it going to be picking you up in a little while and you don't want to make him wait. You still haven't heard about where you will be staying when you get there?"

"Not yet. But hopefully soon. We have to make plans."

"It will work itself out."

"Oh yeah, how do you know that Pappy."

"The Bible says so."

"It does huh? It says Robert and Holly don't need to worry about where they will be staying because it will work its way out. Hmm, I don't right recall where that verse is Pappy."

"You don't?"

"Nope, not that particular one."

"Well it is found in 1 Corinthian 2:9 *"But as it is written, Eye hath not seen, nor ear heard, neither have entered into the heart of man, the things which God hath prepared for them that love Him!"*

God has something prepared for you, why, because you love Him. You just keep the faith. Keep seeking after Him and he will reveal it to you."

And he was right! He always was!

CHAPTER 34

Robert was tired when he picked me up from work. A week off had made him appreciate his muscles.

He told me that I was going to have to take him to work the next day.

Lance had not been at work that day and unless he could talk to him at home, he was going to need a ride to work.

"No problem. I was born for this. Husband taxi service."

He laughed and said as long as he was the only husband that got to use that service, he was fine with it.

"Besides," he said, "you look better and smell better than Lance does."

He went straight upstairs to shower and change.

I went to clean up and help finish dinner. The frying chicken smelled delicious.

I wasn't super hungry because I'd had such a late lunch with Pappy.

"Where's Robert?"

"Taking a shower. He'll be down in just a bit. Will it be okay if I wash his clothes tonight? They are pretty greasy and I don't want to leave them in the dirty clothes hamper."

"Sure, why not? It is going to take some getting

used to having a man in the house."

"Do you want us to leave? I know married couples are supposed to be on their own. If we are in the way mom, please tell me."

"Oh no Holly, that isn't what I meant at all. I am so glad you are both here. The house is so empty when you leave. It just seems to echo. I just meant. I don't want to be intrusive to you guys. You are newlyweds and you are going to want to be alone a lot. I want you to know that if you need to just be alone together or I am being too much, just let me know. I perfectly understand."

"I love you mom."

"I love you too Holly."

Robert interrupted, "Sorry to intrude, but I hope you don't mind, I am washing my dirty laundry that I wore today. It is pretty greasy and I didn't want it to stay in the dirty clothes hamper."

"Where did you get him Holly," mother said as she stared at him shaking her head? "He does his own laundry."

"Next door. He helps make the bed too. This morning he threatened to make it with me in it if I didn't get out of it."

"He's a keeper."

"Ladies, you are making me blush. Here let me set the table while you two finish up whatever you are doing in there. And may I say, it smells divine."

"Oh, yes, he's a keeper.

And as good as it smelled, it even tasted better.

Mother was turning out to be a pretty good cook. She could almost give Aunt Jessie a run for her money on the meatloaf.

We were just finishing up dinner when the doorbell rang.

It was my new mother-in-law.

She came bearing a gift.

Dessert.

Lemon meringue pie.

Neither one of us wanted to share but we did.

Robert went to put his laundry on to dry and his mother set the mail on the table.

"This came in the mail."

It had Roberts name on it so I figured he could open it when he came back.

I made a pot of coffee to drink while we devoured the pie.

"By the way," mother asked her, "good job on raising this kid."

"Oh yeah, how's that?"

"He washed his own laundry and set the table for dinner. What else did you teach him to do?"

"I didn't teach him that. His dad did."

"His dad did?"

"Oh yeah. He told him that there was no such thing as man's work or woman's work. In this family, everyone pulls their own weight around here. He showed both boys how to do their own laundry when they turned 10. He told them if they wanted clean clothes then they had better learn how to use the machines. I wasn't their maid and that if he ever caught them disrespecting me that they would regret it. Not that I didn't do their laundry on occasion or help them by changing their bed linens and such. But yeah, for the most part, they know how to take care of things."

"Where did you find him?"

"I don't know. Just blessed, I guess.

I wasn't raised like that. My dad didn't do anything to help around the house, inside anyhow. My poor mother had to do it all. Well, with the help of us four girls.

Now that we are all moved out with families of our own, it is back to just her.

I remember one Thanksgiving in particular. We were all at my mother's house for dinner. We had been cooking all morning.

Ryan came into the kitchen and we got the kids plates fixed. My sister's husbands were helping a bit. My brothers weren't there that year for some reason. Anyways, all of us were working together, well, except for my dad.

When we all were getting ready to eat, he didn't have a plate prepared. My mother, who had been helping get the kids plates ready as well, was still in the kitchen, getting their plates ready.

My dad pipes up, "I guess I don't get to eat today."

Whereas I piped up, "I am sorry. I didn't hear that you had broken both of your arms and legs."

I thought Ryan was going to choke on his food. But my dad, no. He never would have done the things that Ryan does or has taught my sons to do. He's a keeper."

"Who's that? Dad? Yeah, he's a keeper. Did she tell you he showed me how to get grease stains out of my shirts?"

"No, but I will be more than happy to let you show me how that's done. I might need that little trick for a couple of my blouses after I eat at the Burger Joint."

CHAPTER 35

The doorbell rang.

Mother answered.

"Well, come on in and join the party."

"Is she in the kitchen?"

"Yes. Come on in. We are about to cut into that Lemon pie she brought over and have some coffee. Are you going to join us?"

"Pie and coffee. Try and stop me."

"What are you doing over here?"

"What do you mean, what am I doing over here. You brought my Lemon pie over here and you didn't cut me a slice of it."

"Are you crazy? I have a whole Lemon Pie for you sitting in the fridge."

"I looked in there and I didn't see a pie."

"Well, of course you didn't. Do you really think that I would make a Lemon Meringue Pie for someone and not make you one too? What kind of person would I be to do that to you?"

"Well, I couldn't imagine that you would do that but the only pie I saw in the fridge was Chocolate and as much as I like Chocolate Pie, it isn't the same as Lemon. Ooh, it is making my mouth water just thinking about it."

"Well sit down and I will get you a cup of coffee to

go with it. How do you take it," I asked?

"Just a little cream."

No wonder I loved this family.

A man that raised his sons to do laundry and know how to clean house. A man who taught him that Lemon pies beat Chocolate pies, hands down. And a man that taught his son that coffee with a little cream is the only way to go! And a mother-in-law who can bake circles around just about anybody, especially when it comes to Lemon Meringue Pie!

This is my kind of family!

We were enjoying the pie and coffee when Robert noticed the mail.

"Oh, yeah. This was in the mail today."

"I think it is from the college."

He opened it and read it.

"We regret to inform you that there are currently no openings in family housing at this time."

"Awe man, what are we going to do?"

"Well, we have a bit of money saved. I say we go down a couple of weeks early and see what might be available."

"I don't see that we have any choice."

"What are you talking about?"

"Mom, we have to find jobs and a place to live while Robert is going to college next year."

"Okay, but why are you so concerned?"

"Well, we have to have money to live on and it costs money to rent an apartment. And right now, we don't have either one."

"I mean, I know you will have to have those things. You neither one will have problem getting a job. Robert aren't you going to be working at the same place you've been working?"

"That is the plan, but it didn't pay very well, so now I'm not sure. If we had been able to stay in married student housing, then it would have been fine with Holly working. But now, I just don't know."

"Holly, money shouldn't be a problem. I mean, you have plenty of money in savings. And you have all those savings bonds that your grandparents have been giving you all these years. They may not be worth millions of dollars, but I would imagine that most of them are at full maturity."

"I guess I didn't think of that."

"Okay, then, let's plan on heading out at the end of July. That gives us time to find a place and try and get jobs."

"Then it's settled. We leave at the end of the month. That should give us plenty of time to find a place to live and jobs."

"Okay then, who wants more pie?"

Robert, his dad, and I in unison, raised our hand, "Me" we all said at once.

Robert asked his dad if he knew where Lance was today. He hadn't been at work and Coop wasn't there either so there was nobody to ask."

"No, I don't know where he was other than I knew he wasn't going to work. He just said he had some business to take care of. Why? Did you need him for something?"

"Yeah, I was going to see if I could bum a ride off of him in the morning."

"Yeah, he hasn't made it home tonight so far. Well he might be there by now. We've been over here for a while. If he's home when we get there do you want me to have him call you?"

"Nah. I'll just have Holly take me one more time and ask him tomorrow if he can start taking me."

"Okay son. Love you guys."

He hugged us and headed for the door.

"I love you too. Now I need to get your dad home so I can show him where that pie is."

"You kids go on up and spend some time together. I'll clean up."

"We can help."

"You both did the dinner dishes. I think I am capable of washing a few plates and a bit of silverware. Go on with you."

"Hey maybe tomorrow you could meet me at the bank, and we could see if any of those savings bonds are worth anything.

Sure, how about I come by and pick you up after the Bible Study and we go to lunch? I could go for a good greasy burger from the Burger Joint."

"Sounds great! See you in the morning."

"See you in the morning. Do you think Robert would like the rest of this chicken for his lunch tomorrow?"

"Are you kidding me? I am sure he would, but I don't see him eating four pieces of fried chicken?"

"Are you sure? He works pretty hard."

He came in carrying a basket with his warm dry clean clothes in it.

"Robert, do you want to take the rest of this chicken in your lunch tomorrow? Holly and I are going to have lunch together so she won't need any of it."

"Sure, yeah, I'll take it. Was there any of those

biscuits left? I would take a few of those too."

"Where do you keep that extra stomach of yours? You eat like this and still stay so fit. I don't get it. I even look at an extra helping and I gain 10 pounds. Life is unfair. So unfair!"

CHAPTER 36

Mother kept her word. After Bible study she came by the store to pick me up.

I had already told Pappy that I was going to have to make it a short day because I had to take care of some business at the bank.

"No problem. So where is she taking you for lunch?"

"You are not going to believe this, the Burger Joint. She said she hadn't had one in a while and I didn't want to disappoint her."

"I am going to have to find something around here to eat. I don't go home on Tuesdays for lunch since your Memaw does the Bible study. Too much work for her. I am sure I've got something here. Maybe I'll call Shorty's and see if they can bring me a sandwich."

"Uh, well, if you really want a sandwich, I have mine in the fridge from yesterday."

"What is it?"

"You are awfully picky for someone who has nothing to eat."

"Yeah, but I've got means, girly."

"Well, do you "means" to eat my roast beef sandwich or not?"

"Well, now, that does sound mighty good. I just might have the means to eat it. Do you need me to pick up Robert and take him home for you?"

"No. He dropped me off today. I'll just ride home with mom."

"You're a good girl Miss Holly. Looking out for me like that. Now, where is that sandwich?"

He had just finished eating it when Mother showed up.

"See you in the morning Pappy."

I didn't want to say anything to him about Robert and I having to leave earlier than planned to have to find a place to live before they were all gone. We didn't want to leave it up to chance that we would be able to find something affordable and close to the school.

That would be determined by how much money I did have in savings and how much some of the savings bonds were worth.

I should have at least 6 or 7 years-worth of them that might help us through.

We would soon find out.

The Burger Joint was just about finished with their lunch crowd when we got there.

The kid behind the counter, of course the one and only time they would have a most observant employee, pipes up, "Weren't you in here yesterday?"

Mother looked at me, "Were you here yesterday."

"Uh..."

"Yeah, I remember. You were here with that old guy. He is in here a lot. I remember. You ordered the cheeseburger with extra onions."

"Oh, you must be mistaken. She hates onions. She would never order a burger of any kind with onions."

"Then why did you order one like that yesterday if you don't like onions?"

"I didn't order one like that yesterday. I ordered it

without onions, and you put onions on there. A lot of them. But if you know the old man that came in with me since he is here a lot, why would you make his burger with no onions?

"So, you were here yesterday?"

"I told you she was here yesterday. What do you think, I would lie to you?"

"No. I was just surprised that she was here yesterday since she had a roast beef sandwich to eat.

What happened to the sandwich I sent with you?"

"Pappy ate it."

"Who is Pappy?

"The old man that came in with me yesterday. My grandfather"

"Your grandfather ate a roast beef sandwich and a double-double cheeseburger yesterday? Do you guys not feed him at home?

By this time I was getting frustrated.

"No! I mean yes, we feed him at home. I mean my grandmother feeds him at home. He ate the sandwich today.

Can we order?"

"Oh, sure. Welcome back. What can we make for you today?"

"We will have 2 single cheeseburgers, NO ONIONS, 2 medium fries and 2 large sodas."

"And what will you have?"

"Oh brother. I will eat off of her tray."

We paid, after reiterating, NO ONIONS.

"We'll have that right out."

We were trying so hard not to laugh as we found a place to sit.

"So, the roast beef sandwich wasn't so appealing

yesterday huh? We could have gone somewhere else, sweetheart."

"No. This is fine. And no, I was looking forward to eating that sandwich yesterday. It was good Sunday night and I am kind of sad that I didn't get to eat it. Pappy and I came here because I needed to talk to him about something important. Rather than try to find a moment where we would be getting interrupted, we decided to come here. He didn't bring anything for lunch today so I gave him my sandwich from yesterday. I know it was good. He devoured it right before you got there."

The food arrived right about then so the conversation came to a stop for a bit.

Thankfully they got it right. No onions.

After we had eaten a few bites to stave off starvation, Mother asked, "So what did you need to talk to your Pappy about? If it isn't any of my business, just say so. Just curious."

I guess it wasn't much of a secret. So, I told her.

"They know."

"Wow! That must have been a lot to take in. Are you okay? How do you feel about that?"

"I'm not really sure. I mean, I guess I'm glad they know, but then again, I don't know what they think of me. I mean, do they think I was some wayward girl that got pregnant and gave my baby away? I don't know. It kind of weighs heavy on my heart, but I'll figure it out. Now, how do you feel knowing that they know you are her grandmother? I mean, if they know I'm her mother, then they know who you are. Right?"

"Well, yes. I guess you're right. I guess I am not sure how I feel about that. I guess I am going to have to figure it out too. You know, I'm sure it isn't as hard on me as it is on you every time you see her. I just want to scoop her up and love on her and pour all the love I can into her, just like a grandmother should be able to. I keep myself at a distance because I am afraid that I just might do it. I don't know how my mom and dad do it."

"Me either. She sure is cute. Did you see her Sunday in that red dress? She kept calling it her "wedding dress." She said she had gotten married to the "ring bear." Lisa had to explain to her that she had not gotten married. I wasn't sure if she was buying it or not. She sure makes my heart happy every time I lay eyes on her.

Tony and Lisa are doing an awesome job of raising her and little MJ. I don't think I could have hand-picked better parents for her. For either one of them.

Mom, you know I have the photo album of her in my room. It is under my pillow at all times. If you ever want to just get it and look at the pictures, please feel free to do so."

"Holly, really? Do you mean it?"

"Yes, I mean it. Afterall, she is your granddaughter."

"That she is. I do love her Holly. I would like to look at it sometime."

"Any time you want. You know where it is."

"We better hurry," Mother said after she looked at her watch. "I am not sure how much time this is going to take."

We finished up and headed to the bank. Mr. Crawford greeted us. He was not a bad looking guy.

His wife had passed away a while ago and he just

seemed sad. It broke my heart to see him so sad.

Not that I really knew him to really know. He had just always seemed to be a bit more chipper.

"How can I help you ladies today?"

Mother explained to him our dilemma, she and he set to work to see exactly how much we had and how we would be able to access it.

"Well, you had a substantial amount in your savings. Your mother has invested your portfolio well.

"All in all, once you cash out the matured bonds and with what you have in savings already, plus the life insurance policy that paid out, you have a little over $100,000.00 in savings. Plus, your savings account that you opened yourself a few years ago. All in all, the exact amount is $122,094.57."

I just sat there stunned.

"See, I told you that it wouldn't be that bad. You and Robert should be able to find a place to live with that much money."

"Mother, I think we could buy a couple of houses and a brand-new car with that kind of money."

"Yes, I guess you could."

"What happens if I leave it in there and do nothing?"

"Well, you should cash out the bonds that have matured and just deposit it in the savings. It will continue to earn interest. If you need some to live on, then you can transfer what you need into a checking account."

"Okay then. I will need to talk to Robert and see what he thinks we should do. We will be back in touch. Thank you so much Mr. Crawford for all of your time and help."

"It was truly my pleasure. You are two of the most pleasant customers I have had in here all day!"

"Thank you, Charlie. You made this very easy."

"Anne, you are very welcome. You and your daughter come back any time. And congratulations Holly on your marriage. Speaking of that. At some point you need to change all your accounts to your new name. Davis is it? Right?"

I hadn't even thought about that!

"Yes, I will get that taken care of really soon. My husband and I will come and make sure it is taken care of as soon as possible. Thank you again."

We waved at him as we walked out to the car.

"So, do you think that will get you by while you find jobs and an apartment?"

"Yeah, I think it will do."

"How about let's order a Pizza for dinner when Robert gets home?"

"Sounds good to me."

She could have said, "Let's have boiled alligator liver for dinner tonight and I would have said, sounds good to me. I could not get my mind wrapped around the fact that I, well Robert and I, had over $100,000.00 in the bank.

CHAPTER 37

Robert was home around six that evening and after a quick kiss and deciding what kind of pizza he wanted, he went upstairs to get a shower and get cleaned up.

"Boy do I have something to talk to you about tonight. Let me get cleaned up and I'll tell ya."

"Well, I've got something I need to talk to you about too. So, hurry up and get changed."

Mother left to go get the pizzas.

I took Roberts clothes to the laundry room while he showered.

I scrubbed some of the dirtier spots with the bar of pink soap that mother kept on hand.

I had just turned on the machine when I heard him close the bedroom door.

I went upstairs.

Pretty exciting news. I wonder what he is going to say.

I opened the door just as he dropped his towel.

"Seriously! We are going to have to stop meeting like this," he joked.

It didn't take him long to get dressed.

"So, what is your news? What did you need to tell me?"

"Guess what?"

"Okay, what?"

"Lance is buying Coopers Auto Shop."

"He's what?"

"He's buying it. Yeah, Coop finally decided to sell and him and Lance went down yesterday to get the paperwork going. I think he is going to be getting a VA loan or something. Can you believe it.

Lance told me today.

He said he is going to change the name of it to "Wheels" since that is what everybody is calling him lately. Pretty cool huh?"

"That is pretty cool."

"He is going to be needing some help. I mean with us leaving soon and Cooper leaving, it's just going to be Lance and Matthew. Matthew is pretty good, but I don't think he will be able to handle it all. Lance is going to be needing at least one more person. We need to pray that God sends the right guy."

"Is it a done deal?"

"It is if he can get the VA to loan him the money. He has about $4,000.00 dollars of his own. So, all he needs is the balance. I guess him and Coop have been talking for a while about it. I hope it goes the way he wants it too. I hope more than anything this is where God wants him to be and that he is doing what God wants him to be doing.

I tried to tell him that, but he didn't want to hear me. All he told me was, "We can't all be you now can we Robert."

I'm not sure exactly what that means but I sure hope whatever demons he's fighting don't win this war.

He's already lost a leg to one war. I don't want to

see him lose his soul over another one."

"We'll just have to pray extra hard for him babe."

I kissed his forehead.

Mother came home and hollered up, "I've got pizza."

"Oh, pizza. I'm starving."

We went downstairs and started setting everything out.

Robert was just about to take a bite of his piping hot, everything pizza when mother asked, "So did you tell him?"

"Tell me what?" He took a big bite.

"We have over a $100,00.00 in savings.

"What?" Robert started choking on his pizza.

Mother started pounding him on his back.

After a minute or so he got himself under control.

"Are you trying to kill me? Now what did you say? Say that again!"

"We have over $100,000.00 in savings. Oh, and we need to go to the bank and have our accounts joined in both of our names. Maybe we can do that sometime this week?"

"Uh, are you kidding me? Is this some kind of joke?"

"No. Mother and I met with Mr. Crawford at the bank today and he went over everything with us. He assured us that we have to have everything changed into both of our names."

"Very funny Holly. You raised a comedian here, now didn't you?" He laughed as he looked at mother.

She thought it was pretty amusing herself.

"No, he really did say that."

"Oh, come on now. You both are a couple of

comedians. Tell me what you are talking about. What is going on?"

We both told him everything we could remember.

He said that he would talk to Cooper to see if he could take some time off one morning so we could go get it taken care of.

We would be okay.

We would have enough money to live on while we looked for a place to live and jobs.

It was going to be hard saying goodbye to everybody, but we really didn't have a choice.

We were going to be on our own for the first time in a few weeks, as husband and wife.

I hoped that I would be able to live up to the examples I had been shown.

Maybe Mother had not been the example of what a wife should be, but I had others that I could look up to.

Memaw, Aunt Jessie, even Robert's mother.

That night after we ate and cleaned up, we decided that it was a good a time as any to open the gifts we had received.

Robert called his mother and dad to see if they wanted to come over and help. His mother was more than happy too but his dad was helping Lance navigate his proposal and vision for his new business.

"Wheels"

It had a good ring to it.

Lance was going to be a success! We were sure of it.

Robert was a good mechanic, but Lance surpassed him.

He was able to listen to a car and almost always he was able to tell you what was going on.

And the older the cars the better. He loved working

on vintage cars.

Once news got around that he was going to be the owner, business was going to boom.

We spent the rest of the night opening presents and writing thank you notes.

What in the world we were going to do with all this stuff was a mystery to me?

Mrs. Davis and my mother laughed.

"You'll figure it out. Most of this stuff will come in pretty handy."

"Well, except for the Dolphin with the clock in its belly. I don't know what to tell you to do with that," Mother said.

We all laughed, well except for Robert.

"Hey, I kinda like that."

Then we all laughed again.

"You are kidding right?"

"No."

"Then it's yours. You can put it anywhere you want to, just not in the living room or the bedroom. Or any place that I have to look at it."

"It's that bad huh?"

"Yes, it's that bad. But it is all yours."

"Well, if it is that bad, then I don't want it. I will give it to Lance when he opens his business. He can have it."

"Who gave us that anyways?"

"I don't know. There isn't a card."

CHAPTER 38

I was beginning to feel like a part time employee. I knew that I had missed a lot on Monday because of the long lunch that I'd had with Pappy. I had missed all afternoon Tuesday from having lunch with mother and all the banking I had to get done.

And now, it was only Wednesday, and if I could get in touch with Lisa, I was going to see if she and I could have lunch.

I so needed to talk to her.

My heart had been heavy ever since I had read the letter.

It was now or never, well, maybe not never, that I would get a chance to talk to her.

We were going to have to be leaving soon and I didn't want to let time and distance get between us before letting her know how I felt.

Robert and I had talked about it and he realized that I needed to let them know.

Pappy understood, of course he did, I knew he would.

I waited until eight to call her. I wasn't sure of her schedule.

"Good morning, Henderson residence."

"Hi Lisa. This is Holly Ab... Davis. Is it too early to call? I didn't want to wake you."

"Oh, honey, you think you're my wake-up call? MJ has been up since 5:30 this morning building things, God knows what, with his building block things and then shooting them down with the slingshot his Pappy got him.

Thank God for Captain Kangaroo or I wouldn't have even had a chance to bathe this morning.

But hallelujah! Mission accomplished.

Were you needing something this morning?"

"Well, I was just wondering if you would be free for lunch today?"

"That sounds so good, but it would have to be a late lunch. I have some shopping to do this morning. Hannah is starting 1st grade and I need to get her some new clothes and school supplies and a few things for MJ. Those kids are growing like crazy. Must be something in the water. I am dropping them off for a playdate with my neighbor while I shop.

I will be watching hers while she does the same tomorrow.

It would be nice if we could shop together but we've found we enjoy our sanity much more than we love company.

Would 12:30 work for you?"

"Yes, that would be just fine. Where would you like to go? You choose!"

"Honestly! I would love a burger from the Burger Joint. I love that place. I don't get there often. The kids prefer McDonalds. Not that I couldn't eat a Big Mac but there is something about the burgers at the Burger Joint. I think they must add extra grease to make it so darn tasty. Does that sound ok too you? We can go anywhere if you prefer something else."

Are you kidding me? Yes!!! Anything else.

"No, Burger Joint is fine. I'll see you there at 12:30."

I had no longer hung up the phone when I turned around and Pappy was standing behind me.

"Did I just hear you right? Are you going to the Burger Joint again?"

He just laughed as he walked away after I nodded in the affirmative with a pained look on my face.

She was just getting out of her car when I arrived.

She hugged me.

"Let's go eat. I am starving. I just love how this place smells. I don't even like onions, but they sure smell good when you mix them with all the other wonderful smells.

You won't believe one of the things I am looking forward too."

"What's that?"

"Not having to share my French fries."

We laughed.

I didn't have the heart to tell her what I was looking forward too.

Someone else to be taking the orders.

Thankfully one of us was going to be very happy today.

"Welcome to the Burger Joint. What can I get for you today? Hey, weren't you here yesterday? Yeah, yeah! Double-Double extra onions! I remember." He smiled so proud of himself for remembering.

Too bad he remembered wrong.

Lisa looked at me as if to say, "You were here yesterday? You can eat a double-double? I did not even think you would like onions."

"No. I don't eat onions. Sorry."

"Oh, I must have you mixed up with someone else."

"Quite alright."

We ordered our food with the emphasis on "NO ONIONS"! and found a place to sit.

Lisa was excited to be out to lunch.

"Such a rare treat. I love this place. Tony and I used to come here when we were dating. Now we just come on occasion. It's like coming home."

"Yeah, it's pretty special."

We had just barely started small talk when the kid brought the food over.

"I remembered you. You were here yesterday with that other lady. I remember because you made sure to say, "NO ONIONS" just like now. Enjoy your food!"

He started to walk away when Lisa stopped him.

"Do you have any lemons?"

"I think so?"

"Would it be a problem if I asked you to bring me some?"

"No, no problem at all."

"Have you ever had lemon in your soda or tea? I just love it. Tony and I were on one of our rare dates one Saturday afternoon. Have you heard of Paulie's? Love that place. Anyways, we were having a late lunch and I looked across and there was this elderly couple sitting there. They looked familiar but I couldn't place them. Anyways, the lady asked for lemon and she squeezed it into her soda. I love lemon. Anything lemon!

So, I thought, why not? I loved it!

Have you ever tried lemon in your soda?"

"I have. I love it as well. I just forget to ask for it.

Do you get to Paulie's often?"

"I think we have been there maybe five times. It is always so good. It's a place that you can go and have a conversation and good food."

The kid brought the lemon. A whole lemon!

Lisa looked at it and then looked at the kid.

"Do you think we could get a knife so we could cut it please?"

He looked at the whole lemon for a second and then it hit him.

"Oh, yeah, sorry about that. I should have known you would need a knife."

We lost it.

I am sure he thought we were terrible when he came back with the knife and could barely utter "Thank you."

As we ate, I told her I thought I knew who the older couple might be.

"She is the same person that I learned to put lemon in my soda from. They are my other grandparents."

"I knew they looked familiar. They have come to the church a few times. They were just at your wedding."

"Yeah, that would be them."

"Have you tried the Lemon Tarts? I always tell myself. Order that first, but I never do. One of these days I am going to. It will probably shock Tony, but it shouldn't. We've been married forever. Nothing I do should surprise him now. But I have to do something like that every great once in a while to keep him on his toes. Besides, life is too short. You should eat dessert first. At least sometimes. Right?"

"Right!"

CHAPTER 39

"Are you in a big rush to get home?"

"No. I have some time."

"I really want to talk to you about something."

"I thought you might. Did you read the letter?"

"Yes. But not until we got back. As a matter of fact, we didn't get a chance to read it until Sunday night after church."

Lisa reached her hand across the table and took my hand.

"Are you okay?"

"That is so funny. I was wanting to ask you the same thing."

"Why wouldn't I be okay?"

"Well, I just thought maybe you would want us to leave and go away and not be around us now that you know."

"Oh, Holly. I have known for a long time. At first, when I would see you two together, I felt like the intruder. But as I watched and realized that you were, well, for lack of a better way to put it, walking on eggshells around her, and Tony and myself, I knew you were having a hard time dealing with us being this close to you.

There were plenty of times these last few months when we really knew who you were, that we thought maybe we should find another church to go to. But it seems that the more we prayed about it the more we felt that we were to stay.

I don't know why. Tony and I both feel the same way.

We were willing to go anywhere else to make all of you feel more comfortable.

Even your mother has a hard time being there.

She knows right?"

"Yes, she knows. She didn't at first. Not when she first started going there. Not when she first got saved. She may have suspected. But she didn't know. It wasn't until later when I told her. She told me that when she had first seen Hannah that she couldn't get over how much she looked like me when I was little."

"Yeah, I see her wanting to play with her and interact with her. Tony and I would not have a problem with that.

Neither one of us have any family out here. My parents were killed in an automobile accident right after we were married and it's just Tony's dad. He never comes and visits. So, if you want to tell your mom that it would be okay for her to talk to Hannah, play with her, please let her know we would be okay with it."

"I'll be sure and tell her."

"Yeah, we don't want her or you or now even, Robert, to be uncomfortable. The only two people that don't ever seem uncomfortable are your grandparents."

"Yeah, they have a way of making everybody feel like family."

"That they do. Did I tell you, or maybe they did,

they asked us to call them Memaw and Pappy? Did you know that?"

"Welcome to the family!"

We both laughed.

"Holly, all we ask though is that you or your mother, or any of you to not let her know that she is your daughter. Please! We will let her know in good time. I mean, like I said in the letter, she knows she is adopted. They both do. But we want to be the ones to tell them."

"I would never tell her. Cross my heart!

Lisa, I want you to know something. The first time that I saw you with her, do you know when that was?"

"No, when?"

"It was right after she had gone to live with you. She was just a baby. I was with Memaw and Pappy. We were shopping at Sears. Memaw and Pappy knew right away that I would recognize her. How could I not? That birthmark on her neck and well, how could I not.

You don't know how bad I wanted to grab her from you and run. I couldn't do it! I just couldn't. I wanted to though.

All I could think is, "she's mine". But she wasn't.

She didn't belong to me. She belonged to you and Tony.

Memaw and Pappy took me home that day and told me how they had found out and they told me about you and Tony.

How you had been wanting a baby for so long. They told me that you two were awesome people and that you loved God. I have to admit, that loving God part didn't really matter that much to me. But that you had wanted a baby for so long and the way you looked when you held her, I could tell, she belonged with both of you.

When Memaw gave me the photo album with some pictures of her in it, my heart was made whole.

She looked so healthy and happy!

I knew that I had made the right choice.

I really didn't have a choice. There was no way I could keep her. But even if I'd had the choice, I was so young, there is no way I could have given her what you and Tony have.

I could have given her love, but I couldn't have given her home.

Ever since I met you, not at the store, but at the church, I have watched you, both of you. You are awesome parents. Hannah and MJ are truly blessed to have you both as their parents."

Lisa wiped tears as she sat there listening.

"To be honest I thought now that Robert and you got married that he and you would be wanting to try and take her back."

"Why would we do that? Robert and I will have our own children, someday, hopefully. Then he will know what it's like to love like I found out, with Hannah."

"He's not Hannah's father? I feel so foolish. We assumed that you had gotten pregnant by him and when he went into the Army, you had gone away to have the baby. I am so sorry we jumped to that conclusion. We never even asked your grandparents who the father was."

I lowered my head and got a little quiet.

"She isn't Roberts. Not many people know who the father is. There is a reason for that. I haven't told many people.

My grandparents know, as well as my mother and just a few more people. I told Robert when he and I first started dating. He just found out that Hannah was my daughter Saturday night.

He thought I should tell you that I knew that Hannah was my daughter and couldn't understand why I hadn't. I guess I hadn't told you because of what you said. I was afraid you would leave and take her away and I would never be able to see her again.

But no, Robert isn't her father."

"Do you want to tell me who it is? If you don't, I will understand."

I felt the blood drain out of my face as I volleyed my choices inside my heart and my head.

I prayed as I sat there until a stillness came over my heart.

A peace if you will.

"If I tell you, please don't hate me."

"Holly, I don't believe that I could ever hate you. Honestly, if it is too hard for you, you don't have to."

"No, I think you should know."

I told her everything. Every sordid detail.

And we cried. And she came and sat by me and put her arms around me and held me and we cried some more.

CHAPTER 40

Thursday morning, I felt so bad having to leave Pappy again.

Robert and I wanted to get to the bank as soon as it opened to take care of all the banking business.

They opened at nine, so I dropped Robert off at work and went straight on to get things going before I had to leave.

He knew that we had to get these things taken care of, so it didn't really bother him.

Honestly, he only had me working because I was his granddaughter. Nobody did the job but himself while I was at college. And when Robert and I leave he will have to do it all by himself again.

His parting words as I left were to bring him lunch when I came back.

I promised.

Robert was getting a little cleaned up when I got there to pick him up. He had been elbows deep in monkey grease, him and Lance, all morning, trying to get some old car to run.

Lance went to hug me.

"Don't you dare!"

He laughed.

"Robert should be ready in a couple of minutes. He even brought a clean shirt to change into for ya."

"I know. I told him too. By the way, I hear congratulations are in order."

"Well, not yet. I am in the process. I should know if all the financing will go through in about three weeks. If it does then I will be the proud owner of, he looked around, "well, all of this."

"Well, all of this will be blessed to have you. Lance, I don't know if I ever told you how much I appreciated all you did for me by taking care of Roberts car like you did. I don't know a thing about cars, but you sure did. This place is going to be great. Robert tells me all the time that he's is a pretty good mechanic but that he can't hold a candle to you. If you promise not to touch me, I want to give you a kiss."

"Cross my heart," he blushed.

I kissed his cheek.

"I am truly blessed to have you as a brother-in-law. It will be great having you as our chief auto shop. Toby and Patty know they can trust to bring the car in here. Who better to work on it than you?"

He really was blushing then. His face almost matched his hair.

Robert cleaned up nice.

"Ready to go?"

"Yeah." I tossed him the keys.

"Bring me back some lunch."

"Me too," Matthew yelled.

We signed in and had to wait about thirty minutes for Mr. Crawford to finish up a phone call.

It took a while for us to transfer all our money into one checking account. I cancelled mine and was added on to Roberts. Then we had to put both of our names on the savings account. Sign so many papers.

Dot so many I's and cross so many T's.

We were there for a little over two hours and by the time we were done, we were starving.

"I could eat a horse," Robert said.

"I'm pretty hungry myself."

"That is because you only eat a bagel for breakfast."

"Well, a lot a big breakfast does for you. You are starving right now, and I know what you had for breakfast.

Where do you want to go?"

"Honestly, I could go for a double-double cheeseburger at the Burger Joint. It is on the way back and Lance and Matt want me to bring them food. I know they would love a burger. Doesn't that sound really good?"

No, no, no! It did not sound really good. But Robert sounded like if he didn't eat there that nothing else would do.

"Sure, why not?"

"Let's go then. Ooh, I can't wait 'til that grease is pouring off that burger and into my mouth."

"Don't let me forget when we order food for Matt and Lance that I need to get Pappy food as well."

This was not happening!

I mean, I loved the Burger Joint as much as anyone, but please, too much is too much!

"Hey, weren't you here yesterday?"

"You were here yesterday?"

"Yeah."

"Then why didn't you say something. We could have gone somewhere else."

"Well, you seemed like you really wanted it and I just wanted to make you happy."

"Well, that's all sweet and everything, but nobody wants to eat at the same place two days in a row."

Before I could even say, "You don't know the half of it", the boy behind the counter decided that he should help the conversation along.

"Oh, she hasn't been here two days in a row."

"But you just said she was here yesterday."

"She was."

"Well, in my calculations, that is two days in a row."

"No, she hasn't been here two days in a row. It's been four days in a row. Right lady? Remember, the first day with the older man, then the next day with the other lady, then yesterday with your sister and now today with your boyfriend. See, I remembered."

All I could think of as I looked at Robert and smiled was, "You can remember all of that, but you can't remember to keep your mouth shut?" Really?

Robert ordered the double-double cheeseburger, extra onions, large fries, and large coke. I ordered the single cheeseburger, as always with NO ONIONS, medium fries and a large coke, and lemon.

We sat down and I told Robert the story of the four-day feast at the Burger Joint.

I had just finished up when he brought the food to our table.

"Look, I remembered the knife this time."

He then walked away so proud of himself.

I unwrapped my burger and onions were spilling off the sides.

Robert unwrapped his and not one single onion.

If it hadn't of been such a long day already, I would have thought it funny.

Robert thought it was hilarious!

I scraped the onions off my burger and onto Roberts.

Then I cut my lemon for my soda.

This had to stop!

Friday I was going to be able to give Pappy a full-days-work.

There was absolutely nothing on the agenda that would take me away from getting everything caught up.

Robert and I decided that they were going to be leave on the 29th of July.

That would give us a little over a month to find a place get settled in and find a job before school started back up.

We were so busy that morning. We'd had a lot of customers and I had a lot of catching up to do to get the work that I had neglected that week done.

We were trudging along when I heard the most beautiful voice walking up behind me.

"Holly, are you hungry? Pappy said you guys were too busy to leave the store today so I thought I would surprise you both with burgers from the Burger Joint."

I thought Pappy was going to split a gut he was laughing so hard.

Memaw just stood there with a perplexed look on her face.

What could I say?

I looked at Pappy and we both started laughing all over again.

We thanked her and we all sat down to a feast of greasy cheeseburgers.

CHAPTER 41

It was so good to see Toby and Patty when they got back. Even if just for a few days.

They were not going to be back before we left to go try and find a house or an apartment.

I also needed a job.

They were so excited about what God was doing in their lives.

Just in the time they had been gone, they had received quite a few offers to come hold revivals.

God was truly doing great things.

Robert had preached his heart out that Sunday night.

He had so wished that Toby and Patty had been there. But they weren't coming home until the next day and would be leaving to go to another revival the following Saturday and we were leaving the Monday. We were going to have to make the best of our time together.

I missed Patty so much.

We had spent the four years as roommates.

It wasn't the same not having her around to talk to.

There were so many people that came to the altars that night after Robert preached. It was great to see what God was going to have in store for his ministry.

It wasn't the same as when Patty and Toby were

there. They always had a song or two, but not tonight.

Robert reminded me that I had promised to practice with him.

"Who knows, God could be using us to minister just like Toby and Patty someday?"

"Who knows," I smiled.

I could not imagine us, or should I say, me, ever sounding that good.

It had been easy enough to get everything changed over at the bank. They had given us a package of checks with our names on them.

Mr. Robert Davis

Mrs. Holly Davis

Wow! It never got old seeing my name written like that.

I had to admit though, it did take me a while to remember to write it that way when I signed anything.

It was so funny when I had introduced myself to a new couple at church, "Hello, my name is Holly Abernathy, and yours is?"

Robert said, "No you are not."

"Yes I am."

"No, you're not."

"Why are you saying that? Yes I am."

"You are not Holly Abernathy. You are Holly Davis now, remember?"

"That's what I said."

The couple that I had introduced myself too, shook their heads.

"No, you said Holly Abernathy."

Robert put his hand out to shake theirs.

"We just got married. Apparently, it is going to take

some time."

They laughed and we all went inside.

"Abernathy?" Robert shook his head as he laughed at me.

"Well, at least I got the Holly right."

We both laughed.

We made sure to take Toby and Patty out to eat on Thursday after we got home from work. We didn't want to keep them all to ourselves. Really that wasn't true. We did want to keep them all to ourselves, but we didn't want to be greedy.

I am sure Aunt Jessie and Uncle Joey and Patty's parents were wanting to spend as much time with them as possible.

It was such a joy listening to them tell of the wonderful things that God was doing.

It lit a fire in our hearts knowing that God was moving in such mighty ways.

They were having great crowds show up every night.

But the thing that thrilled them both was the young people that were coming.

To see God moving in their lives and the Holy Spirit filling each of them.

It was so amazing what God was doing in the young people.

We hated to say goodbye.

We told them as soon as we knew where we would be staying, we would let them know. If they were in the area holding services, they were more than welcome to stay with us to save on the cost of hotels and such.

We all hugged and prayed and cried together. Well

Patty and I cried.

Saying goodbye to them that night was almost as hard as saying goodbye to our families.

We weren't sure how long we would be gone. We weren't sure how long it was going to take to find a place to stay and for me to find a job.

We had talked it over.

Just because we had the money in the bank, didn't mean we wanted to be stupid and wasteful.

We were going to try and not spend as much of the savings as possible.

We left the following Monday.

We made reservations at a hotel close to the college.

We were going to try to get everything taken care of as soon as possible so we didn't have an added expense of the hotel as well.

We were going to have to come back and get our belongings before we could move into any place.

First point of business was to find a place to live.

With his GI bill, we would be ok. College would be covered. We might even have a little left over to help cover other things. He would be working part time again and I would be working full time if I could find a job.

But really first things first, we needed to eat.

The Whistle Stop Café was first on the agenda.

It was like coming home.

Vicki was so glad to see us.

Angie, her niece had graduated the same time that Patty and I had. I was going to miss her. She had gone back home and someone else had taken her place. A new girl that didn't know who we were.

But Vicki set her straight.

"You be nice to them. They are two of my favorite customers."

We gave her a big hug and a tin full of her favorite cookies.

"You guys are back a little early aren't ya'? School doesn't start for another month does it?"

"No, but we were rejected for family housing so we wanted to beat the rush and try to find something we could afford before everything got snatched up."

"Oh, that's right! Congratulations! How was the wedding? How was the honeymoon?"

We told her everything as she sat down with us at our booth.

She listened to every word.

"Awe. It sounds lovely."

"It was."

"But now to real life. I need to get a job and we need to find a house or an apartment. Hopefully we can find one that is affordable and furnished."

They brought our food and Vicki disappeared with her cookies.

CHAPTER 42

It saved us a little money being able to have a continental breakfast. But the coffee was not that great.

It wasn't horrible but it just wasn't great.

"How about we go back to the Whistle Stop and have some coffee while we look at a paper to see what is available?"

"You are a mind reader. I cannot drink this coffee. There is not enough cream in the world to make this taste better."

"Ok but grab another apple and banana and one more of those bagels. Just in case we get hungry while we are out."

"Really?"

"Yeah. Put it in your purse."

"Oh, my word!"

"Just do it!"

The Whistle Stop did have some of the best coffee in town.

So, we ordered a cup and sat down with the paper.

"Here's one. They want $200.00 a month for it. Does that sound doable?"

"Circle it and we will start writing some of them down."

"How many bedrooms did it say? Was it

furnished?"

"It didn't say."

"Okay."

"Oh, here's one. $195.00 a month. 2 bedrooms, 1 bath. Unfurnished."

"Yeah, that isn't going to work. We need a furnished one."

"Well, there are a lot of them in there. Let's keep looking."

And we did.

We found several possibilities.

We made a list of pros and cons for them and we were just about to leave when Vicki came from the back.

"They told me you were here."

"Yeah, we've been here for a while. Looking at apartments and houses to see if we could find something we could afford."

"Well, I am glad you came in. I might have found you a place."

"You just found out we were looking last night. Are you a miracle worker or something?"

"Or something," she laughed.

"Well, where is it? Is it an apartment?

"No. It is a little house. A little two-bedroom cottage. A minister friend of mine was in this morning. We were talking and his wife said they were thinking about renting out the cottage on the church grounds. They used to use it for missionaries at times, but it hadn't been used in a few years. The church had finally decided that it could generate a little income and voted to let them rent it out. Only problem is, they didn't want to rent it out to college kids. They didn't think they would take care of it or the grounds that the house sat on. I told them your situation and that I would vouch for you. His wife seemed to like the idea, but he wasn't too keen. I asked them if they would at least talk to you and they agreed. Here is the good news. It is only three blocks from the college."

"You mean Trinity Church?"

"Yeah, that's the one."

Are you talking about Pastor Carson?"

"Yeah, that's him. Do you know him?"

"Well, sort of. Toby used to preach there when he was going to school here. Holly and I used to go with him and Patty sometimes. He is a pretty good man. Maybe he will change his mind after we talk to him."

"Maybe he will. Here is the address. Well, I guess you don't need the address. He said he would be at the church until about one this afternoon. You should go on over there."

"Yeah, I think we will."

We got up to leave after we paid.

"Wait," Vicki called after us. "Here, take this Lemon Meringue Pie to him. Lemon Pie is his absolute favorite, and a little bribery never hurt anything!"

Robert and I smiled a knowing smile at each other.

We went to pay for the pie, but she would not let us.

"Let's call it a little love back to you for all the wonderful cookies you guys bring me. I am going to miss my little Angie. Do you know she got a recipe and learned how to bake those cookies just for me? Love that girl!

Now you two go on. If he says no, tell him that I said for you to take the pie back. But I don't think he will say no."

She winked at us as we left.

We sat in the car and held hands and prayed that if this was where God wanted us, then for Him to open the door.

CHAPTER 43

Pastor Carson was in and his secretary ushered us in to his office.

"I understand that you two might be looking to rent the cottage on the church grounds here?"

Then he looked up and saw that it was us.

"Oh, I'm sorry. I was expecting someone else. Come on in."

He came from behind his desk to greet us.

"How have you two been? I heard that you were getting married this summer. How'd that go? Did you have a nice wedding?"

"Well, yes we did," Robert answered. "And I don't think you are waiting for someone else."

"No. A friend of mine. She owns the Whistle Stop Café, she told me that a couple of college kids might be wanting to be renting our little cottage we have here. We are not sure we want to rent to college kids. Not sure how well they would take care of it. It has been there a long time, but it hasn't been used for years. I don't even think anybody has been in there to clean it in at least two years."

"Yeah, she told us that you had talked to her this morning and that she told you about us."

"About you? I thought you had both graduated?"

"No. Just me. Robert has one more year to go. So,

we are here a little early trying to find a place to live. We weren't able to get family housing. It was already full."

"Well, I'll be!"

He pushed on his buzzer.

"Nancy, get my wife on the phone and then bring me the keys to the cottage please."

"Yes sir."

Within a couple of minutes Sister Carson was on the phone.

"You are not going to believe who is in my office right now."

We felt like celebrities the way he told her that we were there, and why we were there.

"Okay, we'll wait."

"She is coming over. She should be here in about 10 minutes. Can you wait that long? She really wants to see you and go with us when I show you the cottage."

"Sure. We can wait. Oh, by the way, Vicki sent this to you as a bribe."

Robert handed him the pie.

"Oh, be still my heart. Lemon Meringue is my all-time favorite. Anything lemon and I can't get enough."

"Us too. Lemon is our favorite."

"Well, this day keeps getting better and better. We really just voted to do this last Thursday night at our monthly staff meeting. Do you mind waiting in the outer office? Dean Matthews is coming over to discuss something with me.

They are looking for someone to work in the Bookkeeping Department and he was wanting to know if I knew of anyone looking for a job. He always runs these things by me, and we pray and put it before the Lord. God always comes thru.

It is hard to keep people in some of these positions because the jobs only last while school is in session."

"Really, they are looking for someone in the bookkeeping department?"

"Yes, but at this time all of our parishioners are fully employed. But God will send someone to fill the position. He always does."

"Well, if I might be a little bold, I am looking for a job."

"You are? What kind of experience do you have? I mean, bookkeeping is not up everyone's alley."

"Well, I have a little experience. I am the bookkeeper for my Grandfathers porcelain store. I have worked for him for years. If I was not at college, I was worki--ng for him. I also graduated college with a degree in Mathematics."

"Um, well, I would say that makes you pretty qualified. Tell you what. You two wait in the front office. I will pray with Dean Matthews and if we feel that God has put us together then I will introduce you. Deal?"

"Deal."

We went to the outer lobby and held hands and prayed as we waited.

It wasn't but a couple of minutes before Dean Matthews walked in.

"I'm here to see the pastor."

"He is waiting for you."

Just as he was to go inside, he noticed Robert.

"Hey man, how are you?"

Robert stood up to greet him.

"Good, I'm doing really good."

"You are looking good. What, it's been about a year now since I saw you last. I didn't hardly recognize you. What are you up too these days?"

"Well," he reached down and took my hand to stand me next to him so he could introduce me, "I recently got married. This is my new bride, Holly.

I am about to start my last year of college here and we just met with Pastor Carson regarding the cottage they have for rent."

"They are finally going to do it. They have been talking about that for a long time. Nice to meet you, by the way." He shook my hand.

Pastor Carson came out to see what was taking so long.

"I'll talk to you guys later. I need to go over some business with Pastor Carson. It was so nice to see you. Both of you."

"Nice to see you too."

They went into the Pastors office and shut the door.

What's that old saying, "When one door closes, another door opens."

I laughed as that thought came to my head.

No sooner had they closed the door than Sister Carson opened the other one and came in.

"Oh my, you two are a sight for sore eyes. Newlyweds, now are you? Oh, I love it. I can't wait to show you the cottage. You are going to love it. When do you want to move in? It is going to need a good cleaning. Oh, I just can't wait to show it to you."

She hugged us again.

"What is taking that husband of mine so long?"

Nancy told her he was in a meeting with Dean

Matthews.

"He's a good man."

"Yes, yes he is."

"You know him?"

"Well, yes. He helped mentor me when I first got saved. He helped me get home. I really owe him a debt of gratitude. He really is a good man."

"Where did you get saved?"

"Right here in this church. Toby and Patty were preaching here, and I went to the altar when he asked for anyone that wanted to be saved to come down. I did. And the rest, as they say, is history. That was almost four years ago."

"What a lovely testimony."

"Yes. He's the one that mentored me while I was here right after I got saved. I didn't know he was the Dean at that time. As a matter of fact, I just found that out when he went inside for his meeting."

"This is amazing. You used to come here with Patty and Toby these last few years. You four are the cutest little couples. How are they doing? They are newlyweds too, right?"

"Yes ma'am. They are already booked up for the next several weeks, if not months now holding revivals. God is doing something amazing in their lives. In their ministry."

"You wouldn't believe how any young people are getting saved and filled with the Holy Spirit!"

"Oh, that is what I love to hear."

Pastor Carson and Dean Matthews opened the door to the office.

"Holly, could you come inside for a moment. Dean Matthews wants to talk to you."

I went to see what he might want, praying that he was going to offer me a job.

After about a fifteen-minute interview, I was employed!

CHAPTER 44

"Oh, I so hope you like this little cottage. Did I tell you, Pastor Carson and I stayed here many, many years ago? We were just starting out in the ministry. We graduated from this very college. Anyways, we were invited to be the Associate Pastors. We needed a place to stay and they let us stay here. It was lovely. I was so excited to be staying here. I was a new bride, much like yourself and was the most horrible cook ever. I don't want to even remember how many dinners I burned in that little kitchen. But he ate them. Didn't you de-ar?"

"Yes, and they weren't that bad. But praise the Lord you got better."

I think there is a scorch mark on the wall behind the stove still. What do you mean they weren't that bad? Sweetheart, you are going to have to repent over that one."

We all laughed.

Pastor Carson unlocked the door.

It was the most charming dust covered dirty little cottage that I had ever been in.

It was as if a storybook had just opened up and we were being invited to step inside.

"Oh, it's lovely."

"I know, huh," Sister Carson laughingly agreed. "I

just love this place. It brings back so many memories. We lived here for two years before we took a church two towns over. But this, this will always feel like home. It has two bedrooms! But only one bathroom.

After we left, they mainly used it for missionaries that would come to town or an evangelist holding a revival."

"Yeah, anymore, the evangelists who come would rather stay at a hotel or they have a little camper that they get around in.

"It's so nice. So now what were you going to ask for rent."

"Well, the church was thinking $200.00 a month. Now, that would include water and electricity. Also, you would need to take care of the lawn and such."

"Does it have a washer and dryer?"

"Well, it has a washer, but it has a clothesline out back. Also, it has a really nice fireplace."

"I noticed that."

"And the furniture comes with it?"

"I don't know why anyone would want to use this old furniture, but yes, it comes with it. Do you have any furnishings?"

"Well, yes. We received many gifts at our wedding, but we haven't used any of them yet. We haven't needed to. But no furniture, like tables and chairs and such."

"When can we move in," Robert asked.

"Well, anytime. When would you want to move in?"

"Yesterday!"

We all laughed.

"Well, let's talk about what it is going to cost to get

you in here. It will be first and last month's rent and a cleaning deposit."

"I think we could swing that. What if Holly and I cleaned it, would we still need a cleaning deposit?"

"I think that could be arranged. So, it would just be first and last month's rent and you two will clean it. Are you sure you want to do that? It is a big mess."

"Well, if we spend the next few days while we are here. We can leave on the weekend and go get our things and come back the following week. That would give us time to get settled before school starts and I had to start my job. I think it would work out great."

"Okay. You two come by first thing in the morning and we will have the papers ready for you to sign."

Sister Carson hugged us both.

"I am so glad that it is you two that are moving in here. Ever since they said we would be able to rent it I have been praying that God would send just the right people. You two are just the right people."

We thanked them both and went and sat in the car and held hands and thanked God for His hand of providence on us.

CHAPTER 45

We were packed and ready to leave the luxuries of our little hotel room and move into the lap of, well, not luxury. Not yet anyways.

After we had eaten our celebratory dinner of a new job and a new house, we went shopping for cleaning supplies.

We left them in the car so we would be ready to go as soon as we signed the papers in the morning.

We couldn't wake up early enough.

They had given us permission to go ahead and move in when we signed the lease if we wanted to. We wanted to.

We could hardly fall asleep for talking about how cute it was and how much cuter it was going to be.

After a quick bite at the Whistle Stop, we were off to sign the papers.

Pastor Carson welcomed us in.

He had everything in order.

"Is Sister Carson around?"

"Oh, she's around here somewhere, I suppose. She said something about having to take care of some church business or something this morning. She was on the phone when I left to come to work."

Then he handed us the keys.

"Shall we Mrs. Davis?"

"We shall Mr. Davis."

He took my hand and we walked to our car that smelled of Pine Cleaner and headed to our new abode. For the next year anyways.

I was not expecting Robert to be such a traditionalist.

He unlocked the door and as I started to go in, "No. This is our first home together. Would you please do me the honor of letting me carry you over the threshold.?"

"Oh, Robert, I love so much."

I could not keep my eyes off him as he scooped me up and we walked into a room full of dust and cobwebs.

It seemed a lot dirtier without the storyteller there to weave her magic into the room.

"Wow! Where are we going to start?"

"Pick a spot."

"Let's go get the supplies and then we'll decide."

He put me down and we headed back out only to be greeted by Sister Carson. Well, Sister Carson and the whole women's ministry it looked like.

They came loaded.

Sister Carson was smiling from ear to ear.

"I just could not let you two little sweeties clean this place yourself. I called a few of the ladies to see if any of them were willing to come and help. Here we are. Where do you want us to start?"

"Oh, thank you so much! Actually, we were trying to decide that very thing ourselves."

"Tell you what, let's divide up into teams and tackle this thing. How about that?"

It sounded awesome.

These ladies were a cleaning crew.

We thought we had brought cleaning supplies, but we did not have half the things these ladies came equipped with.

"Lucy, how long do you think it is going to be before we have that kitchen spic and span. Janey and Polly are going to be showing up with supplies in about an hour."

"Oh, we should have it done by then. It wasn't that dirty. Mostly needed to just have a good scrubbing. Are they bringing liners for the shelves?"

"I told 'em too."

These ladies were a force to be reckoned with.

The linens that were left, that were still in good condition had been put on to wash. That is, after Robert hooked the water line back to it.

Then the sheets were washed, and the curtains taken down to be washed.

We were fast running out of room on the clothesline.

A couple of the ladies took Sister Carson aside and had a conversation with her. They all looked in our direction. It seemed serious. They all nodded in agreement and the two ladies left.

"Did we upset them," Robert asked me?

"I don't know, but they sure seemed serious didn't they."

Lucy and her crew finished up the kitchen just in the nick of time.

Apparently, the supplies had shown up.

"Janey and Polly are here," someone yelled as the front door came open.

"Did you get everything?"

"Oh, yes, and a couple of other things too."

"Ladies, Robert, Holly, can you all stop for a minute? Janey and Polly went shopping this morning to get the supplies. Holly, you and Robert go on into the kitchen. We'll be right there."

We did as we were told.

They all went outside.

"What more supplies did we need?"

Robert said he was sure he didn't know.

They all came in carrying bags of supplies.

But they weren't cleaning supplies.

They sat them on the newly cleaned table and counter tops.

Bags and bags of groceries.

Canned goods.

Coffee.

Dried goods.

Shelf liners

A mop

Dish liquid

Toilet paper.

Salt and pepper and pretty much any spice you could imagine.

Bread.

Ketchup.

Mustard.

Mayonnaise.

Vegetables.

Milk.

Cream.

Eggs.

There were new towels. New bed linens.

Clothes detergent.

So much more. So much more!

I couldn't believe what these wonderful women had done for us.

I stood there as tears rolled down my face.

Robert wrapped his arms around me.

"We don't know how to thank you, all of you for what you have done for us today. We come from a little town. The church we go to has a women's group much like you ladies. You never think about the family of God being everywhere. You all have made us feel like family today. More than you'll ever know."

Now we were all wiping tears.

Everyone started putting things away when there was a knock on the front door.

"Can I come in too," Pastor Carson asked with a grin.

"Come on in," Sister Carson said. "But if you do, be prepared to work."

"Oh, I came prepared. Emily and Leah stopped by the office and I just got back with them. Robert, I think I am going to need your help."

Robert went to see what Pastor Carson needed.

He stepped back in.

"Holly, could you come here for a minute?"

"Excuse me ladies. I'll be right back. What is it Robert?"

"You are not going to believe this."

He covered my eyes and led me outside.

"Ta-da!"

It was the most beautiful used clothes dryer that I had ever seen in my life.

"Are you kidding me!"

Emily said her and her husband had just got a new

one and they were needing to get rid of the old one.

She had gone to the church office to call her husband to make sure he didn't care if she gave it to us. He said yes.

Pastor Carson and Robert had it unloaded out of Leah's truck and hooked up in no time.

In a total of about four hours this little dusty, dingy, cobwebbed house had been turned into a storybook cottage.

And it had two of the most grateful, exhausted, starving, but in love with the each other, people the world and God, that anyone had ever known.

CHAPTER 46

We were tired. So tired. And dirty. So dirty.

We really weren't sure if we were more tired or dirty.

With the house in spic and span shape. Both beds were made. The curtains were hung back up to frame beautifully washed windows that was letting in the greatest beams of sunlight.

Not a speck of dust or dirt to be found.

The beautiful wooden floors had been swept and mopped and a quick polish.

The beautiful braided rugs had been taken outside and the ladies had made sure they were not brought back in with one iota of dirt in them.

Every dish had been washed and put away.

Every towel, wash cloth, doily, if it was washable, it had been washed.

The only things that were left in the house that were dirty at all was Robert and me.

We decided to bring our luggage in and put away our clothes before we showered.

We didn't even want to lay on the beds or sit in the chairs until we could bath and get cleaned up.

"You go ahead," Robert said. "I'll take a shower after you."

"No, I insist you go first. You take quicker showers

than I do."

"It's okay. I can wait."

"Robert, I really do insist."

Robert moved in closer.

"How about this," he said, as he wrapped his arms around me and pulled me close to him. "How about we take a shower together?"

"Together?"

"Why not? We're married now. Have been for a while now. I think we could take a shower together."

I thought about it for half a second.

"Okay," I blushed.

"Go get the water running. I'll go lock the door."

And he did.

And we did.

It was a most glorious shower.

After a while we realized we hadn't eaten since early that morning.

We had time to make a sandwich before we got ready for church.

We cleaned up everything and turned out the light.

It was perfect. Just perfect.

Yet, I couldn't help but feel that something was missing?

That it needed something.

I just couldn't put my finger on it.

It would come to me. I'm sure it would.

Pastor and Sister Carson were there as well as the women that had been there helping that morning.

"We didn't expect you two here tonight."

"It's Wednesday night and since we were so richly blessed today, we were able to join you all tonight, if you'll have us?"

"Oh, you little sweetheart! We are so blessed that you would join us," Sister Carson said as she hugged us both. "Come on in. Let me introduce you to some of the young people around here. You met most of their parents or grandparents today.

When school starts back up there will be even more. I hope you both feel at home here and want to call this your home church away from home church."

Robert and I looked at each other.

We both knew.

This was home.

Pastor Carson took Robert aside and had a little conversation with him.

While they were gone one of the ladies came up to Sister Carson and me.

"Honey," she said, "I don't know about you. But I love a good cup of coffee in the morning."

"Me too. The day just doesn't seem right until we've had that first glorious cup of coffee."

"That's what I thought. You two look like coffee drinkers."

"Oh, we are. We are."

"Well, darlin', I got to noticin' your place ain't got no coffee maker. It broke my heart. I hope you don't mind. I got you a coffee pot."

With that she handed me a bag with a brand new, drip coffee maker in it.

I started crying.

"If it's not the one you want, I have the receipt. You can exchange it."

"No ma'am. I love it. It's perfect. I appreciate it so much. It just hit me how God looks out for the little things.

When we were leaving to come here tonight, I looked around that beautiful home that you ladies helped make possible. All the wonderful gifts of food, cleaning supplies. Everything that we had because of your love to us. And I thought to myself, as perfect as this is, it seems as if something is missing. I could not put my finger on it. But God knew all along. We are really going to appreciate this in the morning! Now, what was your name again?"

"Jenna, they call me Jenna. And if you ever need someone to have a good cup of coffee with, you just call me. You know, I've got a secret to make coffee even better. You want to know what it is? A pinch of salt."

"I know that trick. I do it all the time. My Aunt Jessie taught me that."

"Oh, we are going to get along just fine. Just fine."

She took my arm and led me inside the church.

I looked back and Sister Carson just smiled.

CHAPTER 47

Robert and I stayed for a couple of more days getting to know the lay of the land. The cottage was set back a little way from the church. It had a bit of a woodsy area that we were able to take walks in.

The mornings were beautiful.

It wasn't quite fall and school was not going to be starting for a few weeks.

We had been so busy acclimating to our new home that we had barely thought about home.

I guess it had felt like home as soon as Pastor Carson put the key in and opened the front door and we had walked in. We didn't feel like we should be anywhere else.

The little place held a lot of little surprises.

"Holly, have you been in the spare bedroom?"

"No, not really. The ladies cleaned that room. I cleaned ours. Why, is there something wrong with it. We need to let them know as soon as possible so it can be taken care of. We don't want them to think we destroyed something already."

"Are you finished?"

"Okay, so what is wrong with the room?"

"Did I say there was something wrong?"

"Didn't you?"

"No. I asked if you had seen it."

"Oh. Then the answer is no. I have not seen it. Is there something wrong?'

"Oh, please don't start that again. Come on, let me show you."

He covered my eyes.

"Are you going to tell me there is another clothes dryer in here?"

"Are you serious," he laughed.

"Here. Ta-da!"

He took his hands away.

It was another bedroom.

"Very nice. It is lovely. Do you want this to be our bedroom? I thought you liked the other room?"

"Holly, are you even looking?"

"Yes, Robert, I am looking."

"Okay then, tell me what you see."

"Well, I see a bed, two nightstands, a dresser, a rocking chair, a closet, pretty curtains, a piano, a, a, what? A piano. Robert, there is a piano in here. How did I not see that?"

"I don't know. I just noticed it this morning when I walked by. I had to do a double-take my self. Let's see how it sounds. It probably needs a tune up."

"Can you play me something?"

"What do you want to hear?"

"I don't care, something nice."

He started to play.

"I haven't played for years. I'm a bit rusty."

"It sounds lovely to me. I wish I could play an instrument."

"I wish I could sing like you. Your voice is beautiful Holly. I can't wait for us to be able to sing in church together and minister like that.

Do you know this song," he asked, as he started playing "How Great Thou Art"?

"I love that song. It is one of my favorites."

"I thought it was. I hear you singing it in the shower."

My face turned ten shades of red.

"Sing it for me."

I couldn't.

"Come on Holly. Sing it for me, please."

After a little convincing I told him I would try, but he couldn't look at me.

He promised!

After transposing it a couple of times to find a key I felt comfortable singing in I gave it my best shot.

I was so engrossed in singing this beautiful hymn that I was taken a little off guard when he joined me singing harmony.

I put my hand on his shoulder and we completed our first duet.

He didn't move from the stool after we were done.

I didn't know what he was thinking. He was so quiet.

"Holly," he said without looking at me, "that really touched my heart. It is one of my favorite songs. I think we sang pretty good together. Sure, the piano is a little out of tune, but if you're willing to practice with me, I would love for you to work side by side with me when we start our ministry. I mean, even now, we don't have to wait to be out evangelizing like Toby and Patty. They had to start somewhere.

Will you be willing to go to churches with me when they ask and sing with me in front of people? Will you? Would you?"

He turned to look at me with pleading eyes.

"Robert, when I sang to you on our wedding night, I was sure that I would never do that ever again. Ever! But you know what? That song I sang wasn't just a song. When Patty showed it to me and reminded me of the story, and I listened to the words, I knew it was more than just a song, it said everything.

So, even though I am only taking your word and Patty's word for about how I sing, the answer is yes. If you want me to sing with you in churches, on the street corner, in the park, wherever, that's what I'll be willing to do."

We went back home on Saturday morning after a quick breakfast at the Whistle Stop. We wanted an early start and we didn't want to have to clean the kitchen before we left.

We ate a good breakfast.

Well, I ate a good breakfast, Robert ate a great breakfast.

Then it was home to pack and then back home.

CHAPTER 48

It was sad knowing this was going to be our last service in our home church for a while.

I was going to miss so many of these sweet people.

But mostly I was going to miss Hannah.

I told her and MJ that we were going to be leaving and going to live in a cottage by the forest. I told her that it was the sweetest little cottage and that I would take pictures of it and send them to them so they could see it.

"Does it have bears," Hannah asked?

"Yeah, bears," MJ echoed?

"Does what have bears?"

"The woods. Does it have bears?"

"I don't know. I guess it might. I didn't see any."

"Does it have roses?"

"The woods?"

"No, the cottage. Does it have roses?"

"Not right now. But we can plant some."

"Can you plant red roses and white roses?"

"I suppose we could. Do you like red and white roses?"

"Yes, and so does the bear."

"Which bear would that be?"

"You know, the one in the story that is a Prince."

"Yeah, a Prince," MJ helped.

I looked at Lisa and she was smiling.

She explained that they had been reading the story of Snow White and Rose Red and how they lived in a cottage by the woods and a bear came and stayed with them and protected them and how the bear turned out to really be a Prince.

It had been the favorite story for a few nights lately.

At least now the inquiry made sense.

I was at a loss for words.

That was a story that I was not familiar with.

Lisa took over. She told them that it didn't have a bear that turned into a Prince in the woods. She told them that if there were going to be red and white roses that they would be real roses, not people.

"Oh."

"Oh."

They both seemed disappointed. Even I was a little disappointed. I mean, who wouldn't like to live in a magic cottage with a Prince, even if he was a bear.

One last attempt. "Is that where the ring bear lives? In your woods?"

"No. No. He lives in a house with his family."

"Oh." Disappointed again.

Lisa was just rolling her eyes.

But Robert and I knew how to leave a lasting impression.

We gave them both a roll of lifesavers.

Lisa promptly took them and put them in her purse and told them they could have them after lunch.

Hugs and kisses all around and they were gone.

I watched them walk away and a little piece of my heart went with them.

Robert just pulled me closer to him and I wiped the tears.

Mother came along beside me and said she would keep an extra good eye on them.

Memaw had already promised to send pictures as soon as we got them the address.

We had left the clothes we took with us so that we would have room to bring more back with us.

We were going to be needing our winter clothes before too long and all our wedding gifts.

Now we knew how handy a hand mixer, a toaster, towels, our own dishes, and silverware, all the things we could not figure what we were going to do with, was going to come in handy.

All but the dolphin clock.

That was not coming with us.

Robert wrapped it up and gave it to Lance.

He told him not to open it until the business was his. It was a gift for his office.

Lance thanked him and he and Robert did a thorough investigation of the car.

He told him he couldn't have his big brother go off into the unknown in an unsafe car.

It passed inspection and after many hugs and tears from everybody, we started on our new adventure.

Even Aunt Jessie and Uncle Joey had come over. They had even brought Josh. I finally had a chance to ask him about his little girlfriend and why he was with her and not the other one.

"She was too fickle. She would act like she liked me and then she would act like she liked Mason. Back and forth. She couldn't make up her mind, so we made it up for her."

"Oh, so Mason got her, and you got Janey, huh?"

"Nope. I got Janey because, well because she really loves God and she has standards. Mason got Danica, a friend of Janey's who really liked him for a long time."

"Then who got the other girl, I forget her name?"

"She got herself."

"Well, there you go!"

"I sure am glad you are my little brother, Josh. I love you so much. You are not supposed to be this much taller than me. I am going to miss you."

I hugged him and he hugged me back.

It was a hug-fest and crying-fest.

We were going to miss them all terribly.

It was still up in the air as to whether we would be able to come back for Christmas. So that made the goodbyes harder.

We left after a good breakfast and headed out on the highway to our new little cottage.

We would be there early enough to get everything brought inside and unpacked.

I didn't have to start work for one more week.

The girl whose place I was taking was not leaving for another two weeks so they said I could start then.

It gave us a whole week to get things put away and for Robert to make sure what his hours were going to be at his job.

It was always going to be Saturday mornings. But we weren't sure what other days.

He would have to drop me off at work and then he would have the car most days.

I could walk the three blocks home.

We would work it out.

But first things first.

We could now turn our little cottage house into our little cottage home.

We began by making a pot of coffee!

Life was good!

Tiring, but good!

CHAPTER 49

We were tired but up and ready for church on Sunday morning. Even in time for Sunday School.

Sister Carson was the first to greet us.

So many people she introduced us too. We would never remember them all. Hopefully we weren't expected to. But it was good to see some familiar faces.

The ladies that had so lovingly helped us get our little cottage cleaned and ready for human living were all there.

Jenna, my coffee friend, was there. She reminded me that any time I needed someone to help drink a pot of coffee she would be happy to oblige.

Dean Matthews was there. He and Robert spent a little time together before someone showed us where the Young Marrieds class was.

That was us!

Young and married.

The couple teaching the class were just a few years older than we were. They reminded us a lot of Tony and Lisa.

Thinking of them my thoughts quickly turned to Hannah and little MJ. I smiled as I pictured them running down the aisle to greet everyone with Lisa telling them not to run in church.

Pappy would be scooping them both up to smother them in hugs and kisses.

Robert reached over and took my hand, "You okay?"

"Yeah. Just thinking about things."

"I love you!"

"I love you too."

He squeezed my hand to let me know everything was going to be okay. And it would be okay. At times it would be marvelous. And I am sure there were going to be times it was going to be a chaotic mess. But for now, this very second, it was a bit bittersweet.

"So, would you two like to introduce yourself to the class? We are so glad to have you here this morning. My name is Blake, and this is my wife Gabby. I did not give her that name. It is really Gabrielle, but when you get to know her you will know why they call her Gabby."

She playfully hit at him.

The class chuckled.

Robert did the introductions for us.

"Good morning! It is so good to be here with all of you. My name is Robert Davis, and this is my new bride, Holly. We have been married for about six weeks now. Still newlyweds. I am going to the college here and my sweet lovely wife graduated from there. We look forward to getting to know all of you better. Thank you for having us this morning."

I just smiled and nodded.

They all seemed like very nice people, but it wasn't home, yet.

After class a few of them came up and shook our hands.

It might not take that long for it to start feeling like home.

Dean Matthews was waiting for us. He reintroduced Robert to his wife and introduced her to me.

They invited us to sit with them in the service.

What a service it was too!

It was a full house.

We were impressed.

Dean Matthews said just wait until school starts back up. It will really be packed then.

A lot of the kids, or I guess I should call them young people, would call this their home church when they got there.

There were a lot of churches in the area but this one was the closest and a lot of them didn't have cars.

If they didn't want to go to church on campus a lot of them would come here.

Sunday evening services were not quite so full.

When Toby, Patty and I were going there we chose to go to church on campus because we lived on campus.

Doing that gave Toby and Patty, and myself and Robert, the luxury of going to different churches on Sunday evenings to minister.

I didn't always go on Sunday evenings with them, that is until Robert started going to school there. Then we all went.

But this was going to be even better.

Here we could go to Sunday School and really get to know a few people.

And get to know each other a lot better.

CHAPTER 50

Robert was getting used to my cooking. I wasn't half bad. I had learned from the best.

I missed Aunt Jessie, a lot.

I loved getting letters from her.

I was going to have a hard time keeping up with the letter writing.

Now that I was a married woman, I wasn't going to have as much time for correspondence as I once had.

I was so blessed that Mr. Davis had taught Robert how to do laundry.

He was good at it.

It was my least favorite chore.

He even enjoyed ironing.

We had gotten two irons for wedding gifts but no ironing board.

We had to make a list of things we were going to need.

Ironing board was at the top.

His jeans had the perfect crease. I don't know how he did it. He even ironed my clothes. Not that I would have gone outside in wrinkled clothing, I mean, I knew how to iron. I just didn't want to iron.

Robert didn't seem to mind it at all. I think a kind wife should try to make her husband happy, and that seemed to make him happy, so...

The best part of being a newlywed was the waking up part.

Waking up next to the man that held my heart and made me feel loved every minute was the best part of the day.

How he would kiss my neck and whisper in my ear, “Good morning beautiful!”

Then he would pull me in close.

Morning breath and all.

And for some odd reason, I thought I had needed coffee to wake me up in the morning.

All I needed was Robert.

Well, Robert, then coffee.

We knew we wanted a routine in our lives so we decided that we would start each morning reading the word and praying for everyone and everything.

Then he would help make breakfast and we would have a jumpstart on the day.

With the love that we had for God, and each other and a good pot of coffee, we could conquer the world.

Robert had made inquiries of Pastor Carson if it would be okay if we got the piano tuned.

He told us no.

That piano was not worth tuning, but if we were willing to help load it, there was a better one that no one was using in storage. They had moved it there when they got a new one in the children’s church.

He told him the one that was here had been here since he and his wife stayed there and that was a millennium ago. Well, maybe not that long but a long time.

Robert said he would be glad to do so.

Tuesday morning after we had cleaned up after

breakfast, he met one of the groundskeepers for the church and they swapped out the pianos.

He was right. This one looked a little shabby, but it sounded great.

They had told us we could get a phone put in, so I had stayed behind to wait for the person that was coming to hook everything up.

We needed to add a phone to our list.

Ironing board

Phone

What else could we need?

Time would tell.

We spent the rest of the week putting our things away.

We would need to find someone that could get us wood for the fireplace.

We were going to have to add a cord of wood to our growing list.

It wasn't cold yet, but it never hurts to be prepared.

Also, I had promised Hannah and MJ that I would plant a red and a white rosebush.

So, now roses were added to the list.

Robert and I planned a shopping trip for that Wednesday morning.

We went to Montgomery Wards to get an ironing board and phone.

Then we stopped at the Whistle Stop Café for some lunch.

She was so happy to see us.

She congratulated us on our new home!

"How did you know."

"Well, I'm a genius you see. I figured that if you hadn't gotten it you would have been back in here to still be looking and also for the simple fact that you came in and told me the morning you were signing the papers, remember," she laughed?

"And, if you hadn't told me Pastor Carson and his wife did. Aren't they just the sweetest people? If it hadn't been for them when my Travis passed away, I don't know where I would be."

We were at a loss. We didn't know she had lost someone.

"We're so sorry for your loss," Robert said.

"Oh, it's okay. It was fifteen years ago. When he died though, I went through a really hard time. We had only been married ten years. He was a truck driver and he came in here all the time to eat. One day he asked me out. It took him forever. We got married six months later.

Pastor Carson married us.

We went to his church on Sunday mornings when Travis was in town.

He was a Godly man, my Travis. He was always reading his Bible.

I still go on Sunday mornings if I have the extra help here.

I know it is one of my busiest days, but I just love going and hearing him preach.

It is hard sometimes to make it.

But Pastor Carson comes in on Mondays and gives me notes on what he preached on so I can study it.

He keeps telling me that someday he is going to start recording his sermons for me so if I have to miss then I can at least listen when I get the chance."

"That is pretty nice of him to bring you those notes. It would be pretty great if he could record those sermons too."

"Maybe someday. But for now, I am satisfied with the notes and he is satisfied with a piece of Lemon Meringue pie."

"Ooh, that sounds so good. I think I will have a piece of that."

"Holly, you haven't eaten lunch yet. You know, lunch then dessert?"

"Well, just so you know, I was recently enlightened by someone that I truly admire. She told me, life is short, sometimes you should eat dessert first. So, that is what I am going to do. A piece of that Lemon Meringue pie please!"

Robert just looked at me like I

had just grown a new head.

You could see the wheels turning.

And then, "You know, your friend is right! I will have the same! Lemon Meringue pie for me too!"

"And coffee," we both said.

She walked away shaking her head and smiling.

It wasn't long before we had two scrumptious pieces of Lemon pie in front of us and two piping hot cups of coffee with a little cream!

"We can get a burger when we're done right," Robert asked?

Yes Robert," I smiled, "You can get a Burger when you're done. I will just share some of your fries. Deal?"

"Deal!"

CHAPTER 51

We had no luck finding who sold firewood in town so we thought we would ask at church that night. We were also needing rose bushes!

"Jenna, she would be the one to ask about both of those things," Sister Carson told us. "She lives with her oldest son and his wife. You've met them. They teach the Young Marrieds class. She will be able to get you some information. That is what they do. They have their own nursery. They sell trees and plants and they even have someone that will plant them for you. He also sells firewood. Just let him know what you are needing and he will get it for you. It's called Walker Farms. They really do have nice plants. And good prices."

"Thank you. We are going to have to get over there tomorrow and check it out. We have to get those roses planted this week if at all possible."

"Oh, yes. If you want them to survive these winters, you need to get them in the ground as soon as possible."

"Not only that. We've got to get as much done this week that we can. We both have to start back to work on Monday and we have to get everything done this week that we can."

"Robert is still preaching on Sunday night for us,

right? I am so looking forward to hearing him preach. If he is anything like Toby, we are in for a real move of God."

Robert showed up just as she was asking.

"Robert is still doing what," he asked?

"Still preaching on Sunday night for us. I was just asking Holly if that was still the plan."

He shot me a sideways look and smiled.

"Yes ma'am. That is still on the agenda."

"I am so glad to hear that."

She leaned in and hugged us both.

I didn't say a word, but I kept looking at him.

"I was going to surprise you. I thought you might like it if I surprised you. That's why I didn't tell you. I was going to surprise you. Surprise! Oh, and would you mind practicing a song with me. I told them we might sing a song when Pastor Carson got us the good piano."

"Are you kidding me? This Sunday night? When were you going to tell me that?"

"Right now! Surprise! So, will ya? Huh?"

"We'll talk after church."

And we did.

After we talked to Jenna to find out more about her son's business.

She was more than happy to tell me all about the good deals.

They sometimes missed coming on Wednesday night services because of the business closing so late.

We told her we would definitely be going there to get the things we needed.

"Maybe I can come over when they plant them and we can have a nice cup of coffee," she asked?

"That would be lovely!"

And when we got home Robert was true to his word.

He told me everything.

"Pastor Carson had asked if we sang like Toby and Patty. I told him we were working on it and he asked if maybe we would like to practice on them. I thought, why not! So why not?"

I really couldn't think of a reason "why not" so I said we could practice and give it a shot.

"What about the preaching? Why didn't you tell me about that?"

"I already told you. I was going to surprise you. Surprise!"

"So, is that what you have been doing when you disappear out in the woods in the afternoons? Are you studying for your sermon?"

"Well, yes and no. I am studying and praying of course."

"Well, what else are you doing?"

"Practicing."

"Practicing? Practicing what?"

"Preaching."

"Who are you practicing too?"

"The ring bears, or whoever else will listen."

We both laughed, remembering little Hannah's question.

Ring Bears!

"Let's go to bed."

CHAPTER 52

Sister Carson and Jenna were right!

This place was fantastic!

Blake was looking for us to show up that morning. His wife was in the office taking care of the books when we arrived. They both came out to greet us.

They truly were a very sweet couple.

Blake was very knowledgeable about all the plants and he showed us a lot of them.

But we had to have roses. Red ones and white ones.

"There is a little girl at our home church who asked if our little cottage had a red rose and a white rose. We told her it didn't. She seemed disappointed."

"Like in the book. "Snow-White and Rose-Red"?

"You know that story?"

"Oh yes. My mother used to read that to me and my sister when we were young. My sons don't seem to care for it so much. But they do like "Robin Hood" and stories like that. So, at least I get to read to them. They are almost too big to be read to anymore. They are eleven and fourteen. Right about the age when my sister and I started really reading for ourselves."

"I had never heard of this story before. But Hannah, the little girl I was telling you about, just loves it. She was for sure if we lived in a cottage that we had to have a red rose bush and a white rose bush. Her and her little brother both seemed a little disappointed that we didn't know if we had a bear or not. I will gladly plant the rose bushes, but I am not going to go see if we have any bears."

She laughed. "I hear ya. I think there are bears out there, but I would not want to be the one to find out. And if there are bears out there, I am sure they are not magical bears. Besides, why would you want a bear when you already have your Prince charming? Right?"

"Right!"

"Right what?"

"Right that you are my Prince Charming."

"Yes. Yes, I am. Now, will these do?" He showed me two beautiful rose bushes. A white one and a red one.

"Blake helped me pick out two really nice ones. He said he has a teenage boy that works for him that could come by tomorrow and plant them for us. Would that work for you?"

"It works for me. We'll take them. Or should I say, we'll have you deliver them. What about the wood?"

"Got that taken care of too. It will be delivered by the end of September, right before the first frost."

"Ugh. I do not want to think about the first frost. This summer has been just too glorious! I don't want it to end."

"Well, one thing about it. Once winter sets in you won't have to worry about bears," Gabby said.

"Why would they worry about bears?"

"Yeah, why would we worry about bears?"

"So, they don't eat you before you convert them all."

"Don't worry so much about it." Robert said. "I'll

convert them all. They haven't got a chance against a man of God and a good sermon."

We all laughed.

We stopped by the Christian bookstore on the way home to pick up a music book to see if we could find some songs that we could practice. We found a few.

We were going to have a hard time picking just one.

After a quick lunch we began to look through the books.

I told Robert, "I don't think we are going about this the right way."

"How's that?"

"Well, aren't you the one that is always telling me that we should pray about everything. EVERYTHING. You know, everything?"

"Okay, yes, I do say that. What are you getting at?"

"Well, I guess I am just wondering if this is supposed to be part of your ministry and you pray about what you are going to preach about. You did pray about that right?"

"Yes. I prayed about that. I wouldn't want to say or take a step that was not directed by God. If I am going to be His voice, then I want what He wants me to say to come out of it."

"Well, that is what I thought. So, if this is part of how you are going to minister, then don't you think you should pray about what you are going to sing?"

Robert was quiet.

"Don't you say all the time that the steps of a righteous man are ordered of God? You say, that right?"

Robert nodded. "Yep, that's what I say."

"Then don't you think you should pray about it so

God will tell you what song we are supposed to sing?"

Robert was still silent.

I could tell something was stirring in his head.

Then he smiled at me.

"You are right. This is part of our ministry. We should be praying for what God would have us say and do. But you see Holly, it isn't just my ministry. We are a team. You and me. When you said "I Do" to me, you didn't just say it to me, you said it to God. It is a joint covenant between me, you, and God. It isn't just my ministry Holly it is our ministry.

We are in this together.

I don't want just a wife. I want a Godly wife. A wife whose feet are ordered of God. A wife who is willing to pray for guidance as well as I am for what she thinks the Lord would have us do."

"Oh, Robert, I am not that woman. I am not that bold that I could do that."

"Why not? Holly, the Word of God tells us in *"Hebrews chapter 4 that we are to come boldly unto the throne of grace, that we may obtain mercy and find grace to help in the time of need."*.

Because we are His children, and we are willing vessels, wanting to do His will, then we need to approach Him daily, hourly, minute by minute if need be, boldly into the throne room of grace to find help in the time of need.

We need to know what He would have us do. We need to hear from Him."

"Yes, we do. What was Pastor Carson talking about on Sunday? Wasn't it about Paul who said, "I die daily"? Doesn't that mean that we die so that Christ might live in us. Does that mean that we put who we are away to put Christ first in everything? In all of it? That we are supposed to maybe say the things He wants us to say and not just words because they can so easily be spoken?"

"Yeah, that pretty much is what that means."

"So, we just give up who we are and what we want and let Him tell us what He wants us to do?"

"It isn't quite like that. It is more like we are saying, "God, you are much wiser and knowing than I will ever be. I am going to become a willing vessel, a conduit if you will for the Holy Spirit to use. By utilizing all the gifts that you have given me. I want to be used of you. I want to serve you to the best of my ability by letting my abilities be used by You. Because I love you so much for all that you have done for me, I want to serve you."

"Then I think we should pray before we keep looking through these books. Robert, I don't want to be just a wife that sits back and lets her husband be the one that is working for God. I want us to be like Toby and Patty. They are a team. They work together, they pray together, they present God together. I don't know if I will ever be as bold as any of you. But I do know that I am willing to allow God to use me. I want to serve Him with all my heart, my mind and soul."

And we prayed. We knelt on the floor in our little cottage and we sought God in what He would have us present to the people of this church that He would want us to give to them. We prayed that He would really and truly make us one.

We prayed together that He would bless our ministry, not just Robert in his ministry, but our ministry, as husband and wife.

When we finished, we started looking again; and it wasn't long before we found it!

CHAPTER 53

We heard the knock on the door around eight-thirty. We had almost forgotten that the young man was coming to put the rose bushes in.

We were just finishing the dishes from breakfast and Robert was going to wash a load of laundry.

I went to answer the door and there they were. Miss Jenna and JoJo.

"Gabby told me JoJo would be coming to plant your roses this morning so I thought I would tag along and enjoy a cup of coffee with you while he worked. I hope that is okay?"

"It's more than okay. If you hadn't have come this morning who knows when we would have had the opportunity. Come on in."

Jenna called out to JoJo. "Her husband will be out to show you where he wants them in a bit JoJo."

"Yes ma'am."

We came inside and I shut the door just as Robert came from the laundry room.

"Well, look who we have here. Don't tell me he sent you over to plant those rosebushes?"

We all laughed.

"No. JoJo is out front waiting for you to show him where you want them."

"Well, Holly is going to have to show me first then.

I just know they have to be in the front yard. Holly, can you show me where you want them?"

"I was just about to make a fresh pot of coffee. Can you give me just a minute?"

"I can make the coffee. You two go out there and show the young man where you want them."

"Are you sure?"

"Absolutely! Now go on!!"

We went on.

I wasn't absolutely sure where I wanted to put them.

We could plant them on either side of the front door or on either side of the little gate out front.

I decided to plant them on either side of the gate. That way, when I looked out the front window, I would be able to see them every day. And if they had a lot of bees, then at least I would be able to get inside without being stung.

Robert offered to help JoJo as long as I promised to bring him a fresh cup of coffee.

JoJo said he didn't drink coffee, but he accepted the soda when I offered it to him.

He seemed like a nice kid. Him and Robert hit it off pretty good.

I left them to their job while I went inside to make them their coffee and soda.

Jenna was not in the kitchen, but the coffee was finished.

I hurried out with their drinks and asked if they had seen her come out.

Neither one of them had.

Where in the world could she be?

I found her as soon as I opened the door back.

Well, she told me where she was.

Just as I came back inside, I heard the piano.

"So, this is where you went off to," I said as I walked into the room.

I startled her.

"I'm so sorry. I didn't mean to make you jump like that. Keep playing. You play so beautifully."

She started playing again.

"Thank you. I just love playing the piano. It just brings such pleasure to my soul. I don't always get to play. My arthritis acts up so bad sometimes that I just can't do it. Today is a good day. My daughter-in-law plays. She is really good. She took lessons most of her life, I think. I love to listen to her play the piano and Blake play the guitar. They don't get much opportunity to do it anymore. Their business is doing pretty good and most evenings they spend with the boys at some sports thing or studying for the Sunday School class they teach.

They really love the Lord and are doing their best to raise those boys to be Godly men.

I am so proud of them."

"Sounds like you are. They are pretty blessed to have you there with them."

"Oh, I hope they feel that way. After my husband, Gerald, Blakes dad, passed away, I was all alone. Blake is an only child. Our daughter died when she was three of pneumonia. Blake was five. We never had any more children, so, Blake was pretty much raised as an only child.

Him and his dad were best buds. They did everything together. They were both sports nuts. Gerald had him involved in Pee Wee Football. But then he found that he loved baseball even better, so, him and his dad became baseball fanatics.

He played first baseman and third baseman. Boy, he had an arm on him.

I think it was when he was in high school that he realized that he liked the guitar.

I never could get him to sit down and play the piano at all, but get some new girl to come to church that liked to play the piano and he was all about learning an instrument and how to sing.

That is how he got her to go on their first date. Him and Gabby."

"How's that?"

"Well, he saved up his allowance and went and bought a secondhand guitar. The best one he could afford. Then one night after youth group was over, he asked her if she knew how to play the guitar. He already knew she did. Somebody had told him. When she told him she did, he told her he had one but hadn't learned how to play yet. He rooked that poor girl into teaching him how to play the guitar. If that was all that came out of that relationship it would have been good. He picked it up pretty quick and before long they were playing duets in the youth group and then in church.

And as good as they are together when they play music, the best thing to come out of it is them. She is the sweetest daughter a person could ask for.

You'll see. The more you are around them you'll see.

Anyways, when Gerald died, they insisted that I come and live with them. The youngest one was only two at the time. But those boys made room for their

Ami. That is what they call me, Ami.

I clean and fix the meals and pick up the boys from school and take them to the places they have to get to so that Gabby and Blake can work and make a living."

"Awe, that is so sweet. How special you are that you get to love on them, and they get to see you and be around you. I didn't get to be around my grandparents much when I was younger. I really missed out on that. Thank you for sharing that with me."

"Do you think that coffee is ready yet?"

"It's been ready. Let's go get a cup."

Robert was making himself a fresh cup when we walked in.

"How did you get so dirty? I thought JoJo was planting the roses?"

"He is. I'm helping. Can you bring him a fresh soda? It's hot out there."

Then he was out the door.

"You go on ahead and do that and I will fix us a cup of coffee. A little cream, right?"

"You remembered!"

"Hey, I might be old, and I might have a tendency to forget somethings, but when it comes to coffee, I pay attention!"

We laughed.

Sure enough, when I went outside, they were both still digging.

"Thank you, ma'am," JoJo said when he took the fresh drink.

Ma'am. That made me feel old.

"You're welcome."

Robert must have seen my face when he called me ma'am. He was smirking when I turned to come back inside.

I stuck my tongue out at him.

Ma'am!"

"Can you believe what that kid JoJo just called me?"

"What was that?"

"He called me ma'am. Do I look like a ma'am?"

"Well, you don't look like a sir now do ya?"

"No, I guess not. It just feels strange being called ma'am. I don't feel old enough to be a ma'am."

Jenna chuckled, "Oh, honey, ma'am isn't a matter of age. It is a matter of respect. JoJo would have called you Miss if you weren't married. He is a very respectful kid. He has two younger brothers that he helps provide for. His mother is extremely ill, and his dad is working two jobs to help cover medical costs. So, him and his brothers do what they can to earn extra cash. He will only be able to do this job for about one more week. He lives over in this area. He rides his bike to work every day. But it will be too far to ride after school starts.

He is going to have to find another one closer to home.

Blake is going to be losing a good man."

The little talk made me realize ma'am was not too horrible after all.

It wasn't too long before they had it finished, and they were beautifully planted.

JoJo had told Robert all about what he would need to do to take care of them.

He also told him what he could do to take care of the lawn. Now that Robert was going to have to take care of it, he was open for any pointers.

It was needing to be mowed and we were going to

have to get it done on Saturday morning.

Thankfully they had a lawn mower on the grounds that we could use so we weren't going to have to buy that. They had rakes and hoes and all those good things.

The front yard was not that big, but the back yard was. It would take him a good hour or more just to mow it.

Robert had already commented that he wasn't sure how he was going to manage once he started back to school and was back to working in the shop.

We would have to worry about that when the time comes, I guess.

JoJo and Jenna left, and Robert and I admired the handywork.

"Oh, baby, you need a shower."

"I do?"

"Oh, yes! You do!"

"Wanna come wash my back?"

Robert raised his eyebrows trying to imitate Grouch Marx.

How could I resist?

I couldn't!

CHAPTER 54

First time grocery shopping is not an easy feat.

I don't think either one of us had ever done the shopping.

This was going to be a real first for both of us.

Not that we hadn't gone to the store to pick up a few things, but to do actual shopping that would sustain our lives, uh, no!

"Don't you think we should make a list?"

"Probably? That is probably a good idea. I know my mom always makes a list."

"Mine too. What were we thinking? How could we have gotten to be this old and never shopped for groceries?"

"I don't know? It just never came up."

List in hand we headed to the store.

Of course, we found plenty of things that we had forgotten to put on the list and plenty of things that we had not put on the list but when we saw it, we had to have it.

There were plenty of things that we missed that were going to have to wait for another trip.

After we had everything put away and were enjoying the fruits of our labor by eating the bag of cookies that we just had to have, we realized that we needed to make sure all the laundry was done.

"That's what we forgot!"

"Pink bar of soap?"

"Yeah, the one to get the stains out when I do laundry."

"Oh, do you need it?"

"Do you want the stains out of your blouses?"

"Do we need to go back and get it?"

"Nah. I will figure something out. What is this anyways?"

I looked at my blouse and shrugged my shoulders.

"I have no idea. Is that going to be a problem?"

Robert just looked at me.

"I'll figure it out. Next time though, try to remember what you got into. It makes it easier to get the stain out."

"I'll do my best."

I helped him sort the laundry while we talked about different things.

I told him about Miss Jenna playing the piano and playing it well.

He told me of how JoJo did such a good job planting those roses.

Robert was impressed with JoJo's knowledge.

"Jenna told me he has two brothers and they all three work to help support the household."

"That's impressive."

"I'll say. Especially with his dad working two jobs to take care of his wife."

"What's wrong with his wife?"

"I'm not really sure. Miss Jenna didn't elaborate. Just said she was very sick, and that JoJo's dad was working two jobs to take care of the medical bills and the boys all worked to help make ends meet."

"That's too bad."

"Yeah, especially since JoJo will be out of a job in about a week."

"Why? He seemed to really know his stuff. He was telling me all about what kind of fertilizer I was going to be needing and when I should do it and what other kinds of plants would work in this area. He said when the snows come, we need to cover the roses out front and to mulch the ground around them."

"Mulch? What is that?"

"Well, I don't know. What is it?"

"Never mind! How come he is going to be out of a job? Is he not doing a good enough job for them?"

"No. They live over here, close to the church. He only has his bike and it is too far for him to ride it after school and home when it starts getting so dark in the evening. He is going to be looking for something in the area."

"Hmm."

"Hmm what?"

"Well, I was thinking that I was going to have to try and find someone to take care of the grounds here. With going to school full time and working like I will be, I was trying to figure out when I was going to have time to do it. It has got to be taken care of. We agreed to do it. Do you think we could find it in our budget to pay him to do it?"

"I don't think we could pay him what he is making working for Blake, but we could see if he is interested. He seems like a pretty good kid."

"Let's see if Blake will talk to him tomorrow after church and see if he might be interested?"

"Or maybe he will come to church tomorrow night

and we can ask him ourselves. I invited him to come and hear me preach."

"Did he say he'd be there?"

"No. But he didn't say he wouldn't. He said they used to go to church here a long time ago but not in a while. Probably since his mother got sick."

"Well, let's just pray that he comes."

"Let's pray that we can get the stains out of your blouses as well. What did you get on this one?" He held up my favorite shirt.

"I don't know. But it is my favorite shirt so pray extra hard."

He threw it at me.

CHAPTER 55

I truly had never been more afraid in my life.

The one and only time that I had performed in front of anyone at church was many years ago when I had been thrust into the role of Mary the Mother of Jesus in a Christmas play.

Singing at my wedding was a first as well, but at least I had my back to everyone, and they couldn't all see me sweating bullets.

I thought I would never be doing that again.

Yet here I was.

We had practiced all afternoon.

I don't know why I had agreed to do this. How did I let him talk me into doing this?

Pastor Carson introduced us. Soon to be Reverend and Sister Davis.

We went up and stood beside him as he gave more of an introduction.

"Some of you might know this young couple right here. You might remember them when they came with Brother Toby and his new bride Patty. Well, they are newlyweds and young Robert here is finishing up his college years here and they are now renting the cottage on the grounds here.

They are here tonight because Robert and his new bride here are going to be ministering to us tonight.

I am not sure, but I do believe that tonight, for the first time as a couple, they are going to launch their ministry.

How blessed are we that God has placed them in our care!

Brother Davis the service is all yours."

Robert looked fabulous. Nervous, but fabulous!

"Good evening! Pastor Carson, thank you for inviting us to minister here tonight. You are right, tonight, for the first time as a married couple, my beautiful bride and I are starting our ministry.

We could not be more honored than to start it here.

Many of you do not know this, but this is the very church that I first gave my heart to the Lord. That would be almost four years ago now.

Brother Toby was speaking that night and I responded to the altar call.

Praise God for men like Toby and Pastor Carson that are not ashamed to stand up in a pulpit and tell the truth. To preach the Word unashamedly. To compel sinners to give their hearts to God.

Because of men like them and men like Dean Matthews that will come alongside young Christians and mentor them, guide them, teach them, I am here today.

Now, I hope you won't be too disappointed tonight.

My wife, Holly, say hello to the people Holly."

"Hi." I smiled and waved.

"We are going to sing for you tonight. We have been practicing for the past few days a song that I hope you will enjoy. Like I said, I hope you won't be too disappointed.

We are not Toby and Patty. Up until this week I

had not played the piano for years and to tell you the truth, neither one of us have ever sang in front of an audience.

So, if you would bear with us tonight, we are going to try and sing a song that we hope blesses you."

We went to the piano and Robert began to play.

This piano sounded like heaven. Not that the one we had been practicing was horrible, but this one sounded like it would cover a multitude of my musical sins.

We began to sing,

"I will serve thee
Because I love thee
You have given life to me
I was nothing
Before you found me
You have given life to me
Heartaches broken pieces
Ruined lives are why you died on Calvary
Your touch was what I longed for
You have given life to me"

We sang it through twice in perfect harmony.

They all applauded when we were done.

I took my seat as my husband took my hand and helped me down the stairs.

I caught Miss Jenna's eye.

She was wiping tears away as she smiled at me and mouthed, "Good job."

Robert began his sermon.

Could you all please stand for the reading of the Word.

Please open your Bibles to *Romans 12 verses 1-2, "I beseech you therefore, brethren, by the mercies of*

God, that ye present your bodies a living sacrifice, holy, acceptable unto God, which is your reasonable service. (2) And be not conformed to this world: but be ye transformed by the renewing of your mind, that ye may prove what is that good, and acceptable, and perfect, will of God.

Let us pray.

After he prayed, he had us all sit down and then he began his first sermon as a married man.

He preached his heart out that night.

"Many of you don't know me, a few do. I hope to get to know more of you better.

Like I said earlier, I got saved right here in this very church not quite four years ago.

Toby and Patty were here that night ministering to you and I happened to come in.

There was something in the way he presented God that night that compelled me to give my heart to the Lord.

I was raised in church. I had heard all the Bible stories. As a matter of fact, my sweet wife Holly, her grandmother was one of my Sunday School teachers. My mom and dad love God with all their hearts and raised me in a Godly home, so it's not like I didn't know about God, I just didn't know God.

I had no relationship with Him, with my maker.

I had played all the little church games. I knew how to do that, and I did it well.

I had pulled the wool over my parent's eyes, over my Sunday School teacher's eyes.

They all thought that I was a good boy.

And I was for the most part.

I never did things in my hometown that would

have brought shame to my family, outwardly anyways.

But we all know man is only capable of looking on the outside. God looks on the inside. I could not fool Him.

When I graduated high school, I decided that I would do my part, I joined the Army.

I mean, here I was, the biggest, baddest, football player that ever was.

Strong.

Big man on campus if you will.

Man, I knew I had it going on.

I was going to win this war.

The Army was just waiting for me to take care of things for them.

They were not!

I found that out at basic training. But by then it was too late to back out.

This little hica fide, country bumpkin, football playing kid, was in for a rude awakening.

I thought I was tough, but I was not that tough.

Trust me, I wanted to leave, but I knew that my parents would have been disappointed in me, and truthfully, I would have been disappointed in myself.

I was going to see this through.

I might not have been as tough as I thought I was, but I was bound and determined to get there.

And I did!

I conformed my way of thinking from civilian to service man in a matter of weeks.

I was no longer a country bumpkin kid straight from the farmland, I was a country bumpkin man that was going to take on the world.

When I got to Vietnam, there is no way I was prepared for what was ahead of me.

So many young men my age, most of them fresh from Bumpkin land, just like myself.

We had been told to make a will before we got there because most of us would not be coming home.

Most of them didn't.

And those that did, have not come home untouched by the horrors that we saw and lived through.

But for those of us that did survive those first few weeks, months and even years, we changed to fit in.

By fit in, a lot of them turned to drugs, alcohol, and other things.

We became wild.

Like caged animals that had been let out of our cages for the first time in our lives.

We had lived a protected life, most of us anyways, and had not been exposed to the things that went on there.

But even the ones that had been exposed had not seen it on this grand scale of things.

For some reason, the drugs and alcohol, those things just weren't appealing to me.

It seemed to me that the young men that took part in those things, were the ones that made too many mistakes and cost them or those around them their lives.

By now I was in charge of a lot of men and I did not want to have their lives on my conscience.

Well, one day we got a newbie.

A new guy.

A fresh from the farm one.

This guy was not like the other kids that came with him. No, he was special.

What we had in our midst was a real, genuine, born again, Holy Spirit filled Christian.

His name was Sam Lewis.

Many of you know his brother, his twin brother at that, Toby Lewis.

Well, as the Lord would have it, Sam Lewis became one of my charges.

I was now responsible for this target.

You see, that is what he was.

He was different.

And as we all know, different isn't always easy.

And it wasn't.

Sam became the brunt of a lot of jokes and ribbing and he took it.

They were brutal to him.

They stole his Bible on several occasions.

A Bible that I came to find out much later that had sentimental value as well as being his guidebook.

Now, Sam, he wasn't going to fight these men, these comrades of his. He would just pray about it. Lo and behold the Bible would show back up.

I asked him one time why he didn't just go get another one.

He told me that it was special and that he had pretty much memorized it anyways.

There was something about Sam.

He led many men to Christ while he was there.

Men that had tried to destroy him and his testimony.

Men who had laughed at him and mocked him, called him names.

They were the ones that he would share his cookies that he got sent to him on a weekly basis with.

He just loved them back.

They would come to him when they could get him alone and he would counsel them.

He would tell them they didn't have to live like they were living.

He showed them a different way. He shared verses in the Bible with them. He showed them by example what it was like to be different. To not be one that conforms to the world but that they could be transformed by the renewing of their mind by the power of the Holy Spirit.

That they could be set free from the sins and chains that would bind them.

That they no longer had to live in bondage.

He would tell them that because of Jesus and His love for us, and His willingness to die on the cross for our sins, our multitude of sins, that we could be washed white as snow and we could live and walk in newness.

So many of them listened and were set free.

Many of them gave their hearts to God and were even baptized in water and in the Holy Spirit.

It was amazing to see.

I had many conversations with Sam.

I told him that he was doing good, leading these men to the Lord and everything.

He asked me on more than one occasion was I ready to give my heart to the Lord?

I wasn't.

I could not believe that God would still love me or want me with all the hate I had in my heart for these people.

I couldn't believe that He could forgive me, especially if I could not forgive myself.

Besides, there wasn't enough room for Him in my heart and all the hatred and bitterness that I had building up inside me.

He would always tell me he was praying for me.

I would tell him, "you keep doing that Preach."

That's what we got to calling him, "Preach".

Well, as time went on Preach didn't have the opportunity to lead me to Christ.

I did have the privilege of him saving my life though.

Because of his sacrifice I am here today.

I was entrusted with that Bible to return it to his family. But I got sideways in my thinking.

I wandered for a long time after they discharged me trying to figure it all out.

"Why would this happen to such a guy as Sam?

Why did he have to die?

He was a good guy?

One of the best?"

I didn't understand it.

To tell the truth, I still don't.

But I know that beyond a shadow of a doubt, that day when Sam took his last breath on this earth, he took his next one in heaven.

I know that because of the blood he shed that day out in the fields of Vietnam I am here today.

And I am here today to tell you of the love of Christ, that because of the blood that He shed on Calvary that day, when He hung upon the cross, when he so willingly gave His life so that I could have a new life, so that I could know of His forever faithful love, that is why I am really here today.

Yes, Sam had the power to lay down his life for mine.

The word of God tells us in *John 15:13-Greater love hath no man than this, that a man lay down his life for his friends.*

And that is just what Sam did. He laid down his life and I as well as others are alive because of it.

But Jesus, He laid down His life as well.

He was wounded for our transgressions.

He bore all our sorrows, not just some, all.

He was the greatest, the ultimate sacrifice, so that we could not just have life but eternal life.

John 3:16 tells us For God so LOVED the world, that He gave His only begotten Son that whosoever believeth on Him shall be saved.

Not can be, not should be, not might be but SHALL BE saved.

My wife and I just sang a beautiful song tonight about serving the Lord.

Why do we serve the Lord? Because He first loved us!

Because He gave us new life and not just life, but life abundantly.

Full of joy and running over. Joy that can splash all over when your cup runs over.

We can serve Him because no matter what heartaches, what pain, what broken pieces that we bring to Him, it was covered at the cross.

We can bring our nothing of a life, a life we thought was really something but under the scrutiny of the cross it is just rags.

We can be made white as snow.

The Word tells us that our sins can be washed away, we can be white as snow.

What are you holding on to?

What have you got that is so worth holding on too that God can't do you one better?

He is calling you, just like He called me, just like He called my wife, just like He has called all of us that would heed to that call.

He is calling you from brokenness into wholeness.

He is calling you from fear to boldness.

He is calling you from bondage into freedom.

These altars are open tonight for anyone that is wanting to be set free. For anyone that is willing to become a servant, a child, a friend, of God.

Please come."

Many came that night.

Many lives were changed as they came and prayed and gave their lives to the Lord.

Robert and I as well as many other prayer warriors prayed over them.

But what spoke volumes to both Robert and I were the young people that came and prayed.

They prayed for each other and they prayed for anyone that would come down.

Robert got my attention as he noticed a young man at the altar that night.

He had many young people praying for him and with him.

JoJo had come home.

CHAPTER 56

That night after church Robert and I met JoJo and his younger brothers.

When he came home that Friday after work, he had told his brothers about the cottage and how Robert had asked him to come and hear him preach.

He asked them if they would come with him and being the little brothers, they said they would.

We invited them to come out with us after church as our guests to get to know them. What better place than the Whistle Stop Cafe.

They said they would have to go by their house and ask their dad if it would be okay.

They got in the backseat and we drove them to their home.

Miss Jenna was right. It wasn't that far from the church. Just a couple of blocks.

JoJo went inside and asked.

His dad came out to meet us.

"Are you sure you want to take these ruffians with you?"

"Yes, sir we are. JoJo put in my rosebushes for me the other day. He did such a good job that we really would like to take them with us."

"Okay, try not to make too much noise when you get in boys."

They all promised.

We promised to try and get them home before midnight. We both had to work in the morning, and we didn't want to oversleep.

Vicki was working that night. She was so happy to see us and seated us right away.

"Do you guys know everybody in this town?"

"No," Robert answered, "just the special ones."

"So, what will you guys be having tonight," our waitress asked?

"What can we have," JoJo asked?

"What do you want?"

"Really?"

"Yes. Really!"

JoJo looked at the menu with his brothers and they discussed it at length.

"Would it be okay if we had cheeseburgers and fries and a chocolate milkshake?" JoJo asked for all of them.

"You heard the man! Matter of fact that does sound good. I think I'll have the same. What about you babe?"

"I think I will have the meatloaf dinner with a side salad. Oh, and a coke please."

We handed her the menu's.

"Okay, so, JoJo we know, but we haven't met you two yet. My name is Robert, and this is Holly, my wife. So, what's your names?"

JoJo started to answer for them, but the youngest one said, "JoJo, I think we know our names. We can answer." He looked at us and smiled. He stuck out his hand to shake Robert's hand, "My name is Frankie. I'm 14. But I'll be 15 soon."

"Nice to meet you Frankie." Robert shook his hand.

Then the other one put his hand out.

"I'm Willy. I'm 16."

"Well, it's really nice to meet you all. I am glad that you all came tonight."

"So, really this was your first time to preach?"

"Well, not my first time to preach. But it was my first time to preach at this church. I have preached a few times at our church back home. But it was our first time to sing together."

"You did a pretty good job, ma'am," Frankie said.

"Well, thank you. I was a bit nervous."

"Yeah, you did real good at singing. You sing like my mom."

"That is so sweet of you to say that. That is if you like how your mom sings."

"Oh, we do. She doesn't sing much anymore, but when she can, I love to listen to her. I don't think she knows that song. But she knows some like it," JoJo said.

"Yeah, she used to sing all the time, but not so much since she got so sick."

My heart was breaking for these three precious boys.

"That's too bad. I am sure you miss it."

"She used to sing to us at night when she would put us to bed. Then we got too big for her to be tucking us in so much and now I miss her singing to us."

"I'm sure you do. My mom used to do the same thing. I think all moms do that."

I smiled as I remembered that mother had done that for me for a while.

Our food arrived and we had three hungry boys. Well, four if I counted Robert.

That was the quietest they had been since we got there.

Robert told JoJo that he'd heard he would be looking for a job in the near future.

"How'd you hear that?"

"Miss Jenna told us that when school starts back up you were going to have to quit working for her son. She told us they were sorry to see you go. They think you are a pretty good worker. From what I saw of it on Friday I would have to agree."

"Yeah, I don't want to quit but I can't ride my bike that far in the dark. As it is it takes me about 30 to 40 minutes to ride there now, but at least it's daylight and I can still see where I am going. I don't want to have to chance it in the dark and snow."

"I don't blame you. Where have you been looking?"

"Not anywhere yet. My dad works two jobs right now, so someone has to be home with mom at night so we all three try to work our schedules so that someone is mostly there."

"Well, that is pretty nice of you boys to work together like that."

"Yeah. That's what family does. We work together pretty good."

"Willy and JoJo work a lot more than I do right now. I only work mowing lawns and such right now. JoJo is teaching me a lot about plants and such. He's a pretty good teacher."

I looked at Robert. We knew that we would no longer be needing JoJo to do our lawn work.

"Would you like to add another job to your workload?"

"Do you know somebody that might be needing

their lawn done?"

"Well, sort of."

"I work real good. I will do a real good job for them. I have my own tools and everything. I have a lawn mower and all kinds of things. If you think they would want me to do their yard you let me know who they are and I will go and meet them. Do you think they might like me to do their yard?"

"Well, maybe if you didn't talk 'em to death." Willy nudged him.

"Hey, watch it now."

JoJo cleared his throat.

That seemed to settle them down.

"Well as a matter of fact I think they would. How about coming over to our house tomorrow around six and looking at it and let us know how much you might charge us. We have to maintain the grounds that the cottage we are living in is on and with my work schedule and school, I don't know how I am going to work it in."

"Really?"

"Well, only if you want to."

"I'll be there."

The waitress brought the check over.

Vicki came to say goodbye to us.

"How was your food? Did you boys like the cheeseburgers?"

They all agreed that they were very good.

"Sorry to talk and run but one of my busboys quit on me and I am having to play clean up as well as cook and hostess."

"How old do you have to be to work here?"

"Holly, I couldn't afford you." She laughed.

"No, not for me, for my friend JoJo here. He is looking for a job. Well in another week he will be. He works for Walker's Nursery right now, but it is too far for him when school starts back up. Do you think he might do?"

JoJo put his hand out, "Nice to meet you ma'am."

"Oh, this boy was raised right. Tell you what, can you come by tomorrow after work and we can talk. If we can work things out, I don't have a problem holding the job for you for another week. Is that doable?"

"Yes ma'am. It will be around seven though. They don't close until six and after we get everything put away it takes me about thirty or forty minutes to get here. Will that be okay?

"See you tomorrow around seven then."

It was eleven-thirty and we needed to get these boys home and we needed to get home.

We were not going to wake up at six in the morning if we didn't leave.

"Thank you for the dinner," they all said.

"Oh, you are so welcome. Thank you for going with us. You were great company."

Then to home, to bed, to sleep.

It had truly been a long day.

And God had been in it all.

CHAPTER 57

Pleeeease shoot that alarm clock!!!!!

I do not want to get up at six in the morning!

Who does?

But then I felt those arms around me.

Pulling me closer and the kisses on my neck.

"Good morning beautiful," he whispered in my ear.

I rolled over for a good morning kiss.

"Good morning handsome."

Then the best words ever. Well most of them anyways.

"I'll make coffee while you get your shower first."

The first part was great.

"Coffee!"

I reluctantly rolled out of bed.

I had just finished when he came in with a steaming hot cup of coffee with a little cream.

I was in love!

I had married the man of my dreams and he makes me coffee!

It didn't take long before we were both ready and had settled down to our morning devotions.

We made sure to thank God for our new little friends.

Then we made the bed, grabbed our lunches and hi ho, hi ho, it was off to work we go!

We both had to be at work by eight.

Robert was working a full schedule this week. Next week his schedule would change and he would just work on the days he didn't have classes and work around the hours that he did.

Evenings would be full of homework and whatever else we could fit in.

It was going to be a lot different than when Toby, Patty and I were all going together. When we would spend most of our nights and evenings at the Pizza Mart and then the Whistle Stop. After Toby graduated and it was just us three, we spent most nights at the Whistle Stop.

Vicki didn't mind us taking up a back booth. We always bought food and then helped clean up. It always seemed like the right thing to do.

It was closer to the garage that Robert worked at so he could come there right after work and we could all study together.

But now with Toby and Patty gone and Robert and I had our own little place, we could come home from work or school and Robert could study and I could, well, clean house while he studied.

I might even have to learn how to do the laundry.

I shuddered. Ugh. That would not be my favorite chore on the list.

But like Robert said, "It was a dirty job, but somebody had to do it."

I was going to be a bit early for work. It really was only a couple of blocks from the house, but Robert had insisted on driving me my first day.

He was going to be a bit early too but we both had paperwork to fill out so a little early was not going to kill anybody.

Dean Matthews was there to introduce me to everyone.

Imagine my surprise when one of the men in the Bookkeeping Department turned out to be a familiar face.

"Holly let me introduce you to Noah Masters. Noah, this is Holly Davis. She is the new girl we hired to take Priscilla's place."

"We've met."

"You have."

"Well, sort of. Her and her husband took the boys out to eat last night. I met them but I didn't quite catch their names. Nice to meet you, again."

He shook my hand.

"Nice to meet you as well."

"Priscilla, meet your replacement."

"So nice to finally meet you. Your husband did a great job preaching last night. And I loved that song you sang. I am going to miss getting to hear more of you guys." Then she flashed her ring. "I'm getting married in two weeks and we are moving to Montana."

"Congratulations! You are going to love being married. Well, at least I do."

We all laughed.

She showed me around the office. All the machines and how they all worked.

Most of them I was familiar with, but some were new to me.

She assured me that if she could figure out how to work them then anybody could, and besides, Noah was awesome, and he would be glad to help me out.

Right Noah?"

"Absolutely."

He sounded chipper enough but there was a sadness in his eyes.

My heart went out to him.

She was only going to be here until the end of the week, so we had a lot of ground to cover.

It didn't take long before I figured out the things that would need to be done and I knew the job would be a pretty good job.

Noah was the only one that worked all year round.

Which meant we would be able to go back home, if we had the money, for Christmas.

CHAPTER 58

True to his word, Frankie showed up around six. He was inside drinking a soda when Robert got home.

Robert took him outside and showed him all around. He told him that it was going to need fertilizing and mowed and weeded and all kinds of things. Since it was part of the church the grounds had to be kept up.

Robert wondered if the job would be too big for him to handle.

He showed him where all the tools were kept. He let him know that if there was a tool that he didn't have then he could borrow one from there but to make sure and put it back when he was done.

While they wandered around the grounds looking at all the different plants and grass and such, I prepared dinner.

Fried chicken, mashed potatoes and green beans and cornbread.

When they got back after settling on a price, I could see Frankie's face as the smell of the food hit his nostrils.

"Care to join us? You will be our first dinner guest."

"Really?"

"Sure. You can help set the table while Robert gets a shower and cleaned up. Do you know how to do that?"

"Yes ma'am. My mom showed me how."

"Well, good for your mom. She sounds pretty amazing."

"She is. She is a good cook too. Well, she was. But we get by."

Robert wasn't too long getting cleaned up and Frankie had been telling the truth.

He set a mean table.

"Sweet tea or Soda?"

"Sweet tea please."

"I'll take sweet tea as well," Robert said as he helped me put the food on the table.

"This looks good!"

"Wait until you taste it. I didn't just marry a pretty face. The girl can cook."

After we were all seated Robert took my hand. I reached for Frankie's and he looked perplexed.

"We are going to say grace over the food. We hold hands while we do so." Robert explained.

"We haven't said grace in a long time. I almost forgot."

"Lord we thank you for your many blessings,

For the day that you have given us and your bountiful supplies.

Lord we thank you for this food. May it bring nourishment to our bodies and bless the hands that prepared it. In Jesus name. Amen!"

"That was some prayer. I haven't heard prayer like that over food since well, last night I guess."

"Well, it is good to be thankful."

"Yep."

His eyes got so big when I put food on his plate.

"So how was your new job?"

"You started a new job?"

"Yes. I did. And you are not going to believe who my co-worker is?"

Robert shrugged his shoulders, "Probably not. I don't know a lot of people in this town. Is it someone we met recently?"

"Yep. I am now a co-worker of Mr. Noah Masters."

"I don't remember meeting a Noah Masters."

"Yes, you did. It's my dad. You got a job working with my dad? That's pretty cool."

"I think so."

"Wow.

I wasn't as good at having dinner and dessert made but we had bought ice cream, so we all had a bowl of that. I made sure to get Roberts attention and asked if we could send the rest of the food home so the other two would have food to eat.

He looked at the left-over chicken that was to be his lunch and he looked at Frankie.

"What do we have to put it in?

We found containers and Robert loaded Frankie up in the car and drove him and his leftovers home while I finished cleaning up the kitchen.

I knew he had his heart set on fried chicken leftovers for his lunch, but he was going to have to be satisfied with another roast beef sandwich.

I think he would survive.

Robert said JoJo was just getting home when they pulled up.

The boys were glad to have the food and best news of all, JoJo was going to be working at the Whistle Stop after school starting on Monday and work after school every day and Saturdays as well.

He would not have to ride his bike in the snow after dark either.

Vicki said she would throw his bike in the back of her truck and drive him home when the weather started getting bad.

Yes, indeed we had much to be thankful for.

CHAPTER 59

Our schedules changed after school started.

Robert had school every day but not all day.

We would ride to work together, and we were able to have lunch on most days together.

Then he would take the car to work and I would walk home.

I would have dinner ready by the time he came home and would clean while he studied.

Saturday's though, I kept the car so that I could do the grocery shopping.

Saturday afternoons and Sundays were our only time to really reconnect.

We were both tired by then.

But we never failed to make sure to start each day with the Lord.

And just to think, we would get to do this for the rest of our lives.

Frankie was true to his word.

He worked hard on our yard.

He picked Saturdays to do it.

He would show up early, just about the time I was taking Robert to work and was well on his way of doing a fine job on the grounds.

It was a lot of mowing to be done and weeding.

It was at the stage that it was needing to be

fertilized as well.

I took him with me to Walker's Nursery to get it and helped him unload it under his protests.

"Hey, just because I'm a girl doesn't mean I can't help, does it?"

"No ma'am."

"Well, alrighty then."

So, I helped.

While he worked, I would prepare him a good lunch.

I also made sure he had plenty to drink in between time.

He was a good worker and earned every penny of his pay.

He had two or three other jobs every week after school.

He said when he turned 16, he was going to try to get a job with Willy at the grocery store. "They pay really good."

"When will you be 16?"

"In two years, next June."

"Two years from next June? I thought you told us you would soon be 15. I guess I thought you meant real soon."

"Well," he shrugged his shoulders, "that is pretty soon. It ain't like it's in two Augusts."

"Well, you got me there."

"Well, at least we'll have a nice-looking yard for a while. That is if you like working for us. It is a lot of work."

"Yeah, but you guys pay really good. Mr. Jacobs has a big yard too, but he only pays me $15.00. I don't have to do as much. But he has me pick up the dog flops before I mow, and he has two Great Danes. That is not my funnest job. I mean who wants to pick up dog flops? Not me I tell ya."

Yeah, he was a good worker and we were blessed to have him.

"Oh, yeah. The mailman came. Do you want me to go get it and bring it in?"

"Thanks."

"I gotta go after that. Mom has been home by herself for a while and I need to get home and check on her. See if she needs anything. Then I gotta start cleaning the house."

"Alrighty."

He brought in the mail and dropped it on the table by the front door.

"See ya tomorrow night."

"What's tomorrow night?"

"Church!"

"Well, that's right. Are all three of you coming again?

"We talked about it and we kinda liked it, so, since that is the only night we all have off together, we decided to come to church. We used to go here you know."

"I think I did hear that."

"When mom got sick, real sick, a couple of years ago, we kinda quit coming.

Sometimes I miss it. I liked coming, but it's hard when we have to get everything ready for the week on Sunday mornings. Willy sometimes has to work on Sunday mornings, and dad, well, he works as much as he can. Mom's medicine costs a lot of money."

"I'm sorry to hear that. Your dad must be

exhausted."

"He is. He drives a cab in the evenings and on the weekends. He makes pretty good money plus sometimes people pay him tips. Us guys, we work too. So, we get by."

"Your mom must be so proud."

"I think she is. She has good days and bad days. This morning was a good day. Hopefully she was able to stay up for a while."

"I am going to have to get over there and meet her."

"She would like that. We all told her about you and Mr. Robert. We told her how pretty you sing."

"That is very sweet of you."

"Well, it's true. You do sing good. Do you know the sparrow song?"

"The sparrow song. I don't know that I do know that song. Do you know some of the words?"

"My mom sings it. She used to sing it loud, but now she sings it more to herself when she is reading her Bible. I love my mom."

"Sounds like you do. How does the song go? Do you know?"

"It says something like, I sing because I'm happy, I sing because I'm free, His eye is on the sparrow, and I know he watches me." Do you know it?"

"You know, I do know that song. I have never sung it before. Now I am going to have to find the words and see if Robert will teach me all of it."

"If you do, can you sing it for me? Would you sing it real loud for me?"

"I promise to do my best."

"Oh, I gotta go. Willy had to be at work an hour ago, so she has been alone for a while now. See ya tomorrow night."

"Okay. See you all tomorrow night."

CHAPTER 60

Robert was excited to see we had gotten a couple of letters.

One from his mom and one from Lance.

His mom was telling us to make sure and call more often. Even if we needed to call collect.

She missed hearing our voices.

We made a point of calling her that evening.

But Lance had the best of news.

He was going to be the proud owner of a used Auto Shop.

Everything had come through for him and he would be signing papers to be the new owner on October 1st. He had already talked to a guy that made Neon signs and was having a couple of them made.

He was wondering if maybe he knew of someone that might be looking for a job. With Robert gone and him taking over the business they were going to be needing one more guy at least.

We were so excited for Lance.

We called both his mom and Lance to talk to both of them.

After spending a good amount of time on the phone with his mom and begging for cookies he got a chance to talk to Lance.

"So, I hear you are going to be an entrepreneur.

That's great. So, what kind of sign are you going to be putting up?"

"Well, I am just going to modify the one that Coop has up their now. His has that big tire. I am going to spruce that up and take down the one above it and have it say "Wheels"."

"That sounds cool."

"Yeah. They said they could make it so that tire looks like it is rolling."

"I can't wait to see it."

"Yeah. Then they are going to make me one for that big window in the front of the store. It will look like the big tire out front, but they are going to put the word "Wheels" right in the middle of it. Coop already has the one that says open, so I won't need one of those. It is still in good condition."

"Man, I can't wait to see it. Take some pictures of it and send them to us. Holly and I won't be coming back until Christmas and we don't want to wait that long to see what it looks like."

"Well, you might have to. It might take that long for them to get them made and up."

"Well, take pictures if they get it up sooner."

"Hey, you know anybody that might be looking for a job out here? With you gone and Coop gone we are gonna be super busy. I know Coop was getting up there in age, but he at least got here and did some oil changes and changed tires on occasion."

"I can't think of anyone, man. If you ask mom, she probably knows someone at church who has a kid or somebody looking for work. Too bad you can't find a vet like yourself to work. That would be the thing to do."

"Yeah man, I don't need a vet like myself. I need a vet like you. Somebody who can get in there and get the job done."

"Man, I might have been able to get in there, but you, you can work circles around me when it comes to this. Lance, man, I am so proud of you. This is going to be great. What about Louise, is she gonna still run the front when Coop sells?"

"I doubt it. As old as Coop is, I think she is old enough to be his mother. I think he said she would probably be quitting too. I'm gonna need to find someone to take her place. I'll ask mom like you said. Your right, she probably does know someone."

"Later bro."

"Later."

With a promise from his mother to send cookies we hung up the phone.

Robert could not have been prouder of Lance, and neither could I.

CHAPTER 61

Frankie was right, all three of them did show up to church the next night.

Frankie noticed a couple of guys from when he had gone there before.

They motioned for him to come and sit with them, so we motioned for Willy and JoJo to come and sit with us.

After church we drove by one more time to make sure they could go out for a bite with us.

Noah was wondering, were we sure that we wanted to do that?

We assured them that we most definitely did.

He gave his permission but reminded them that they would need to be quiet when they came in.

They promised.

Robert and I both had the day off the next day. It was Labor Day and the boys all had it off. Well, except for JoJo. He was going to start work tomorrow at his new job.

Vicki was excited to see all of us when we came in. She hugged us and seated us right away.

It wasn't very crowded.

"Where is everybody tonight?"

"Labor Day weekend. They are all out of town for one last hurrah! It will all be back to normal on

Tuesday when they all get back. Sometimes it's nice to have a breather."

She looked at JoJo. "Are you about ready for your new adventure?"

"Yes ma'am." He nodded to her.

"Where did you find these three fine gentlemen? They have more manners that some of the college crowd that comes in here."

"Hey there," Robert joked.

"Not you guys of course, but some of them."

"Your mama must have raised you boys right," she said to them.

"She likes to think so ma'am. We aim to make her proud."

"You are doing a pretty good job of that boys. You are doing a pretty good job."

Our waitress came over. "You take good care of these folks. They are my favorite customers. Hey," she said to Robert and myself, "did I tell you? Angie is getting married."

"She is?"

"Yep, to some guy she met here at school. He is really a nice-looking man. He is going to be a minister. His name is Jerry Jenkins. No that's not it. Wait, it's not Jenkins."

"Is it Jerry Denkins?"

"Yes! That's it! Jerry Denkins. Do you know him?"

"Uh, no. But I've heard of him. Toby knew him. Toby thought highly of him."

"He is a really good man. He treats her nice. He is going to be the youth leader at their church and then in a few months he will be the associate pastor. They are getting married in March I think."

"Tell her congratulations for me."

"I will."

This time around we all ordered the same thing. Meatloaf meals. The boys chose to forgo the salads. That was one of my favorite things of the meal.

But they didn't forgo the milkshakes.

I still had a soda.

"So, are you excited about starting your new job here?"

"I guess so. It is going to be a lot more different than working in the nursery for Mr. Walker. I liked working for him. They are nice people and I was learning a lot. But it wasn't gonna be doable now that school has started."

"I think you will like working for Miss Vicki. She is one of the nicest people that we've met in this town. She seems to know everybody."

"Yeah. She is so nice. I'm sure it will be fun. She insisted that I take Sundays off unless they are in a pinch. She said it was important for us boys to be able to go to church on Sundays. I forgot how much I liked this church."

"Yeah. Mom and Dad used to take us every Sunday morning and night. Sunday School was fun. But it was nice on Sunday nights sitting in church with them and listening to mom sing. I miss that."

"Guess what? Miss Holly is gonna learn the sparrow song and sing it in church for me!"

"You know the sparrow song?"

"That'll be so cool. I think that is my mom's favorite song. She don't sing it that much anymore but she does sometimes. Just not very loud."

"Yeah, that's what I told her."

"What is the sparrow song.," Robert asked?

"You don't know the sparrow song?" I winked at the boys.

"I guess not," Robert looked at me puzzled.

"Sing it to him Frankie," I nodded to Frankie.

"No! Not in here." He looked all around like everyone could hear our conversation.

"I'll teach it to him, and he can learn it on the piano and I promise we'll sing it."

"No! Not him. Just you. Just you sing it, okay?"

"Uh, well, I'll see what I can do."

Luckily, we were saved by the meatloaf dinner.

Next day Robert and I went through all the songbooks looking for the sparrow song.

"I know this song," Robert exclaimed once we found it. "My mom sings this song too. Do you want to learn it?"

"I've heard it before, but I would like to learn how to sing it since Frankie and the boys seem excited for me to learn it."

We practiced it every chance we got and by Sunday evening I was ready to sing it for the boys and by that time the word had taken hold of my heart and I was singing it as unto the Lord.

CHAPTER 62

Bailey showed up for work on October 1st promptly at 8 am.

Lance's mom had truly come through.

When she announced at the Tuesday morning Bible study that Lance was looking to hire a new employee for his business and wondered if anyone knew of someone needing a job Aunt Jessie told her she thought she knew just the right person.

Brayden had returned from the Army, but he was in no condition to work too far from home.

He had made it through unharmed, but with a lot of shell shock. He was needing a job, but he had not been able to find one for a couple of months.

Bailey, his brother, was concerned for him.

He had asked if there was any way that he could come back to work on the farm for her and Uncle Joey, but they didn't need an extra hand at that time.

Bailey understood but you could tell he was worried about his brother.

Her and Sara talked after the service and she said she had a plan they both had prayed about it.

That night she had talked to Uncle Joey about it and they decided to run it across Brayden and Bailey and see if they were game.

They asked if they could pray about it and they all

did.

Bailey came and talked to Lance about the job and showed him some of his skills.

He started work promptly at 8 am even though he had a thirty-minute drive. And Brayden got his old job back working for Aunt Jessie and Uncle Joey.

Bailey was a natural.

He wasn't as good as Lance, or even Robert, but he ran a close 3rd.

Lance had a full crew, well except for the front of the place.

But that position didn't stay open long either.

He had no sooner put a sign in the front window looking for help when a girl he recognized from the Burger Joint came in.

She had worked there for about a month and was looking to make a change.

She seemed to fit right in.

At first.

The male customers loved her.

But she didn't keep books very well and her phone and organizational skills were not the best.

But she was pretty and that kept the clientele coming in and so Lance looked the other way.

"She'll get better," he told himself. "Everybody needs a chance to prove themselves."

His business was going to be a success.

Lance, Matthew, and Bailey worked well together. They all got along and knew how to work together and around each other.

The customers never had a complaint about the work. They had plenty to say about the girl who always messed up their invoices.

She might be pretty to look at, but she was costing the customers money and time with the mistakes she kept making.

Lance kept holding out hope.

Sometimes the stress would get to him. Especially if his good leg was giving him a problem.

Those were the days that everyone knew it was not going to be a good day.

After Bailey had been working there a month, he decided it was time to move closer to his job.

He found a little furnished apartment. Well, more of a studio apartment.

He thought it was just perfect.

It had a bed, a couch, a chair, a dining table and chairs, a kitchen, and a bathroom. It even had a T.V.

"Who could ask for anything more? Besides, this way, I don't have to get up an hour early to get to work. I am only ten minutes away and that suits me just fine."

"Can you even cook," Matthew asked him?

"I can open a can of soup. I like soup."

"You can't live on soup."

"Yeah, but my girlfriend will come and cook for me sometimes so there."

"So, you're telling me that your girlfriend is going to be willing to drive almost a half an hour to come and fix dinner for you?"

"Yeah, she loves me. She tells me I'm a winner."

"Oh brother! It is a good thing you know how to work on cars."

CHAPTER 63

"Noah, what are you guys doing for Thanksgiving?"

"Nothing. Probably just stay home like last year."

"Would you all like to come over to our house? We are not going out of town this year. We are staying here rather than drive for just a week's stay. With the school closed down next week I have the time off, but Robert has to work. He will have Thanksgiving off but that is it.

We are used to having a lot of people around for the holidays. I'm a pretty good cook. If your wife is feeling up to it, we'd love to have you all over."

"That's pretty nice. I guess I can ask. I've got to work that morning on my second job, but I will be done at noon. Would that be too late?"

"No, that would be perfect. You ask her and see if she would feel like it and let me know. You have our number, just call. There is going to be plenty of food."

I was hoping they would be able to come.

Blake and Gabby and their two boys and Miss Jenna were coming and so were the Carson's.

Even Vicki was going to be coming since she closed the diner down on Thanksgiving.

She only closed it down four times a year!

New Year's Day, Christmas Day, Easter, and

Thanksgiving!

She said those were days that she felt her employees deserved to be spending with their families.

We considered her family and since she had no one else here, we invited her, and she agreed to come.

We were going to have a full house if they all showed up.

We bought two turkeys.

Robert was sure that we would need to have two big turkeys so we would have plenty to have turkey sandwiches and anything turkey leftovers.

Apparently, Robert loved turkey!

Little did we know that it was going to be even a fuller house.

Monday morning while I was elbow deep in pie making there was a knock on our door.

Toby and Patty were there.

They had finished up a revival nearby and were going to be starting one the following Sunday at another local church.

They had stopped by hoping we'd be home.

I was.

I found out over a fresh pot of coffee that they were going to be staying at a hotel.

They were not going home to have to turn right around and drive in the snow to get back.

We hadn't seen them since before we left.

We had spoken on the phone, but we had not heard they were not going home.

I would not hear of them staying in a hotel.

They were going to be our guests.

Well, working guests.

I really was glad to see Patty. I could use all the help I could getting pies and desserts made for the next two days.

They agreed to stay with us.

Robert was going to be so happy to see them.

Patty and I cooked like fools all the rest of the day until Robert got home.

He hurried inside. He knew they were there.

"Toby, Patty! When did you guys get here?"

"How did you know they were here?"

"You don't think I recognized that car out there? Who else could it be, right?"

"Go get cleaned up. We are going out to eat tonight. Patty and I have been baking all day. They are going to be our houseguests for a few days."

"Yes ma'am."

Patty and I covered all the pies and put them out in the laundry room. It stays a cool 30 degrees when the dryer was going. I think they should be fine out there.

"Tomorrow we tackle the cookies and the cobblers."

"Are you feeding an Army?"

"Pretty much. If everybody shows up that is invited, I want to have plenty of food. I don't want anyone ever to go away hungry."

"I don't see how they could."

"Then Wednesday we can cook one of the turkeys and Thursday we can cook the other one."

"She is feeding an Army."

"That's ex-Army," Robert said as he came out ready to go.

"I'm ready," he said, "but you two might want to go freshen up. You both have flour on your face and stuff."

Patty and I looked at each other.

We were a mess, but not such a mess that it was going to take us forever to get ready.

And in no time, we were ready to go to our favorite diner.

Vicki was so happy to see Toby and Patty.

JoJo was there working. He smiled and waved as we came in.

"He is such a hard worker. He never complains about anything that I ask him to do. I wish I had a dozen of him. I encourage him to get his homework done on his down time. His mom and dad should be so proud of this young man."

"Oh, they are. Him and his brothers are three of the best kids I have ever met."

"Come on in and get seated. What are you two doing here?"

Toby explained the situation.

Vicki was elated that they would be there for Thanksgiving dinner.

We spent the evening eating and catching up and the next two days cooking and cleaning and Toby and Patty caught up on their laundry.

Thanksgiving was going to be awesome!

CHAPTER 64

Thanksgiving morning was so cold! We'd had a good amount of snow fall through the night.

Toby and Robert got a good fire going that morning as Patty and I made coffee and breakfast.

It was going to be a long day, so we decided to get up early to get a good start on it.

We made a good hearty breakfast as it was going to be all hands-on deck to make this come off. Who better to have help than Toby and Patty!

Pastor Carson had said we could borrow some tables and chairs from the church. Toby and Robert had headed up to the church to get them.

Two tables and at least 20 chairs.

It was going to be a tight fit, but it was going to be a huge success if it turned out.

Patty and I had made six pumpkin pies, two pecan pies, two lemon meringue pies, and two chocolate pies. We had a chocolate cake, an Italian Cream Cake, a Pumpkin Cheesecake, and cookies galore. We even had lemon bread and banana bread.

We had prepared the green beans for the green bean casserole and the sweet potatoes for the sweet potato casserole. We had peeled potatoes for the mashed potatoes, and everything was ready to make the dressing.

One turkey was already cooked and needed to be reheated as needed and one more to cook.

We had splurged and purchased an electric oven to bake the turkey in so to free up oven space. So that was going to be a lifesaver.

All the dishes had been washed and prepared.

We had cooked all morning and the boys had gathered pinecones for us to make centerpieces.

Truthfully it was going to be one of our first dinner parties ever, for any of us.

Patty and Toby had not been in their own home since they had married and Robert and I, even though we'd had Frankie eat lunch with us a few times, this was our first dinner party.

It felt like a group effort and it felt like it should be. Family!

It was one-thirty when our first guests arrived.

We had moved the furniture to make room for the table and chairs.

Pastor Carson and his wife were our first guests.

Patty took their coats and put them in the bedroom.

While she was in there Vicki showed up.

We had made it clear that she was not to bring anything but herself. She deserved a day to be fed and not have to worry about a thing.

We had told our guests to just come and be blessed.

And thankfully she listened.

Robert took her coat and put it in the room with the other ones.

By two o'clock we had a full house.

The Walkers and the Masters' all showed up around at the same time.

Gabby took the boys to the room to help them put their coats away. Miss Jenna took Blakes coat and was going to take them to the room, but Toby insisted that she let him do the honors.

JoJo, Willy, and Frankie made sure to take their coats and put them away as Noah helped Gina into the house.

Patty took their coats and we were at capacity!

"Please make yourselves comfortable around the table," Robert told them as Patty and I started putting the food on the table.

We had been pretty clever we thought. Knowing there would be so many people we had made two pans or platters of everything so that no one would be left out.

The rolls were the last things and they came out piping hot. Robert sat them out while Toby set out the butter.

Patty had made homemade cranberry sauce.

The table looked as if there should be enough food to feed a small Army.

Robert asked Pastor Carson if he would please ask the blessing over the food.

He obliged.

It was so good to watch the food being passed around and plates were becoming full, emptied and then full again.

"Save room for dessert," Patty told them.

"Whatcha got for dessert."

"Mind your manners Frankie," Gina told him.

"Yes ma'am."

"Well, honestly, we have too much to even list. But it is going to all be good. Holly and I have been baking all week. Vicki, we even made those cookies you like."

"Oh, my! I might just have to take me a few of those home."

"You just might have to. There are a lot of them as well as pies and cakes and cobblers."

"And whipped cream?"

"Yes Frankie, and whipped cream."

The atmosphere was lively and after everyone had eaten their fill, Robert asked if the guys wanted to go play football out in the front yard.

He looked at me as if to say, will you be okay doing the dishes if we do that?

I smiled and nodded, go ahead.

Pastor Carson said he wouldn't play but he wouldn't mind watching for a while.

Even Noah went out with them.

Patty and I cleared the table.

The other ladies started to help and as much as we would have liked to have them just sit and be our guests, we knew that the more people that helped the faster we could get to dessert.

Sister Carson helped Gina move to a more comfortable chair and kept her company while the rest of us made fast work of it.

It truly only took about an hour to clean a mess that had taken days to create.

The boys came in just as we finished making hot chocolate and coffee.

Robert and Toby got the boys to all come help bring in the desserts.

Patty had made fresh whipped cream. A lot of it and I had heated up the cobbler.

It was a feast fit for, well for anyone who thought

they could have one more bite.

The boys had worked up an appetite and so had the women.

Even with all of us eating like we did we did not put a dent in it.

After everyone had eaten their fill, Toby and Robert took down the tables to make room for everyone to sit and visit.

Gina was getting very tired.

She looked like she could cry. I wanted to cry with her.

JoJo sat on the floor by her and wouldn't leave her side.

Each of the boys kept asking her if they could get her anything.

You could see the love on their faces.

But before long she said she felt like she needed to go home.

I could tell the boys didn't want to have to go yet so I asked if they could stay a while longer.

"I'll bring them home after a while, if that's okay." Robert asked?

"Please dad," Frankie pleaded?

He and Blakes oldest son were the same age and had hit it off.

Noah agreed to let them stay but made them promise to not be a bother.

Patty found their coats and I hugged her.

"Gina, I am so glad you felt like coming out today. Your boys talk about you all the time you know."

"I am so glad you invited us. We don't get out much, really at all, anymore. Noah tells me all the time that you and your husband are pretty good people."

"We like to think so," I joked. "And Gina, just so you know, we love those boys of yours. You have done an excellent job of raising three fine young men. You and Noah should be very proud of yourselves. Thanks for letting them go with us on Sunday nights after church. We just love hearing what God is doing in their lives."

We hugged again and they thanked everyone for having them and with a parting shot to the boys to "be good."

They were gone.

Pastor Carson and Sister Carson and Vicki left a little later.

Vicki took a bag of cookies with her and Pastor Carson talked himself into the remaining Lemon pie.

That left us with one whole one so Robert was okay with it.

The boys had gotten some cards from somewhere and they were playing some game that Willy knew called spoons and they were all having a good time.

The rest of us gathered in the living area and visited until late.

Miss Jenna was getting tired and falling asleep during the conversation, so we loaded them up with goodies and they left.

It was close to eleven and Robert made sure to send a lot of food home with the boys so they could make turkey sandwiches and whatever else they wanted.

He knew that Gina was not going to feel like cooking, and they should have the luxury of Thanksgiving leftovers. They chose the rest of one of the chocolate pies and some of the cookies and Willy asked if he could take some of the peach cobbler home.

They could take whatever they wanted.

Toby and Robert loaded them up and took them home.

While they were gone Patty and I covered the desserts and put them away and then started washing dishes again.

We had just finished putting the last dish away when the guys came home.

We were just about to turn out the lights and go to bed when Robert asked, "Toby, you hungry?"

"I could eat."

"You have got to be kidding me?"

"No, I'm a little hungry. I could go for a turkey sandwich."

"Me too. That sounds good."

"Well, I tell you what. You two go on ahead and make yourselves a sandwich. We are going to bed," Patty told them.

"And clean up your mess when you are done," I chimed in.

Patty and I hugged goodnight and went to our bedrooms and shut the doors.

Robert and Toby celebrated with one last hurrah.

CHAPTER 65

Turkey hangovers are tough, but Robert survived.

He made his lunch before he and Toby went to bed.

He even cleaned the kitchen.

I barely heard him getting ready the next morning.

I started to get out of bed to help him and he kissed me and said he had it taken care of, to go back to sleep.

How I wanted to, but he had done the unthinkable. He'd made a pot of coffee.

That glorious morning aroma permeated the house and I couldn't resist.

I made us both a cup and since I was already up, I made him a simple omelet.

I couldn't send him off into the cold without at least a little breakfast.

"What were you going to eat if I hadn't made you breakfast," I asked.

"Pumpkin pie."

"Are you serious?"

"Well, and coffee!"

He grinned and winked at me.

We had time for morning devotions, and he headed out after stoking the fireplace.

I finished my coffee and went back to bed.

It was about an hour later that I heard Patty and Toby stirring.

I got up to make a fresh pot of coffee.

Patty was not doing well this morning.

She was very sick.

She went back to bed after a quick trip to the bathroom.

Toby came into the kitchen for a nice hot cup of coffee.

“Patty doesn’t sound too well this morning.”

“No,” he yawned. “She’ll be okay though.”

“I hope so. I hate to see her sick like this. I hope it wasn’t something she ate.”

“No,” he grinned. “It wasn’t something she ate.”

He wouldn’t look up at me. But he didn’t look too concerned for her at all.

It was starting to get me a little upset that he didn’t seem even a little bothered about how she felt.

And besides, how would he know if she was going to be okay?

All he had done was get...a..washcloth..and hand it to her..

I looked at him and he still would not make eye contact with me.

Sitting there like the cat that ate the canary!

“Patty. Patty,” can I come in? I stood and knocked on her door.

“Come on it.”

She was covered up with the washcloth cooling the back of her neck and a sleeve of saltines on the nightstand.

“Toby, did you tell her,” she yelled feebly at Toby as he came into the room behind me?

“I swear I didn’t babe. I swear. How do you know she knows anything?”

We both looked at him.

"Alright, alright! But, Holly, I didn't tell you, did I?"

"Well, yes and no. You both told me in so many words. Just call me Nancy Drew."

Patty sat up in the bed a little. She did not look well at all.

"Could you please shut the door. The smell of that coffee is not going over to good this morning."

"Sure babe." Toby shut the door behind him.

I sat on the edge of the bed.

"How long have you known?"

"We found out for sure last Friday."

"How far along are you? Do you have due date yet?"

"He told us that we are due in June around the 19th. I don't always get sick like this. I think it is bad this morning because of all the food I ate yesterday. Too much of a good thing as they say."

"How exciting! What did your mom say? I bet she can't wait. What about your mom Toby? I bet they are going nuts."

"They don't know yet. We haven't told them. Toby wasn't supposed to tell you.

We are trying our best to not tell anyone yet. We were going to surprise all of you at Christmas."

"Cross my heart. I will not tell anyone, well, except Robert, if that's okay?"

"Sure! But just Robert. By the way, how did you figure it out."

"Well, doofus here didn't seem concerned about you at all and when I asked about you, he wouldn't even make eye contact with me. I had my suspicions then. But when I came into your room and saw the washcloth and the saltines, I put it all together. I'm not just a pretty head you know."

We all laughed, well, until she had to run to the bathroom again.

I followed her and held her hair back and got her a fresh washcloth.

It felt strangely awesome to be on the giving end of this.

I couldn't help but smile as I thought of Aunt Jessie and how kind she had been to me while I went through the same thing.

Tears rolled down my face as the sweet thoughts ran through my mind.

"I'll be okay," Patty said.

"I know. Just remembering what love feels like when it is freely given."

I need to send her a card. I loved her so!

Then I rinsed out the cloth for Patty.

She was feeling a lot better a couple of hours later. So she ate a little something.

"What are you going to do with all that turkey you have left over?"

"I sent a bunch of it home with people last night. I don't know. I mean, we are going to have enough turkey to make all kinds of turkey dishes.

Robert knew we would need two. He thought one would not be enough. He wanted to make sure we had a lot left over for turkey anything."

"Well, I think you have more than plenty."

"Do you want to take some with you when you go tomorrow?"

"Uh, we might take a couple of sandwiches, but I don't think it will make that big of a dent in it."

"I know. I am not going to eat turkey sandwiches

for a month! There has to be something else besides a sandwich?"

"Too bad you can't make Mexican food out of it. I could really go for some tacos." Patty said.

"Ooh, tacos do sound good."

"Why would you girls make tacos when you have perfectly good turkey?"

"Ooh, turkey tacos sound good."

"Oh, yeah, yeah the do."

"Do you feel like going to the store? We can get tortillas and all the stuff to make it. Do you feel like it?"

Patty and I went to the store and got everything you could possibly need to make turkey tacos.

Robert and Toby were pleased to say the least.

"Now, aren't you glad I had you make two turkeys?"

"Hey, can we come back next year and eat turkey tacos with you?"

"You can come have turkey tacos with us any time you want, well, anytime we have turkey. Right Holly."

Traditions!

Turkey taco night was born!

CHAPTER 66

We hated to see them go. But they had to get to the next church for the weeklong revival.

They promised to stay with us after the first of the year when they were scheduled to hold a revival in town.

With tears and hugs and a promise to see them at Christmas they left.

Frankie had shown up while they were leaving.

We must have looked a sight with all of us hugging and Patty and myself crying.

Patty hugged him and told him how happy she was to have met him and his family.

"Holly and Robert talked about you all the whole time we were here. You make sure she makes you a batch of cookies every once in a while. She's a pretty good cook."

"Yeah, she is. Have you had her fried chicken? It is so good!"

"I have not. Next time we are here I am going to have to have her make me some."

"Yes ma'am. She is a real good cook."

"Guess what we are having for lunch when you finish out here?"

"Something good I hope."

"How about turkey tacos?"

"Turkey tacos?"

"Trust me," Toby smiled, "you are gonna love 'em."

Frankie worked while I washed bed linens and prepared a turkey feast for him and Robert when he got home.

He worked up an appetite.

And just like Toby had predicted, he loved them!

He and Robert ate their fill and then helped clean up.

We drove him home after lunch and I asked about his mom.

"How is she feeling today?"

"This morning was a good morning. She had a real good time at your house the other night. Thanks for asking her to come too."

"Oh, sweetheart. We were just so blessed that you all came. We had a full house now didn't we.?

"You sure did. Mr. Walkers son, the oldest one, he seemed nice. We got along. I remember him from Sunday school. He was in my class with me when my mom taught my class."

"Your mom taught Sunday school?"

"Yeah. She would sing songs with us and we had to learn our memory verses and everything. If you learned your memory verse and read the lesson, you would get a gold star and a piece of candy. She was a good Sunday school teacher. I liked her class the best. She had these pictures that she would put on this board and she would tell us the story about the pictures."

"Your mom sounds pretty special."

"She is. I really love my mom!"

"Sounds like it. Do you think she would mind if we

came inside and said hello?"

"Let me go ask her. She might not be feeling too well now. You never can tell."

"You go inside and ask, and we will wait for you to let us know."

Frankie ran inside and was in there for a few before he motioned for us to come inside.

"Are you sure you want to do this," Robert asked?

"Sure. Don't you?"

"I do. But remember, she may have been putting her best front on when she came over. She may not be feeling as well as she did then."

"Oh, I see what you mean. Well, we won't stay long. But if she'll let us, will you pray for her?"

"That I can do."

We went inside.

Frankie was telling her about the turkey tacos.

She was smiling at him as she listened to him go on and on.

Toby was right, she didn't look like she was feeling all that great.

I hadn't noticed the deep dark circles under her eyes the other night.

Honestly, I had been so busy that I had not gotten much of a chance to talk to her.

The house was immaculate!

"Please come on in," Gina motioned.

She was too weak to stand.

"Thank you for letting us come inside. I feel like we are imposing on you, but we didn't get much of a chance to visit the other night and I really wanted to thank you all for coming. It was our first dinner with invited guests."

"Hey, I eat there," Frankie exclaimed!

"Yes, you do! But you are not a guest anymore. After that first time you ate with us, you were family after that!"

He grinned and so did Gina.

"Would you care for something to drink or eat? Willy made fresh tea before he left this morning and there is lemon for it if you like."

"As tempting as that sounds, we just ate, and we have a few errands to run. We are going to go look for a Christmas tree. We are still debating on a real one or a fake one. We are thinking a fake one because we are going to go back home for Christmas and will be gone for a couple of weeks and we don't want to come home to a dried-out tree. I would rather have a real one. That is all we've ever had, but if we aren't going to be here to take care of it, well you know what I mean."

"Mom, when are we going to put up a tree? We put it up in front of the window last year, remember?"

"Oh, I remember. I just don't know if your dad is going to have the energy to get all the ornaments and lights down this year. With all the hours he is working now, I just don't know sweetheart."

"Okay. Well, hopefully he'll feel like it. It sure would look nice there in front of that window though wouldn't it?

You could see the tree through his eyes.

When we got ready to leave, Robert asked if it would be okay if we prayed for her, she gladly accepted.

CHAPTER 67

We found the perfect tree!

We could not fit a huge tree in our little living room so we found a little tree that fit perfectly on a table that we could pull in front of the window.

We found a little string of lights and a box of lovely ornaments.

Our first Christmas tree together!

We wanted it to be special. Even though it was very small, not like the ginormous trees that we both used to have in our homes growing up. But then again, we were not in the ginormous houses that we grew up in either.

It didn't take long to decorate it, but it was beautiful when we were done.

We went outside to admire the view.

It truly was lovely!

Robert put another log on the fire, and we made turkey noodle soup for dinner.

After we cleaned the kitchen, we sat on the couch together and snuggled and enjoyed a cup of coffee.

It was the first time in a long time that we felt like we had just been alone together.

It was nice being held so close and feeling the quiet as it engulfed us.

The crackling of the fire and the lights flickering on

the little tree made it the most perfect moment.

"I am so happy for Toby and Patty."

"They are going to make great parents!"

"I know. Patty is so excited. Did you know she knits?"

"No. I did not know that. And that is important because...?"

"She is going to knit booties and blankets and things for the baby."

"Didn't you say the baby was due sometime in June or something?"

"Yes."

"Ok, won't it be a little hot for a knitted baby blanket?"

"Do you think that babies only stay little for a couple of months? The baby will be needing blankets for a long time."

"I see your point. Holly, we really haven't talked about it but, have you thought about us having a baby?"

"Honestly, I really haven't given it a lot of thought. We have been so busy since we got married that I guess we haven't really talked about that. It is kind of an important thing. I mean, I want a baby, but I am not sure that right now is a good time. With you working and going to school and me working full time I'm not sure that we would either one have the time to give a baby if we had one. Have you thought about it?"

"Honestly?"

"Yeah, honestly."

"Well, to tell you the truth, I have kind of thought about it. I kind of feel like you do. I want to have a baby with you, our baby, a little Holly, or a little

Robert. But right now, we could provide for a baby I guess, but I don't think that we would be able to devote the time it takes for a baby, like you just said. Do you really feel that way or were you just saying it?"

I was quiet for a second as I really thought about my answer.

"Robert, when I had Hannah, and I held her for just those brief moments, once they took her and I never got to see her or hold her, my arms never felt so empty in my life. After I had her, I never thought that I would have a chance at motherhood ever again. Much less be married. Then I met her. And my heart ached for her. It still does. It made me want to have a baby to hold and love and would be mine forever. Mine to hold and love and just have. Then I met you and married the man that I had always loved. A dream that I never thought would happen. I guess I think in my heart, that, if the dream of being in love with you and marrying you and you will be mine forever. You will be mine forever, right?"

"Right!"

"Well, if that dream can come true then the dream of having a baby will come true as well. But I want it to be when we can devote all the love that we have on our own little Holly or little Robert. Until then, I am just going to have to be content holding this dream in my arms. I think we are good to wait. If that really is okay with you?"

"Holly."

"Yes?"

"Have I told you that I love you?"

"Not today."

Then he kissed me.

CHAPTER 68

We only had three weeks before we were going to be going back home for Christmas.

Christmas shopping was always fun.

We had to cut back a little on what all we wanted to get everyone.

I had got the letter from Lisa telling me what dolls Hannah was into now.

She had her eyes set on a Shirley Temple doll that she had seen. And MJ was really wanting a Tonka truck.

Those were easy enough.

I had called her and asked her to send me a what they would want.

Since she knew it was me that had been buying them, I wanted to be up front about things.

And now that we loved MJ so much it just didn't seem right to not get him what he wanted as well.

Robert was glad we were getting MJ something too. He wanted to be the one to get just the right thing.

I had to remind him that they wouldn't know we got these things for them, but he reminded me that they might not know, but we would.

He always knew just the right thing to make my heart fall in love with him over and over again.

We wanted to get something nice for Noah and

Gina and the boys. We just weren't sure what they would want or need.

It was hard not being around family too.

It wasn't as if anyone needed anything, but we couldn't not get them something.

Then we figured it out.

We decided to give them all gift cards with money in them.

It sounded so cheesy, even to us, but other than MJ and Hannah, we just didn't know what they would need or want.

But shopping for just the right cards was kind of fun too.

Robert had preached at a couple of churches on Sunday nights, so we hadn't seen JoJo or Willy in a couple of weeks, but Frankie came every Saturday just like clockwork.

He was always checking on the plants and making sure they were covered and just making sure the yard was kept looking good.

He was such a joy to have around.

The Saturday before we were going to go out of town we asked if we could take him home.

He was more than happy to oblige.

After a good lunch I grabbed the tin of cookies that I had made for them and we drove him home.

What a surprise for us.

The tree was lovely all lit up shining in the window.

"I love your tree. It is so big!"

"Yeah," Frankie beamed, "Dad got it for us last weekend. Me and him got the decorations out of the attic and all of us decorated it last Sunday. Mom couldn't help much but she felt good enough to sit and watch. She said it was the prettiest tree we ever had."

"Do you think she would mind if we came in to say Merry Christmas. We are leaving to go home on Monday and we wanted to see her before we left."

"Let me check."

After he had been inside for a few minutes he motioned for us to come inside.

Robert carried the tin of cookies and the Christmas card.

Gina looked tired. Really tired.

She smiled weakly as we came in.

"Merry Christmas," she managed through a forced smile. The words had such effort behind them.

"Merry Christmas to you!"

"We aren't staying long. We just wanted to bring you and your little family a little something. It isn't much, but we just wanted to let you know that we were thinking about you and that we love you all so much."

I gave Frankie a little side hug when Robert told her that.

He blushed.

"You didn't have to do that."

"We know, but we wanted too. I hope you enjoy them. And don't eat them all before your brothers get home Frankie," I joked.

He lifted the lid and saw the cookies.

"Then they better hurry and get home. I make no promises."

He took the tin into the kitchen.

"Your tree is lovely. It looks like you all did a great job of decorating it."

"Yes, the boys and their dad did an awesome job.

It made my heart sing just watching them work together like they did. I have a pretty good crew around here I must say."

"Yes, you do. They are great boys. You and Noah have done an awesome job with them. They are such well-mannered boys, and so sweet. We just love them."

"Thank you for saying so. Those are the words that make a mother proud."

"Well, we wouldn't say it if it wasn't true."

"Well, we're not going to keep you. We just wanted to step in for a minute and bring you the cookies and this card. We weren't sure what you might need so we put just a little something in there for the family. You guys get what you need."

"You didn't have to do that. We know. Please take it and use it for something you need or want."

"Thank you both so much."

She wiped a tear that had escaped.

"Holly, I have a letter on my nightstand in my room. I was going to mail it but since you are here would you mind going in there and getting it instead?"

"Sure."

She told me where it was and sure enough there was a letter sitting there.

"Please come and see us when you get back and let us know how your trip went."

"Thank you. We definitely will."

Robert and I prayed with her and Frankie before we left.

We had a few more stops to make before we went back home to pack and make sure everything was in order for when we left on Monday.

I put the letter in my purse to read later.

It was a very heavy letter.

More so than I even could perceive.

Vicki loved her tin of cookies and so did Pastor & Sister Carson.

We paid our rent for January since we would be back a few days after the first and we did not want to be late.

Pastor Carson said they would drive by the house a few times and make sure everything was okay.

We knew everything would be okay.

Then home to pack and wrap the presents we got for Hannah and MJ.

This was going to be a great Christmas!

I couldn't wait to see Patty and Toby.

We hadn't really heard from them since Thanksgiving, but we could hardly stand to keep the secret every time we talked to anybody.

We'd heard from Lance. He had told us the Neon signs he'd had made were up but that since we were going to be home in a few days he would rather us see them in person. That a picture just wouldn't do them justice.

We could hardly wait.

But the best part about the conversation was when Lance thanked Robert for the gift his mother gave him from Robert.

"Oh, so you liked the dolphin clock did ya'?"

"Well as a matter of fact yes, yes I did. I liked it when I gave it to you and Holly for a wedding gift too."

"So, it was you! You're the one that gave us that. Brother, I loved it. Mom and Holly and her mom said no. But I liked it. That is why I gave it to you. I figured you would like it too since they said I couldn't keep it. I thought you might like it for your office. We didn't know who gave it to us. It didn't have a card, so we didn't know who gave it to us. I am so going to give Holly such a hard time over this. No hard feelings?"

"Nah! Like I said, I do like it. And as a matter of fact, that is exactly where the darn thing is, right on my desk. It works as a clock and a paperweight. Love ya man!"

"See ya in a few days."

He found me in the kitchen washing up the dishes.

"Holly, guess who loves that dolphin clock?"

"Who would that be."

"The person who gave it to us for a wedding gift, Lance!"

"You're kidding right?"

"Nope. He thought it was a hoot that we gave him back the same gift that he gave us."

"We didn't. You did!"

"Don't even go there!" Robert laughed at me.

"Is he angry that I didn't like it?"

"He didn't seem to be. He probably thinks you don't have very good taste anyways."

"Why would he think that?"

"Because you married me."

"Well, yeah, there is that." I joked.

"Very funny Mrs. Davis! Very funny!"

CHAPTER 69

We were so glad that we had put snow chains on the tires. It wasn't that there was a lot of snow everywhere, but some places had more than others. It took us a while longer than we had anticipated.

Mother and Sara were waiting for us when we pulled in. They both came outside and nearly slipped in the snow.

We grabbed our bags and hurried inside.

They must have known we would be needing something warm.

The aroma from the fresh brewed coffee smelled so good.

They wanted to know everything. And I do mean everything!

Did we take pictures of the house?

Did we take pictures of the yard?

How is school going?

How is work going?

How many churches have you been invited to preach at?

Are you both really singing together?

Is she a good cook?

Does he help around the house?

How are we set for finances?

So many questions, and that was just the first five

minutes.

You could tell they were excited to see us just as we were excited to see them.

We were exhausted and after Roberts mother went home, we took our bags to our room.

That sounded so different to me.

"Our room."

Even after all these months.

Mother said she would have a nice warm meal for us after we rested.

And rest we did.

The aroma of something cooking in downstairs lured us awake.

It took a minute for us to get our bearings.

We were just about to head downstairs when we noticed the tree topper glowing.

We hurried down to admire the handiwork.

Mother came in, "I missed your help this year. I had to commandeer your dad to come put the top on for me again. Your mom helped me decorate. We had a good time making it look all fancy for you both.

Look, your mom tucked an ornament in there that was yours when you were small.

She wanted you to have something special on here."

"Awe, that is so cute."

"You both did a very good job. I am going to have to tell her thanks for thinking about me. But as lovely as this tree is, and it is, it can't be near as lovely as whatever it is you have cooking in the kitchen. Can we eat? I am starving!"

We laughed and mother led the procession.

"Your mother brought over a fresh pan of

cornbread for you to go with your stew. She gave me the recipe. She said it is one of your favorites."

"Stew? You made me stew? You are absolutely my favorite mother-in-law in the whole world!"

"Well, thank you Robert," she laughed. "I hope I did it justice."

"Awe, it smells so good!"

He helped set the table and he ate like I had never fed him one ounce of food since we moved away.

"Mother, do you think anyone will be upset that we didn't do any actual Christmas shopping? We are giving cards with cash this year. With our schedules the way they were we simply didn't have time to shop. And, honestly, we didn't know what anyone would need or want this year."

"Oh, sweetheart, don't you know, we are all just happy to have you home. No one needs anything. The only thing we need is to see you."

"I hope so. I love shopping for everyone and just getting them the right thing, but we just couldn't get it done. I am so sorry."

"Holly, just having you both here is the best present ever."

She wiped a tear from her eye.

"I miss you both so much."

"Awe, mom, don't cry."

I put my arm around her and hugged her.

"We missed you too."

We hugged each other for what seemed to be forever.

Robert, I'm sure didn't know what to think.

Finally, he broke the ice.

"Um, would it be okay if I had some more of the

stew?"

We both started laughing through our tears.

CHAPTER 70

After we helped clean the kitchen and put everything away Robert called Lance.

"Hey, wanna take me up to the shop and show me those signs?"

Lance must have agreed to do so because Robert asked if it would be okay if he went with Lance for a little bit.

"Go. Have fun. I'll put our clothes away while you are gone."

He kissed me and grabbed his coat.

"What time are we going to Aunt Jessies on Christmas morning?"

"I figured we would go over there around nine or ten. Would that be okay? There is going to be a lot of people there. There always is.

You do know Brayden is living with them again, right?"

"I do know that. Bailey is working for Lance. I'm glad it worked out for them. Bailey is really a good guy. I remember him helping Josh with that go cart we got him that Christmas. They kept that thing running. I'm glad Lance hired him."

"That girl they hired though. She is not the most congenial of people. I hope she starts doing a better job for Lance.

I had to take my car in for an oil change and she was going to charge me $20.00. I didn't think that should be right, especially since the sign on the wall said $9.95 for the deluxe oil change.

She was almost in shock that the price was posted somewhere. I guess she thought she had to make it up as she went."

"Oh my! That won't be good for business. I hope they get it straightened out."

"Me too. That kid deserves a break. I will say that sign of his is awesome! It is like a big Wheel that is just rolling in place. Then he had the word "Wheel's" put under it. The one in the window is pretty too."

It was so nice just to sit and visit and make small talk.

I really did miss her.

I know all the things from the past. The things that happened. The mother she used to be. But thanks to Calvary, she is not the same person.

"Hey, did you hear back from Grandmother and Grandfather Abernathy? They are going to be at Aunt Jessies for Christmas, right?"

"The last I heard they were. They called yesterday afternoon to make sure you were still coming here for Christmas. I think they are as excited to see you as the rest of us."

"Good. She sends me letters all the time. I called her after Thanksgiving to let her know how it went. She seemed interested and happy that we'd had such a good turnout.

How is Memaw and Pappy? I can't wait to see them. We brought Hannah's and MJ's Christmas presents for them to give to them. I can't wait to hear if they like them."

"I'm sure they'll both love them. What did you get them?"

I was in the middle of telling her when Robert came home.

He seemed concerned.

"It's a good thing we went there."

"Really? What happened?"

"The girl that works for him had turned all the lights off, including the Neon signs. They are not supposed to be turned off. And on top of it she left the door unlocked."

"Oh my! That isn't good. What did Lance do?"

"He about lost it. He was so angry. He called her and told her she was fired."

"Right before Christmas?"

"Yeah, I don't think she really cared. She had a few choice words for him and then she hung up on him."

"Did you get everything back up and running?"

"Yeah. I am going to go in with him in the morning and help him try to make heads or tails of the office."

"Do you want me to go with you? I could probably help get the books in a little order?"

"That's up to you. We are going to leave early."

"Would that be okay mom? I know we just got here but I think we should go and try and help. Is that alright."

"Of course. You both go. I was just going to bake tomorrow anyways.

Robert, your family is coming out to Jessies for Christmas. We are going to have dinner in the barn. I didn't know if you knew that or not."

"That's good. The more the merrier. I can't wait to see

Toby and Jessie."

Robert shot me a look.

"Didn't you just see them a few weeks ago?"

I realized I had just about let the cat out of the bag.

"Yeah, but I still miss them."

"Well, you guys better get to bed. You are going to have to get up awfully early tomorrow."

"We have to get up early every day. What's one more day?"

But truthfully, I had wanted to sleep in, at least one day!

CHAPTER 71

Robert was right. The office was a total mess. But it was "pretty groovy" as Josh would have put it, pulling up to the shop while it was still dark and seeing the Neon signs shining like they did.

It was a good thing we had gotten up early enough to make a pot of coffee at home.

We worked until noon and had barely made a dent.

There were invoices everywhere. There was trash piled on top of trash that had been mixed with parts orders.

It was going to take longer than one morning.

By noon we were all starving and decided to close it down for the day.

We all knew where we were going to have lunch, the Burger Joint. Us and the rest of the town had the same idea.

It was a bit crowded, but not so crowded that I didn't recognize a familiar voice.

Why, Miss Hannah, Mr. MJ! What are you two doing here?

"Eating lunch with mama and daddy," MJ said as he pointed to his daddy.

They were standing behind us in line.

I bent down and hugged them both.

"Did you see any bears yet?"

"Any bears?"

"Yeah, bears, at your cottage. You know, bears."

"Oh! No Hannah. I have not seen one single bear. But I have seen a couple of rabbits and I think there is a squirrel living in one of my trees."

"Really?" They sounded excited at the thought.

"Yep! And guess what?"

"What?"

"Mr. Robert and I planted a white rosebush and a red rosebush in our yard. I told you we would."

"Did you take a picture?"

"I think we did. But I don't have one with me right now. But I will send you one if you want me too."

"Yeah." MJ said.

"Yeah, send one. One for me and one for MJ, 'cause he wants one too. Okay?"

"You got it! So, what are you going to eat today? A double-double with extra onions?" I joked.

"No," Hannah laughed. "Daddy might but I don't think I could eat one that big. Daddy can. MJ, can you?"

"I can. "Cause I'm big like daddy. See," he held up four fingers, "I'm four like daddy."

I hugged Lisa.

Robert shook their hands and introduced Lance to them.

They told them all about the Neon signs in front of the shop.

"Those just got put up a few days ago, didn't they?"

"Yeah, you've seen them already?"

"Are you kidding? I think MJ here knew as soon as they were ready. He noticed they were working on them a while back and asked a thousand questions. As soon as you turned them on, we had to go by there. We parked outside and watched them.

We've done that a few times. He loves how the wheel goes around like it does. Very impressive. So, you own it now? Coop was a pretty good mechanic, but I hear a lot of good things about it since you took over. Congratulations!"

"Thanks!"

"If you hear of anybody looking for job, send them my way. I just had to let the office girl go."

"Oh, that's too bad."

"I didn't have a choice. She has made a mess of things in the office. I need to get someone in there pronto."

"If we hear of anyone, we will sure let them know."

"I appreciate that."

We ordered our food and went to find a place to sit.

They ordered theirs to go.

I guess they didn't want to fight the crowd for a place to sit.

It was so worth the wait.

They tasted, well, they tasted like home!

CHAPTER 72

It was going to be a white Christmas. The snow had not melted, and fresh snow had fallen through the night.

We had helped bake goodies when we got home from helping Lance and had everything packed and ready to load so we wouldn't be getting a late start.

Our first Christmas as husband and wife.

It felt like the best present ever, waking up in his arms.

The very thing that I thought would never happen, having a husband and the possibility of having children, a family, well, that was the best present ever.

I am sure he thought I was a little foolish as I laid beside him, snuggling into his arms as he held me, and wept.

"Why are you crying babe?"

"It is too hard to explain. I am just feeling overwhelmingly blessed. I love you and I never want this feeling to end. I never want to know what it feels like to not have you with me. I can't find the words to express this, this feeling. I just know that the word love just doesn't cover it, and yet it does. I'm sorry you married such a cry baby but thank you for marrying me and making me the happiest I have ever been in my life."

"Thank you for marrying me. Can we just lay here a bit longer before we have to get up and go?"

"Or at least until we need a cup of coffee!"

"Deal!"

"Deal!"

Mother had gotten up and made a fresh pot of coffee.

The aroma wafted to the room.

"Can you smell that?"

"Oh, yes! And it is calling our name!"

"I guess cuddle time is over."

"I guess it is."

Mother had played Santa and the tree had presents underneath it when we came down for the first dose of civility.

"Good morning! Merry Christmas.!"

"Merry Christmas to you too Mom!"

Robert made us all three a cup of coffee.

It was easy enough. We all took it the same way.

"Do you want to open presents?"

"Mom, we didn't get presents for anyone this year, well, except for Hannah and MJ."

"Oh, I know, but I did, and I can't wait for you to open them. Come on."

We headed for the tree and sat down on the floor just as we had done the last few Christmases. The only difference was now we had Robert.

Mother was as excited as a little kid to be handing out presents.

Some were for the both of us and some for each of us.

New sheets for the bed. A new towel set.

Dress shirts and ties for Robert and a couple of

pairs of dress slacks.

She told him if he was going to go to different churches to preach that he needed to look the part.

A couple of dresses for me.

Way too many items.

Then there was one for each of us left.

A little box.

She handed one to each of us.

"Now, I know the boxes are little, but open them at the same time.

Robert shook his.

It didn't make a lot of noise at all.

We opened them to find a keychain with a set of keys on them.

We looked puzzled.

"Ok, let me explain. I know the car you have probably doesn't have but maybe thirty-five or forty thousand miles on it. And I also know that you take really good care of it. But I really wanted to get you a newer car, one that you could have for a few years that was just your own, for both of you. Is that okay?"

"Oh, mom! That is way too much. You shouldn't have done it."

"Well, it isn't just from me. Your Grandmother and Grandfather Abernathy asked if they could help pay for it. They knew you were going to be going to school for another year and that money would be limited to take care of any repairs so they suggested that we pool our money and get you a new car. Do you want to see it?"

"Yes, I want to see it," Robert said.

"Me too. But it is still too much, even for all three of you."

"I'm surprised you didn't see it when you walked by the window."

We went and looked out the window.

A brand new, maroon Ford LTD with a big bow!

"Oh, my word! That is beautiful!"

Robert headed to the door.

"Robert, don't you think we should get dressed first before we go out in the snow?"

"Uh, yeah. You are probably right. But, man oh man, that is a nice car."

He hugged mother and thanked her profusely!

I hugged her and thanked her as well.

She was beaming!

"Mother, as beautiful as this car is, you have got to stop buying us cars. You are going to go broke!"

"No, I won't. I got a job!"

You got a job? Where?"

"I am working for Pappy while you are away. Well, part time. I don't work on Tuesdays. I have Bible study and if I need time off, well, I am going to take it. Like while you are here. I can get everything caught up after you leave. I don't need the money. I just need something to do."

"Oh, mom! You are a treasure! I love you!"

We cleaned up the vestibule and took everything upstairs.

It didn't take us long and we were down for another cup of coffee and breakfast.

"Can we go look at the car first?"

"Yes, let's go look."

Mother got in the backseat and Robert drove us around the block.

"This is fantastic!"

“It is nice mom. Thank you so much!”

“Be sure and thank your grandparents. They went with me to pick it out. Your Grandfather knows his stuff. He asked questions that I would not have even thought to ask. He got it at a good price too. I think they know everybody in town. Do you like the color? Your Grandmother thought that you would. She loved the color. She said, since they didn’t have a pink one, that maroon was the next best thing.”

We laughed. That sounded right. Pink was her favorite color.

Robert loaded the car with all the baked goods while Mother and I made a quick breakfast.

Well a quick breakfast for she and I. Robert had ham and eggs and home fries and toast.

“You are going to be eating in just a few more hours. Are you sure you can eat all that?”

“Really? Have you ever seen me not be able to eat?”

“You and Toby run a close second on who can eat the most. I can’t wait to see them.”

“Me either. Let’s get this show on the road!”

CHAPTER 73

Josh was the first one to come outside when we pulled up.

After helping take all the baked goods into the barn he talked Robert into driving him around in it.

Pappy talked his way into a ride with them.

Aunt Jessie called out to them to go to the store and get some bags of ice.

With that they were gone.

Everyone was busy.

The barn had been transformed into Christmas magic.

There were candles everywhere and lanterns.

The heaters had all been turned on and it was a toasty cozy little place.

Tables and chairs were set with beautiful tablecloths.

The centerpieces were beautiful, as always and it was going to be the best Christmas ever!

Toby and Patty had not gotten there yet.

They were staying with Patty's parents and would be there in a little while.

Mother and I put the finishing touches on the table.

Arranging the silverware, or I guess I should say plasticware.

The amount of people that were invited had grown

into a multitude and Aunt Jessie did not have that much silverware or dinnerware for that many people.

Mother had brought the silver plated plasticware and some fancy disposable dinner plates.

It may have not been good china, but it was lovely.

My heart was so full that I began to sing as I helped her.

My favorite Christmas carol, “Silent Night”, started to escape my mouth as I worked.

I didn’t even realize that I was singing until I heard mother harmonizing with me.

She came up behind me and put her arm around me and we sang our first song together.

I turned to see her wiping her eyes.

“Holly, you sing so lovely.”

I was embarrassed.

“I am so embarrassed. I didn’t even realize I was singing.”

“Please don’t apologize for singing. I should have told you at your wedding how beautiful you sounded. Time and everything just got away from me.

But you do have a very lovely voice. Thank you for letting me sing with you.”

“I didn’t know you sang like you do either. I guess I should have. You played the piano at church before, well you know. I guess it has been such a long time that I forgot.”

We heard the car pull into the driveway.

We went to see how they had enjoyed the drive, but it wasn’t Robert, it was Toby and Patty.

I hurried out to see them.

I hugged Patty but she seemed a little distant.

We went on inside to get out of the cold.

After they hugged everyone, they asked to speak to Aunt Jessie and Uncle Joey alone.

I was so excited for them.

I could just imagine how excited they would be to hear that they were going to be grandparents!

They were upstairs for a while.

Long enough that Robert returned with the bags of ice.

Josh grabbed all three bags and took them into the barn and put them in the cooler that was set up by the tea pitchers.

Roberts parents and Lance were the next to arrive, followed by Patty's parents.

I had expected to see them beaming from ear to ear, then I realized, maybe they just hadn't told them yet.

It was starting to get to be a full house.

Memaw commandeered the men to start carrying the food over to the barn.

While they were doing so, Grandmother and Grandfather Abernathy showed up.

Robert and I thanked them over and over again for the car.

They seemed pleased that they'd had a hand in it.

Then Pastor Taylor and his family showed up.

His girls were getting so big now and their sweet baby boy was no longer a baby.

They still had their little dolls and he had some cars that he had brought with him to keep him occupied.

Brayden and Baily came and their parents.

I had only met their parents at church, so it was a pleasant surprise that they showed up.

Yes, it was going to be a full house, or barn.

But it was going to be family!

Everything had pretty much been taken over to the barn with the exception of the Turkeys. Toby, Patty, Uncle Joey, and Aunt Jessie came downstairs.

They did not look like they were excited about the good news.

"Before we all go to the barn to eat," Uncle Joey said, "I know it is really crowded in here, but Toby and Patty just told us some news. We would like to share it with all of you."

Patty's parents came and stood by Patty and Toby as well.

Patty looked like she was going to be sick. She was pale. Toby put his arm around her and pulled her to him.

I took Roberts hand in anticipation!

"Let me dad," Toby said.

"Okay son, go on ahead."

Toby paused, looking at Patty.

"A few weeks ago, Patty and I found out that we were expecting a baby."

"Congratulations!" A couple of people said.

"Thank you," Toby said, still looking at Patty as she raised her gaze to meet his. "But it was not meant to be. We lost the baby about two weeks ago. Patty miscarried."

Patty let the tears flow.

I squeezed Roberts hand and he pulled me close to him.

My heart fell into my stomach.

The tears flowed, and I couldn't stop them.

"We didn't want to put a damper on this joyous occasion. Although we are sad and disappointed, we know that it was just not God's timing."

Patty smiled at Toby.

"Please don't let this news take away from our time together. We wanted to let everyone know now so that you wouldn't be wondering why we weren't very talkative or if we just looked sad. We would rather you know than to wonder.

So, all we ask is that you keep us in your prayers while we walk through this. God will see us through. He always has and He always will. He has never failed us yet and I don't think He is going to start now. So now, let's eat. We are starving."

Everyone headed for the barn. Uncle Joey and Toby carried the platters full of turkey over.

I excused myself and went upstairs to the restroom.

I heard the footsteps coming up the stairs.

Patty knocked on the door.

"Can I come in?"

I opened the door and we fell into each other's arms and cried.

"I am so sorry Patty!"

"Me too!"

"I didn't tell anyone. My heart aches for you right now. I am so sorry."

"I know. It is so hard right now. Everything Toby said is true though.

We've got to trust that God knows what is best. It was a blow though.

I don't know why I am reacting like this. I was only about three months along. Not even that far really. I never knew that you could already love someone that wasn't even here yet. I don't think this baby was connected to the umbilical cord. I think it was connected straight to my heart."

"I'm sure it was. That is exactly how I felt when I was, well you know."

"You just keep praying for us. God has a plan. That I am sure of. If I didn't believe that, then there would really be no reason to move forward."

We wiped our faces and went to the barn while there was still food to be had.

We both knew there was no fear in all the food disappearing before we got over there. There was truly enough food to feed an army.

CHAPTER 74

Robert and I had a lot to discuss.

One of them was what were we going to do with an extra car?

We didn't need the expense of an extra car.

It didn't have but fifty-eight thousand miles on it.

It got great gas mileage and was still a great car.

Mother didn't seem to mind that we spent our mornings helping Lance.

Robert helped in the shop while Lance worked in the front office with me.

He and I tried to make heads or tails of some of the things that she had done.

Which clearly was just piles of paperwork on top of paperwork.

We were busy working on Saturday morning when we had unexpected visitors.

Toby and Patty came to the shop to have Lance work on the Fairlane.

It had been making a noise and it was clearly time for a tune-up.

Lance told them he should be able to have it ready for them by that afternoon.

They were going to leave it and go get some badly needed shopping done.

Patty had followed him over in her parent's car.

They pulled it into an empty bay and Lance joined Robert to see what was wrong with it.

It was going to take some work.

Even though Toby had taken care of it, changing the oil and everything the engine was going to have to be replaced. It had thrown a rod and that was no easy repair. On top of that, it needed new tires and a couple of hoses.

He didn't want to be the bearer of bad news, but it didn't look good.

Both Robert and Lance agreed, it was going to take a bit of money and a few days to repair the car.

Robert came into the office to let me know.

"Yikes! Can it be done cheaper than that?"

"That is cheaper. Lance is giving them a big discount. I am going to do most of the work. But it is still going to cost them.

That car has around two-hundred and thirty thousand miles on it. It is about worn out. I mean they have been driving it all over for the last few months and Toby was driving it a lot himself before then. Not to mention the miles it had on it before I bought it.

It would almost be better for them to buy a new one rather than throw money into this one. It is not going to last much longer even after we rebuild the engine."

"I don't think they can afford that right now."

"Probably not."

I picked up the phone and called my mother.

"Who are you calling?"

"My mom."

"You can't ask your mother to buy them a car. That

just wouldn't be right."

I looked at him and shook my head.

"Mom? Can I ask you a question?"

"Sure."

"I know you bought us this new car and everything, but now we are kind of stuck with two cars."

"Yeah."

"Well, we just learned of a young couple that are in need of a car. They can't afford to buy one and the one they have right now is beyond their budget to repair. Before we say anything to them, I wanted to make sure you would be okay with it."

Robert just looked at me with a perplexed look on his face.

"Would you care if we gave them our old car? It is still in great condition and doesn't have many miles on it. They really need it. I wouldn't just give it away to anyone without talking it over with you and Robert. Would you care if we did that?"

"Oh, honey, that car is yours and Roberts to do with as you will. You both pray about it and if you feel that it is the right thing to do then I am sure that you should do just that."

"Thanks mom. We will. I will give you all the information when I get home. Love you!"

"Love you too baby!"

I looked at Robert.

"Robert let's pray. I feel like it is the right thing to do but I don't want to do so if you don't think it is the right thing."

Robert moved in closer and took my hands and we prayed.

We both new that we were supposed to give it to them.

We just weren't sure how they would feel about it.

Robert talked to Lance and they came up with a plan.

They moved the car out of the bay and parked it behind the shop.

A plan was in place.

Toby and Patty came back to pick up the car after they had lunch with Pappy and Memaw.

"Is the car ready," Toby asked?

Robert said, "Yeah. Your car is ready. It is still in the bay. Lance is just finishing up on the tune-up."

"How much is it going to cost me?"

"He hasn't said to me. Holly, did he tell you?"

"No. He didn't give me a price."

"Let's go see if he is done and maybe he will let us know then."

We all went outside to the bay that Toby had pulled he Fairlane into.

Robert knocked on the door.

"Is Toby and Patty's car about done?"

"Yeah, open the door."

Robert and Toby raised the door.

"Uh, where is my car?"

Patty looked inside.

"Where is the car?"

"Right here. Isn't this your car?"

"No, this is your car."

"I don't think so. Holly, is this our car."

I looked at it. Walked around it. Looked inside it.

"Well, it does look familiar. It kind of looks like a car we had at one time. But didn't we give that car away just a few minutes ago?"

"What?"

"Yeah, I think I remember. Yep, this is the car we just recently gave away."

With that he reached out and handed Toby the keys.

"I don't get it," Patty said.

"Well, truth of the matter is, the Fairlane was going to cost a lot of money to repair. It had thrown a rod and the engine was going to need to be rebuilt. It had some hoses that needed replaced and it was in dire need of new tires. It has way too many miles to be on the road without a much-needed overhaul done on it.

Holly and I prayed about it and we feel that God would have you in this car.

It is low in miles and runs great. Lance and I just gave it a once over and much needed tune-up. It has snow chains on it and the tires are fairly new.

You guys need a safe vehicle to travel around in.

You need to be able to get from place to place safely and we don't need two cars.

So, if you would be of a mind to do so, let's trade cars.

Lance said he would keep the Fairlane here and work on it when he had the opportunity.

Would you both be willing to do that for us?"

"Are you kidding? Is he kidding Toby?"

"I don't think he is. You're not kidding us, right?"

"Not kidding."

Patty and I started crying while Toby and the guys cleaned out the Fairlane and she and I cleaned out their new car.

It was a good thing we did.

The letter that Gina had given me had fallen out of my purse and was between the seats.

CHAPTER 75

Mother was so happy about what we had done once we explained the situation.

"You two just made my heart smile. That was awfully nice that you did that for them."

"We would not have been able to bless them like that if you had not have blessed us with our new car."

"Maybe that is why I kept feeling like I was supposed to get it. God is so good! Even before we know we have a need He is always there to meet that need. He is so faithful."

"Yes, He is!"

"I just know that He has something planned for them. Something great! He is providing for them and opening doors for them to go to so many churches. After Patty recuperates, we may not see them for a while. They have a lot of churches lined up. God is moving in their lives and their ministry. I can't wait to see what all God has in store for us Holly.

We have a few churches that we are going to be ministering in when we get back."

"That is so good to hear," mother said. "Do you know what path He is leading you in? Are you going to be an evangelist or preach in a church?"

"You know, honestly, I don't know yet. We keep praying but I just don't have the answer. I love being able to go and preach at different churches and seeing God move. I have to say, when I see people coming down and giving their hearts to the Lord it thrills my heart. I miss seeing how their lives change and seeing how they grow in the Lord.

It is great when we go back to these churches and some are still there. Like when I got saved and Dean Matthews was there to mentor me and walk along beside me. I miss knowing if there is someone there doing that for these new Christians.

But whatever it is, I am, we are," he said as he pulled me closer, "willing to do."

And we were.

We were willing to go anywhere He would lead us.

It was so sweet to see Miss Hannah and MJ the next morning.

Hannah was carrying her new doll. MJ was carrying his new action figure.

GI Joe was his new favorite toy now.

They made sure to tell us everything they had gotten from Santa.

It was a list as long as your arm.

"Miss Holly, do you like my new baby? Her name is Becky."

"Becky huh? I like that name."

"You do? Me too. I have another baby that Santa got me. Her name is Shirley.

Well, this doll was named Shirley. But she didn't like that name. And my other baby had a name called Becky. But she didn't like her name. So, they traded names."

"Well, what a coincidence that they both wanted to change names. That was pretty nice that they just traded like that."

"Yep. They are good friends like that. I let them do that because they are my new babies and it is hard to come to a new name for babies. So, I let them just change names."

"Well I think that is very nice of you to do that."

"I know. I am very nice. Where is Pappy and Memaw. I want to tell them my new babies name. Memaw gived her to me."

"I bet she will love it. They should be here any minute now. Do you want to sit here and wait for them?"

"Can MJ sit here too?"

"Of course. MJ do you want to sit here too?"

"Where is Pappy? See my GI Joe?"

"I do. I bet Pappy is gonna love him."

"He is in the Army. GI Joe. He has a Jeep."

"I didn't know that."

"Yeah. He has a... Pappy!!!!"

They both took off running to show off their new toys and to give explanations.

Lisa leaned over and told me that they both loved the toys.

She said Hannah had dressed the doll in all the new outfits that we sent, and MJ had maneuvered the Dump Truck all over the house moving things from one place to the other. Mostly Lego's.

I thanked her for letting us know.

I turned to her. I wanted to make sure that she understood exactly what I wanted to say to her.

"Lisa, I want you to know that I do not ever want to overstep any boundaries. I would rather that you let me know what you are wanting to get them before we buy something. I will always ask or try to find out from you what they want before I buy it. You and Tony are their parents and I just want to thank you for letting us have this little bit."

She hugged me and thanked me.

Then she went and rescued Memaw and Pappy and took them to Children's Church.

Memaw and Pappy had heard about the car switch.

"You two are such a blessing! Toby and Patty really needed to be blessed. Are you sure you didn't want to sell the car? You could have put the money in savings or invested it?"

"We did invest it," Robert smiled.

"Well, I guess you did, didn't you," Pappy said.

It was so great to see Grandmother and Grandfather Abernathy at church that morning.

They invited us to have lunch with them the next day at our favorite place, Paulie's.

"I could go for a good Lemon Tart," I said.

"Me too," Robert licked his lips. "They still have them, don't they?"

"Oh yes they do, and they are every bit as good as you remember," Grandmother said with a twinkle in her eye.

It was a date.

Roberts mother had invited us to come over for Sunday dinner. How could we not go?

We were both going to gain ten pounds before we went back to our home away from home.

Mother joined us and as was expected, dinner was spectacular.

We couldn't stay and visit because Robert had been invited to preach that night.

We went home so he could prepare a sermon.

Mother said he could use her study. So, he used her study and she went to take a nap.

I was left alone to fend for myself.

I remembered the letter that Gina had given me.

I figured now was as good a time as any to read it.

CHAPTER 76

Dear Holly,

First off, I want to thank you so much for inviting us to your Thanksgiving Dinner.

You and your friends were such gracious hosts.

I had not seen Pastor and Sister Carson in a while. It was so good to see them. It made my heart happy that they were there.

They have already come by the house since then to see us and pray with us.

I had asked them not to come a while back because I was going through so many treatments that I never knew when I would be home.

Sister Carson does calls occasionally to check on us but still, I just haven't been up to seeing anyone.

I'm glad she and I had the opportunity to visit that day. There were many things that I needed to tell her. She is one of the sweetest ladies that I have ever met.

I am getting off track as to why I started this letter.

I do get a bit tired and a little sideways in my train of thought on occasion, so please forgive me if I start to prattle on.

Holly, I want to thank you and Robert for taking such an interest in my boys.

I knew you were special the way they talked about you.

Tell Robert thank you for inviting them to come to

church.

Jonah, or JoJo as everybody calls him, came into my room that night and told me all about going to the altar and giving his heart to the Lord.

I cried and prayed with him.

It was an answer to prayer.

He is such a sweet boy.

All three of them are.

Hard workers too. Just like their dad!

They have all three had some sort of job since I became sick.

They have all pitched in and cleaned house and did odd jobs until they could find jobs.

They have even mastered laundry.

They have had to take up a lot of slack with their dad working two jobs.

When Willy started working for the grocery store, he decided he would do the grocery shopping. He has gotten quite good at it.

He works with a lot of women who are more than happy to tell him how to cook something.

Mostly he cooks spaghetti and meat sauce.

It is easy and there are usually leftovers, and everybody gets full.

But it does get redundant, I'm sure.

I haven't had the energy to cook in a long time. The treatments take a lot out of me.

It seems as if I stay tired.

For a while I thought the treatments were working.

They had told us that things had turned around for us. It was going to be a long road to recovery, but at least it looked possible.

Then about three months ago they told us that the

treatments were no longer being effective.

I was out of remission and the cancer had returned with a vengeance.

Now it was going into my spine and my lungs and I would have to start doubling up on the treatments to try to shrink it.

They wanted me to have surgery and then more chemotherapy and then radiation.

There was no guarantee that any of it would work.

They said that if I did nothing that I could possibly have six to eight months to live.

With it, there was no guarantee that I would have longer than that. If it went well, then I could live another two to five years.

Noah did not take it well.

We came home to discuss what our options were.

We did pray about it. A lot!

I told him that I was not strong enough to go through more surgeries and chemo and radiation. Especially if there was no guarantee.

He wanted me to fight. And I am. Just not the way he wanted me too.

How could I put my family into any more debt? My children, my sweet babies have missed out on so much.

Children should not have to take care of their mother, not like this.

They have done far and beyond what they should have had to do.

And I know, if it had been my mother or my father, that I would have done the same.

We do these things because we love so hard.

Oh, how I love them!

I never knew that your heart could walk outside of

your body until I had those boys. But it does.

When I look into their handsome faces and see the hurt in their eyes when they look at me, my heart breaks into a million pieces.

I know what it is like to lose your parents. Both of my parents were killed by a drunk driver when I was just seventeen years old.

Noah and I had been dating for a few months.

He was going to college here. He was almost through his third year when they were killed.

He was working his way through college and was going to be working in finance.

He is a very smart man.

But when they died, I was left all alone. My older brothers had moved away when they got married. They had families of their own. I didn't want to go live with them.

I had one month to go before I finished high school.

My parents had life insurances that paid off the house.

My oldest brother came out to take care of everything.

He made sure that the house was paid off and then come to find out they had left the house to me.

This old house we live in right now has always been my home.

I turned eighteen two weeks after they died.

Noah knew he loved me, and I knew that I loved him.

As soon as I graduated, we got married.

Not a big wedding. Just the Justice of the Peace.

I got a job working in a Department store and he worked full time already.

I really don't know how we had time to date.

He was going to school full time and working full time. Somehow, we had made it work.

We debated on whether he should finish school the next year.

His parents weren't happy that we had gotten married.

They didn't really care for me.

We knew we couldn't count on them for any support.

But the one thing that my parents had taught me to do was to pray and even though Noah's parents weren't happy with him, they had taught him to pray too.

That is where we met, was at church.

He had move out here to go to school and had started going to the Carson's church. Our family went there. I had a major crush on him as soon as I saw him.

It took him a while, but he finally came around.

So, that is what we did. We prayed!

We both felt that God wanted him to finish school.

So, he did.

It was hard. It is hard to take care of a house, pay bills, go to school full-time and be married.

But we did it.

JoJo was born two months after he graduated.

What a blessing it was when the school called him and offered him a full-time position working in the Bookkeeping department.

He has been there ever since.

But it didn't help that I had little stairstep children.

A year after JoJo we had William, Willy, and a year later we had Franklin.

Three boys.

I know that things would have been different if my parents had not been killed.

I do wish they were still here. I miss them terribly!

But only God knows the reasons for some things.

After a while it looked like we were going to have breathing room.

He started getting raises and everything was getting better.

I was able to teach Sunday School and we went to church every Sunday and Wednesday.

The boys were always excited to go to church.

Noah even taught their Wednesday night boys class.

Then a little over two years ago, I thought I was pregnant again.

To tell you the truth, we looked at it as a blessing.

We thought that maybe finally we were going to get our little girl.

We both wanted a little girl so badly.

When I finally made it to the doctor, it was not the news we were hoping for.

I was not pregnant after all.

They sent me straight to the oncologist.

I had uterine cancer and they scheduled surgery right away.

My chances of having a little girl were gone.

Everything was gone.

I had to start chemo right away as well as radiation.

Then they found it was spreading so they doubled the chemo and the radiation.

Even with insurance it wasn't enough.

We had never had a mortgage on the house since we were married.

We do now.

Noah works two jobs and the boys are doing everything they can.

The house payment gets paid and so does everything else.

Above all, we pay our tithes first and foremost.

I was too weak to go to church. I barely have the strength to leave the house to go to the doctor or hospital.

And Noah was working on Sundays and any time that he had off in the evenings and weekends.

So, we quit going to church.

At first the boys would walk on Sunday mornings.

But one Sunday after they had left to go to church, I tried to get up to go to the bathroom and fell.

I hit my head and laid there until they returned and found me.

Now they only leave me while they are all at school or for a very short period of time.

Most always someone is here with me since Noah can't be.

Well, now you know the whole sordid story.

Well, most of it.

You see, Noah and I know that I am out of remission, but the boys don't.

We are not going to tell them.

I have written each of them a letter.

They are in this envelope.

I know that I am asking an awful lot of you.

You see, I barely know you and you barely know me.

But I do know God, and I have been praying as always for guidance.

I have felt so compelled to ask you to do this huge favor for me.

You see, Noah won't be able to.

He is going to need someone to come alongside him and help him when the time comes.

I hope Robert can rise to that occasion.

But Holly, for some reason, my boys have taken to you

and your husband.

I may be wrong, but I don't think so, but I believe that you both love my boys.

When we were at your home for Thanksgiving, that was honestly the first time that I have gone anywhere besides the doctor or hospital.

I have not had that kind of energy in a long time, and I have not had it since.

But I am so glad that I got to see them interact with you.

They don't have aunts or uncles or really any family around at all.

Once Noah's parents turned their backs on us, the whole family did as well. Our boys do not even know them.

But when I saw them with you two, I knew they had a place where they could take their broken hearts and find healing.

Frankie told me that you sing, according to him, "almost as good as you mom."

He told me he asked you to learn my song.

Well, it isn't my song, but it is one that I sang to them when I would rock them to sleep. And I sing it when I have my alone time with the Lord.

You see, no matter what I am going through, I can sing because I am happy, and free. And I truly do believe that if His eye is on the little sparrow, then how much more He watches over me and cares for me.

Holly, if you could, learn this song and please sing it at my funeral, I would appreciate it.

Please let my babies know that I am in a better place and that I am longing to see them there.

Please let them know that they were loved by me. That

I might be in heaven, but a part of my heart has stayed here with them.

Also, please take care of Noah.

He has been my rock.

I love this man with all my heart.

He is going to be at a loss as to what to do.

I have already made the arrangements with Pastor Carson and Sister Carson.

They will talk with Noah when the time comes. But I am counting on you.

Please love my boys for me.

Thank you, Holly!

If it is too much to ask, I understand.

Just pray about it is all I ask.

Sincerely,

Gina

CHAPTER 77

I sat there stunned. I wiped tears that had fallen from my eyes.

I fell on my knees and cried and prayed.

My heart was broken.

I could barely fathom the pain she was feeling.

To know that you were going to have to leave your babies and never see them again.

I could understand that.

I remembered that night so vividly when Hannah was born.

I remember when they took her from me in the hospital, the tugging in my heart as it was ripped from my very soul.

I never thought that I would see her again.

I never thought that I would have the opportunity to know that people that were pouring into her little life.

But God did know. He knew the very plans that He had always known from the beginning.

I reached under my pillow and touched every picture. Looked at every sweet, quirky little smile.

That face! Oh, how I loved that little face.

Then I thought of MJ.

I wondered what his mother thought.

Did she miss him half as much as I missed

Hannah?

I couldn't know her story.

MJ might never know it.

But he had people that were around him that were going to pour love into him just like JoJo, Willy and Frankie were going to need.

I didn't need to pray about doing that.

I was going to love those boys forever.

But I knew that Robert and I would need to pray for guidance.

We would need to pray for the right things to say.

We would need to pray that our hearts would be open to hear their tears and know how to respond.

We needed to pray on how we could be a representative of Jesus to them.

Yes, we were going to need to pray.

Robert came upstairs to start getting ready for church.

He saw that I had been crying and wanted to know why.

"I read Gina's letter."

"Are you okay?"

"No, well, yes. My heart is just broken. You need to read it later or tomorrow. Now is not the time."

"Okay. Well, let's get ready so we will have time to practice a song or two before church. Do you think your mother will mind if we practice on her piano?"

"I don't think so."

It didn't take us long after praying and practicing a couple of songs that we knew which one we were to sing.

It was a packed house that night.

The young people were all sitting up front.

Robert and I were introduced for the first time to our little church as Mr. and Mrs. Robert Davis.

Grandfather and Grandmother Abernathy had even come back that evening to hear Robert preach.

They didn't know, well actually, no one but Mother knew that we were going to sing that night.

Toby and Patty had come to hear him preach.

It was a bit overwhelming to say the least when Robert announced that we were going to sing a song for them.

We had sung together a few times but not really in front of people that we had known.

I was so nervous.

I wanted to tell them to all close their eyes and not look at me.

I think Robert could feel the apprehensiveness in me.

He reached over and took my hand which got my attention.

"Just sing as if you have an audience of one, sing it for Jesus," he smiled at me.

I took a deep breath and we began to sing.

The words fell from my heart as I felt the Holy Spirit begin to minister through the song.

"If you've knelt beside the rubble of an aching broken heart,

When the things you gave your life to fell apart,

You're not the first to be acquainted with sorrow grief or pain

But the Master promised sunshine after rain

Hold on my child, joy comes in the morning

Weeping only lasts for the night

Hold on my child, joy comes in the morning

The darkest hour means dawn is just in sight

To invest your seeds of trust in God in mountains you can't move
You have risked your life on things you cannot prove
But to give the things you cannot keep for what you cannot lose
Now, that's the way to find the joy God has for you
Hold on my child, joy comes in the morning
Weeping only lasts for the night
Hold on my child, joy comes in the morning
The darkest hour means dawn is just in sight!

The song penetrated the hearts of so many that night that after Robert preached so many came to the altar.

So many with hurts that had dared to linger and stay, were given a promise.

They would have joy in the morning.

I needed to hear that myself.

To know it myself.

I had to believe it deep down in my soul because I was going to have to live that out in front of three young men down the road and I needed to know that this was truth spoken into my heart and my soul so that I could speak it into theirs.

CHAPTER 78

New Year's Eve was going to be especially hard this year.

There were a lot of things that I had been able to conquer these last few years, but for some reason it was still hard for me to make it to church on a Tuesday night.

"What is taking you so long to get ready? We need leave in a short time to make it to church. Toby and Patty wanted us to come. Hey, what is a foot washing service."

I smiled when I remembered the first time I experienced a "foot washing service."

"Sorry. I don't mean to take so long."

I really didn't. But this would be the first time I had ever been to church on a Tuesday evening.

I thought I was going to be sick.

"Are you okay?"

I looked at him, almost pleading with him to not make us go.

He came and sat down on the side of the bed.

"What is going on?"

I turned away as I felt the tears come to my eyes.

"What is wrong with you girl?" I thought. "It's just church!"

He took my hand and pulled me to the bed to sit by

him.

I was trembling.

"Are you sick? Do you not feel well? Do you need to go to the doctor?"

I shook my head.

"Holly, then what is going on? Are you upset about something? Did I do something to upset you? Did Lance say something today to upset you? I know he can be a little crass, but I don't think he would do something to hurt you. What is it?"

I felt foolish.

Why was I letting this get to me?

I hadn't even realized that it was Tuesday until Robert had asked if we were going to leave on Friday or Saturday to go home. I counted the days and realized that today was Tuesday and we were supposed to go to church tonight.

"Holly?"

"I feel like a stupid fool letting myself get upset like this."

"What happened? Did somebody say something? Really, did I say something or do something?"

"It isn't you. It's, well, I guess it's just me."

"What are you talking about?"

"Robert, I know that I told you what happened to me growing up. I don't know if I ever let you know that the things my Father did to me was always on Tuesday nights at our church."

"The church down the street? The church that he preached at?"

"Yes, that church. Every Tuesday night after my mother would leave the house, he would take my hand and walk me to the church and do the things that he did to me. It was a rare Tuesday night that we missed going there.

Since he died, I have not been to a church service on a Tuesday night. Ever! Tonight, well, it will be the first time."

"Oh, Holly, I know you told me the things that he did. I just didn't realize that he did those things to you at your church."

He pulled me close to him and held me.

"If you don't want to go, I totally understand. We can stay here. We don't have to go."

"That's just it. I want to go, and I don't want to go at the same time. Does that even make sense?"

"Yeah. I mean. You are not that little girl anymore. You are a born-again child of God."

"I know. I want to go and pray the old year out and the new year in. I want to see Aunt Jessie and Uncle Joey. I haven't hardly had any time with Josh. And I would love to see Toby and Patty tonight and hear them sing and preach. But when I think about walking in through those doors, I feel like my head is going to explode. I have this fear that comes all over me. I don't want to live like this. I don't want to walk in this fear. The more I have thought about it today, the more it has felt like chains are being wrapped around me.

Will you just stay with me when we get there?"

"Oh baby, like glue. I will not leave your side. Babe, you know this is not what God wants for you? His word tells us that He has not given us a spirit of fear. We know that because it says so in 2nd Timothy. He has given you power, love, and a sound mind. Satan wants to rob you of that. He is the one that is tormenting you.

When these things come to your mind, when the devil starts beating you up with these thoughts, that is when we put on our helmet of salvation and we dwell on the whatsoever's."

"The what so whatsits?"

"The whatsoever's. You know, *Philippians 4:7-9 says, "7: And the peace of God which passeth all understanding, shall keep your hearts and minds through Christ Jesus. 8: Finally, brethren, whatsoever things are true, whatsoever things are honest, whatsoever things are just, whatsoever things are pure, whatsoever things are lovely, whatsoever things are of good report, if there be any virtue, and if there be any praise, think on these things. 9: Those things, which ye have both learned, and received, and heard, and seen in me, do: and the God of peace shall be with you.*

The whatsoever's.

Nowhere listed in those things is fear.

Don't let him rob you of the things God has in store for you. For us!

Do you want to pray before we go?"

"Yes, will you pray with me?"

Robert took my trembling hands and prayed.

"Heavenly Father, Lord, we come to you in need of peace. Satan has been doing his thing on Holly all day. Lord, we both know that you do not want her to walk in fear or condemnation any longer. We come to you and ask that you would set her free from this bondage that he is trying to keep her in. We pray in Jesus name that Holly would have joy in her heart, peace of mind and that she would walk in Your fullness. That the whatsoever's would fill her very soul. In Jesus name we ask these things. Amen"

"Amen!"

He kissed me and then we had to go.

Mother was going to go with us.

She was waiting downstairs with a meatloaf and a load of mashed potatoes.

We had baked cookies to bring as well.

I was so glad that she was coming with us. I felt like I had neglected her since we were there.

Working with Lance at his shop pretty much every morning was taking away the time I could spend with her.

I had told Lance and Robert that I was not going to come back on Thursday and Friday. I was going to spend the time with my mother and his.

"Fine! Desert me in my time of need."

"Time of need indeed! You need to put a sign in your window. "Slave wanted!"

They laughed.

We had made a dent, albeit a little one. Some things were mostly sorted. Whoever he hired was going to have to know what they were doing to get this place in order.

I told him I would pray that God would send just the right person.

"You do that Holly! I need all the prayers I can get."

Memaw and Pappy were there, of course. They always came out to help Aunt Jessie get things cooked to bring for the dinner. They were carrying in boxes of food, just like always.

Robert got the box out of the trunk that Mother had so lovingly packed. I carried the tin of cookies.

Josh came out to greet us. He always gave the best

hugs!

"Hi sis!"

"Hi baby brother! Where is your girlfriend?"

"We broke up."

"You broke up? Why?"

"Well, it is kind of a long story. Short version is, she isn't sure that she wants to be with someone that might be a preacher someday. She thought that it would be better if we didn't see each other for a while. We broke up right before school started up."

"How come you didn't write me and tell me? Man, that is tough."

"Yeah, but you know. I would rather know that now than a few more months down the road. You see, I know that God has called me to preach. Either in a church or as evangelist, like Toby. And if she doesn't feel that calling in her heart, and on her life, then she is not the one I am supposed to be with.

God has a plan for my life. I may not always be walking one hundred percent in it, but I sure do try."

"Josh, have I ever told you that you are my favorite little brother? You are right. God does have a plan for you. A perfect one. One of these days you are going to meet the perfect girl and God is gonna say, "You see that one, she's the one. She's the one I had planned for you all along. Now go get her!"

He turned red.

It felt funny calling him little brother when he was already a head taller than me.

Robert came back outside after putting taking the food to the kitchen.

Josh said he would take the cookies in for me. I watched him sneak a couple of them out of the tin before they made it inside.

"You ready?"

"As I'll ever be."

I took a deep breath and my heart leapt into my throat as Robert took my hand and walked inside with me.

As we passed through the doors I silently prayed.

"Lord you have not given me a spirit of fear. Lord, thank you for setting me free of this. I am no longer a prisoner of this. Lord, break this chain of fear that has come upon me. I thank you Lord for your peace and joy. I thank you for filling me with your fullness. In Jesus name!"

I could see Patty and Toby and others that I knew. Pappy was standing just inside.

As we walked inside, the chains that had so tenuously enveloped my soul, choking the very air out of my lungs, seemed to fall by the wayside.

There was a love, a perfect love, a peace that I was never going to be able to explain, that swept over me like a wave.

Like a breath of fresh air breathing into my heart. It felt like freedom.

I know my countenance changed.

It had been too long that I had let fear and anger and the lies that Satan had tried to strangle me with, had controlled my life, my thoughts.

I felt the love of God wrap around me and through me.

I knew that I was set free.

I was no longer going to walk in that weakness.

I felt such an urge to just praise Him.

"Are you okay," Robert asked?

"Oh, yes! I cannot explain what just happened. But Robert, I am never going to let Satan have that control over me again. Did you feel what I felt when we walked inside?"

"I don't think so. What did it feel like?"

"Deliverance!"

CHAPTER 79

I had not had much time to visit with Memaw and Pappy.

I missed seeing them.

We'd had such an awesome time when we had lunch with my grandparents.

Grandfather said he felt like the lone man out when he was the only one to eat the chocolate mousse.

Robert took care of that and ordered a lemon tart as well as a chocolate mousse.

They asked a dozen or more questions about how school was going and how we liked our little house.

They were genuinely happy to see us happy.

We thanked them again for the car.

"Glad to do it, glad to do it," Grandfather said.

"Did you like the color? They didn't have pink so I thought maroon would have to do. Did you like it?"

"It is beautiful."

We told them that because of their generosity we were able to bless Toby and Patty.

"That is the loveliest thing."

"It is hard being in full time ministry like they are. They needed a reliable car to get around in."

"My heart broke for the poor girl when they announced their news. We are praying for them. We have put them on our daily prayer list."

"I know. We had found out that she was pregnant at Thanksgiving. But we were under strict orders not to tell anyone. I was so excited for her and Toby. She is like a sister to me. I was devastated when they broke the news."

"Not to be nosy, but when are you two planning on, well, you know?"

"Mother, now, we are not gonna pry into their private lives like that. If they want us to know, then they will tell us."

"We don't mind saying. We did talk about it. We are going to wait until Robert graduates from school. That way we can devote the time that a baby will need."

"It's not like we don't want one now," Robert interjected, "but it wouldn't be fair to do that to a baby."

"You two kids have a good head on your shoulders. Just don't wait too long afterwards. We won't be around that long." He winked at us.

It was really a pleasant visit.

Thursday though, that was going to be just a day for mother and myself.

After Robert left to go help Lance one more morning, mother and I got dressed and decided to go shopping and have a nice lunch.

Mother didn't seem to shop at Mardell's anymore. We found another little shop that had opened that was built with her in mind.

Only clothes and they were oh so fashionable!

We spent plenty of time and plenty of money there.

It was quite a pleasant experience.

We didn't have to drive everywhere to shop.

This little store was inside a mall that had just opened.

We found a shoe store and spent both time and money in there as well.

Robert was needing new shoes. His were starting to look a little worn.

Mother begged me to let her pay for them.

I relented and hence she became his favorite mother-in-law.

There was a new little Mexican food restaurant that we had never heard of, "Tortilla Flats" it was called.

It smelled even better than it looked.

Neither one of us were familiar with the menu so we ordered the number one platter.

We should have ordered only one.

There was so much food. We were wishing we had a way to call Robert so he could come up and finish both of our plates.

He was going to enjoy the wonderful leftovers when we took them home to him. We even bought him a jar of their salsa.

"I am going to have to learn how to make this. Robert is going to want to eat this all the time."

"I am sure he would eat just about anything put in front of him," mother laughed. "That boy can eat. I don't know how he keeps looking so trim."

"He is always on the go. Even though Frankie comes and does the yard every Saturday, if he is still out there working when Robert gets home, he goes out there and helps him. He helps do the housework. He works and goes to school. He has more energy than a toddler."

"Yes, he does. I watch him run up and down the stairs two or three times every morning while you are getting ready. He takes you a cup of coffee then he comes down to drink a cup with me, then he is back up with you to finish getting ready, then he is back down. And he isn't walking, he is running. Makes me tired just watching him."

Neither one of us was hungry when we got home.

Robert was taking a nap, so I decided to take a nap with him.

Mother went next door to see Sara so we could make plans to spend time with her the next day.

I felt bad for waking Robert when I snuggled next to him on the bed, but I didn't feel that bad.

We only had two more days and then we were going to have to leave.

I was going to miss them all so terribly much.

I guess there was never going to be enough time in the world to love on all the people that you wanted to.

I wanted to stay there forever and visit and love on all of them, but I knew that we had to get back home.

We both had to be at work on Monday.

We had both taken time off without pay.

We couldn't afford to stay gone longer than that.

Robert had one more week before he had to start classes and I had to make time to see Gina.

As much as I loved and missed everyone here, my heart longed to see those boys and love on them.

Gina was right. We did love those boys.

Robert had read the letter and we both prayed for all of them.

I could not imagine what it would be like to lose my mother like that.

To see her so sick and hope that she was going to get better, not knowing.

Robert went with us the next day so he could spend time with his mother.

I am sure she enjoyed seeing him.

She was so proud of him.

And why wouldn't she be?

He was tall and handsome, and that red hair. Be still my heart.

And he was mine, well, ours.

We were not above eating at Tortilla Flats one more time.

This time though we really looked over the menu and we picked a bigger platter for all three of us to share and Robert ordered the number one all for himself.

That night we went to eat dinner at Memaw and Pappy's. It was nice to finally sit and just be loved on by them.

They were my rock.

It was always a heartwarming feeling when they would hug me and Memaw would call me her little Holly Del.

She had more pictures for my album.

I always knew they were going to be watching and praying over my little pieces of heaven. It was funny, I never realized that now, whenever I thought of Hannah, my heart always went to MJ too.

I loved both of those little angels.

My dreams weren't built around little Hannah so much. But when I did dream of her, MJ was always there.

"Thank you for watching over those babies like you

do," I whispered in Memaws ear.

She wiped my tears and said, "Oh, darlin, it is our greatest pleasure."

I knew she meant it.

Saturday morning came too soon.

We didn't leave right away.

The roads were icy. We knew we would be driving on slippery roads most of the way home.

We had so many tins of cookies to pass out when we got back plus all the new clothes and everything else.

This was going to be the first time for the long trip home in the new car.

Lance had come home from the shop to say goodbye and to thank us for all the help.

"We'll be praying for the right person to come along. She's out there somewhere. Just be nice to her."

"I will. I will."

"And pay her good money."

"Hey, let's don't get carried away here!"

We all laughed and then we hugged and said our goodbyes.

I know I cried for thirty minutes while Robert held my hand.

Goodbyes are the hardest when you love them.

CHAPTER 80

Even with the snow chains we had slid several times.

There were trucks salting the roads, but it only helped a bit.

We were blessed more than some. Our car never slid completely off the road.

We talked about how glad we were that Toby and Patty would have a better car to travel in.

God works in mysterious ways.

Who would have known that they were going to needing a vehicle and that we would be able to bless them just as we had been blessed?

They had cancelled a couple of revivals to let Patty spend time with family so she could heal.

Her body would be just fine, but her heart needed mending.

She and Toby were going to be just fine.

Before you know it, they were going to have a family.

Robert and I prayed for them as we drove home.

Our thoughts and prayers went to Gina and Noah and those three boys.

"We should go see them tomorrow after church don't you think?"

"We probably should. Robert, I am not sure what to

say to her. What do you say in a situation like this?"

"That is a good question. I don't know the answer, but it is a good question. I haven't been around anyone other than when I was in the Army that was dying. Out of all of them, Sam was the only one that I knew that had a relationship with the Lord. I don't mean to sound horrible, or like I am prying, but what did people say to you and your mother when your dad died that brought any peace to you?"

"That is a whole different scenario. When my dad died it had been a horrible life with him up to that point. There was no love there between him and me. I guess there really wasn't any love between him and my mother either. So, anything anyone could have said wouldn't have meant anything to either of us. We had to pretend like we were sad that he died.

Now, after all this time, I guess I really don't think about him much, only that it is sad that he died without knowing Jesus. That he is spending eternity in a place that was never intended for him. So, I guess I don't know how to answer your question. They could say nothing because there really was no grief."

"Yeah. I don't think this is going to be the case."

"Me either. One thing I do know."

"What's that?"

"When she leaves this earth, when she takes that last breath, she will take a new one in heaven."

"I think you are right about that one babe. I think you right about that one!"

We made it home early enough to take everything inside and get a fire going.

Frankie had done a great job clearing the sidewalk for us.

He had the yard looking pristine. Well as pristine as you could make a yard full of snow. He had made sure the sidewalks were clear and that the plants that needed covered were covered, especially the roses.

Neither one of us felt like cooking so we grabbed the tin of cookies we had brought for Vicki and headed over to the Whistle Stop for dinner.

It was a pretty good crowd.

We were greeted by a familiar face.

JoJo was working!

He smiled and waved at us as he cleaned off the tables and headed to the back of the house.

Vicki appeared out of nowhere and hugged us.

She hugged us again when we handed her the tin full of her favorite cookies.

We were seated quickly and ordered our favorite. Meatloaf!

She was busy working but joined us when things started settling down.

"How was your Christmas?"

"It was really sweet. How was yours?"

"It was awesome. Angie and her new husband came into town for a few days. He is going to be an assistant Pastor in a church over in Oklahoma. They were on their way and stopped by here to see me. I love that girl. Her new husband is a very nice guy. They seemed to be made for each other."

"I forgot to tell Toby about them. He is going to be so happy when we tell him. I think they were friends."

Robert just looked at me.

I smiled.

I was going to have to explain to him how blessed he truly was later tonight!

"How is JoJo doing? Is he working out for you here? He seems to be a hard worker."

"Holly, that boy is a Godsend! He is one of the hardest working young men that I have ever had working here. He doesn't complain. He goes above and beyond anything that is asked of him.

I am thinking of asking him if he would want to be a waiter a couple of nights and see if he likes it. He could make some good tips. The people that come in here seem to really like him. He is so handsome too.

We have a family that comes in about once a week. They have a teenage daughter that is always smiling at him when he walks by. His little face always turns red. I think he could have just about any girl he wanted. But all he does is study when there is down time and work.

A few times he has taken some cheeseburgers home with him. He said, Willy makes decent food, but he was really tired of spaghetti."

"Those boys are a treasure."

"Yes, they are. JoJo calls home every evening to make sure one of the boys is home with their mom. Their dad is always working.

She didn't look to well at your house on Thanksgiving. But you could sure tell that those boys love her and that she loves them."

"That's for sure."

"Is his shift just about over?"

"Yeah. He should be done in about thirty minutes or so."

"Do you mind if we take him home? I know you usually do, don't you?"

"No, I don't mind. I can stay here and finish up.

You have outstayed most of the guests. Do you want a piece of pie and coffee while you wait for him?"

"Do ya got any lemon pie?"

"Robert, I believe I do."

And she did. And it was so delicious.

Robert went and got JoJo's bike and tucked it into the trunk of the car while I paid for our dinner.

"You got a new car? Wow! That is so cool!"

"It was a present from my mother and grandparents. They wanted to make sure we had safe transportation while we were here."

"Man oh man! Willy is going to love this. He loves cars you know. This is sharp!"

He didn't really talk much about anything other than the car all the way home.

Robert helped him get his bike out of the trunk when we got there.

"Tell your mom and dad and your brothers we have a big tin of cookies for all of you. We will be bringing them by sometime after church tomorrow afternoon."

"I'll tell 'em."

He put his bike away and went inside as he waved to us.

We were home!

CHAPTER 81

Memaw answered the door. “Amy? Amy!! Get yourself inside here. What on earth are you doing in town?”

Amy came inside. Had she been right to come here? Had she really heard the voice of God? She felt like it was the right thing but what if she had made the biggest mistake of her life.

“I am so glad you remembered me.”

“Remembered you? Ha! Oh sweetheart, we pray for you all the time. I am just so happy that you are here. Pappy will be too. We are so happy every time we get one of your letters. It is so heartwarming every time we read one that lets us know the great things the Lord is doing in your life. What brings you here to see us?

“Well, this is going to be kind of awkward. Do you remember those many years back when I first came to your house?”

“Absolutely, like it was yesterday. You were just a wee bit of a thing and we were so happy to have you here. We hated to see you leave. You just walked right into our hearts. Those few days seemed like a lifetime. You belonged to us now!”

Amy wiped a tear that had escaped.

“Well, I hope you remember telling me that if I ever

came back that I could come and stay with you."

"Absolutely! Are you going to be staying here for a few days? Are you on a vacation? No matter what. You stay with us as long as you need to or want to."

"Do you think you should ask Mr. Lewis?"

"Well, first off, no. He will be just as happy to have you here as I am. And secondly, if you are going to call us Mr. and Mrs. Lewis, we probably won't know who you are talking about. When you are family, and that is who you are, and don't forget it, you call us Memaw and Pappy. Is that understood?"

"Yes ma'am."

"Now, what brings you to us?"

"Mrs... I mean, Memaw, I have been seeking the Lord on what He would want me to do with my life, what He had for me to do. I felt Him telling me that I was supposed to come here. I have been really fighting it for a few weeks now. I finally went to my Pastor and his wife and talked it over with them. They said if I felt like that is where God was telling me to go then I had better do what He was telling me to do."

"Sounds like you have good Pastors."

"They are the best. I had a hard time letting go of the only job that I ever had. I have a little money in savings but not a lot. I wasn't sure where I was going to stay but I felt like God was telling me to come straight here."

"I really like this God of yours. Sounds like He was calling you back home to us."

Amy smiled.

"I hope so. Do you think I could stay here until I find a job and a place of my own?"

"Oh honey, you can stay here as long as you need.

Are you hungry?"

"I am starving. It isn't that far of a drive, but I had to drop off the keys to my duplex this morning and I just headed out with my full car and a full heart and

an empty stomach."

"Then let's go get Pappy and get some lunch. He is going to be so happy to see you! Do you like good old greasy burgers?"

"I adore them!"

"Then grab your coat."

Amy did as she was told.

True to her word Memaw was right. Pappy was as happy to see her as Memaw was.

Amy remembered this little burger place, "The Burger Joint" they called it.

She remembered her first burger there. Pastor Toby had bought it for her. And yes, it was greasy, but it was one of the best burgers she had ever eaten.

Her stomach growled just a little in anticipation.

They found a place to sit while they waited for their food.

Pappy and Memaw listened to Amy tell again how she had felt as if the Lord was calling her there. She didn't know why but she knew she had to be obedient.

The food arrived and Pappy prayed.

"So, you don't have a job, or anything lined up?'

"No. I know that is not how you are supposed to do things, but I just felt an urgency, like I was supposed to get here. Does that make any sense? I mean, what if I am all wrong? What if I am just wishful thinking that God talks to me and has a plan. What if..."

"Oh honey, life is full of what ifs. What if you hadn't listened to God, to that still small voice? What if you had stayed put because you were unsure of your relationship with Him?"

"I am never unsure of that. I pray and read my bible. I study it. It is my very life. I would be lost without it."

"Then don't question whether or not you heard your Father speak to you. You know His voice."

"Yes, I do. Just like I knew when I left your home those years ago that I was supposed to go home. It was not always good. But God had a purpose. I had so many Godly people pour into me. To lead me and guide me and help me grow into the godly person that I am now. I am not the same person that left here. I know who I am now. I am a child of the Most High King. He does have a plan for my life and I always want to be in the center of that plan."

"Memaw, I do believe we have a little preacher here with us. Amy, you are truly a remarkable woman. You could not have put what you said any more succinctly than you just did. We should all strive to be in the center of God's will."

"Thank you, Pappy, for saying that. I may be in the center of God's will, and I hope a remarkable woman. But right now, I am in the center of God's will without a home or a job."

"Now that is just not true. You have a home. Our home is now your home. Please say you will stay as long as you want or need. And as for a job, I think I may know of something. Are you willing to work hard?"

"Hard work does not scare me."

"Well then, I know of an auto mechanic that is needing a front office person. Do you think you would want to go by and see if they are still needing someone? I think you know his brother Robert. Holly and Robert told us they stayed at the resort you were running."

"Holly and Robert, oh yes. So, it is Roberts brothers' shop?"

"Yeah. So ok, after lunch we can go by there."

"No, just tell me where it is and I will go there myself. Do you think I have a chance?"

"Oh, yeah, you have a great chance."

"Wow," Amy thought to herself. "A place to live and a prospect of a job, and I hadn't even been here three hours."

CHAPTER 82

Bailey came into the shop office, "There's a lady out in front to see ya, boss."

"What kind of car does she have? What's wrong with it?"

"Uh, yeah, I don't think she needs her car repaired. She is asking for you."

"Okay then."

Lance walked into the front and there she was.

Man was she gorgeous.

She wasn't dressed all showy. She was dressed really modest like. Not like the girl that he'd just fired. She had been a flake. She was rude to the customers and dressed like she, well, like she had lost half of her clothes in a windstorm.

"How can I help you? My guy says you were asking for me."

"Yes," she said as she stuck out her hand for him to shake.

He started to but realized they were covered in monkey grease.

"Better not," he said showing her his dirty hands. "Anyways, what can I do for you."

"I am staying with the Lewis's. Brother Lewis told me that you might be looking for someone to help in the front here. Are you looking to hire someone right now?"

"Well, huh. Do you have any experience?"

"Well, not experience in an office like this, but I was a manager at a resort. I think I know your brother and sister-in-law. Robert and Holly? They honeymooned at the Spa that I worked at."

"Oh yeah, I think they talked about you. Do you have a Fairlane?"

"Yeah, that's me, Amy Pinkerton. Like I said. I am looking for a job and he told me you might be looking for someone."

"Well, he was right. When do you think you can start?"

"Well, I could start right now if you needed me too. From the looks of things, you need me too."

"Yeah," Lance smiled, "I could have used you two weeks ago."

"Well, I'm here now. What do you need me to do?

"Can you make a decent pot of coffee? That would be a great start."

She laughed.

"That is always a good place to start."

And she did.

She made the best coffee.

But first she had to clean the pot and the coffee cups.

Amy set about getting the office sorted. It looked like someone had made an attempt, but it was a still a huge mess.

Lance stuck his head up front a few times to see what she needed.

All she could do at the moment was to sort things into like things. It looked as if someone had already started doing that, so she just continued from there. She had a good handle on it. Before too long it was quitting time.

Lance hoped that the work would not be too much for her. It was still a huge mess, even after the last two weeks of Holly working on it.

That last girl had been a piece of work.

He should have known not to hire her.

She might have a had a pretty face, but she had an empty head.

This girl, Amy, well, she had a pretty face and she looked like she might be pretty smart too.

He sure hoped she was.

Bailey had stuck his head in there a couple of times as well.

They went through two pots of coffee.

And it was good coffee too.

Around five he came in and told her that was enough for the day.

"How was it? You put in a full afternoon. Are you willing to come back tomorrow? It is a lot to ask. The last girl was truly useless."

"Well of course I will be back. Unless you don't think I will work out."

Lance looked around the office. It already looked better. The best-looking part was Amy. Sitting there behind the desk with piles of paper in front of her. Neat piles! That is what counted.

"No, I really think you will be a good fit. I don't think we talked about pay. What are you expecting in pay?"

Amy hadn't even thought about that.

"You know, I don't know. I just knew I needed a job

and I didn't think about that part. What did you pay the last girl?"

Looking around at the mess he said, "Way more than she was worth. She couldn't even make a pot of coffee."

"Well, Mr..uh, what do I call you?"

"My name is Lance. Some call me "Wheels." So, either one will be fine."

"Then Lance it is. Well, Lance, I think I will leave it up to you. At the end of the week, if you think I am doing a good enough job then I trust that you will pay me what I am worth. If you think that I am not doing a good job or that my coffee making skills are lacking, then you can say it isn't working out and I will be on my way. No hard feelings. Does that sound like a deal?"

"I can already tell you that your coffee making skills do not lack anything. You made some darn good coffee, and even in just these short few hours, I can see a difference in here. I think you will be a great fit. I just hope you stick around."

"What time do I need to be here in the morning?"

"Can you be here by eight?"

"I will see you then."

Amy picked up her purse and walked out the door.

Bailey stuck his head in one more time.

"Is she staying?"

"She said she would. At least until the end of the week."

"Why only until the end of the week?"

"She said if we didn't think it was a good fit then she would go on her way, no hard feelings."

"Wheels, don't you let this one get away. I think

she is a keeper."

"Me too Bailey. Me too!"

CHAPTER 83

It had been a week since Robert and Holly had gotten home.

When they had stopped by after church that Sunday, Frankie was there with her.

She was not looking too great, but she seemed happy to see them.

Frankie had seen the car when they drove up.

"Nice car!"

"Thanks. You want to go look at it?"

He looked at his mother. She nodded.

They were out like a shot.

The dark circles under her eyes were worse now than they had been just a couple of weeks before.

Holly sat beside her on the couch and held her hand.

"I read your letter Gina. I really do not have words to say."

"I am asking a lot of you, both of you. If it is too much please say so. I would not want to ever impose on you or anyone for that matter. I would not have asked but I know that my boys adore both of you."

"Oh, Gina, they have captured our hearts as well. It is like a burst of energy when they are around. The room is so alive. You are a very blessed woman."

"Yes, yes I am. I have been blessed with an amazing

husband as well. I don't know how he does it. He is at work early in the morning. He only takes off to take me to doctors' appointments. He comes home to check on me after work every day and then off to his other job. I know he's got to be exhausted. We didn't take that much of a loan out to help us get by, but with the treatments costing like they do and all the medicines and now a funeral to pay for. Well, it starts taking its toll.'

"I'm sure."

"What breaks my heart is that he doesn't have the sparkle in his eyes that he once had. You didn't know him before all of this. He is the biggest teddy bear that ever there was. His smile could light up room. You knew he was around because he was always joking and making people feel good about themselves. Now, well now, he is just too busy to even take time for himself. He has lost about forty pounds because he doesn't eat right. I worry about him like he worries about me. He is the love of my life. I pray for him all the time. He needs a friend Holly. I hope when this is all over that he lets you and Robert be the friends that he needs."

"We are going to do everything we can to show him how much he is loved. We will show the boys as well."

"Would you mind doing one more thing for me then?"

"If I can."

"I know I gave you letters for each of the boys to give them after I, well after. But it took me some time to write one to my Noah. I finally have it finished. Would you get it and give it to him when the time is right?"

"Where is it?"

"By my bed."

Holly went and got it.

"I will." After we talked for a bit more, I realized that no one had eaten lunch.

"Now, I know you have to be a little hungry. What do you have in this kitchen?"

Holly went and looked. It was a nice clean kitchen.

Those boys really did do a great job of taking care of the housework.

She found a chicken that had been thawed.

"Do you mind if I make you a fried chicken dinner?"

"I might not be able to eat it, but I know Frankie and the boys would love it."

Holly got busy.

Frankie and Robert came in after a few trips around the block in the new car.

They came in and went straight to the kitchen to seen what they could do to help finish dinner.

Robert showed Frankie how to mash potatoes and before long they had the table set and food was ready to eat.

True to her word, Gina couldn't eat the chicken, but she was able to eat a few bites of mashed potatoes.

"I told you mom! I told you she was a good cook."

"Yes, she is!"

After we cleaned up and made Frankie promise to save some food for his brothers when they got home, we left.

I cried all the way home. Soft tears that wouldn't stop. It felt as if they were coming from my soul.

Robert seemed to understand.

He gently held my hand all the way home.

We only had time for a quick nap and then we would be back at church.

The boys didn't come that night.

We kept looking for them, but they didn't show up.

We decided to go home after church. It had been a long day.

The phone was ringing when we were coming in. Robert answered.

"We will be right there," he said.

"Let's go."

I put my coat back on and followed him out the door.

"What is going on?"

"That was JoJo. They had to take their mom to the hospital. She is not doing good. He asked if we could come there and pray for her."

I felt a lump in my throat. All I could do was cry.

"Pull yourself together. They are going to need us."

I wiped the tears and put on the bravest face I could muster as we entered the hospital emergency room.

We told them who we were, but they said we could not go back unless we were family.

Robert asked if they could let JoJo know that we were here. He explained that he had called us and wanted us to come down.

She sent a nurse back and within a few minutes we were ushered back.

Frankie melted in my arms.

"It's bad Miss Holly. It is really bad."

Willy had joined him, and I had them both wrapped in my arms. Robert went on in and JoJo nodded at him.

Noah reached out and shook his hand and thanked us for coming. Then his eyes turned back to the love of his life.

He sat by her bed and held her hand.

I had seen that look before.

When Grandfather had been in the hospital with Grandmother. That look of undying love. The pain that was written on his face said it all.

"Do you want me to call Pastor Carson and have him come down?"

"I already did," JoJo said.

And sure enough, before too long Pastor and Sister Carson were there.

We all crowded around her bed and held hands and prayed.

They admitted her and Noah said he was going to stay with her.

He asked if we would give the boys a ride home.

We told them we would bring them to our house for the night if that would be ok.

He agreed, mostly because I don't think he heard what Robert had said.

The boys piled into the car and we headed for home.

They didn't say a word all the way home.

What could they say?

The words were written on their pained little man faces.

JoJo was trying to be strong for his brothers.

Frankie and Willie just let the tears fall.

CHAPTER 84

The boys missed school and Noah and I missed work.

I called Dean Matthews and explained everything.

School would not be starting up for another week, so he wasn't too concerned.

There were plenty of people that could take up the slack for a few days.

I told him that I would come in the next day after we knew everything was ok. I wasn't scheduled but I knew that Noah might need to stay with Gina.

As soon as I took Robert to work, I went back home and got the boys some breakfast.

They didn't have too much of an appetite, but I made them eat anyway.

They helped clean up and I told them I would take them home to clean up so we could go to the hospital to see their mother.

Noah looked like a man who had been through hell.

He appreciated the coffee that we brought him.

He told us she'd had a bad night but that she was sleeping peacefully now. They had given her morphine for the pain and it had helped a little.

They were thinking of letting her go home the next day.

"Is she going to be ok?"

"No, you little idiot! She is not going to be ok! Look at her! Can't you see for yourself. She is dying! She is dying right dad? Right!?" JoJo had finally lost it.

Frankie was shaking.

"That will be enough of that JoJo. Yes, she is dying."

"Why didn't you tell us? We thought she was getting better."

"Dad, why didn't you tell us."

"She said she didn't want you boys to worry. She didn't want you to have that weighing on you."

"How long has she known? How long did you know," Willie asked?

"A couple of months. They told her that she was out of remission and that it had spread. They wanted to do more chemo and such, but she told them no. She said her body couldn't take it."

"You should have told us. Even if she didn't want you to, you should have told us."

"I'm sorry JoJo. She made me promise. Some promises you don't ever break."

Gina stirred in the bed.

Noah turned and gently reached for her hand.

"Hey babe. How you are doing this morning?"

"I have been better. Are my babies here? I need to see my babies."

The boys moved in closer to her.

Noah stepped away to give them room.

"Hi mom. You gave us quite a scare last night." Willie reached up and gently moved her hair away from her forehead.

"Sorry about that sweetheart. I guess you all know now, huh?"

Frankie moved in closer. Trying to be as close to

her as he could without actually getting in the bed with her.

"Noah, would you mind if I see the boys for a few minutes? Go with Holly and get a cup of coffee or something please. I need to talk to them."

Her voice was barely a whisper.

Noah didn't want to leave. Holly took his hand and led him out of the room and too the cafeteria where they both drank a cup of hospital coffee.

Holly didn't know what to say. She just sat there with him.

"Do you know she is the only person that I ever dated?"

"Really? No, I didn't know that."

"She was seventeen and I was twenty-one. My parents didn't like her for whatever reason. Their loss. They don't even know my boys. They don't know what a great mother she has been. They never knew what a great wife she has been. She could have used a mom. Her parents were killed right before she turned eighteen. She has two older brothers. They lived a good distance away. They came down for the funeral and helped her out.

Her parents had left her the house and everything. She turned eighteen two weeks after they were killed. We were going to wait to get married after I finished college. I only had one more year to go. But I couldn't bear the thought of her being all alone. So, we got married. That was what made my family decide that since I had not conceded to their wishes that they would have nothing to do with me. I was already paying for my own schooling and since we had a place to stay it really didn't matter.

She got a job and I finished my last year and not long after that I got a job at the college. Been there ever since. Almost nineteen years now, or is it twenty? I don't know. I just know it has been a long time.

We had JoJo about a year after I got the job at the college. Then Willy, then Frankie. Thank God they gave me raises. That allowed for Gina to be able to stay home with the boys and be a full-time mom."

"That sounds like a lovely thing."

"It was, I mean, it is. Gina wasn't supposed to get sick. Why did God let that happen? Why Holly?"

"Why do you think?

"What? I don't know. I mean, I don't know."

"That is the right answer Noah. Nobody knows. But I do know something."

"What is that?"

"I do know that you are a Godly man."

"How do you know that?"

"Gina told me."

"Gina? My Gina?"

"Yes, your Gina. She told me that is why she loved you so much. She said that she knew that you were a real man of God. That she loved you even more because of it. She said you were a true lover of God and that she knew this was going to be hard on you but that because of your faith in God you would be able to get through this. She asked me to remind you of something."

"What is that?"

"She said to remind you that you had told her once that with God you could do all things. That He was your strength. And that without Him you could do nothing."

"I did tell her that. I told her that when she first got sick and I was having to work two jobs. She saw how tired I was and made a comment about it.

Holly, I meant those words when I said them. But now, now I don't know. I mean I have prayed for her healing for the last two years and look at her. She isn't healed. She is about to die. My sons are going to be without that wonderful woman.

He failed me Holly."

"Did He?"

"I don't know what you mean."

"Noah, the Word of God tells us that it rains on the just as well as the unjust, right?"

"Yes."

"In those dark moments, those moments when you felt like you were not going to make it, God saw you through. Think about all the people that have come into your lives that have prayed for you. You haven't been forsaken. God does not forsake us. Especially in our darkest hour. He is the one that will sustain you. Did she get her healing on this side of heaven? No! But just think about what it will be like for her when she steps into heaven. Healed! Complete healing. She will not be in any pain. She will be with her Heavenly Father. She will have left a legacy for you and your boys.

Bad things happen to good people. Gina is a good person. A good person that loves God with all her heart. You know that. If her faith hasn't wavered in this, then why would yours? She knows that God has always been there. You showed her that. She is a lovely woman, a Godly woman. You have been blessed to have had a wife like Gina. You two have raised three boys. Three boys that will need you more than ever.

Robert and I will be here for all of you. But you Noah, are going to have to step up and show those boys what a Godly man does in a time of trial and in a time of hurt.

He trusts God. It is not going to be easy, but you can do all things, ALL things through Christ that strengthens you.

Gina would expect nothing less."

"No, she wouldn't. I do love God. I just feel abandoned."

"I know how that feels. I have had that same feeling. But I do know that God can sustain you. God will keep you. God has not forsaken you and He never will."

Noah's eyes filled with tears and they spilled over.

"I am going to miss her so much. Holly, please pray with me."

I took his hands and we prayed.

The peace that permeated the room felt like a blanket of love that engulfed both of us.

Noah looked at me and wiped his eyes.

"Holly, I don't know what just happened, but I do know that no matter what, God is going to see us through this."

"Yes, He will."

Frankie walked through the door.

"Dad, mom said to come on back up."

We stopped and got them each a soda before going back up.

CHAPTER 85

Gina had come home from the hospital and the boys were back in school. They were not too happy to leave her for anything.

Noah had taken off work for a few days.

He had vacation time coming.

I went to work so that the workload would not be so bad when he came back.

I didn't realize how much he did.

He had that place running like a well-oiled machine.

The hospital had sent her home with a plethora of pain killers.

We all knew that the pain killers only took the edge off. But Gina did her best not to complain too much.

Noah had quit his job at the Taxi Stand.

He was not going to miss any more time with Gina.

Dean Matthews told him to take all the time he needed. Dean Matthews was a good man.

Sister Carson had been by to see her and the ladies of the church had made meals.

No one was going to go hungry.

I had called my mother and she had said they would have everyone praying. She said she would let Memaw and Pappy and everyone else know.

Then she hit me with some good news.

Lance had hired a girl for his mechanic shop. When she told me I knew her, I could hardly believe my ears.

"Amy? Really?"

She told me that she had started working there right after we came home and was living with Memaw and Pappy.

I was thrilled.

She said Memaw had written me.

"I had gotten a letter from her, but I hadn't read it yet with everything going on. Robert is going to be thrilled. Is she doing a good job?"

"Lance said she was. He said the place never looked better. Even when Cooper owned it. He said she makes a mean pot of coffee. I am going to be going there to get an oil change in the next few days."

"Tell her we said hello and we can't wait to see her. Mom, you are going to love her."

"I think I already do."

I did find the letter, unopened, along with a letter from Lance to Robert.

I so wanted to open that letter, but I thought better of it.

I opened Memaws.

"My Dear Holly Del,

I am not going to beat around the bush. You are not going to believe who showed up on our doorstep.

Amy! Our Amy!

Remember the girl that you met when you and Robert were on your honeymoon?

Well, she is the girl that stayed with us a few years back, right after Robert came home. She only stayed with us a few days. But during those few days she just walked right into our hearts.

I know that sounds strange, but it felt like she belonged to us.

Your Pappy and I are so happy to have her here.

She just showed up.

She said that she felt as if the Lord had been leading her, calling her if you will, to come back here.

I am so glad she listened.

She is the sweetest little thing.

If you could have had a sister, I think she could have been it.

Well, except for her dark hair.

She is a beauty.

You will never guess in a million years where she got a job!

She is working for Lance in his front office.

I have heard from a couple of people that have stopped in there that she is just perfect for the job.

She has the office looking ship shape and not a smidge of trash anywhere. She has gotten Lance caught up on all his filing and all his bills are getting paid. On time!

I don't think Lance knew how much he needed her, but I guess the Lord did.

She has grown so much in the Lord.

She had just gotten saved that first week that we met her and now, well now she is one of the Godliest women that I have ever met.

She is always smiling and singing and worshiping God.

It is a treat to have her help in the kitchen.

She hasn't got baking down but she can make a mean pot of beans and cornbread.

I am so thankful to God that He brought her back to

us.

Lift her up in your prayers.

Praying that all is well with you and Robert.

That little family that you told us about, we have been praying for them.

They have been heavy on my heart.

We will keep them in our prayers.

Love and miss you both to the moon and back.

Love, Memaw

"Wow!"

Now that was a letter if I ever read one.

Amy truly was a remarkable person. I wonder why God had led her to go back to Memaws and Pappy's? It didn't really matter. I think I was as happy that she was there as Memaw and Pappy.

I would include a letter to her when I answered Memaw.

Right now, I had to get dinner going.

Robert would be home soon, and we wanted to go see our extended family.

CHAPTER 86

Robert had read Lance's letter.

He told him all about Amy. Amy, the girl from our honeymoon.

She was still driving the Fairlane. It was in much better shape than the one that Toby and Patty had left behind.

He told Robert that Amy was sharp too.

She had pretty much pulled the front office together after we left.

He also told him to thank me for getting so much done while we had been there.

He seemed to be impressed that she could make such a good pot of coffee.

He said him, Bailey and Matthew went through about two pots a day themselves. Not including the customers.

He told how the customers were already talking about how happy they were with her. "I mean, why wouldn't they be. She was a real sweet girl."

He mentioned many times over in the letter that she was "a real sweet girl."

Robert chuckled.

"I think my little brother might have met someone. A girl!"

"Oh yeah, why do you say that?"

"I just read his letter. You are not going to believe this. He hired a new girl for his front office. You will never guess who it is. Not in a million years. She is pretty. She is smart. You will never guess?"

"Do I know her?"

"Yes, yes you do."

"You say she is smart and pretty. Who do I know that is smart and pretty?"

Robert looked like he would bust, "Go ahead try and guess?"

"Hmm... smart and pretty? If I guess right what will you give me?"

"If you guess right, I will do the dishes tonight, all by myself. But you are never going to guess. Go ahead guess."

"Smart and pretty you say. Well, of all the girls that I know that are smart and pretty the only one that comes to mind would be Amy Pinkerton. Did I guess right?"

He could tell by the way I was trying to not smile that I already knew.

"Smarty pants. How did you know?"

I pulled out my letter from Memaw and told him that mother had called before he got home.

"Now about those dishes..."

"Nope. A deal is a deal. I said if you guessed right that I would do our dishes tonight. So, get dressed. We are going out to eat."

"Cheater!"

"You're calling me a cheater? Now that is too funny! Go get dressed! I am starving."

JoJo was there. He had been working all day and was about to get off. We asked him to join us for dinner. We told him we would take him home afterwards.

It had been a rough week for him and his family.

He reluctantly agreed. I think it was because he was tired and didn't want to have to ride his bike home and he just probably needed a break.

Vicki wasn't there but the waitress that was there was extra attentive.

She took our order and before long we all had a salad in front of us while we waited for our meatloaf dinner.

"How are you holding up, JoJo," Robert asked?

"I have been better."

"I bet you have. How are your brothers?"

We had told Frankie not to come by this morning. One week wouldn't hurt. It wasn't like he could do too much anyway, with all the snow on the ground.

"They are holding up about like all of us."

"We are praying for all of you."

"Thanks. I don't know why though? It isn't doing any good."

He moved the salad away.

Robert reached over and touched his arm.

"I know this is rough. Probably one of the worst things you are ever going to have to face. But prayers aren't always answered the way want them to be. We have to trust that God is in control and that He is going to see you and your family through this."

"I sure hope so. It doesn't feel like it."

"Not right now it doesn't. It rarely ever feels like it when you are in the midst of the storm. It is when you come through it, when the storm is over, that you realize that God was with you all the time. He said

He would never forsake you. He is a friend that sticks closer than a brother. He will see you, all of you, through this."

"What does your dad say?"

"He said the same thing as you. I don't know what happened in the hospital the other day when he went with you. But he came back a different person. Him and mother seemed to be at peace about everything. Our world is falling apart and yet they aren't stressing. What did you say to him Holly?"

"The same thing Robert has been saying to you. God is still on His throne. That He loves you. That men of God, men that trust God fully, and make Him Lord of their lives are able to sustain anything that the world throws against them. I reminded him of who he is in Christ and who Christ is in him. Your dad is a godly man. A man of faith. A man that truly loves God. He realized that without God he would not be able to go through this. He would not be able to help you and your brothers when the time came.

JoJo let me ask you something. When you came to the altar a few months ago, did you really mean it? I mean. Did you believe that Jesus really died on the cross for your sins? That He wanted to have a relationship with you?"

"I thought I did. Now, well I am just not sure."

"What are you not sure of?"

"I am not sure that any of it is real."

"Why not?

"Because why would a good God allow such bad things to happen to my mother."

"Did you ask her?"

"My mom. No, I didn't have to. When you and

my dad left the room, she told me and my brothers that she was so proud of us for starting to go back to church.

She said that of all the things that had ever mattered to her in this life, raising godly young men that would love and serve God, just like our dad, was the most important thing. She told us that God had a plan. A master plan! We may never fully understand what it is, but it didn't matter as long as we learned to listen to God and follow His guidance then we would never be lost or fail. She told us that she would love to stay here on this earth with us and watch how our lives turned out, but that was not going to be Gods master plan for her life. She said that any question that we would ever have about life would, could and should be found in God's Word. She said if we had questions as to why this happened to her to take it to God. He might not give us the answer we wanted, but He would give us the answer we needed."

"Do you believe her?"

"I want to. I mean, even with all the pain and suffering that she is going through, she still doesn't seem to blame God."

"Why do you think that is?"

"To be honest, I really don't know. Why do you think it is?"

"It is because of her relationship with Him. She has come to know that she can truly rely on Him. That day to day relationship where she has talked to Him and allowed Him to talk to her has grown over the years. She has a built-up faith in God the Father. She knows she can turn to Him, for anything. There is peace in knowing God like that. You don't always get that peace, that peace that passes all understanding, until you have walked with Him, talked with Him, built a relationship with Him. It isn't a onetime trip to the altar. It is a day in day out, moment by moment thing. When you start talking to Him and letting Him talk to you then you will know the answers. You see, He loves you, just like He loves your mother and your dad, just like he loves Willy and Frankie. He wants to have a deeper relationship with you. With each of us. Not just a surface relationship."

"It's not that easy," JoJo whispered.

"Nothing worthwhile ever is. But just like any relationship, it is worth it in the end when you learn that you can lean on Him, trust in Him. That He can be your everything. And that He wants to be."

"I just want my mom. I want her to be healthy and here. Is that too much to ask?"

"No, it isn't too much to ask. But you know as well as anyone that we don't always get what we ask for."

"I know. But I can still want it can't I?"

"Yes. But don't let it completely break you when you don't get it. When you do that, then Satan always wins the battle. Don't let him win this one JoJo. You are too important and special to allow that to happen."

We had been so engrossed in our conversation that we had not noticed the little waitress with our food.

She sat our food down in front of each of us.

By now JoJo's appetite had come back.

We all pretty much ate in silence.

While Robert and JoJo were getting his bike to put in the trunk of the car, I paid our bill.

The little waitress came running up to the counter

where I was paying.

"Excuse me."

"Yes. What can I do for you?"

"I am sorry that I was eaves dropping in on you, but I couldn't help but overhear. Did you and your husband mean all those things that you were telling JoJo?"

"Well, of course we did."

"All of it?"

"Every bit of it. Why do you ask?"

"I, I just, well I just wanted to know if you think that God would want to know me like you said He wants to know JoJo? I mean, do you think He would?"

I had finished paying. I took her by the hand and led her to an empty booth.

I looked at her name tag.

"Billie, right?"

"Yes ma'am."

"Have you ever heard about Jesus before?"

"Well, I have heard of Him, but not like you and your husband were talking about Him. Not like He was real and personal. I mean I just thought He was some religious guy that you just talked about at Christmas and Easter. Not like He was a real person."

"Well Billie, He is real. He is as real as the air that you breath. He is as real as the rustling of the leaves in the trees. He is real as the sound of a baby's pure delight. He is as real as the refreshing rippling water that flows through the streams. He is real. And yes, He wants to have a relationship with you. Not just you, but everyone.

That is why He came and died on the cross for us."

"He did what?'

I explained to Billie how God in His ultimate love for us had offered His only Son as a living sacrifice for us. A sacrifice for our sins so that we could have everlasting life and live in right relationship with Him. It was a free gift. All it took to receive this gift was to ask for it and believe that it was true, and that God would cleanse us from all unrighteousness and that we could be set free.

"Do you think that you would like to ask Jesus to come and live inside your heart and be set free? Billie, He loves you more than you will ever know. He wants to have a relationship with you and fill you with His joy, His righteousness, and His peace. All you have to do is ask."

"Yes. Yes, I want all of that." Tears were streaming down her face.

So right there I led her in the sinner's prayer.

She hugged me and I held her and we both cried together.

I invited her to come to church and gave her directions.

She said she would be there."

Robert and JoJo were wondering what had taken so long.

Robert was smiling from ear to ear.

JoJo just sat back in the seat and took it all in.

The ride home was silent.

Robert helped him get his bike out.

"See you at church tomorrow night?"

"Yeah, sure, I guess."

I rolled down the window.

"Tell everyone that we love them. Give your mom a hug and kiss from me."

"Will do!"

He went inside and Robert and I went home with full hearts.

CHAPTER 87

True to his word, JoJo was at church the next night, and he brought Willie and Frankie with him. Billie was there too.

She had a little beat up car, but it got her there.

We were so happy to see them all there. They sat closer to the front with the rest of the teenagers.

JoJo motioned for Billie to come and sit with him and his brothers.

She said she was sure glad to see someone there that she knew. JoJo said he was glad she came.

It looked like he was glad that she came for a lot of reasons.

She was a real cute little girl. She couldn't go wrong in getting to know JoJo.

Church service was as good as it could ever be. JoJo and is brothers went to the altars to pray. Billie was unsure of herself.

I went and talked to her about what was going on while Robert went and prayed with the young people that were seeking after God.

So many of them crying and pouring their hearts out.

Not just Highschool kids, but College kids as well.

Wanting more of God.

Wanting to know Him.

Seeking a better relationship with Him.

A real relationship.

JoJo was relentless. He laid on the altar until he was sure He had the answer.

Billie had said she wanted to know God like that. She and I went to the altar.

"What do I do? Last night was the first time I ever prayed. How do I do this?"

"Just talk to Him like you would if He was your friend. You can tell Him anything. You can just talk to Him. He wants to hear from you what you want from Him. What do you want from Him?"

"I want that peace that you were telling JoJo about last night. I want it to come inside me and never go away. Do you think He would do that for me?"

"He wants that more than anything. More than anything in the world for you He wants you to know Him so personally that nothing else in the world matters to you but pleasing God and having a right relationship with Him. It is not always an easy road to walk, but it is so worth it."

Billie began to call out to God. She sought after Him that night, just like so many of the other young people were.

Parents were coming down and laying hands on them and praying for them.

God was moving and heaven was going to be moved that night.

After church was over, the boys said they would rather go home than go out to eat. They wanted to spend as much time at home as possible.

We took them home and hugged them and thanked them for coming to church.

JoJo lingered behind after Willie and Frankie went inside.

"I just want to thank you for what you told me last night. I came home and was just sitting in the living room thinking.

Dad had fallen asleep in the recliner. Willie and Frankie had already gone to bed.

I was enjoying the quiet when I thought I heard a small voice. It was so low that I thought at first that I was hearing things. I got up and as quietly as I could I tried to move closer to where the sound was coming from.

It was my mother. She was singing. It wasn't loud but it was beautiful.

I could hear her singing the song that she used to sing us to sleep by.

"Why do feel discouraged, why do the shadows come, why does my heart feel lonely, and long for heaven and home?

When Jesus is my portion, a constant friend is He.
His eye is on the sparrow, and I know He watches me,
His eye is on the sparrow, and I know He watches me.
So, I sing because I'm happy,
I sing because I'm free.
His eye is on the sparrow, I know He watches me
His eye is on the sparrow, and I know He watches me."

Then I heard her as she started to just talk to Jesus.

She was thanking Him for being her friend.

She was thanking Him for her children.

She was praying that we would know what it was like to have a friend in Jesus just like she'd had all these years.

She thanked Him for everything and told Him over

and over how much she loved Him and how grateful she was for His love for her.

She fell asleep soon after that and the peace that filled our house was so thick that you could almost feel it.

When I went to bed Frankie was sitting up in his bed and Willie was just lying there.

"Did you hear her singing," Frankie asked us?

"I heard her."

"Me too," Willie whispered.

We all just laid down in our beds and fell asleep.

Dad had gone to bed at some point because they were still asleep when we woke up and made breakfast.

Dad came out of the room and told us that Mom had slept through the night.

"Uh-huh," Willie said.

Dad looked at us as we sat the table.

"Did you boys hear her singing last night?"

"Yes sir."

"Me too. I love to hear your mother sing. We don't get to listen to that much anymore. What a blessing that was."

We were all ready to cry, but we didn't.

Dad said, "You boys are the closest thing to heaven that she has here on this earth. I know that she might not be here with us much longer, but we are going to make the best of every day, every hour, and every minute. We don't quit living. She would not want that, and it is not going to happen. Do you boys know what I am talking about?"

We all nodded.

He asked if we would mind staying with mom this

morning while he went to church.

Willie had to work so Frankie and I stayed with her so he could go.

Did you see him there this morning?"

We had not.

"Well, he came home with a bucket of fried chicken and all the stuff to go with it."

After checking on Mother we all sat at the table and ate.

Willie came home and finished off the rest of it.

Dad said he wanted us to go to church tonight and he would stay home with mom.

So, we went.

I am so glad that we did."

"We are too," Robert told him as he hugged him.

"I know that I have a peace like I have never had before, and I don't ever want to not have it. I feel like a load has been lifted off my heart and that I can breathe again. I feel like I could sing. That song makes so much such sense to me now. I want to sing because I happy, I want to sing because I am free. I know beyond knowing that His eye is on me. That He sees me. That He cares for me."

"Yes, He does."

"I just wanted to say thank you for sharing with me last night. And thank you Miss Holly for praying with Billie. She is a really nice girl. She just always seems sad. Now she doesn't have to be. I better go inside so you guys can go home. Sorry I kept you so long."

"Don't you be sorry. We are so glad you shared that with us. I hope you and your brothers, your whole family knows how much we love you."

"We do. We love you both so much too."

"We know. Now go inside and warm up."

He waved as he went inside.

CHAPTER 88

"Ok."

"Ok what?"

"Are you going to ask her?"

"Am I going to ask her what?"

"Don't go playing that game with me?"

"Bailey, what are you talking about? What game?"

"Listen Lance, either you ask her out or I am."

"Who? Amy?"

"Who my foot! Yes Amy!"

"Uh, correct me if I'm wrong but aren't you dating Cheryl Jones from your church?"

"Yes. But she wants to get married. I do not believe that I am of the marrying kind. Not right now at least. So, what's it going to be?"

"Do you think I should? I mean, I have been thinking about it."

"Well, don't think too long, 'cause if you don't, I'm gonna!"

"Well don't, because I think I am going too."

"Alrighty then!"

"You're darn tootin' alrighty then!"

"Then go do it!"

"Don't get pushy! I'll do it in my own good time."

"Come on man. She has been working here over two weeks now. What more of your own good time do you need?"

"Get back to work!"

"Right on boss!"

Bailey chuckled at how red Lances face had got.

Was he blushing?

Probably.

It was too funny!

Lance sat in his office trying to figure out how he could bring it up.

"Hey Amy, would you like to go have dinner with me some time?"

"Hey Amy, would you like to go see a movie?"

"Hey Amy, want to have a picnic in the park?"

"Hey Amy, do you want to marry me?"

What? Where were these thoughts, these emotions coming from?

He had never seen a more beautiful girl in his life.

She was so pretty. She smelled so nice! She smiled at everyone. She had only been working there for two weeks and already the regulars were in love with her.

How could they not be?

There was something about her.

No matter how hectic the day was, she always seemed to keep her cool. There was no getting away from it. Amy was special. She was different from anyone that he had ever met.

He had dated before he went into the Army, but not since, well not since he had got out.

Who would want to date him?

Who would want to be with a half man?

He was hoping Amy would.

He was going to do it.

He would just march himself into that front office

and say, “Amy, would you like to have dinner with me tomorrow night?”

“I guess I would. Where would you like to go?”

How long had she been standing there?

“Uh…well..uh..I, uh, well, where would you like to go?”

“You asked me remember. I don’t really know this town. I will let you decide.”

“Uh, okay.”

“How about I pick you up around fivish? You are still staying with the Lewis’s, right?”

“Yep. Fivish it is.” She smiled and turned to walk away.

She realized she had some invoices in her hand that needed a signature.

She came back to the door.

“I almost forgot. I need signatures on these invoices so I can file them.”

That is why she was there!

Lance signed them and asked her to close the door when she left.

The stupid door squeaked as she shut it.

At least next time he would hear her when she came to the door.

He really didn’t want the door to be shut.

If it was shut, he couldn’t hear her singing. She was always singing. He could listen to her sing all day.

He got up to open the door a little so he could hear her, but his good leg gave out and he fell to the ground.

“What was I thinking? She is not going to want to be seen with a cripple!”

Amy came running to see what the commotion was.

Lance was trying to get up and was almost there when she came back into his office.

She hurried to help him up.

Lance was ten shades of red.

Once he was settled back in his chair, he figured he better break the date now so she wouldn't have to later after she thought it over.

"Amy, maybe I misspoke. Maybe we shouldn't go out to..."

Before he could finish Amy interrupted.

"Lance, are you trying to break our date already? Do you not want to be seen with me? I mean, I guess I understand. You don't really know me, and you probably don't want people to see you with me. I understand."

"No, you don't. I don't want you to have to be seen with me. I mean, look at me."

"Don't be silly. You don't look that bad. I mean a little monkey grease on you, but you clean up real nice. You don't look near this bad when you come in in the mornings. And after a couple of cups of coffee, you almost seem human. So, fivish it is right?

"Uh, yeah, fivish."

Amy turned to leave and shut the door behind her.

"No, leave the door open."

"You got it!"

CHAPTER 89

"What did I agree to?"

Amy looked in the mirror.

She had nothing to wear on a date.

"Really! What was I thinking?"

Memaw walked by.

"Thinking about what dear?"

"What was I thinking when I agreed to go on a date with Lance. My mouth had agreed to go before my head could talk me out of it. I mean, I think he wanted to break the date two minutes after he made it and I wouldn't let him. What kind of person does that? I should have let him."

"Why?"

"Why what?"

"Why should you have let him break the date? Do you not want to go out with him? Do you not find him attractive?"

"No. Of course, I want to go out with him. And yes, he is attractive. I mean that red hair. I have always had a thing for red headed men."

"Then why should you have let him break the date?"

"Because look at me. I am a mess. I don't really have clothes to wear on a date. To be honest, Memaw, I have never been on a date before. I don't know what

I am supposed to do."

"Well, that is going to change. You go get a shower and wash that beautiful hair of yours. I know just who to call."

She shut the bathroom door on her and went and called her daughter.

"Hi mom. What can I do for you?"

Memaw poured out the whole scenario.

"I will be right there."

Within twenty minutes she was there with everything a girl would need to go on a date.

She had raided Holly's closet and had found a couple of outfits that should fit Amy. She even found some boots.

Anne and Memaw knocked on the bathroom door.

Amy had finished showering and she had her hair in a towel and a robe on.

"I hope you don't mind," Memaw said, "but I called my daughter Anne, Holly's mom. She came over with plenty of things to get you ready for a date with Lance."

"She what?"

"Come on. Let's go to your room so she can show you what she brought you."

Anne showed her three outfits that would look gorgeous on her.

"You look them over and decide which one then we will work on your hair."

They left her to her own devices to get dressed.

She had picked a maroon midi with a long-sleeved tan shirt that went underneath. It had a cowl neck on it, and it fit her like it was made for her.

The boots went perfect with it.

"Are you sure she won't mind if I wear these?"

"I am sure."

They both admired the beauty that was standing before them.

"Here, let me blow dry your hair. I have a curling iron that will just do wonders."

It didn't take long until all that dark hair was blow dried and curled.

Amy looked in the full-length mirror that hung on the closet door.

She could scarcely believe that it was really her that was staring back.

"You look gorgeous," Memaw said.

"You do look lovely," Anne chimed in. "Where is he taking you?"

"I have no idea. I really am nervous. I don't know what to say to him. What do I say to him?"

"Well, just talk to him like you normally would. He is just a person. That is all he is. A person."

"Yeah, but he is a guy person."

"Is he some other kind of person when you are at work?"

"No," Amy smiled shyly.

"Then talk to him like you would anyone else. He is just a guy. You do not have to impress him. I think you may have already done that."

"What do you mean by that?"

"Well, to be honest, I don't think Lance would have asked you out if you had not have impressed him. He is not that kind of guy. He is a real down to earth guy."

"He seems nice to work for. Maybe I shouldn't date my boss. I mean, what if we don't hit it off, or he realizes that it was a mistake. It could make things awkward at work."

"I tell you what, we are going to hold hands and we are going to pray."

"Thank you."

Memaw did just what she said she would do.

They had just finished praying when the doorbell rang.

Memaw went downstairs with Anne. Amy put on a quick spritz of her favorite perfume. Cachet. She always felt as if she wasn't quite dressed without a little spritz of perfume.

Pappy had opened door and was standing in the entryway when Amy came around the corner.

Lance almost lost his breath when he saw her.

She was the loveliest creature that he had ever encountered. She smelled so good.

His head was swimming.

"Well aren't you a vision," Pappy said. "What do you think Lance?"

"Yes, a vision," Lance repeated.

"Do you have your key?"

"Yes ma'am."

"Just let yourself in when you get home."

Lance helped her with her coat.

It was cold outside. The sun was going down and it was starting to get a little dusky outside.

Pappy shut the door behind them.

"Let's eat. I have been smelling that stew all afternoon. You staying to eat with us?"

"Yessir I am. If I'm invited. I have smelled it ever since I walked in the door.".

"Of course you're invited. Come help Pappy set the table while I add finishing touches."

They did as they were told.

Lance helped Amy with her car door. Then he hobbled over and got inside.

"So, where are we going?"

"I hope you like seafood. I have heard about a restaurant that serves lobster and fish that I thought we could try. If you don't like fish, we could go anywhere else."

"I love fish."

Lance seemed pleased with himself.

Lord she smelled good and she really was a vision.

He didn't always pray but he shot a quick one up to God.

"Please let this go good God. Don't let me mess this up! Amen"

CHAPTER 90

They both were quite nervous.

I mean, now who wouldn't be.

Lance could tell that Amy seemed to be as anxious as he was about the whole thing.

They had to wait for a table for about ten minutes.

They looked at the lobster tank while they waited.

"Do you like lobster?"

"It's okay. I would rather have crab legs."

"Really?"

"You don't like crab legs?"

"Nah, I mean they are ok. I like crab cakes and such but not necessarily crab legs."

"Why not?"

"Well, I don't want to have to fight with my food to be able to eat it. If somebody else wants to go to all the trouble and take all that crab out of the shell, then I'll eat it. It isn't that I don't like the taste. I just don't like all the work."

"That is too funny."

"You think so."

"Yes. I have never heard anyone say the reason they didn't like a food is because it was too difficult to get it out to eat. I guess that is as good of a reason as any though. I love the thrill of cracking open the crab legs and making sure to get every last piece of meat out of it that I can, then dipping it into some rich butter sauce."

"Well, you make it sound delicious, but I still think it is too much work."

They were calling them to their seat.

They seated them in a booth with the blinds raised.

The sun had finally gone down and there was a sprinkling of stars in the sky.

"Look how beautiful it is tonight. It takes my breath away."

Lance was looking at Amy when he answered her.

"Yes. Tonight is a night of rare beauty."

Amy looked at Lance. He quickly looked out the window.

Then he looked back at her.

"The night sky is beautiful tonight, but Amy, I have to tell you, it really can't compare to you."

Amy blushed.

"Thank you for saying that. That was so nice of you."

"It was true. You are looking more beautiful tonight than ever before."

The waitress showed up before they could even really look at the menu.

They ordered a meal that was fit for a ship's captain. Lance ordered a side order of crab legs for Amy.

"You didn't have to do that."

"I know. But I figured if you enjoy them then maybe you will look at this date a success and go out with me again some time."

"Well, then, ok."

Before long they were talking about a lot of things.

Mostly about work. How Lance had come to own "Wheels."

Lance was sure to tell her everything.

She let him do most of the talking.

He did let her know that he was glad that she had come in that day for a job.

"Best thing I ever did was to hire you."

"Yes. Yes, it was."

They both laughed.

After the meal and they were just sitting there, Lance asked her if she had enjoyed her dinner.

"It was really good."

"How were your crab legs."

"Delicious, just like I knew they would be."

"Well, that is good to hear. So, does that mean we are set for another date for next Saturday? Say fivish?"

"Fivish it is."

Lance smiled.

They had sat there for a while and Lance decided he better take her home.

She had already told him she got up early every morning to pray and read her bible.

She would be at church tomorrow morning.

He hadn't been to church since Robert and Holly got married.

Maybe he would go tomorrow.

Maybe he would.

He drove her home extra cautiously. The roads were getting iced over.

"You have tire chains on your car, don't you?"

"No. I can't afford them."

"You need to talk to your boss about a raise."

"Now that is funny. I think my boss pays me just

fine."

"Well, Monday we are going to look and see what we can do for you. You are one of my prized employees. I can't have you sliding around all over town and getting into an accident. I don't ever want to have to find someone to replace you."

He walked her to the door.

It wasn't very late at all.

Pappy and Memaw were still awake.

Lance was about to unlock the door for her when Pappy opened the door.

"Come on in you two. Get in here out of the cold."

Lance came inside with her.

"Did you have a nice dinner?"

"Yes sir we did. We had fish."

"And crab legs. They were yummy!"

"Did you have dessert?"

"No ma'am."

"Would you want some. Pappy and I were just about to have a piece of Chocolate Pie and some coffee."

"That sounds good. Would you like to stay and have some pie?"

Lance was all in.

I mean it was chocolate pie!

They sat around the kitchen table while they ate the most divine Chocolate Meringue Pie they had ever tasted. The coffee helped it go down even smoother.

After a little small talk, mostly about cars and such Lance bid his goodbyes and thank-you for the pie and coffee.

Amy stood at the door and waved goodbye to him as he drove off.

Memaw could tell by the look on her face that the date had been a success.

They cleaned up and they all went to bed.

After her nighttime prayers Amy's head hit her pillow like rock.

She barely remembered dreaming.

But she did sleep like she hadn't in a while.

Contented.

CHAPTER 91

Sunday mornings were a rare time to get to sleep in and today would not be that day either.

Robert hurried to answer the door.

Holly was hurrying to get a robe on so she could see who was at their door.

"Toby, for goodness sake. Where is Patty? Is she with you?"

Holly could hear Toby and Robert, so she hurried even faster.

"Where else would she be? She is just putting on her shoes. She told me to go on ahead and make sure you guys were awake."

"Well we weren't but we are now."

Patty showed up at the door just as Holly was coming out of the bedroom.

Holly went to hug her, but Patty ran on past her and into the bathroom.

The heaving was horrible.

"Is she sick?"

Toby responded, "Not exactly."

He wouldn't look them in the eye.

"What do you mean not exactly?"

As soon as she asked the question, she knew the answer.

She ran to the bathroom to help her friend.

Robert and Toby went and made coffee.

After a few more heaves Patty was ready to try a little bit of crackers and ginger-ale while the rest of us enjoyed coffee and breakfast.

"What brings you guys by here? We thought you were in Tucson?"

"Now why would we be in Tucson when we could be in this lovely freezing town?'

"We don't know," Robert said, "that is why I asked."

"Honestly we had been heading home for a couple of weeks so that Patty could go see Dr. Shackleford. We were going to just push through, but Patty started to not feel well so we decided to see if we could stay here for the day and rest up a bit and head out tomorrow."

"Oh, we would be so pleased to have you here."

"Do your parents know about this baby?"

"Yes! They all know. I couldn't keep it a secret this time. I figured I wanted them praying for us and this baby from the beginning."

"I am so glad you stopped by. We will have to celebrate by going out to eat for lunch."

Patty went pale again and barely made it to the bathroom.

She asked if she could go ahead and clean up and start to get ready for church while we finished our breakfast.

Toby went and brought in their suitcases while Robert stoked the fireplace.

Then he helped me finish the dishes.

After we all had showers and were ready for church, we all quickly prayed for Patty. She threw some saltines in her purse and a handful of mints.

The Carson's were so happy to see them.

He asked if Toby would at least give a testimony of what God was doing across this great big country.

He agreed.

Noah was there and Frankie was with him.

It was so good to see them. It had been a few weeks since Gina had been taken to the hospital.

Noah was coming to church on Sunday mornings. Sometimes one of them came with him. Usually it was Frankie.

All three boys came on Sunday evening.

Gina was holding her own.

Not better, but not worse.

They had to hire a nurse to come and sit with her during the day.

Luckily for them, they had good insurance.

Noah had to get back to work.

He had taken off for two weeks.

He had plenty of sick and vacation days coming but he didn't want to use them all up.

Gina had been right. He was a most pleasant Godly man. Ever since that day in the hospital, he had been smiling a lot more and you could tell that he had come to an understanding.

They weren't really struggling as much as you would have thought since Noah had quit his second job, but I guess since she wasn't doing chemo and such then the cost wasn't so bad.

Toby and Robert sat up front while Patty and I sat at the back. She didn't want to disrupt the service if she had to leave.

Pastor Carson introduced Toby and he went up to the pulpit.

"Where is that lovely wife of yours?"

Just as he asked Patty was heading for the exit and making good time of it.

"Uh, well, uh...she just left the building Pastor."

"Was it something I said?"

"No. Nothing like that."

Toby leaned in and whispered into Pastor Carson's ear.

Pastor Carson nodded.

Ladies and gentlemen, please excuse Toby's wife. Miss Patty is in the family way and she is not feeling up to par at the moment. Please pray for her."

Toby's face turned three shades of red.

You could hear the women twittering. "Family way."

Sister Carson met me in the vestibule, and we went to check on Patty. She had finally finished her final round and was laughing uncontrollably.

"Family way."

We all three started laughing.

Toby took the mic and began to tell of the glorious things that God was doing with him and Patty as they went from church to church to minister. He told of young people filling the altars.

Revival was filling the land.

CHAPTER 92

The weather stayed cold all through February and a little into March. It was just beginning to warm up a little when the inevitable happened.

Gina had not been doing well. She had been in a lot more pain.

The boys were staying with her as much as possible. Noah had been leaving work earlier so he could be home with her as well.

Dean Matthews had told him to take any time he needed. Noah didn't want to abuse the generosity, so he only stayed home with her when he felt she needed him to.

Not because he wanted to but because the boys needed to, did he allow them to miss school on occasion to stay home and be with their mother. At least once a week they were all missing a day off to help.

Robert and I had been by to sit with them that Tuesday evening. She asked me to visit with her by myself for a few moments.

"Holly, do you still have those letters that I gave you?"

"Yes ma'am I do."

"I believe you are going to have to have them ready soon."

"Please don't say that Gina."

Gina laid a tired hand onto Holly's.

"Oh sweetheart, I know my time is coming to an end. It isn't going to be much longer. I am so tired. I feel as if the only thing holding this tired old body to this earth is the love that my family keeps wrapping around me. I don't want to leave them. I see their faces and I see the sadness in their eyes. It is not going to be easy on them, but they will get by. It will take some time I know, but my God is going to see them through this.

I know when my parents passed away, I was just a bit older than JoJo, I thought my heart would never heal. But it did. Funny, but I still miss them. My mother was so sweet. She was a godly woman. She is the very reason I have such foundational faith."

Gina smiled remembering, "She used to tell me, "Gina, when you are feeling like you are at the end of your rope, you make sure the other end is connected to God then hold on for dear life. Hold on to Jesus baby,"" she would say, "Hold on to Jesus and you will never be lost or sorry." My dad would reiterate, "And if you feel yourself slipping, tie a knot in the end and don't let go, baby, don't let go!"

Holly wiped a tear or two as it escaped.

"You tell my boys that will ya? You tell them to hold on to Jesus for dear life. If they can do that, they will have the dearest life. I know I have."

"I'll tell them. I promise."

"One more thing. Have you learned my song? I believe that it will bring the boys and Noah comfort if you would sing it for them."

"Yes ma'am. I have learned it."

"Will you sing it for me? Right now, would you sing it for me?"

Holly picked up Gina's frail little hand and began to sing.

It wasn't long before the bedroom door opened and the boys were standing in the doorway listening.

Frankie came in and sat on the floor by Holly and reached up and put his hand on Gina's arm.

Willie went to the other side of the bed and sat down and tenderly picked up her other hand. He brought it to his lips and kissed it.

JoJo just stood there looking at his mother. Tears flowed down his face.

"Thank you, Holly," Gina said. "Boys, I hope you know how much I love you. You are three of the handsomest young men I know. I have been so proud to call myself your mother. God truly blessed me when He gave you to me."

They all told her they loved her and that they were the blessed ones.

I felt like a blessed one at that moment.

Just being able to witness such love. Not just the love that these boys had for their mother or that she had for them, but the love that had permeated the room from a heavenly Father that loved us all so much that His peace filled the place.

Robert and Noah had joined the little party at some point and we all prayed together before we left.

Noah told me the next morning that Gina had slept most of the night so peacefully. She hadn't slept like that in days. He thanked us for coming over.

He didn't come to work on Thursday.

Friday morning, Robert had already left to go to

work and I was just heading out to walk to work, when the phone rang.

"Frankie, what's is going on?"

"Can you come over? Please? Can you come over? She is in a bad way this morning. I don't think she is going to last through the day."

"Yes baby. I will call Robert and we will be there as soon as we can."

I called Robert. He had just got to work.

He told his boss what was happening and came home and picked me up.

I had called Dean Matthews to let him know the situation. He told me that Noah had already called. He asked me to let them all know that the whole staff was praying for them. I assured him that I would.

Pastor and Sister Carson were just pulling up when we arrived.

We all went in together when Willie opened the door.

He fell into my arms and we all walked into the bedroom where the doctor and her nurse were.

The doctor gave her an injection for the pain. It wasn't that she was crying out or even screaming, but you could tell that she was hurting. Her breathing was so much slower and shallow. She had wanted to be home when she left this earth and the doctor couldn't see any reason why she shouldn't.

He and Noah stepped out into the hallway and spoke for a few minutes.

Robert reached over and held my hand.

Frankie was half laying on the bed with his head resting next to Gina. He wasn't sobbing. He was just lying there. JoJo was sitting on the bed behind

Frankie. His hand was on her leg. Willie knelt at the end of the bed and laid his head by her feet.

The doctor and nurse went into the living room to give them privacy.

Pastor Carson asked Noah if it would be okay if he prayed and Noah agreed.

Sister Carson came and stood on the other side of me as Pastor Carson prayed.

Gina opened her eyes and looked off into the corner.

I didn't know if anyone else had seen her or not.

It seemed as if she was looking at something. Something that I couldn't see. A smile came to her face.

She looked at Noah.

"I love you. I love you all so much." She could barely whisper. "I've got to go now. He is waiting for me."

She turned her gaze back to the corner.

This time we all looked.

We could see nothing. But clearly Gina could.

She reached out her hand towards it.

"I'm coming. Oh, thank you for coming to get me. Thank you. I have been waiting for you."

It was barely a whisper.

Then her hand fell to her side and her breathing stopped.

I felt my heart beating out of my chest. I couldn't seem to swallow the lump that was in my throat.

Sister Carson squeezed my hand tighter as we both stood there and cried.

"Mom? Mom?" Frankie was now crying. Sobbing.

JoJo put his hand on his back.

"It's ok. It's ok. Look at her Frankie. Look at her face. She isn't in pain anymore."

Willie started to cry as he still laid at her feet.

Noah went and got the doctor.

He came and listed to her heart and checked for a pulse.

Time of death for Gina on this earth 10:32 AM.

Time of life for Gina in heaven 10:32 AM.

CHAPTER 93

The funeral was about as lovely as it could be.

More people showed up and filled the church up.

Gina's oldest brother and his wife came. Her other brother and his family couldn't make it due to him being sick as well.

Flowers filled the front of the church.

Noah had asked Robert and me to sit with them. We were family.

Frankie sat next to me and Willie sat between Robert and myself.

JoJo sat on the other side of Robert between him and his dad.

We had them covered.

Many people came up and talked to Noah and the boys. Offering condolences.

Sister Carson and I had gone shopping to find a dress for Gina.

She had been sick for so long that none of her clothes fit on her emaciated little frame.

But there was something about Gina's countenance. I had only ever been to two funerals in my life.

My father and Sam's.

Sam had that same look on his face. It was a look, no, not just a look, it was more than that.

It was a feeling. As if they were at rest. Peaceful. Honestly, I really could never give it justice to try and describe it.

They had done a fine job of making her look beautiful.

She did. But in just the few short months that I had known her, I knew her to be beautiful. It was her inner beauty that had always shown through.

The boys didn't seem to really notice anyone that came up to talk to them. Noah would smile and acknowledge them, but honestly it didn't seem to be that he was listening either.

No one from Noah's family came.

I think Noah would have been more upset if they had.

The boys seemed to be holding up okay.

I knew their hearts were broken but I also knew that they would eventually be, well, never fine, but they would be able to resume life at some point.

They had a dad that loved them and a Heavenly Father that loved them just as much.

Life for them would never be the same but it would be fine.

I hated that Robert and I had to even get up and leave their sides for even a second. But we had to when Pastor Carson asked us to come and sing Gina's song.

Frankie looked at me and I kissed his forehead.

He was just a little taller than I was and the other two were even taller. Yet they were still just children.

My heart ached for them.

I wasn't sure that I would be able to sing this song without breaking down and crying through it.

But as I sang, I remembered Gina as she laid in the bed and I sang it to her. How her face had shined with light that only people that knew what it was like to have a relationship with a heavenly Father that had His on a little sparrow, and the importance of knowing. Knowing that if He cared for the little sparrow, how much more He cared for us.

That was more than enough to make anyone happy enough to sing.

Gina had that happiness. That freedom.

And truly now she was free.

Free from pain. Free from suffering. Free to worship at her Fathers throne.

She was free.

I am sure she was singing right along with me.

So, I held on and sang it for her. I sang it for her boys and Noah.

But in the end, I sang it for myself.

I sang it because now I knew what that felt like.

I was realizing what it was like to really have a close relationship with my heavenly Father.

The air was still a little crisp outside.

It might have been spring, but it still felt like winter with the March winds blowing like they were. It wasn't harsh just a breeze. A springtime breeze with the breath of winter in it.

There was food galore at Noah's house.

So many people came and went.

The ladies that had so generously helped Robert and I make our little cottage a home, were there pouring their hearts into this little family.

Jenna was there making coffee and making sure that anyone and everyone had a cup. They also had cocoa and sweet tea for everyone.

Vicki had shown up with food as well. She brought Billie with her. They had come to the funeral and then headed straight over to help.

Billie, what could I say about her?

She was the cutest little thing.

JoJo had seen her when we got home.

They looked at each other and nodded.

Billie smiled at him and then went back to help Vicki and the other ladies.

Vicki knew that Billie had become a Christian and was so happy for her.

She had started making sure that Billie had Sunday's off so she could go to church.

She said if she wanted to work Sunday afternoons then she would work her into the schedule. Vicki was one of a kind.

Seemed like she didn't know a stranger, even if it was the first time you met her, you were family.

Billie was family to Vicki.

We stayed until everyone left and Sister Carson, Vicki, Billie and myself made sure that the food was all put away. JoJo even came and helped.

The ladies had done a fine job of making sure everything was cleaned up. But there were a few food items that still needed to be put away.

Robert and I hated to leave, even though we were still there until way after everyone else had gone. But we knew that we had to.

It was sad saying goodbye, but we both had to go to work the next day.

We knew we would be back over the next night to check on them and we were.

Gina had been celebrated and she always would be.

We were heartbroken at the loss of her, but heaven was much richer for having gained our sweet Gina.

CHAPTER 94

We had planned on going home for Easter, but adult decisions had to be made.

We knew we weren't going to miss Gina's funeral and be there for Noah and the boys.

And with Noah needing to take some time off for a few weeks it only seemed right that I stay and work to help fill in the gap.

With that decision made Pastor Carson asked Robert to preach Easter evening service.

Robert had been preaching at a few different churches on Sunday mornings as well as Sunday evenings, but it felt like home when he was asked to preach here.

We had not expected to see Noah and the boys that morning, but they were all there.

Frankie even sat with a couple of boys that he knew. Willie and JoJo sat with their dad.

JoJo noticed when Vicki and Billie came in.

She was wearing a beautiful little yellow dress. It didn't go all the way to the floor so you could see her shoes to match. With her hair pulled back in soft curls, she looked like a vision.

JoJo thought so too. He sat up straighter in the pew. He could not keep his eyes off of her.

Vicki and she sat with us that morning. Looking at

her I realized that she was right at the same age I was a lifetime ago.

I smiled when I remembered the first time at Memaw and Pappy's church when my little miss firecracker came to me.

It was the first time I had seen her since she was born. I remember not being able to hardly breathe much less comprehend or even hold a conversation with a toddler.

My heart still skipped when I thought about her.

This would be the first Easter since that day I would not see her or little MJ.

I am sure she was dressed to the nines in her Easter outfit. With her Easter basket, all ready to hunt eggs.

I knew there would be plenty of them. I had talked to Mother and she said that her and Sara had been decorating them since Friday.

They were meeting Memaw, Amy and Aunt Jessie for manicures. Then they were going to Paulie's for a late lunch.

I really envied them. I missed them all so much.

Being an adult is hard.

I didn't feel like an adult most of time. But then there were times that I felt more like an adult than I wanted too. Like now.

I really wanted to be with my family. To catch up with Amy. To spend time shopping with Patty. Having a greasy cheeseburger with Josh. But I was needed here.

Billie reached over and took my hand. She gave it a quick squeeze and church service started.

Vicki and Billie were coming to our house for Easter dinner. So were Noah and the boys.

We had a ham in the oven and potatoes ready to be cooked.

Not as many desserts as we'd had at Thanksgiving. But not as many people either.

The Carson's had been invited to eat with another family so they would not be joining us.

The Walkers were not coming either. They were out of town visiting her family.

A much smaller crowd would be joining us.

We were in the middle of getting food set out when the doorbell rang.

Our first guests had arrived.

Imagine our surprise when the first guests to arrive were none other than Toby and Patty.

They had been preaching in the next town over and wanted to surprise us.

Aunt Jessie had told them we were going to be home and the reasons why.

They knew that if we weren't there that they could get a hamburger and stay at a hotel.

We were so happy to have them.

Patty jumped right in and helped get things set up.

Vicki and Billie showed up with a Lemon Meringue Pie and a Chocolate Chiffon Pie.

No one was going to go hungry.

Noah and the boys showed up shortly afterwards.

Robert blessed the food and it was wonderful.

Patty even enjoyed it.

This pregnancy was going much better than the last one.

She still had a problem on occasion with morning sickness, but it had subsided quite a bit.

I remembered how relieved I had been when Aunt

Jessie had told me that it didn't last forever. I know I thought it would. I thought it was my punishment.

I was so glad she was right.

Patty seemed to be glowing.

It must have been one of those things.

I looked up at just the right moment.

Patty's head jerked up.

She had a funny look on her face.

Her hand went to her stomach.

"Are you ok?"

"I think so. I just felt like a little butterfly flew through my stomach."

"A what." Toby asked.

Without even thinking, I squealed.

Now everyone was looking at me.

"The baby," I pointed to her smiling.

"The baby?"

"Yes Robert, the baby! It's moving! Is that the first time you have felt that?"

Patty nodded and smiled.

Toby reached over and put his hand on her tummy.

Noah smiled a knowing smile.

"I remember the first time Gina felt this big old strapping thing move. She thought she felt butterflies just like you did. She would walk around for days with her hand on her stomach trying to feel it. After a while she was feeling him move all the time."

He looked at Patty, "Now you need to get prepared."

"Prepared for what?"

"Now that the baby is moving everyone is going to want to feel it move. Especially when it starts growing. Gina loved it. She said every trip to the bathroom to throw up had been worth it."

He looked at the boys and winked. "I guess she was right. Most of the time anyways."

"Awe come on dad. We are the arrows in your quiver."

"You're my what?" Noah chuckled.

"Your arrows in your quiver."

"Son, do you even know what a quiver is?"

"No. But I know that is what the Bible says. I think it was Palms."

"Psalms?"

"Ok. Psalms. But it is in there."

"Well Frankie, I guess you are."

"Oh, well, there it goes again. Toby, your little arrow is moving around and it is giving me quivers."

We all laughed.

CHAPTER 95

Amy had made it to church early enough to help set up for the Easter egg hunt.

She loved kids and working with them.

Like in any church they were always looking for Sunday School teachers.

They were needing a teacher for the 6 - 8 year olds.

Memaw had went with her to talk to the Pastor to see if he would be willing to let her teach it.

After he prayed about it and had talked to her old pastor, who gave her glowing praises, she started teaching the class.

Hannah was in her class and of course she loved Amy. Everyone loved Amy.

Sara had even talked to Lance so he would let her off on Tuesday mornings so she could come to their Bible study. She even convinced him to pay her for the time off.

He agreed to it as long as she would bring him a burger when she came to work after the Bible study was over.

Before long she was teaching it sometimes as well.

Lance and Amy had fast become an item.

He had started coming to church and sitting with her during church.

He didn't make it to Sunday School, but he did

make it to church.

Amy sat with Memaw and Pappy so if Lance wanted to sit with her, he had to sit with them, and they sat only a few pews back from the front.

Seems like they always sat in the same place.

After Sunday School Amy came and sat down as always. Lance didn't show up.

She looked around thinking maybe he had come in late.

His parents were there but he wasn't.

She sought them out after church.

They told her that he was not feeling well that morning.

As of late his good leg had been giving him a lot of problems.

He had been cranky and short with everyone.

His language and attitude, towards customers and even Amy, had not been what she was used to.

It made her cringe when she could hear him out in the shop using language that was not words that she wanted to hear. Especially when there were customers in the shop.

Her heart was heavy for him.

She prayed for him but it seemed like her prayers were hitting the ceiling.

She didn't know how to help him. She prayed for guidance for herself.

Was she supposed to stay in this relationship, for it truly was a relationship, or was it not supposed to be?

These questions plagued her.

She so wanted to be in God's perfect will. She knew that the Word of God said not to be unequally yoked. She didn't feel like it was God's will for her to be in a relationship with someone that didn't have a relationship with God, or at least not a relationship like she had.

She knew that God had a plan for her and the more she studied His word, the more she felt like He was leading her to teach the Word to children and anyone that would listen.

As she prayed, she still didn't feel like it was God's will for her to leave.

She did however feel like she was to continue to pray for him. And that she did.

She asked them if she should come over and check on him.

They told her is probably wasn't a good idea.

Sara pulled her in and hugged her. "We are so grateful to God that He brought you here. Keep praying for him."

Amy could feel Sara's heart for her son.

"I will. I definitely will."

Amy went with Memaw and Pappy to help get Easter on the table.

Jerry and his family were there. Joey, Jessie, and Josh would be there soon. Miss Anne was there too. She helped get everything on the table.

Amy had never seen so much food!

It was glorious.

Jerry teased her, "You think this is a lot of food, wait until you have had a feast with all of us here."

"You mean there's more of you?"

"Well, yeah. Robert and Holly and sometimes Josh has a girlfriend. Friends that are family show up."

"Speaking of which, I invited Tony and Lisa and there two little ones to join us today. They should be here in a little bit," Memaw chimed in.

"I hope you don't mind mom, but I invited the Davis's to come as well. She said that Lance wasn't feeling up to celebrating this year so I told her they should join us. She told me she would go home and check on Lance and they would bring what they were preparing for their dinner."

"The more the merrier."

"There is going to be more food? Oh, dear Lord," Amy exclaimed!

"Oh, dear Lord indeed," Aunt Jessie chimed in when she came walking in with even more food. "We're here."

Everyone hugged and Josh and Jerry's older ones slid outside to hide the eggs.

"Make sure you count them," Pappy hollered after them. "We don't want the same fiasco that happened a few years ago."

"There was a fiasco?"

"There was a fiasco. One of the eggs got missed or miscounted and laid out there for a few days baking in the sun. No one realized it because it was painted green."

"Oh yuck!"

"Yuck indeed!"

"How did you find it?"

"We followed the flies."

"Oh yuck."

"Yes ma'am. Yuck indeed!"

Amy suggested that maybe we should go to the highways and bi-ways and invite people to come in and eat.

"We do have more than enough food, but seating is

limited," Memaw chided.

The kids had been relegated to the "kids table. The bigger boys had taken their plates outside to eat and that just left the adults.

It was a glorious time.

An Easter celebration to last a lifetime.

CHAPTER 96

JoJo was going to be graduating Highschool in a few weeks. He'd had a rough year. He was going to be enrolling in college right here where his dad worked.

The tuition was discounted because his dad worked there making it affordable.

After Dean Matthews got him a few grants he was going to be able to afford it.

He was even going to be able to stay in the dorms.

It was kind of a requirement for Freshmen anyway.

And Robert was going to be graduating from College.

It had been a hard year on us as well.

Not so much financially, but just growing up.

We had to learn how to become man and wife.

So far, we'd only had a few words with each other. But we always, always came to each other and apologized. I couldn't stay angry with him and I didn't want to.

It was usually over something that one of us had done not realizing it was irritating the other one.

But once we realized the error of our ways, we always apologized.

I remember the first time Robert got super angry.

It had startled me.

He had asked me to pick up his suit from the dry

cleaners and I had postponed it to the last minute.

When I got there, they were closed.

He had planned on wearing it to the church he was preaching at that Sunday morning.

I didn't see what the big deal was. He could wear a different suit.

After he threw a fit about it and let me know how upset he was that he couldn't depend on me. My heart broke and I went into the room and shut the door and cried.

I remember the phone ringing and him answering it.

Whoever it was got an earful of how inept of a wife I was.

It wasn't a very long conversation.

After he told whoever it was what I had done I could hear him on the phone saying, "yes but" a few times.

About ten minutes later he knocked on the door.

"Holly, can I come in?"

I wanted to say no. Sleep on the couch. But I didn't.

"Yes."

I had my back to him.

He sat on the bed.

"Holly, I am so sorry. I was out of line. You do a lot of things for us to keep us going. It is just a silly old suit. I have another one that I can wear. I was wrong to take my bad day out on you like that. Can you ever forgive me?"

Tears were flowing as my heartache began to subside.

I had cried so much that my eyes were all puffy.

I turned towards him and smeared mascara all

over my face and hands.

"I'm sure I look a mess."

"You do! But you are my beautiful mess. Do you forgive me?"

"Yes. Of course, I forgive you. I love you. You are my favorite husband."

"You are my favorite wife. Can I have a kiss?

"Snot, mascara and all?"

"Snot, mascara and all!"

"No! Let me go wash my face first!"

But he didn't. He kissed me snot, mascara, and all.

Later when I asked him who he had been telling on me too, he told me it was his mother.

"Oh, she must hate me!"

"Truthfully she was angry with me."

"With you? Why you?"

"Yep. She scolded me out. She told me that I was to never tell her anything bad about you ever again. She was not going to have any son of hers bad mouthing his wife. She said surely there had to better things in this world to get upset over than a suit getting left at the cleaners. And if she ever heard me talking bad about you again, she would either hang up on me or just walk away. She wasn't going to have it!"

"Your mom is my favorite mother in law."

"I figured she would be. She is a pretty smart lady."

"Are they coming for your graduation?"

"Her and my dad are. She said Lance has been in a bad mood lately. His good leg has been giving him problems and he has been having to use the wheelchair more often. It is hard to maneuver in the bays and work on cars that way. They already have reservations. I told her your mother was coming with your Memaw and Pappy and they were going to be staying here."

"Are they ok with that, staying in a hotel?"

"Of course!"

We had paid our rent through June so that we could make sure to be here when JoJo graduated.

Pastor Carson had asked us if we would like to stay on for a while and be the youth pastor at the church.

It didn't pay much but they would throw in the cottage as part of the payment.

We asked if we could go and pray about it. And he agreed. He said he would hold the position open until the end of August. If we wanted it then the job was his.

We still weren't sure of what direction God was leading.

Were we supposed to be Evangelists like Toby and Patty?

Were we supposed to be Youth Leaders like Pastor Carson was asking?

Or was He leading us somewhere else?

It was going to have to be prayed over. A lot!

Leaving here was not going to be easy.

We had made family here.

Vicki of course.

The Carson's and the Walkers.

But especially the Masters.

They were going to be the hardest to leave.

But leave we did.

CHAPTER 97

I don't know who was more excited to see who, us or our parents.

It had been months since we had really seen them.

They had all come to the graduation, but that didn't count. Life had been too hectic to really visit.

The one person that ended up not being able to come was Pappy. He had ended up with a flare up of gout. So Memaw and Mother had shared a room.

I am sure they hadn't done that, well, ever. We heard them in bed talking and carrying on.

Robert had wanted to, well, he wanted to, but we realized if we could hear them then they could hear us, and we were not going to have any of that. I think we both would have died of embarrassment.

Mr. Davis, or Dad, as he kept telling me to call him, beat our mothers to the car.

After a million hugs and kisses they helped unload the car.

"Where is all your stuff?"

"Our clothes?"

"No. Your stuff. Your dishes. Your linens. You know. Your stuff."

"Oh, that stuff. We left it there."

"Why would you leave your stuff there?"

Robert and I explained what had transpired.

Pastor Carson said everything would be fine there while we pray about our decision and if we decide that God is leading us elsewhere then we can come pack it up in August.

"What happens in August?"

"Why don't we bring them inside out of this heat and have a soda while we talk about it."

Robert led the way.

We unfolded the whole thing.

As of right now we weren't sure where we were supposed to go.

The invitations to go preach had been dwindling. We would need them to pray with us to find God's direction.

They assured us they would pray.

Sara said she would pray but she was going to pray that God would keep us here.

"Really mom? That is how you are going to pray?"

"Well, yes and no. The mom in me is, but the woman of God is going to pray for guidance. But I miss you guys so much. I can't hardly stand you not being here. I need my babies!"

It was funny to think of ourselves as babies after all these months of adult decisions that we had made.

It was hard leaving Frankie, Willie, and JoJo. It seems as if we had known them forever and it truly had not even been a year. But once you're family, well, you're family.

Robert had to pry my arms off of them. I felt like I was leaving my babies.

With a promise to call as soon as we got here, we had to leave.

Robert called them.

"Frankie! Hey kiddo! Hey, let everybody know we got here safe and sound. Ok! I will tell her. I am sure she will do just that. Ok, bud. Write us. We promise to write back. Yes. That is a promise. You are still going to go and keep the grounds up, right? Yes. You know where everything is. Keep it looking good." Robert laughed, "I promise I will tell her. Talk to you later."

When he got off the phone, he looked at Holly.

"You are under orders, or should I say, it has been requested that you make more cookies and send them."

"More cookies? We just left that tin full of them this morning."

"I know. But Frankie informed me that they would not last the whole week and Willie had already eaten his favorite ones."

"Wille ate a dozen oatmeal raisin cookies? Oh, my Lord!"

"Well according to Frankie, he had six of them and when he got back Willie had eaten the rest of them. So, I am thinking that is brother math. The ones he ate didn't count. It was the ones that his brother ate that counted. Anyway, they need more, so he asked me to please let you know so you could send more."

"I think I will have to make more, a lot more, and send them each their own tin."

"That would be a lot of cookies!"

"Don't I know it. But did you forget who I am related to? Betty Crocker and Suzy Homemaker here can lend a hand."

"Sara, I think we have been rooked into baking," mom winked at Sara

"So, which one am I Betty Crocker or Suzy

Homemaker?"

"I'll let you choose. I am good with either one. As long as she does the dishes then I can bake all day."

"Uh, how did I get dirty dish duty?"

"That's easy. Betty Crocker and Suzy Homemaker only bake. They don't do dishes. Ta-da!"

Well, ta-da! Ok, I don't mind washing dishes, but you better make enough cookies for all three of those boys with enough left over for us. Deal?"

"What do you think Suzy Homemaker? Is it a deal?"

"Yes Betty Crocker. I think that is a deal I can live with."

We all left to go have dinner at The Burger Joint.

Memaw and Pappy were going to meet us there.

She said she would help make cookies too.

I asked her why Amy hadn't come with her? She explained Amy had not been feeling too well and was at a doctor's appointment.

She said if Amy didn't see us before this weekend that she would see us at church on Sunday.

I couldn't wait to see her and catch up.

The talk turned to Toby and Patty and how she was getting along.

Memaw said they had been in town a couple of weeks ago and Patty was glowing. She was finally showing a little. Not a lot but enough that you knew she was going to have a baby.

"You mean, in the family way," Robert said.

I laughed at that.

We all got a laugh out of it.

I couldn't wait to see her, well her and Toby. But especially her. I missed my friend.

CHAPTER 98

Mother had told Pappy that she was stepping down from her position as bookkeeper again.

I was going to start back to work for him, well at least until Robert and I knew what we were supposed to do.

Lance asked Robert if he would like to come back to work for him for a while. Summer months seemed to stay busy.

I guess people went on vacations and they all wanted their cars in tip top shape before they traveled.

We didn't want to wait until the weekend to see Amy, so we had gone by "Wheels" to see the office and well, to see her.

She practically ran from behind the desk.

"Holly! Robert! Lance told me you were back in town. I figured I wouldn't see you until Sunday the way things were going."

"We had to come by and see how this office looked. The last time we were here it was a mess. I had tried to get things in order but there wasn't enough time."

"So, you are the one that had started the piles? I wasn't sure where to start but it looked as if someone had come in and started sorting through things, so I just finished it up. After throwing away the garbage and convincing Lance that the front office could use a new paint job, it turned out pretty nice. I think it did anyway."

"Oh yeah! The walls are white now. Nice! What was the color that was on them before?"

"Dirt! We had to wash the walls before we painted. I don't think they had been washed since this building was built. It smelled nicer and it looked nicer. I hope to keep it that way."

"Good job Amy!"

Lance came into the front office.

"Hey there Amy, no fraternizing with the customers. Get back to work," he joked.

"Oh, I'm not a customer sir. I heard there was some old crotchety bear that was looking to hire a good mechanic is why I am here," Robert teased back.

"Oh really? Do you know somebody that is looking for a job? I mean, we only hire top notch around here."

They hugged each other.

"Come on out back and say hi to the guys."

They both grabbed a cup of coffee and went out back.

Amy was smiling.

"Looks like he is having a good day today."

"Looks like it. His mom told us that his good leg has been giving him some problems lately. Do you know if he has been to the doctor to see about it? Sara didn't say."

"He actually has an appointment on Monday. Robert is supposed to start on Monday, isn't he?"

"That is the plan. Back to the old grind as they say."

"Yeah. Are you going to go back to work for Pappy? I hope you don't mind that I call him that do you?"

"Did they tell you to call them that?"

"Yes."

"Then I would be upset if you didn't. I am going to go back to work for him on Monday. It has been nice having these few days off, but we have to make a living and until God gives us direction then we will be here for a while."

Amy went a little pale.

"Would you excuse me?" She left and went to the bathroom.

"Are you ok?"

Amy looked a little worse for the wear. "I will be fine. Just having some cramps. Sometimes they are worse than others. These last two months they have been a little tough."

"I know what you mean. Sorry about that."

Lance and Robert came back into the office.

I hugged Amy. I was not going to touch Lance the grease monkey.

He went in for a hug and a quick "don't you dare" look shot him down.

"See you Monday," Robert said.

"Won't you be at church on Sunday," Amy asked?

"Well, yeah. I wasn't even thinking about that. See you Sunday then."

As we left, we heard Lance ask Amy if she was ok.

"I'm fine. I can make it through the day. I'll be fine."

My heart jumped.

When we got in the car I told Robert that we needed to pray for Amy.

"Is she ok? Is she sick?"

"I don't really know. I just know that she is not feeling well today. She seems to be in pain from, well, from women stuff. More so than she should be. Can we pray for her?"

Robert took Holly's hand and they prayed.

Then they went home to make cookies! A lot of cookies!

Robert was put on clean up duty with me.

After we made three tins of cookies, one for each of the boys, we boxed them up and made it to the post office just before they closed.

He decided that we would go out to eat for dinner and we both realized it had been forever since we had eaten a lemon tart from Paulie's.

It felt like old home week when we arrived. We were just about to go inside when we noticed a couple in front of us.

"Excuse me sir, but are you and this lovely young lady on a date?"

Tony turned around.

They were so happy to see us.

"Yes, we are. We are on a date with no kids. We could have gone to McDonalds with no kids and it would have been a treat. I mean I love 'em to death but come on. Sometimes you gotta have break."

"I am his amen corner!"

"Do mind if we join you or would we be intruding?"

"Oh, please join us! Date night with other adults sounds so, well it sounds so decadent!"

And it was.

We caught up on the babies and what was going on in their lives.

They were great listeners and wanted to hear everything that had been happening since we had moved away.

They promised to pray that God would lead us in the right direction. We sat and visited forever. We practically closed the place.

"Hannah and MJ are going to be so happy to see you on Sunday. They loved the pictures of the rose bushes. I had to read that story to them forever. They now only have to have it read maybe once a week. Hannah has had to come to the realization that her little brother, as much as he adores her, does not always want to hear stories about Princess and such."

"Life lessons are hard to learn at any age."

"Yes, they are!"

Mother was still up when we got home.

"We brought you something."

"Awe, you shouldn't have."

"We felt bad that we went to eat without telling you. Holly said you loved chocolate, so we got you an order of Paulie's famous Chocolate Mousse!"

"You didn't have to do that."

"Oh, okay then I guess I will just eat it myself."

"Robert, you give that to me right now."

Robert grinned and kissed her forehead as he handed it to her.

"I wouldn't dream of keeping it to myself. You are my favorite mother-in-law!"

"Well, don't tell anybody, but you are my favorite son in law!"

"I won't."

CHAPTER 99

"Hannah, MJ, no running in church!"

"Yes ma'am," they both said, but it didn't slow them down one bit.

Hannah and MJ both made to us right about the same time.

"Mommy told us you were here!"

"She did? Well she was right, we are here."

They scooted in between us and told us everything that had been going on.

"Look," Hannah said as she lifted her lip, "I pulled my tooth. Well daddy pulled it. It didn't hurt much. But it bleeded a little. The tooth fairy came to see me. I got two quarters. Two quarters for one tooth. See this one? See how loose it is? I am trying to get it to come out too so I can get two more quarters. Then I will have four quarters and mommy said that I could add it to my other monies that I have in my piggybank and if I have enough then I can get a Barbie. I really want a Barbie."

"I don't want a Barbie. I want a GI Joe. But I still have teeth. See." MJ lifted his lip to show us all his teeth.

"Yes MJ, but you can't get one yet until daddy pulls your teeth and then the tooth fairy brings you the money."

"I know. But I don't want to not have my teeth. I guess I will have to get a GI Joe some other way then."

He looked so sad.

But not for long.

"Pappy."

He was the first one out so he beat Hannah there for the first scoop up.

Hannah had to show Pappy that she was a toothless wonder. Pappy seemed pleased that she had got two quarters for all her troubles.

Lisa pried MJ out of Pappy's arms and told them it was time for Children's Church.

Hannah saw Amy coming down the aisle. She ran to her.

"Hi miss Amy. I will see you next Sunday."

"Ok. Good job remembering your memory verse this morning! I was very proud of you!"

"Thank you! I practiced it all week. I am going to practice this one too. I will teach MJ so he can go to heaven too."

Amy chuckled, "Ok. You teach MJ too. You tell him that if he learns it then I will give him a treat next Sunday."

"You will? He isn't in our class. He should just learn it to go to heaven."

"Well, you teach it to him, and we will see about a treat for him. Remember, he isn't big like you so it might be a little hard for him to learn."

"I will do my best."

"That is all that anyone can ask of you Hannah, is that you do your best."

Hannah hugged her and ran to catch up with her mother and MJ.

We heard her explain to MJ what Amy had said.

"Maybe it will be a GI Joe."

Hannah turned to look at Amy. Now she wasn't sure she wanted to teach her little brother the verse.

If he was going to get to get a GI Joe for learning a memory verse and she was going to be toothless to get a Barbie, it didn't seem quite fair. Not fair at all.

Like we had discussed, "Life lessons are tough."

Amy was so happy so see us. We all scooted down to make room for her. She kept looking to see if Lance would show up. He did.

Her face lit up.

There was no denying it.

Anyone that looked at her could tell she really liked Lance. He looked at her the same way!

We made room for him to join us. Memaw and Pappy were beaming.

Once Mother sat down, the whole pew was pretty much filled.

Mother motioned for Roberts parents to join us. Once they joined us, we had a full house.

It had been decided that we would have lunch at their house today after church. She had a lasagna ready to go into the oven.

I was getting hungrier the more I thought of it.

Pastor James called Robert to the front to introduce him to the congregation as a newly ordained Pastor.

Pastor Davis! Robert motioned for me to stand.

I quickly stood and waved and sat back down.

Pastor Davis asked if Robert had a quick word for the people.

Never give a mic to a new pastor. They are never quick.

After telling of how God had blessed us so richly over the last few months, he asked the congregation to please pray for God to show us where we were to go. To have our hearts open to His leading. He told them we weren't sure if we were supposed to be here, traveling or if we were to go back home.

As soon as he said it, I mean as soon as he said it, I knew. I looked at Robert and he caught my eye.

As he sat back down, he took my hand. With a gentle squeeze, he looked at me and we both knew.

We were going to be going home.

CHAPTER 100

Robert and I went home to change before we went to his parents for Sunday dinner. It was the first time we had to talk.

"You know right? You felt it too?"

"I did, Robert. As soon as you said go home. I knew that is where we are supposed to be. I can't tell you why or how I knew. But as soon as you said it, my heart exploded with joy of the prospect of what God will be doing when we get back there."

"I know. As soon as I said it, it was as if God birthed it in my heart. I have a heart for those kids. I can't wait to see what He is going to do."

"Should we tell our folks now or wait? I mean if we are going to go back then I don't know if we should wait all summer before we go back. We will need to call Pastor Carson as soon as possible too."

"Tell you what, let's not say anything yet and we will call Pastor Carson tomorrow and see when he wants us to come back. How does that sound?"

"Sounds like a plan."

"A master plan!"

"No sweetheart. It is the Masters plan. Let's always seek to walk in that."

Robert pulled me close to him and we just held each other.

"Have I told you how much I love you Mrs. Davis?"

"Not today! How much?"

"This much!"

Then he kissed me!

Everyone was there by the time we walked over.

We hurried and helped set the table. Amy was already making a salad and Memaw was making a ranch dressing to go with it.

Robert's dad asked to speak with Robert for a few minutes before dinner was ready.

"Ok, but don't take too long. Dinner is almost ready and we will start without you!"

"We won't be long." He ushered Robert off into his study. He grabbed me by the arm. "You come too daughter."

I looked at Robert as we obediently followed. Robert rolled his eyes and shrugged his shoulder as if to say, "I have no idea." Neither of us did.

"Shut the door Robert."

"Sure dad. What is this about? Did we do something to upset you?"

"Nah son. I just brought you two in here to ask you not to tell your mothers yet."

"Tell our mothers? What are we not supposed to tell our mothers dad?"

"Robert, I may be off base here, but if I am not mistaken, you two got your answer this morning."

Holly looked at Robert.

"How did you know that dad?"

"The same way you did. The Holy Spirit told me. Do you two think that you are the only ones He speaks too? As soon as you said you were not sure of where you were being led, when you said go back home, I knew. Your mothers are going to be two unhappy women and I don't want it to spoil our lunch. So, until you know more don't say anything to them. Promise?"

"Yes sir!"

Holly hugged Roberts dad.

He was truly a remarkable man.

Sara knocked on the door.

"Can we come in?"

"Sure! The more the merrier!"

Sara and mother came into the room.

"So, what's the big secret? Mind letting us in on it?"

"Well, don't you think we need to get back out there to our guests?" Roberts dad tried to usher us back out.

"If we guess will you tell us if we are right?"

"Mother, you will never guess. It's ok. We can talk about it later."

"Holly, no, no. At least give us a chance to say what we think it is."

Holly looked at Robert and Robert looked at his dad.

"Ok then, tell us what you think it is ladies," Roberts dad said.

"You got your answer," Sara started.

"And you are going back," Mother concluded!

Roberts mouth fell open.

Sara smiled and reached over and closed it.

"You're catching flies! Really, did you not think that we would know? Do you two, I mean, three, think that you are the only ones that hears when the Holy Spirit speaks.

"Well I'll be!"

"Well I'll be very hungry. Now that everybody knows, let's go eat."

"Not everybody knows. We didn't say anything to anybody in there. So, if you don't feel like saying anything then we can all talk later."

We all ushered ourselves to the table where a piping hot Lasagna had just been set.

Pappy was asked to say grace.

"Heavenly Father, we thank thee for thy bountiful blessings. We thank thee for wonderful friends and family to share it with. But mostly Father, we thank thee for answered prayers. Thank you Father for leading and guiding us and showing us where you would lead us. And we pray that you would keep your hand of blessing on Robert and Holly when they go back home to step into your will. Keep them safe and under your wing as they walk in your directives. In Jesus name! Amen!

Holly looked all around at the people, their family, and friends in disbelief.

"Does everyone know?"

They all nodded. Robert started to laugh.

"Know what," Lance asked.

"Know that I am going to be a short-term employee brother. Holly and I are going to be going back to Trinity to be the Youth Pastors. We will have to call Pastor Carson tomorrow and see when he wants us. Sorry about the short notice."

"Well, I'll be," Lance said.

Everyone laughed.

CHAPTER 101

Summer had come and gone too soon! The highlight had been our anniversary.

A first anniversary celebrated in Aunt Jessies and Uncle Joeys barn was the best.

Toby and Patty were able to be there. It was so nice to have them around.

It was a celebration just like so many that had come and gone. This time though it was Josh and his friends that filled the place.

Josh and a couple of boys from church had the fireworks set up in back, ready for a celebration like no other.

"Remember when we were out here and you rescued me from that snake"

"Oh Lord, yes I remember that. I did not know that I could run that fast."

"Me either!"

Holly shivered impulsively just thinking how close that snake had been to her.

"I hate snakes!"

"Me too," Patty agreed.

"Me three," Amy said. "They give me the heebie-jeebies!"

Lance just shook his head laughing and walked away. "Girls," he muttered.

"Girls what," Toby asked as he came in.

"Girls talking about snakes."

"Oh. Why are you talking about snakes?"

Patty smiled, "We were just remembering the time I saved your cousin from certain death by saving her from that snake."

"Oh yeah, that is when mom found out that dad had given Josh a gun and had taught him how to use it."

"You know, I have been meaning to talk to him about that all these years. Thanks for reminding me."

"See what you started? So much for going down memory lane!"

"Dad, you might want to turn and run," Toby said as he went out the door.

"Why is that son?"

"Mom was just reminded of you giving Josh a gun and showing him how to use it."

"Who reminded her of that?"

"Your favorite daughter in law and your favorite niece."

"Traitors," he called into the front screen.

They went to the barn to finish setting things up.

This would be the last party in here for a while.

They were going to be bringing Josh up to start college in the fall. If all turned out, we hoped he would be able to get a dorm room with JoJo.

We were pretty sure they would be close friends.

They both had been given scholarships and some grants.

Josh would need a job to help make ends meet. Vicki was always looking for help. Now that JoJo was waiting instead of bussing, they might need him.

Robert had called her. She said if she had an opening when he got there that she would be more than happy to talk to him and see if he was interested.

Josh was more than happy with that prospect.

He had heard us talk about Vicki and The Whistle Stop Café for years. Now he would be able to see it for himself.

The food was glorious, and the company was even better.

Lisa and Tony brought the kids out for the celebration, after all, they were family.

Robert and I asked if it would be okay if we gave Hannah a Barbie car for her birthday.

"Of course. She doesn't have one. But I can't guarantee that GI Joe might not take it for a spin on occasion."

Memaw made her a special cake with sparklers on it.

Her little eyes lit up when we all sang happy birthday to her.

It was a glorious day.

Josh thought so too.

Janey and he were on again.

She had realized that she wanted a man of God in her life. Josh was surely that!

They had a long talk about what that might entail, and she told Josh that whatever God had instore for them she was a willing vessel.

He told me that she came to him and asked him out to dinner.

When she poured her heart out to him about how she had been praying and she felt like God was speaking to her and leading her into obedience to

Him. She wanted him to know how she really felt.

Josh said, "I told her I would think about it. Really, I prayed about it. I want a Godly wife. I see what Toby and Patty have to do. It isn't easy. If that is what God calls me to do then I am going to need a wife that will stand side by side with me."

"Josh, you young man, are my favorite little brother. She is going to be one blessed young lady if she ends up with you."

"Yes, yes she will," Josh blushed.

He nodded in her direction and with a quick hug he headed over to her.

CHAPTER 102

Goodbyes are always the hardest.

When we had moved last year, we thought we would be coming back here, at least for longer than a couple of months.

We had been able to visit with everyone on several occasions.

Grandmother and Grandfather Abernathy even said they might come up and see us.

We told them we would be thrilled to have them.

Both of us had gotten our jobs back.

The auto mechanic shop said that Robert could come back to work for them and leave earlier on Wednesdays and Fridays so that he could be available for the youth. The church was going to give him a salary and we could stay in our little cottage rent free as part of it.

Dean Matthews said he was glad I was coming back. He was glad he wouldn't have to try and get someone else.

Noah and the boys were glad we were coming back too.

It felt like we were home as soon as we walked in the door. A little musty and dusty, but nothing a little elbow work wouldn't take care of.

Gabby, Jenna, and Sister Carson came by about an

hour after we got home.

They came with cleaning supplies.

"We figured you could use the help."

We were most grateful.

It didn't need a full cleaning like it had before. We had left it pretty tidy when we had locked the door behind us.

We had thought that day that when we came back to our little cottage, we would be coming back to get our things and move into whatever ministry He had for us. We never dreamed that day that He would bring us home.

Frankie came running through the door.

"You're home!"

My arms went around him instinctively.

It wasn't two seconds later that Willie had joined him.

"We rode our bikes. You said you'd be here and look here you are."

"Hey, what am I chopped liver?" Robert held out his arms.

"It is so good to have you home," Frankie hugged him.

"It is good to be home! Where is JoJo?"

"He had to work today. He said him and Miss Vicki would be coming by in a little while. He said to tell you that Miss Vicki said she would be bringing you your pie."

Sister Cason said she was going to call her and have her bring two so she could take one home to Pastor.

We were taking the week off to make sure everything was in order before we started back to work.

Pastor Cason and Robert needed to talk things over regarding what he really expected from Robert and Robert wanted to pour his heart out for where he felt God was wanting him to do.

It was going to be a great beginning for everything God had instore for us.

Robert was supposed to start working at the church at the end of August but since we came back early, they hoped to have him start early.

Friday nights were going to be Youth night at the church.

Pastor Carson asked if Robert would be willing to allow the college kids to come if they wanted.

Robert thought that would be great.

That way the older ones could mentor the younger ones.

Win - win situation.

We knew that we would have two young men that we truly wanted coming. Josh and JoJo. It would be great if Janey would come as well. And even though Billie didn't go to college here we hoped she would show up too.

We couldn't wait to see what God was doing in her life.

Vicki said she was the most exuberant child of God that she had ever seen.

JoJo and Billie would be off studying the Bible together when it was a slow night.

She still had one more year of Highschool and if she could afford it, she was going to try to get into college here.

We were sure that was going to be doable.

She was a blessing to our heart.

We found out from Vicki that she was being raised by her dad who was an alcoholic. He wasn't abusive or anything, but he just barely provided for her.

She had been working since she was fifteen doing odd jobs to make sure they had food and a place to stay.

Our hearts were broken for her. She was a beautiful little girl.

God was going to do great things in her life. We were sure of it.

God was going to be doing great things in all our lives. We were sure of that too!

We weren't sure how long He was going to have us here, but we knew that we would do everything in our power, or should I say in His power, to teach these kids about God and how they could walk in His fullness!

Willing vessels!

CHAPTER 103

Amy followed Lance into his office after picking up the wrench that had barely missed her.

"What is your problem?"

"What are you talking about? I don't have a problem."

"I beg to differ. You almost hit me with this wrench."

"Yeah, well. Just give it back to me."

"Here." She sat it on his desk.

"Why are you so angry?"

"It's none of your business," Lance snarled!

"Well, it kind of is. Especially when I'm sitting in the front office and customers come in. They can hear you out here carrying on. You have been like this a lot lately. Ever since your brother left a few weeks ago. What in the world is going on?"

"To be honest Amy, it's none of your business, like I said. You can tell anyone that comes in and seems to be bothered by the noises that are coming from the shop, that if they don't like it, they can take their business elsewhere."

Amy just stood there looking at him.

"I just wish you would talk to me. To somebody.

I know you weren't raised to act like this. You know men don't have to act like this right?"

"What do you know about me Amy? How do you know how I was raised?"

"Really Lance, you forget I know your family. I know how they act.

You can't tell me that your dad ever acted or re-acted the way you do.

And I know your mother too, remember? Are you going to tell me that when she gets frustrated at a pan of cookies that doesn't turn out right or they burn, that she throws the pan across the room? Yeah, I don't think so."

"Well Amy, you're right. They don't act or re-act to things like I do.

But then again, they wouldn't have a reason to do so, now would they?

They have both of their legs and can get around and do anything they want to. And as for the wrench, I didn't throw it at you. I just threw it and you just happened to come out here at the wrong time."

"You don't have to be missing a leg to have issues Lance. But you don't have to have a pity party all the time either.

I don't understand how you don't know that. It makes me sad that you choose to live this way. I just don't see..."

Lance cut her off.

"Oh, I know what you see. I see how you look at me."

"And how's that, pray tell?"

"With pity!"

"You're right! I do pity you.

Not because you only have one leg or that you have to use a wheelchair on occasion.

I pity you because I think, how can a man have so much and still have so little?"

"You don't even know. You know nothing of what it's like to have to live like this. To live in constant pain."

"Really, you think so? You think I know nothing of pain?"

"Yeah. That's exactly what I think.

You come in here telling me how I have a constant pity party going on. You know nothing about what I've been through. Or what it's like to watch your friends die, for nothing, Little Miss Perfect!

You come in here all high and mighty. Like Little Miss Perfect Christian!

Oh, so perfect, and try to tell me how to live.

You tell me I can be free of these demons, this anger, this hatred.

Yeah, well, I was raised in church!

I've heard all of that before.

I've seen men and women come and go from there.

Yeah, okay, some were changed, but most of them were like me. We can't all be Robert, now can we?

Don't you think I've prayed?

Do you think I want to live like this?"

Amy was silent.

She bowed her head as tears fell from her eyes as she prayed.

Finally, she raised her head and went and closed the blinds.

"Close the door Lance," she whispered.

"Why?"

"Just do it!"

Lance reached around and closed the door behind

him.

"Lock it."

She had never been this quiet before.

She had his attention.

"You said you think I know nothing of pain. That I don't know what it's like to lose someone I love.

You have only focused on yourself for so long that no one or anyone else mattered.

Well Lance, you know nothing of me or my life.

You assume that my life has been a bowl of cherries!

It wasn't!

Tell me Lance, tell me some of the things you did as a child.

What are some of your favorite childhood memories? Things that left sweet thoughts in your head or bring a smile when you think about them."

"Why?"

"Because I asked."

"Well, I remember a lot of things. One in particular was going fishing with my dad and Robert at the lake. That was always fun.

I remember building model cars with them. I always had to have them just right. Perfect. My dad would help me make sure that they were.

Sunday dinners were always pleasant. My mom is one of the best cooks I know.

I remember playing football with Robert and our friends out in the front yard ever since we learned how.

I remember lots of things."

"So, it was fun? Remembering those things bring a smile to your heart?"

"Yeah. What about you? Didn't you do family things?"

"Oh, yeah. I used to play hide and seek with my baby brother. We would hide from my stepfather, hoping he would pass out before he found us so he wouldn't beat us.

We used to play, let's see if we have anything besides crackers and bottles of booze in the cupboard so we could eat something.

I used to pretend that I was the Queen of Sheba so that I wouldn't have to think about him holding me down so he could have his way with me.

But Lance, my favorite game of all was human ashtray.

It's not as much fun of a game as one might think."

As she spoke, she slowly unbuttoned her blouse, letting it fall off her shoulders. She turned away and moved her beautiful brown hair that covered her back, to the side and in front of her, revealing scars of all kinds all over her back.

Lance was silent.

What could he say?

He noticed she had not moved.

Her head was leaned forward, and he could tell she was crying.

He went to her and bent down and picked up her blouse, carefully draping it across her shoulders, covering her back.

They both stood there for a while.

Amy slowly got her composure.

Wiping her eyes before she turned to face him as she buttoned her blouse.

"You see Lance, you are not the only one to have

had life happen to you.

You are not the only person that has ever been hurt in this world.

And yes, I have seen someone die.

Someone that I loved dearly, beyond words.

I watched my stepfather kill my baby brother. I watched as his little life flowed out of him onto the floor as his blood spilled out of the side of his head.

I watched this, helpless to do anything, as he held me down and raped me and told me that it was all my fault.

I watched my mother die when she fell on the knife she had just tried to kill me with.

So, sweet family memories are not what gets me through.

It's Jesus.

Only Jesus!

You see, Lance, the world is full of hurting people. People that don't deserve bad things to happen to them, yet it does.

Bad things happen to good people and good things happen to bad people.

The book of Matthew tells us that God causes it to rain on the just as well as the unjust!

It is up to you Lance to decide what you will do with the life you have been given.

I choose to give mine to God and let Him make something beautiful from this ash heap.

If I hadn't, then who knows, I could have been just like my mother, if not worse.

I had to quit hating her, to love her, to forgive her.

I didn't want to, but I had no choice.

If I am going to live for Christ, call myself a

Christian, then I must do what He asks of me.

He has told me to walk in love and forgiveness.

Once I realized that my mother had been in as much need of a Savior as I was, my heart broke for her.

I don't know what happened in her life that caused her to be like she was.

I don't know why she rejected the way she was raised.

You see, I know she was raised in church by a Godly woman, my grandmother. But she chose a different path.

Much like you are doing.

You are taking all your hurts, your pain and anger and blaming God instead of laying that burden at His feet.

I can't make you see or understand how or what I feel about living for God and what He means to me. I just know that ever since I gave my life, my heart, my all, every hurt, every grief, every pain, everything to Him, I have not been the same!

When I gave it all to Him, I was filled with a peace and a joy that I am never going to be able to explain.

He filled every void, every emptiness, with His love.

Me, someone so unworthy, He calls me His child.

He calls me His daughter.

He calls me beloved.

He calls me redeemed.

Yes, I am redeemed by His love!

I am so far from perfect Lance.

I mess up all the time.

Sometimes I get angry and say things that I shouldn't.

But, then Lance, there are times I get angry and say things I should.

I loved my mother, but I never had a chance to tell her how worthy she was of God's love.

That she was redeemable.

She went into eternity not knowing the Savior.

My Savior!

So, I made it my life's goal, that if it was in my power to tell someone about God and His amazing, redeeming love, then I would do so.

Especially if it was someone that I loved.

I have already lost too much to Satan.

My heart is breaking Lance."

She looked him straight in the eye.

"You see, I do love you. I made the mistake of letting my heart feel for the first time.

I do love you and I want you to know my Savior and be set free just like I am.

But as much as I love you Lance, I love my Savior more. And I won't compromise!

I have told you everything I could possibly think to tell you, to show you, about how I feel.

But Lance, I can't stay here!"

She walked to the door. She unlocked it and stood there for a moment.

"I will let you know where to send my check."

"Where are you going to go?"

He couldn't take his eyes off her.

"I'm not sure. I just know it can't be here."

She turned to look at him one last time.

"I do love you, leg or no leg. Wheelchair or no wheelchair.

Scars and all!

None of that matters.

I guess, Lance, I fell in love with the man that I know God wants you to be. Only He can make you whole.

Goodbye Lance."

She turned and walked out the door,

She left it open and Lance just stood there and watched her go.

CHAPTER 104

She stopped at her desk and gathered a few things before going to her car. Once she got in, she sat there for a few minutes. He watched as she pulled away from the parking lot.

He wanted so badly to stop her but if she was dead set on leaving then he wasn't going to try and change her mind.

How could he?

What could he even say?

She was right!

Everything she said was right!

But that didn't change how he felt.

That didn't change the anger, the rage, the sadness, the depression.

Just because she was right, it didn't change things.

It didn't change anything!

How did she do it?

How did she manage to live through such hell and not have these same feelings?

These same issues?

Just knowing what that man had done to her, seeing those scars, man, just seeing that, made him even angrier.

Everything in him wanted to run after her and hold her, comfort her. But she'd made it clear that he would not have any part of her life until he changed his.

What could he give her anyways?

More heartache and grief?

She'd already had enough of that in her life.

He was suddenly brought out of his thoughts when the phone rang.

"Hello."

"May I speak to Amy Pinkerton please?"

"You just missed her. Who's calling?"

This is Sabrina at Dr. Shackleford's office. I am calling to confirm her appointment for surgery next week. It is scheduled for Wednesday morning. Can you get this message to her?"

"Um, I can try."

"Let her know she will need to be there by 6:30 a.m. to check in. The surgery is scheduled for 7:30 a.m. Let her know she needs to get her lab work done by Thursday. Can you get her this message?"

"I said I'll do my best."

"Have her call us with any questions. She will need a ride there and a ride home barring any complications. I have a Lance Davis as her contact person. Maybe you can let him know so he can..."

"Listen lady, I already said I'd tell her." He hung up the phone.

What in the world Amy?

What is going on with you?

Why in the world would you put me as your contact person?

Then he remembered her asking him a couple of months back if she could.

Now the hard part, finding her to get her the

information she needed.

And harder yet getting her to tell him what was going on!

CHAPTER 105

Lance was waiting at the church bright and early Tuesday morning.

He knew the Women's Bible Study started at 9 and Amy would be there.

She sometimes taught it. He wasn't sure if she was teaching this morning or not, but he knew she'd be there.

She was always there.

She hadn't shown up yet and he was getting a bit antsy with all these other women starting to show up.

"Lance, what are you doing here? Shouldn't you be at work?"

"Mom, you scared me half to death. Don't sneak up on my like that."

"Sorry baby. Just surprised to see you here. You do know it's Women's Bible Study, don't you?"

"Funny mom. Yes, I know. I need to see Amy."

"She isn't here today."

"What do you mean she isn't here today?"

"Well, you should know. She is going out of town. She called me last night and asked if I would be willing to teach the Bible study today because she was going out of town and wasn't sure how long she'd be gone. She sounded upset. I figured you would know. Doesn't she work for you? She didn't let you know she was going out of town?"

"No. Did she say where she was going?"

"No, just that she had to go and that she would be in touch."

"Where do you think she would go?"

"I don't know. Lance, you have me worried. Is everything ok?"

"No, I just need to know where she went."

"Well, I'm certain I don't know. Maybe Sister Lewis or Anne knows."

"Can you find them?"

"Sure son. I will be right back."

Before long Sister Lewis came outside.

"Hi Sister Lewis."

"Hi Lance. How are you doing this morning?"

"Not well. Do you know where Amy might have gone off to?"

"Well, she left this morning about the same time that I did. She had her suitcases loaded and said she would be gone for a while. She seemed upset. She was crying. Is she ok Lance? She didn't seem to be. I held her and prayed with her before she left.

Lance, we love that girl around here. We don't want to lose her."

"Me either. It's all my fault that she is gone."

"Oh yeah, what happened?"

"We had an argument yesterday and she let me know under no uncertain circumstances that she wants anything to do with me."

"None huh?"

"Yep. None! I don't blame her really. I don't want to have anything to do with me either, but I'm kind of stuck with myself. But that is neither here nor there.

I have to find her. I have a very important message to give her. It's is pretty vital that I get it to her. You don't have any idea where she might have gone?"

"Oh, I have an idea."

"Well, come on then? Tell me?"

"Well, if I was a betting woman, I would bet that she went back to the only other place that she called home."

"She went home. That's right. She went back home!

Thanks Sister Lewis. How long ago did she leave again?

"Close to forty-five minutes I'm guessing."

"Okay then. Hey, tell my mom I probably won't be home tonight," he said as he got in his car and sped out of the parking lot.

He stopped at the shop to let Bailey know that he was going to have to run the shop for a day or two. He told him to make sure him and Matthew closed everything up and locked everything up.

Then he headed for home to pack a bag.

He had to get her back so she could get her lab work done so she could get whatever surgery she needed.

It was only a two-hour drive and she had a good hour on him.

Why in the world would she go back there?

Was she going back to an old boyfriend?

Some guy who would go to church with her and not be so needy?

Some guy with two legs?

Maybe it wasn't a guy after all?

Maybe she was so disgusted by me that she had to get as far away from me as possible.

Well she could be disgusted with me and hate me all she wanted after next Wednesday. If she needs surgery for something, then she can just get it and then leave.

But not until then!

What was she thinking, leaving like this?

Why didn't she tell someone she needed surgery?

Maybe she did, but just not me.

What was I thinking following her up here like this?

Why should I even care?

She doesn't care about me.

Wait, that isn't exactly what she said.

Why in the world would she ever fall in love with me?

I don't blame her for not wanting to be around me.

She deserves a whole man.

Not damaged goods!

She was right. I do have a lot of pity parties.

It was a party I invited myself to every day.

"Pity. Party of one!"

Yeah, that's me.

I mean, I know that I went through a lot. But not any more than most men who fought in wars. Some were much worse off than I was. I only lost one leg and hurt the other one.

A lot of men lost more than that.

Charlie Dickerson lost both of his arms and one of his eyes. He was getting along pretty good. His wife loved him. She stayed with him. They just had a baby boy the last I heard.

Jack Lawson didn't fare so well. His fiancé left him when she found out he was going to be in a wheelchair for the rest of his life.

He said he didn't blame her, but he sure was drinking a lot.

A lot of the guys that came back didn't have it near as good as I did. That's for sure.

My parents had turned the den into my bedroom so I wouldn't have to go up and down the stairs so much. It was more convenient, but I missed my room.

My dad and I just didn't talk sports like we used to. It was hard knowing that he felt he couldn't talk to me about things we'd had in common.

Sure, it made me mad that I wasn't going to ever be able to play football like I had. I had done well in sports in Highschool. Me and Robert were still tied as highest touchdowns ever in that school. I don't think anyone has beaten us, yet anyways.

But just because I couldn't play doesn't mean I don't like watching it still and talking about it.

Mom, man, what can I say about her?

There were a lot of hungry guys left behind when I came home and the cookie source stopped.

She won't let me get away with crap!

I think that is why I liked Amy so much. She reminded me of my mother. Except that she was young and beautiful and that brown hair of hers that was so curly and soft and when she smiled at me in the mornings when she came in to work and said good morning to me, well, it almost made the day worthwhile.

Who am I kidding! It always made the day worthwhile.

Why did I continually let those thoughts, those memories come into my head? Like a flood they would run rampant until I just couldn't concentrate on what I was doing. It frustrated me to the point of confusion.

Like yesterday when I threw the wrench. Just because I couldn't get my one good leg to turn just right so I could get it where I needed it, so I threw it, hard. If it had hit her it could have hurt her bad.

He shivered at the thought of it.

That is the last think I would ever want to do is to hurt Amy.

I loved her.

Wait, what?

I loved her! I really did love her.

Honestly, if I wasn't having a pity party my every thought was about her.

How pretty she was. How kind she was, even to some of our more colorful customers, even to me. How she always seemed to be singing some song in the front office.

I would turn the radio off just to listen. Sure, it was some church song, or some song about Jesus or something, but she sang so beautifully that if I knew she was singing, I always wanted to hear it.

Man, I remember the day I hired her. Gosh, not even a year ago.

Bailey came into the shop office, "There's a lady out in front to see ya, boss."

I remember asking what kind of repair she needed.

I remember walking into the front and there she was.

I honestly had never seen a more beautiful woman. She took my breath away.

She wasn't dressed at all like the girl I had just fired.

She had really been a flake.

My hands were covered in grease. I started to shake her hand but changed my mind. I did not want to get that muck on her.

She told me that she was staying with the Lewis's and was needing a job.

I remember her telling me that she knew Robert and Holly. How they had stayed at her resort, or at least the one she worked at.

Mostly I remembered because they had talked about her owning that Fairlane that she drove.

"Yeah, my name is Amy Pinkerton. Like I said, I am looking for a job and he told me you might be looking for someone."

Imagine my surprise when she was willing to start right then.

I remembered telling her that I could have used her two weeks ago."

She had that place in order in no time.

And coffee!

Man, she made the best coffee in town.

She even had to clean the pot and the coffee cups before she could show off those skills.

Invoices were filed. The place was clean. She'd even talked me into painting the place. Customers were happy. Coffee was made and Bailey was in heaven.

I remember him asking me after she had been there a couple of weeks if I was going to ask her on a date.

If I hadn't, I am sure he would have beat me to the punch.

Once Cheryl decided that if he wasn't the marrying

kind then she would need to find someone who was, Bailey realized that maybe he was the marrying kind.

Their wedding was going to be in November I think

Remembering that conversation brought a smile to his face.

CHAPTER 106

Now to find Amy.

Where in the world is she?

She can't be that hard to find. I mean how many blue and white Fairlane's can there be in this town? Hopefully only one.

He drove all over town looking for her or her car.

He finally realized he was going to have to find a place to stay for the night.

Maybe he could stay at that Spa she'd worked at. Maybe they might know where she might have gone if she didn't happen to come back here.

But she did!

He recognized that car anywhere.

He went into the lobby hoping to catch her but she wasn't there.

The man at the front desk seemed friendly enough.

"Has a girl named Amy Pinkerton been in here recently?"

"Sir, we cannot give away information about our guests. Is she expecting you?"

"No. I'm just a friend. I thought I noticed her car out there. I was hoping to catch her here."

"Well, sir, she is not in here. Would you like a room?"

I was going to need a room. I had to stay here until

I found her.

"Yeah, what do you have available?"

"Well, tonight we have three suites available. They are all the same suite but suite 21 is a bit more secluded than the other two."

"I'll take that one."

"Okay. Just sign in here and I will have the bell boy show you where it is."

Lance signed the book and noticed that the guest that had signed in right before him was staying in suite 20. Amy was not going to be that hard to find after all.

He followed the bell hop to suite 21.

He showed him all around and then of course the best part, the ocean for a back yard.

I could get used to this he thought.

He tipped him and he started to put his clothes away and then thought better of it.

"I am only going to be here one night. No point in unpacking."

He sat down on the loveseat, leaving the front door slightly ajar, hoping to hear Amy when she pulled up.

But he fell asleep instead.

He must have been asleep for a couple of hours because it wasn't quite dark outside, but it wasn't still broad daylight out anymore either.

He looked outside.

Still no Amy.

"I need something to eat," he thought as his stomach started growling.

"Wonder what they got around here that is good."

He drove to the lobby. The same guy was there. But Amy's car wasn't there anymore.

"What's good around here for a place to eat?"

"Well, sir, we have a lot of good restaurants around here. We have one right through those doors or plenty of them downtown. Would you like a list?"

"Where do the locals eat?"

Well, there is Harry's Pizza Palace. There's Tony's. It is a little Mexican food restaurant. Let me think, oh yeah, today is Tuesday! Today there is a little place downtown that everybody goes to. It's Taco Tuesday! They have some of the best tacos in town, especially when they are discounted for Taco Tuesday! I am going to be going there when I get off work myself."

"How would I get to this place? That sounds pretty good."

"You won't be disappointed!"

He gave directions and Lance found it with no problem.

He sat down and ate three of them and realized that he could probably eat a dozen.

He ordered six more to go.

He was just walking into his suite when he heard talking coming from his neighbor's suite.

"Who is she talking to? I know I hear a man's voice.

He went inside and put his food away and stepped back outside hoping to get a glance of who she was talking to. He finally noticed her car pulled up in the driveway, so he knew he was right, it was Amy.

He stepped back in the shadow as the door opened.

What in the world Amy?

An older man, a much older man stepped out of the door. He stopped and I could see her lean into him and hug him and he hugged her back.

"See you in the morning," Amy said.

I hurried and went back inside.

I heard her door shut and then I heard a car drive away.

Really Amy?

What was I going to do?

I knew what I was going to do.

I went next door and knocked on the door.

“Did you forget something,” she said as she opened the door?

CHAPTER 107

"Nope."

Amy's face went white.

"What are you doing here?"

"I might ask the same of you. What are you doing here?"

"Well, if you really want to know, now that I no longer have a job, I was trying to get my old one back, if they would have me."

"And what job was that?"

"Front desk manager. I told you that a long time ago remember. I was just talking to Curly and his wife. I have been praying with them about it all day, well ever since I got here."

"So that is who was here when I pulled up?"

"Oh, you saw them?"

"Well, no, not really. I heard the talking."

"Oh."

"Well, when do you start?"

"I don't."

"They wouldn't hire you back?"

"Nope. We prayed about it a lot. We even went to the church and talked to Pastor Marks. They are two very Godly men. Between them and Curly's wife and myself praying. We all felt that God was telling me this is not where I am supposed to be."

"Where are you supposed to be Amy?"

"First things first. Why are you here?"

I had almost forgot why I came down here.

"Well I have a message for you from your doctor. Yesterday, pretty much right after you left, your doctor's office called, Dr. Shackleford? They wanted me to let you know that your surgery was scheduled for next Wednesday. You have to be there no later than 6:30 that morning and the surgery is at 7:30.

You are supposed to get lab work by Thursday."

"Oh, well, I guess I am going to have to cancel it."

"Why? Why would you cancel it? Why Amy?"

"Uh, because I don't have a job now. If I don't have a job, then I don't have insurance. If I don't have insurance, then I can't afford to have the surgery. You came all the way here to tell me that?" Why would you do that?"

"Really Amy, you have to ask me that?"

"You are not the only one that gets to declare that you love someone then turn around and leave, then expect that the one that loves you back isn't going to try to find you when he finds out you have been holding secrets from him about your health. What is going on Amy?"

She turned away.

"It's just a little surgery that I need. I can do it another time. I mean, I am not going to die if I don't have it right now. So sorry you wasted your trip."

"I didn't waste my trip. I got to see you again and well, I got tacos for Tuesday Taco night."

Amy turned around.

"Ooh, I forgot about those. I am so hungry right now. I wonder if they still have any?"

She started to grab her purse.

"How many could you eat?"

"At least three."

"Would you like to have dinner with me Amy? I just happen to have extra's in my suite."

"Ooh, are you kidding me right now?"

"Nope. Here is my key. I will go down to the lobby and get us some sodas."

She took the key and he drove the Fairlane.

When he got back, they had some talking to do.

CHAPTER 108

"Okay, Amy, now that I have fed you, tell me what's up?"

"Be more specific."

"Okay, specifically, why didn't you tell me you were needing to have surgery?"

"Well, you never asked."

"That isn't going to fly. We have been dating for several months now. I know I have been a jerk. A lot! But we've talked about a lot of things. You never once told me about the abuse you went through. You haven't mentioned once that you were seeing a doctor for something serious. What I want to know is why?

Why didn't you tell me any of this?"

Amy thought for a moment.

She didn't want to speak and say something that she was going to regret.

She always told herself, "Measure your words carefully Amy, they fit better coming out of your mouth than they do going back in."

How could she make him see that the abuse that she took, although it was horrible and no one should ever have to go through it, that is not what was going to define who she was.

She decided that was the path that she needed to take.

"Lance, I was probably out of line yesterday when I showed you my scars. When I let you in on the abuse that I went through. But I did that because I wanted you to understand that just because we go through things, no matter how horrendous they are, that is not what defines who we are. It can. But it doesn't have to.

I am choosing a different path. I choose to forgive my stepfather and my mother for the things that happened in my life.

I would rather walk in forgiveness and have peace and joy than be full of hatred and rage.

Those things are like a cancer that eats away at who you are.

I did nothing to cause the things that happened to me.

Just like you. You were doing your job. You didn't go to war and ask to have your leg blown off. You didn't go to war in hopes that your friends would die right before your very eyes.

We didn't ask for that. But that is what happened.

Now it is up to us to do with that what we will.

If I had not met the Lord, my life would be messed up.

Really messed up.

When my Granny died, she was my last bastion, my last hope.

She couldn't take me to church. My mom wouldn't let her.

She would tell my Granny, "Why do you want to take the kid to church? A lot of good it did me."

So, she couldn't take me. But she could show me.

She showed me what love was supposed to be like.

Love and gentle and kind, it didn't put on heirs.

Love put others above themselves.

She didn't have much, but she was always giving to her neighbors who had even less. She wouldn't buy us new clothes because she knew that my mother would take them back and get the money for them. So, she would find us the best clothes that she could at garage sales and such. She loved on us and we felt it. We knew it.

I was 12 when she died. She just fell asleep and didn't wake up. My mom looted her house before she even called the police to let them know. She took everything of value. All I wanted was her Bible.

She used to read to us out of it when we were allowed to stay there.

But my mother said that it belonged to her and she was going to sell it to get some money so she could buy us some food.

We should have known she was lying. She did sell it, but she just bought more booze or drugs.

After that, I would try to remember the stories she would tell us. My little brother loved the story of David and Goliath. What little boy wouldn't. I am sure I messed it up telling it to him. I didn't have a Bible and I was trying to tell it from memory. But I was a kid and doing the best I could.

I didn't show you those scars to make you feel sorry for me. I don't feel sorry for myself anymore.

I prayed before showing them to you. I felt the Holy Spirit tell me to show you.

Like I said, I don't feel sorry for myself. I used to.

I always felt like I was walking around in lead boots and an iron overcoat.

Then that night when Pastor Toby asked people that wanted to be set free, for people that wanted to let go of the hurts and the pain, that wanted to leave it all at the altar, I had to do it. I had to go forward and do it.

I was so tired of it all.

I truly can't explain how I felt that night when I got up from there.

I mean, I was wearing the same old raggedy clothes that I had knelt down in, but when I got up, it was like I was so clean.

I am not saying all the hurts and the memories went away just like that, but little by little I realized that Satan was just trying to bury me again in all that filth and I was not going to have it.

With the help of a very Godly woman, I called her Mama Jane, she helped me to learn how to study the Word of God and apply it to my life.

She explained that the things that happened to me were not my defining moments.

My defining moment happened when I made the choice.

When I decided what to do with my life.

She told me that I was a new creation. Old things had passed away and I was born again.

I wasn't sure exactly what that meant but I have since found out.

It was like I had a new slate to start writing my life story on.

I could write it, or I could let Christ write it.

My penmanship is a joke, so I chose Jesus.

I sometimes take the pen away from Him and try to do some of the writing myself.

Like yesterday.

Instead of really praying about what I should do I let my emotions speak and I shouldn't have done that.

Do I regret showing you what I did? No. But do I regret walking out on you and saying that I couldn't be there? Yes.

You see, I do my best to listen to what God asks me to do.

Like walking into your business looking for a job.

Brother Lewis did tell me you were looking for someone, but I prayed about it before I went there. I felt the Lord was telling me that I needed to go there. That is why I went.

But when I left yesterday, that was all me.

Curly and his wife were telling me the same thing this evening.

He told me that he did have a place for me, but he knew that I was not supposed to be here.

I knew it too.

You asked me why I didn't tell you before about the abuse, I guess there might be a few reasons.

One is because I don't really dwell on my past. It isn't like I am trying to forget it. It's just that I don't pick it up and wear it around. It is too heavy a garment to wear. I prefer garments of praise.

And Lance, another reason, and please don't get mad or take this the wrong way, but you seemed to not really care about what I might be going through. You were too busy worrying about what others thought about you because you only have one leg. I am going to tell you what people think about you. I hear it all the time.

They say you are one of the best mechanics they have ever been to. You are honest and you don't sell them something they don't need. You treat them like family. They also say they wish you would be more friendly. Some of the men would love to bring their sons down so they could watch you work. They think you are a marvel at your work, but they don't want to expose their kids to your anger.

And I guess that might be why.

"I care about you and what you've been through. And I am sorry that you had to go through that, any of it."

"I am sorry you had to go through what you went through. But I wonder if you have really gone through it?

You see, to go through something, you come out on the other side of it. But you are still dwelling in it.

I am sure you want to be free of it, but you don't know how to get through it.

I guess it is like being in a deep dark forest or a dark cave that there isn't any light and you are walking in it.

Every once in a while, you get close to the edge and you can see a little daylight, but you choose to stay in the darkness.

Not that it is where you want to dwell, but it has gotten comfortable and you feel like there is no escaping it.

You have to make that decision.

Satan will be more than happy to keep you there.

Keep you from freedom of all that.

If you are bound up in all that, in all the chains that he has kept you in for so long, then you are not free to serve the Lord.

Sometimes you have to make that choice, like

Joshua of old, when he said, *"Choose you this day whom you will serve, as for me and my house, we will serve the Lord."*

"You are right Amy. I don't want to live like this. I am so sick of all of it. I feel like I am stuck in a straitjacket. Like I have no freedom.

I was raised in church. I was able to listen to the stories that your Granny read to you. I was taught that you have to have faith and walk with God and that we could be in relationship with the creator. Not that I ever made that choice as a teenager. I knew how to fake it in front of anyone that mattered. Like my parents, but I knew who I was. And then when I went to Vietnam.

Man, I wanted to be just like my big brother. He was some tough guy, but I wasn't going to measure up. I was pretty good at the soldier part, but the faking it there part, well, it didn't much matter.

They were all young, just like me, and away from home for the first time, just like me. So, we could drink, we could smoke, we could do drugs.

It was a coming of age, I guess. The darkness had already started to creep in way before the day I lost my leg and my friends. That just put it over the top.

It was like a death grip in my mind and in my heart. In my very soul.

I feel like I am drowning in a sea of darkness and I can't see my way out. The longer time goes by, the deeper I feel I am falling.

Amy, I don't want to live like this. I am tired of having a pity party all the time.

I just don't know how to break free. How to clean myself up."

"Well therein lies your problem. You can't clean yourself up. You can't break the bondages of sin. Only God can."

"God does not want this mess Amy. I am telling you."

"Lance, you know that is not true. His Word says, *"Come unto me all ye who are heavy laden, and I will give you rest."*

You are included in that all. There is nothing you need to do but to confess that you are a sinner and repent of your sins and you will be made white as snow."

"I know that the Bible says those things, but it is hard for me to believe that He means me."

"In the book of John, we are told that *"Whosoever shall call upon the name of the Lord shall be saved."*

You know these things are in the Bible. It is up to you to believe if they are true or not. You've got to decide, do I want to live in darkness or walk in the light. To be clean and upright before the Lord. To be completely free.

You know the Word also says, *"he whom the Lord sets free is free indeed!"*

Do you want to be free Lance? No one can make that decision for you."

"Do I have to wait until I go to church on Sunday?"

"No. You can pray any time."

"Will you pray with me Amy? I really want to have what you have. I want to forget the past. I want to have whatever it is that gives you the peace and joy that you have. That my parents have. I want that. Will you pray with me?"

"Yes, of course, I will pray with you."

"I honestly do not know how to start."

"You just talk to Him like you would anyone. If you want, I will help you get started."

"Yeah, help me get started."

Amy bowed her head and took Lance's hands.

He bowed his head and Amy began to pray.

"Dear Lord, I just want to take a minute and thank you for this day.

To thank you for your traveling mercies that got me and my friend here safely.

God, you know my friend Lance. He is in a dark place, but he is ready to come out and live for you. He wants to talk to you, to make things right. Please Lord, I pray that you would give him peace and joy and happiness for every sorrow and grief that he lays down at your feet. Amen!"

Then Lance began to pray and call out to the Lord. He made him his Savior. He laid every care and burden at the feet of Jesus. The filthy rags of sin, the garments that had so burdened him and put on garments of praise."

CHAPTER 109

They stayed up and talked for a long time.

It finally came around full circle.

"You know Amy, you still haven't told me what you are supposed to have surgery for. Do you feel like telling me? I know it isn't any of my business, but I really would like to know."

"It really doesn't matter now. I don't have insurance to cover it now that I've quit my job."

"Amy, would you please come back to work then, so that you can get whatever it is taken care of. I will make it easy for you. I do not accept your resignation. How's that?"

"Honestly Lance, I was going to be coming back home tomorrow, well I guess today, to see if you would give me my job back, but then you showed up here."

"Okay then, it's settled. You are not fired, and you haven't quit. You still have insurance. So now will you tell me why you need to have surgery?"

"It is a hard story Lance. Harder than being a human ashtray."

Lance reached over and took her hand.

"If it is too hard to tell then I don't want you to have to tell me."

"No, I will tell you. I have only told one other

person and that was Mama Jane. I was having some issues when I first went to live with her. She took me to the doctor. That is when I first heard of my problem.

When I was almost 13, right after Granny died, I got pregnant by my step-father."

"Oh, Amy, I am so sorry."

"I know, it was traumatic. I was probably a couple of months along. I know it wasn't too far into it.

My stepfather told my mom to fix it.

So, she did.

She took me to visit one of her friends. They tied me to the bed and my mother put her hand over my mouth to stifle the screams as her friend used a coat hanger to cause me to have an abortion.

The pain was horrible. I bled a lot. I remember that.

I missed school for almost a month. No one even came to check on me. With Granny gone, there really was no one.

Then when I was almost 14, it happened again.

This time it was in the summer so no one would have come to check up on me anyways.

It wasn't too long after that when my brother died. I think about 4 months or so.

No one ever knew.

I wasn't going to tell.

I was mortified.

It wasn't like I wanted to have a baby, but even I knew that it was wrong for them to kill these babies, and I was just a baby myself."

Hot tears were rolling down her face.

Lance reached up and wiped them away.

"What they did to me left me with a lot of scar tissue and in a lot of pain. My doctor said that they think they can possibly repair some of the damage that was caused. He thinks that they can get the scar tissue out and the one fallopian tube that has a lot of damage. If they can, then I have a chance that if I ever get married that I could possibly have children.

If they start the surgery and there is so much damage that can't be repaired, rather than leave it as it is, they will have to do a complete hysterectomy. Those are my only choices. They won't know until they get in there. It is a 50/50 chance of either one."

"Then we need to get home so you can get that blood work done. Because you see, Amy, I'm in love with you.

I pretty much have been since you walked into that front office.

And at some point, in our future, I plan on asking you to marry me."

"I can't marry you Lance."

"Not today you can't, not tomorrow you can't. Not even next week or next month.

I haven't even asked you yet.

But Amy, I am not the same man that you came and ate tacos with a few hours ago. I am a new creation, just like you said I would be.

I am going to become the man of God that He wants me to be. You are going to be dating a new Lance Davis.

I have a lot of ground to make up.

Do you think they would let me start coming to those Women's Bible Studies? I hear they have a really pretty, smart, Godly, young woman there that teaches ever once in a while."

"Probably not," Amy laughed. "But if you really want to learn how to walk with God, get your Bible out and start reading Ephesians.

Read it over and over and over and over again.

And when you think you've got it, read it again.

Start writing it on your heart and in your mind.

Let it fall like honey from your mouth.

Start there and then we'll talk."

CHAPTER 110

"Push Amy, push."

"Come on baby, you've got this."

"I can't Lance. I can't do it."

"Yes, you can. You've got this."

"Come on Amy, one more big push. I can see the head."

"Ow, ow, ow. It hurts so bad."

"I know baby, I know. You can do it. Just breathe."

"The head is out. Stop pushing for a second. Don't push."

There seemed to be some kind of concern.

"Try not to push Amy."

"What's going on?"

Dr. Shackleford looked at Lance, the cord is wrapped around him. We are trying to get it undone."

"Lance, what's going on?"

"It's okay baby. Doc has it under control."

In his heart he was praying, trying so hard not to show the concern he had.

"It's in your hands God," he prayed.

"Okay, Amy, one more big push. Deep breath and push."

Amy pushed and felt such a relief as the baby found his way out.

Dr. Shackleford handed him off to the Pediatrician

that was standing there.

We had been calling it a boy, but we had not been 100% sure until Dr. Shackleford announced it.

"You have a boy!"

They didn't show him to us. The doctor had rushed him over to the incubator and was working on him.

"Amy," Dr. Shackleford said as he continued taking care of her, "the baby is having a few complications. The cord was wrapped around his neck and it looks like he was not getting enough oxygen. They are working on him right now to get him to breathe. Now you do what I tell you so can get you taken care of."

"Lance, go see how he is doing! Please, go check on him."

Lance left her side to go see his new son.

He was still not breathing. It had been two minutes.

Lance began to pray, out loud, in the name of Jesus!

The Pediatrician and one of the nurses looked in his direction.

He didn't care. It wasn't their son. It was his. His firstborn son!

He prayed more, reaching over and touching the incubator.

Amy did as the doctor instructed, praying along with Lance.

All of a sudden, the most joyous sound they had ever heard, a baby was crying. Not loudly, but loud enough that the whole room could hear it.

"Thank you, Jesus," Dr. Shackleford exclaimed!

"Yes, thank you Jesus."

Tears were running down most of our faces.

Lance moved over to Amy' side.

"Did you hear that babe? Did you hear that?"

"He's not out of the woods yet," the Pediatrician said. "He was without oxygen for a while. We are going to put him in NICU and have him under oxygen for a few hours and observe him. There could be dire complications from his lack of oxygen. Please don't get your hopes up."

They rushed our baby out of the room.

Dr. Shackleford was just finishing up with Amy and getting her settled in.

"Don't you listen to him. We serve a big God. That is a lie from Satan. Amy, Lance, you both know what a miracle this baby is. You keep praying. Don't you let the devil steal what God has given you! I am going to go down there now and pray for that baby."

One of the nurses that had been helping told us she was going too!

They left us.

Amy and I prayed like we had never prayed before.

We did serve a big God!

We didn't know what God had in store, but we were ready for anything.

If the devil wanted a battle, he was going to get one.

"Lance, you need to go let everyone know what is going on. They need to be praying. Go get our prayer warriors!"

Lance left and found everyone in the waiting room, anticipating news of a sweet new baby.

"Boy or girl," Robert asked.

"It's a boy."

I guess they could tell something was wrong by the look on Lance's face.

"What's going on? Is everything ok?" They all

seemed to be asking at once.

"No." Lance explained the situation to them.

Amy was right, again, they were prayer warriors.

"Do you want to come and see Amy?"

Most did, but Sister Lewis said she would be in to see her in a while. She had something she had to do.

I don't know how they let her in, probably Dr. Shackleford's doings, but she got to stand in the hallway of the NICU. She walked those halls the rest of the night praying, stopping on occasion to put her hand on the window glass to pray.

She didn't just pray for our baby, she prayed for them all.

She came to see Amy early in the morning. She and I were alone when Sister Lewis walked in.

Amy was so glad to see her.

"Where have you been? I was hoping you would have gotten to stay."

"Oh," Sister Lewis said with a smile, "I had an appointment with the King. He and I have been talking all night about that new baby of yours."

Amy smiled. She knew what that meant.

The door came open and they brought in an incubator for the girl in the next bed.

They checked her arm band to match the baby up.

She was so happy to have her baby.

Amy reached up and wiped her eyes.

She had not even been able to see her baby yet.

Sister Lewis reached for a tissue to hand her just as the door opened again with another incubator.

"Wow, twins," I thought.

But nope. This time the nurse pushing the incubator stopped at Amy's bed.

"Amy Davis?"

"Yes, that's me."

"Let me see your wrist band."

She checked it against the baby that was in the incubator.

"Here is your baby Mrs. Davis."

She handed the little wrapped up package to her.

"No," Amy protested. "He can't be here. He is sick. He is supposed to be in NICU."

The nurse picked up his chart and looked at it.

"It doesn't say he isn't supposed to be here on his chart."

"They told us last night that he would be in NICU for a few days."

"Well, he appears to be doing fine. All his vitals are good. Let me go and double check. I'll be right back."

She left.

Amy finally got to look at the face of her new baby.

Tears started flowing, not just Amy's.

"What if he isn't supposed to be here?"

"Well, he is now," Sister Lewis said. "Let's get a better look at him."

Amy laid him out on the bed in front of her, carefully unwrapping the little burrito they had placed in her arms just moments ago.

"Ten fingers, ten toes. Look at that red hair! So much of it. How much did they say he weighed?"

Lance looked at the chart, "It says, Baby Boy Davis - Seven pounds and 2 ounces. He was 19 ½ inches long and born at 12:30 A.M. on May 25th, 1979."

"Good job mama!" Sister Lewis said as she kissed Amy. They were both crying.

"Good job babe. You were awesome in there. I don't

know how you women do that. Just watching you made my whole body hurt. I am so sorry you had to go through that. But thank you sweetheart. Thank you!"

He just laid there and looked beautiful.

Our hearts were full.

"Baby Boy Davis, huh? Well, did you finally decide what we were going to name him?"

"He gets to name him?"

"Yep, we decided if it was a boy, he could name it, and if it was a girl then I could name it. With approval of course."

"Well, I'll be. I guess that is one way of doing it. So, what is his name?"

"Well, I was thinking I would like to name him Samuel."

"Samuel huh? Why Samuel?"

Lance looked at Amy, he reached out and took her hand. Because of Hannah in the Bible.

"How's that?"

"She had waited for a child for a long time and finally God opened her womb and she gave birth to a baby boy and named him Samuel. So, I picked Samuel because God did the same for us."

Amy smiled, "I like that. Now what about a middle name? Everybody needs a middle name."

"Well, if you don't mind, I would love to name him after my dad. Samuel Ryan Davis. Would that be okay?"

"Absolutely," Amy beamed.

"How do you like your name there? Samuel Ryan Davis, you like that," Amy cooed at the little sleeping bundle of love.

"Pappy would have loved to have been here to see

this. He will be so excited when I tell him about this sweet baby. Lance, you guys did really good here. So proud of both of you."

"Thank you, Memaw."

Next day they were able to take their healthy little baby home.

"God is so good to us Lance," Amy said.

"Yes, He is!"

CHAPTER 111

Pappy was finally feeling well enough to come to church. He'd had to miss a couple of Sundays and he had truly been missed.

Especially by Little Miss Hannah and MJ. They saw him and came running.

"Pappy," Hannah cried as she ran down the aisle to greet him.

"Hannah," her mother called after her, "don't run in church."

"Sorry mom," she called back to her. But it didn't slow her down.

My she was getting so big now! She would soon be 11. She was a little beauty!

My heart always skipped a beat when I saw her.

Pappy was her pal, her bud, her comrade in arms so to speak.

They had truly missed seeing each other.

She had come by the house with her mother to check on him.

She and MJ even made him a get-well card and brought him some cookies they made for him.

But it just wasn't the same to be in church and him not be there.

Pappy had been there since Tony and Lisa brought her home from the hospital and they had been an item ever since.

Lisa and Tony had come to accept the idea that these two were made from the same stock. Her little brother MJ adored Pappy as much as she did, and Pappy loved him back just as much.

He had given him another slingshot a few months earlier.

It had already been confiscated twice.

Pappy told him, "Whatever you do with it, never shoot a skunk. One of my grandsons did that and it was not pleasant."

"I won't Pappy," he told him.

And so far, he hadn't, but he had broken the neighbors window and had hit the cat with it. But he had not shot a skunk!

He had given him the same spiel that he had given Josh. Telling him that he needed to be able to knock down giants in his life.

"You have to train them young," he always said.

They sat on either side of him and got all the hugs and candy they could from him before they were ushered off to children's church by their dad.

Lisa leaned up from behind and hugged him.

"I love you," she said. "Thank you for loving my babies."

Pappy reached up and patted her on the hand and told her, "I love you too, little sweetheart. Thank you for letting us."

Church service began as always, prayer, announcements, and songs.

But today was going to be different.

Toby and Patty and their two little twin girls were there. They were a fine mixture of Patty and Toby.

Little Samantha after Sam of course and Patricia after Patty.

They were the cutest little red heads ever. Curly hair galore.

They would be four this coming October!

Wow, how time flies!

I could see why Pappy wouldn't let Memaw name Mother Annie.

No one should have to go through life like that!

Memaw and Pappy were in hog heaven.

But they couldn't hold a candle to Aunt Jessie and Uncle Joey.

They had moved in with Memaw and Pappy to help take care of him after he had fallen and broken his hip.

Uncle Joey was now running Pappy's store.

Pappy came down occasionally, but mostly only to have lunch with Joey.

They were all beaming!

They were going to be holding a week-long revival and it was starting that morning.

Even Josh was there.

He had just finished his last year of college. Janey was right by his side. They were going to be having a June wedding. In just a couple of weeks they were going to be Mr. and Mrs. Joshua Lewis.

They truly were in love.

Best thing about it, he already had a job lined up.

He was going to be the new Youth Leader at Trinity Church!

They were going to have two ministers in the family.

It was so great to see him growing up and watching him become the man of God that he was.

Toby and Patty were finally upgrading to a bigger R.V. now that they were expecting their new baby. They still weren't sure yet if it was going to be twins.

With the twins and one, possibly two more they were going to be needing more room.

It was a full house this morning.

Pastor James called Lance and Amy to the front to bring their new baby up to dedicate it to the Lord.

There wasn't a dry eye in the room after Pastor James spoke that morning.

He told of the complications and how God had come through.

He took little Samuel from Amy and held him up for everyone to see.

"Samuel, what an appropriate name. You truly are a gift of God to Amy and Lance, and to all of us.

We have been praying for you to get here for a long time.

God sent you to this fine couple, this couple of young people that truly love Him and have dedicated their lives to His service. God opened Amy's womb just like Hannah and blessed them with you, Samuel Ryan Davis.

And now they stand here to give you back to Him.

To dedicate you to Him, the gift giver.

Awe, sweet little guy. You are only on loan to them. Sorry Amy and Lance. He doesn't belong to you, but God has seen it in His great wisdom to entrust him to you to raise him in the fear and admonition of the Lord.

He has commissioned you to be the light bearers into his soul, to teach him about Jesus and His love for us.

It is not just your responsibility, but ours as well.

Your family, your extended family, your friends, this congregation.

We are all responsible to live a life worthy of our Lord as an example to this little guy.

To pray for him, to lift him up and to teach him by word and deed.

To let him know that he is worthy of salvation and that he is loved and always will be loved. Not just by us but by a living God. A God that sent His only son so that we could be redeemed by love.

Bought with a price.

Do you accept that commission?"

All the church said a hearty "Yes, and amen!"

"I know you have a few people you want to come up here and stand with you to dedicate this baby this morning. Come on up."

Many people stood and came forward.

Robert and I were there with our sweet twin baby girls.

Sara and Suzanne. Sara after his mother and Suzanne after mine.

They were going to be turning two in August.

Toby and Patty brought their girls with them.

Lance's parents and Memaw and Pappy. And of course, my mother.

We were one big happy family.

"This baby is going to be loved.

So many red heads up here. I feel like I am in an Irish convention.

Lance leaned in, "Not Irish, Scottish!"

Everyone laughed.

Let us pray, *"Heavenly Father, here we are, coming*

before You, much like Hannah did with her Samuel, to offer back to You what already belongs to You.

Lord we pray for this little family, Amy and Lance. May You give these new parents wisdom as they try to navigate parenthood. It isn't easy as any parent would know. But Lord we know that with You all things are possible.

We know that because of You and only You this baby was made possible.

Because of Your divine intervention and grace this baby is here, healthy, and alive.

Lord, there are so many people that are here today that have come around this family.

That love this family.

That will be a support to this family.

Grandparents, Great Grandparents, Aunts and Uncles, friends, church family, so many Lord.

I pray that each and every person that comes in contact with this little fella will in some way or manner show Him who You are.

Lord, let him know his worth as he grows in You and becomes the man You ordained him to be, that You have predestined him to be.

Lord I pray that he will find his way to You and know You as Savior, Master, Friend and Redeemer!

May he always know and walk in Your love. Amen!"

He handed Samuel Ryan Davis back to his mother and she pulled him in so close as the tears fell on his little blanket.

Everyone went to their seats and life exploded in all of us as we were about to be set on different paths.

Robert and I had given up our position at Trinity to take on Pastor Taylors church.

He felt that God was calling him to go pioneer another church.

As sad as his congregation was to see him go, they welcomed us in as their new pastors.

We had just moved all our belongings to Uncle Joey and Aunt Jessies farm.

Well, it would be our farm now. We had bought it from them.

And when the new one gets here in a few months we are going to have a full house.

Memories engulfed me as I sat there that morning.

I was missing Grandmother and Grandfather Abernathy.

They had both passed away just a year ago.

It was so strange that they were only separated from each other for a couple of weeks.

After Grandfather passed, so peacefully in his sleep, then Grandmother did the same.

Two funerals just weeks apart.

They had left everything to me.

Mother had helped me sort everything out.

They had truly been great as grandparents over the years.

I was so grateful that God had healed that pain.

I would never have known how awesome they truly were.

I remembered Gina and my heart was full.

I knew why I could sing so freely.

His eye had truly been on me. And I knew that He had always been watching over me.

His redeeming love had set me free and I could sing.

Tears rolled down my face.

Sweet tears.

Robert took my hand as Toby stepped up to the podium to preach.

Life was good.

It was very good!

ABOUT THE AUTHOR

Darla Kinion

Darla Kinion is a mother, a Darlin (grandma), but mostly a lover of God. She is a teller of stories. Stories that hopefully touch peoples hearts and makes a difference in their lives!

Made in the USA
Middletown, DE
12 April 2023